BOY TOY

BY BARRY LYGA

GRAPHIA

An Imprint of Houghton Mifflin Harcourt Publishing Company

BOSTON

For information about permission to reproduce selections from this book, write to Permissions, Houghton Mifflin Company, 215 Park Avenue South, New York, New York 10003.

Graphia and the Graphia logo are registered trademarks of Houghton Mifflin Harcourt Publishing Company.

www.hmhbooks.com

The text of this book is set in ITC Legacy Serif.

Library of Congress Cataloging-in-Publication Data
Lyga, Barry.
Boy toy / by Barry Lyga.
    p. cm.
Summary: After five years of fighting his way past flickers of memory about the teacher who molested him and the incident that brought the crime to light, eighteen-year-old Josh gets help in coping with his molester's release from prison when he finally tells his best friend the whole truth.
ISBN-13: 978-0-618-72393-5 (hardcover)
ISBN-13: 978-0-547-07634-8 (paperback)
    [1. Sexual abuse victims—Fiction. 2. Emotional problems—Fiction. 3. Baseball—Fiction. 4. Psychotherapy—Fiction. 5. Memory—Fiction. 6. High schools—Fiction. 7. Schools—Fiction.] I. Title.
PZ7.L97967Boy 2007
[Fic]—dc22
            2006039840

Printed in the United States of America
DOM 10 9 8 7 6 5 4 3
4500217780

DEDICATED TO TERRY DAVIS,
FOR SHOWING ME THAT
IT WAS POSSIBLE.

Ten Things I Learned
at the Age of Twelve

1. The Black Plague was transmitted by fleas that were carried throughout Europe by rats.
2. If you first paralyze it, you can cut open a frog and watch its lungs continue to inflate and deflate.
3. There are seven forms of the verb *to be: am, being, been, is, was, were,* and *are.*
4. In order to divide fractions, you invert the divisor to arrive at the reciprocal, which is then multiplied by the dividend. (Mixed fractions must first be converted to improper fractions.)
5. In Salem, the witches weren't burned at the stake—they were pressed to death under big rocks . . . or hanged.
6. Islam was founded in the year 610. It is the third of three world religions worshiping the same God.
7. Each point on a "coordinate plane" (created by the joining of an x-axis and a y-axis) can be described by an ordered pair of numbers.
8. "Monotheism" is a belief system centered on a single deity, while "polytheism" subscribes to belief in multiple deities.
9. The area of a circle can be determined by using the formula πr^2, where r is the radius of the circle.
10. How to please a woman.

Batter Up

Things That Happened
After and Before

"Lucky thirteen," my dad said when I blew out the candles on my birthday cake, and my mom shot down his lame attempt at humor with a disgusted "Oh, Bill!"

But honestly, that's not the important part. Not at all.

The ending began and the beginning ended and the whole mess just got fucked up beyond belief at the party at Rachel Madison's house a few days later. A few days after "Lucky thirteen"/"Oh, Bill!"

The party turned out to be little more than an excuse for Rachel and Michelle Jurgens and Zik Lorenz and me—the Four Musketeers—to hang out in Rachel's basement. Music videos on the TV and sodas and chips and some sort of hot potato casserole that Rachel announced she had made on her own. And three kids sitting around awkwardly trying to be coy with each other. Three kids and me.

It was like watching the mating rituals of retarded birds, clumsily stepping the wrong patterns around each other over and over again. I sat to one side on a brittle office chair and tried not to be bored.

"Something wrong?" Rachel asked at one point, kneeling down next to the chair. My mind flickered for a moment

—dark room and then a light—
and I adjusted my position in the chair.

"No. Why?"

She gestured to Michelle and Zik, who sat on the floor, leaning against the sofa. They were giggling at the TV, sharing a bowl of chips, their greasy fingers slipping against one another. "Well, you're just sitting over here by yourself . . ."

"You're here now."

Her face lit up. "Can I sit with you?"

"Well, I guess . . ." I looked doubtfully at the old chair, which had no room for a second party.

Rachel didn't wait; she planted herself on my lap. The chair squealed. My mind flickered again—

—was—was—was—

and I said, "This isn't a good idea, Rache."

"It can hold us."

She was my size, in a loose sleeveless top and a skirt worn low on her frame. Too skinny, to tell the truth; her skirt was tight enough to emphasize the lack of hips, low enough to expose her concave belly. Her hair was dirty blond and cut short, her face shining, sprayed with an even blast of freckles over the bridge of her nose. Luminous blue eyes. She twisted and put her arms around me. Flicker again

—Was that what you wanted?—

and then Rachel saying, "Is this OK? I need to steady myself."

The chair creaked again, louder, as if to say, "Hey! I really mean it!"

"I don't think this is a good idea, Rachel."

"Come on."

"I'm just worried about the chair."

She wiggled on my lap. I wasn't worried about the chair.

I couldn't let this continue. I struggled to move her off me, our bodies chafing against each other. Her butt slipped and ground against my pelvis in a way that was almost pleasant, almost painful.

"Please"—and I managed to move her off me without dumping her onto the floor.

She fixed me with a glare and a pout at the same time. Rachel Madison was the first girl I noticed when I started noticing girls in fifth grade. Back then, she was a skinny little tomboy with no breasts and the best on-base percentage in Little League that season at .425.

By seventh grade, she'd grown out of the cute tomboy phase, though not much had happened in the chest department. Like so many girls, she emphasized the positive, though, with tight jeans and skirts designed to show off the legs and ass toned over months of beating the throw to first. Up top, she favored the loose blouses and shirts that hinted that maybe, *maybe*, something was starting to sprout under there.

She sauntered over to the snacks, hips swinging in a pathetic attempt to be older than thirteen.

"I have to go to the bathroom," she announced suddenly.

Michelle jumped up and the two girls trooped off to the bathroom together, leaving Zik and me to switch the channel to ESPN, where the Red Sox were clobbering our dear Orioles.

Moments later, the girls returned. Instead of resuming her make-out position with Zik, though, Michelle clapped her hands together and said, "Hey, guys, want to play a game?"

In no time at all, we were all sitting cross-legged on the floor across from each other, an empty Coke bottle between us.

"Whoever gets the bottle pointed at them," Michelle said, as if giving a book report, "gets to go into the coat closet with the person across from them."

That meant Rachel for me, Zik for Michelle. Coincidence? Of course not.

"Are you sure this is how you play spin-the-bottle?" I had never played before, but it didn't seem to jibe with the lore gleaned from older kids over the years.

"This is how my sister plays," Michelle said, and all argument stopped. Michelle's sister, Dina, was drop-dead gorgeous, famous for having had a man offer to leave his wife for her when she was in eighth grade. At least, that was the rumor. No one doubted it, though.

Rachel spun the bottle, giving it a weak little twist that sent it in a quarter-turn before the top of it pointed at me like a compass needle pointing north.

"You and Josh go into the closet," Michelle squealed.

"It didn't go all the way around," I said. "The bottle has to spin all the way around at least once. Otherwise it doesn't count."

Rachel pouted again, but went ahead and spun the bottle once more. It landed perfectly and squarely on me. Again.

"See?" Michelle said, as if something had been proven. She heaved herself to her feet and threw open the closet door. "Get in there, you two!"

Rachel slid in quickly. "How long are we supposed to be in there?" I asked.

"Don't worry about it," Michelle said. "I'm keeping time."

As the closet door closed, it occurred to me that Michelle

would do nothing of the sort. She'd be getting her hands greasy with Zik again.

The closet was nearly empty. A thin sketch of light from under the door made it so that we weren't in complete darkness, but I couldn't really see anything at all, except for those weird dancing color spots that drift in front of your eyes when it's dark.

"Sit down," Rachel whispered. I sat.

I couldn't see her, but I could feel her just ahead of me, sitting cross-legged. I closed my eyes to a new darkness. Flicker

—*turn on the lights if you want*—

and then back to the present.

I opened my eyes. Spots whirled and spun. The dark went to semidarkness. I thought I could see something in the far distance. It shifted.

Rachel changed position, going up to her knees. I felt more than saw her lean toward me in the dark. A sudden giggle penetrated the closet from outside: Michelle.

"Sounds like they're having fun," Rachel said, her breath clouded, warm, against my face. She was practically on top of me. I almost jerked out a hand in self-defense, but I held back.

"I guess so."

"Don't you want to have fun?"

Flicker

—*touch*—

"I guess so."

She giggled like Michelle. "I've been practicing spinning that bottle all week."

"Really?"

"Yeah."

She leaned in even closer; her blouse brushed against my hand. Then her lips pressed to my cheek. They were slippery with too much lipstick. She fumbled for a minute, adjusting, and eventually found my lips. More slimy lip action.

"Don't you like me?" she whispered.

—*touch*—

—*lick*—

—*OK*—

—*yes*—

"Sure." I could feel her trembling—*vibrating*—over me, supporting herself on her hands, elbows locked. Belly pressed to my knee. Blouse drifting against my hand.

"Kiss me," she said, and kissed my lips again, this time probing with her tongue.

I opened my mouth and she sighed deep in her throat when our tongues touched. It sounded familiar. Universal. I closed my eyes again and pretended. Pretended I wasn't in a closet in the Madisons' basement, with Zik and Michelle intertwining their fingers ten feet away through a cheap fiberboard door. Pretended I wasn't sitting cross-legged across from a flat-chested girl with freckles and a too-slutty skirt that looked wrong on her but would have looked so right on someone else.

Instead, I moved forward with my body and my tongue. I heard a familiar grunt of approval. I reached out to touch her

—*touch*—

—*yes*—

and slid my hands down to the bare skin between the blouse and the skirt. I crushed my face to hers, let my hands move the way they wanted, the way they knew . . .

And the next thing I knew, Rachel slammed my chest with both fists. She was too small to hurt me, but she managed to push me away, breaking the hold I had on her, jerking my hands away. "No! No!"

She shoved me, kicked out with her feet, and then the door was flung open and Rachel dashed out of the closet, wailing, tugging at her blouse and skirt, running for the stairs.

Michelle and Zik were sprawled on the sofa, fooling around. They looked over at me, lipstick-smeared, as Rachel charged up the stairs. I heard an adult voice call out. Then another, and then a babble of them—her father, her mother, her brother, home from college.

And that was how one part of my life ended. And another began.

Thirteen years old. Five years ago.

Strike
One

CHAPTER 1

Roland Makes a Decision

COACH KALTENBACH SHOULDN'T HAVE SAID IT. He shouldn't have opened his big, fat, stupid mouth. Because if he hadn't said it, then I wouldn't have heard it. And I wouldn't have hit him so hard that his head left a dent on the lowest bleacher when he collapsed.

We were running laps in the gym—third straight day of April rain, so we couldn't practice outside. Mr. Kaltenbach, varsity baseball coach, was standing near the bleachers, yelling at us to "pick it up pick it up pick it up you goddamn girls!"

"Come on, move it, Lorenz!" he bellowed as Zik ran past him.

"Get the lead out!" he bawled when Jon Blevins ran by.

"Do I have to call the girls' softball team in here to show you how this is done?" he screamed to no one in particular.

As I approached Kaltenbach, his mouth opened and his eyes gleamed, and I waited for the insult.

And then he said it.

Truth be told, I don't even remember deciding to hit him. You'd think that hitting a coach and a teacher would be something that you'd ponder. You'd weigh the pros and cons. You'd really consider it before doing it. Especially if you're me, if you're praying for a scholarship, a scholarship to take you out of this little town that knows far, far too much.

But I didn't think about it. I just stopped dead in my tracks, pivoted on my right foot, and smashed my fist into his jaw.

Kaltenbach made a sound like "Hut!" and staggered backwards, arms pinwheeling, his clipboard dropping to the floor. There was no way he was going to keep his balance; he went over backwards, landed on his flabby ass (good news for him), and then the top half of his body kept on going and he fetched up against the bottom bleacher with the back of his head. *Whonk! Crack!*

I wasn't sure what had cracked—the bleacher, or Coach's head. I didn't really care, either.

Behind me, the sound of running feet squeaked to a stop on the gym floor. Someone said, "Holy shit," loud enough for it to echo.

Zik was at my side in an instant.

"Dude. What the fuck?" He was breathing hard. On the other hand, I was breathing regularly. I touched my fingers to my neck; my pulse was normal.

Kaltenbach groaned from the floor and rolled to one side.

"Oh, man," Zik moaned. "Why did you *do* that?"

Kaltenbach winced as he sat up, probing the back of his head. I think he wanted to say something or get up and get tough with me, but I just stared at him and clenched my fists by my sides. He was *so* out of line and he knew it.

If it had just been the two of us, he would have let it slide. But there were witnesses.

"Office," he said, then hissed in a breath as he touched something tender where he'd fallen.

Which is how I ended up in the office of (according to his desk plaque) Roland A. Sperling, Assistant Principal. Known to students far and wide as "The Spermling."

"Joshua, Joshua, Joshua," he says, sighing as he squeezes into his chair. "Joshua."

"Roland, Roland, Roland," I mimic, right down to the sigh. "Roland "

"We've talked about that before. You need to show proper respect."

"Calling you Roland is better than what the other kids call you, isn't it? An1 at least I do it to your face."

"I don't know what you're talking about."

Sure he does. "If you say so, Roland."

The Spermling 's a fat slug of a man. He goes beyond obese and into "generates his own gravity" territory. I'd say he's a black hole, but black holes are *small*. The Spermling is more like a Jupiter-class gas giant, bloated and round.

On his desk near one sausage-y hand lies my student file—I recognize it instantly from the sheer bulk. It's at least twice as thick as any other I've ever seen. He taps it with his pen and looks at me thoughtfully. "I thought you liked baseball, Josh."

"I do."

"You won't go very far in the game if you punch your coach."

I bite my lip. It's been twenty minutes since I decked Kaltenbach, and my knuckles still hurt. They throb. But that's OK. It's a good kind of throbbing because I know where it came from. It's a justice-throbbing.

"I won't be playing my whole life. I'm not planning on going pro or anything. I just like the game."

"Discipline and respect aren't just about baseball," he tells me. "Or even just about assistant principals. When you're out there in college or in the real world—"

"I know. I won't be allowed to punch people."

He starts tapping his pen again, this time against the plastic Rolodex. "Did he say something to upset you? It's been a while since you've lashed out so . . . physically. He tells me he was goading you boys to run faster."

For a moment, I'm back in the gym. Been like this for years—I get these weird full-body flashbacks that last maybe a second, maybe two. I call them "flickers." So for a second, I'm back in the gym, just as Kaltenbach says *it*.

And then back in the Spermling's office.

"I don't want to talk about it. Just go ahead and punish me."

The Spermling leans back in his chair, finding a new target for his pen tapping: the computer keyboard. "Josh, I don't like punishing you. You're a bright kid, and I think you've got a bright future waiting for you, if you settle down long enough to take it. I've cut you a lot of slack because of your history and because your grades are, quite frankly, better than any other three students' combined."

"I appreciate the vote of confidence, Roland." I get up to leave. "I'll be seeing you, then."

"Sit down." His chair howls in protest as he leans forward against the desk. "We're not finished. Assaulting a teacher is serious business. You could get in a lot of trouble. *Legal* trouble. I don't think you want to be in a courtroom—" He cuts himself off here, as if something has caught in his throat. What the hell?

Oh, I get it. *"Again."* He was about to say, "I don't think you want to be in a courtroom *again*," but he stopped himself.

I say it for him. "You're right. I don't want to be in a courtroom again. Wasn't much fun the first time."

Tap-tap-taptaptap*tap*. The pen goes crazy on the desk. "Mr. Kaltenbach doesn't want to press charges. Says he knows how things can get heated during a practice."

Goddamn *right* he doesn't want to press charges. Because then I would tell everyone what he said.

"Given your history, I think the best thing is for you to talk to Dr. Pierce."

The school shrink? "Aw, Christ, no! Come on, Roland!"

He spreads his hands in front of him as if to encompass the panoply of options in the world. "What would you prefer? What would *you* do in my situation?"

What would I do, Roland? I'd ask the question you don't want to ask: not "Did Coach Kaltenbach say something to make you upset?" but "What did he say?" But no. Not you, Roland. You'd rather just avoid that and play "bad boy" with me, wouldn't you?

"I sure as hell wouldn't send me to Pierce. She doesn't know what she's talking about. Let me call Dr. Kennedy instead."

He considers that. Dr. Kennedy is my usual shrink, the guy I used to see twice a week. Now I'm down to once a month.

The Spermling nods slowly, as if this whole idea were his, as if he somehow manipulated me into this. He doesn't realize I was going to see Kennedy this week anyway.

"That's acceptable," he announces with all the import and

gravity of Moses handing down the Ten Commandments. "Make the call here."

I go ahead and call Dr. Kennedy's office. The receptionist recognizes my voice right off the bat and says, "Confirming tomorrow's four o'clock?"

"Tomorrow at four o'clock." I make it sound like I'm requesting, not confirming.

After she hangs up, I vamp a bit—"Tell Dr. Kennedy I appreciate him fitting me in"—before putting the phone down.

The Spermling grunts. "It's almost last bell, so I want you to get ready and go home. I have to suspend you for a couple of days." Before I can protest, he holds up a hand to stop me. "I know, I know. And I really *don't* want to punish you, but I can't let you hit a teacher and get away with it. Don't worry—I'll make sure your teachers let you make up the work. Come back on Monday. Things should be smoothed over by then."

"This sucks, Roland." I get up to leave. The Spermling is putting my file away, replacing it on his desk with one that's even bigger. I've never seen *that* before.

"Well, suck or not, it is what it is," he says without sympathy. "You've got six weeks of school left, Josh. Try to get by. And try to respect me."

"I'll work on it, Roland."

CHAPTER 2
Releasing Eve

ZIK LORENZ IS MY BEST FRIEND in the world because he's never asked about it. He's never said, "What was it like?" or "Are you OK?" or "Do you ever think about her?" Zik's cool. Which is amazing, because the rest of his family is complete and utter shit. His big brother, Mike, is a real Cro-Magnon type. Played lacrosse and football for all four years before graduating and then flunked out of community college, where he now serves as some sort of coach's assistant, making sure the water bottles are stocked and getting towels for guys his own age. Loser.

Zik's dad is like a grown-up version of Mike, and his mother is hardly ever around. She's always off at yard sales and garage sales and flea markets, buying crappy reproduction furniture that she swears she's going to refinish. She's also so insane that she named Zik "Isaac," with every intention of calling him "Ike" his whole life. Yes, that's right: the woman named her kids Mike and Ike, after the *candy*. It's a miracle Zik hasn't killed someone yet.

I give him a ride home, as usual. He doesn't have a car yet, so he chips in for gas and I drive him to and from school so that he can avoid the indignity of being a senior on the school bus. It also means he can play baseball—he would have no way of getting home or to games otherwise.

"Twelve times one-forty-four," Zik says.

"One thousand seven hundred twenty-eight," I tell him, without even thinking about it. "Cut it out."

"The square root of fifty-two," he says, warming up.

I can't help myself: "Um, seven-point-two-one-one . . . C'mon, Zik, I'm not your personal calculator."

"Distance from Neptune to Venus. In inches."

"Zik! Goddamn it!" Sometimes I hate him. "That depends on each planet's position at the time. Right now, for example, Venus is on the other side of the sun from—"

"In inches," he says again.

"Christ. OK. *Right now,* it's, like, a hundred and . . . eighty-five trillion inches. Jesus."

"How long to get from home to Uranus?"

"You're not going to my anus anytime soon, so stop it."

Having tested my math/astro skillz to his satisfaction (as if he would know if I just pulled the answers out of my ass . . . which I didn't), Zik chortles and kicks back to enjoy the ride. I gun the engine on Route 54, heading to south Brookdale. Zik waits until we're about five minutes from his house before asking, "What happened, man?"

"I hit Coach."

"No shit. I saw that, dumb-ass. What did the Spermling do to you?"

"Oh. That." I watch for the turn into Zik's development. "Three-day suspension."

"That sucks."

"I do 'em on my head. Don't worry."

"Why'd you hit him, J?"

I've been dreading this question. From Zik in particular.

Because if I tell Zik what Kaltenbach said, then that means I bring the whole mess from five years ago back into the light. And Zik has never once made me tell him about it. So do I drag that rotting carcass into the bright, sunny clearing of our friendship, or do I just piss off my best friend?

Just then—it's really embarrassing—I flicker

—slide my hand up her skirt—

and come back to the present. Weird. That was Rachel, in the flicker. From the closet, five years ago. I don't get any sort of erotic charge out of it, but then again, I barely felt anything erotic at the time I was doing it, either.

Zik doesn't know about the flickers. "If you don't want to talk about it, fine. I just want to stay off your shit list. I don't want to piss you off like that."

Not a chance. Zik would never in a million years say to me what Kaltenbach said.

Pick it up, Mendel! You never—

Not quite a flicker. But enough of a pause that Zik just grunts and opens the door. "See you tom— Oh, wait. Never mind. I'll ride the bus."

"No way. I'll still drive you."

"Come on, J. I can't ask you to—"

"You're not asking, dickweed. I'm telling. I'll pick you up same time."

He hovers in the doorway for a moment. "What about practice?" he asks, with the air of a poor kid pushing for one more present from Santa Claus.

"I'll get you. Don't worry."

He hesitates again; he wants to accept the offer, but some polite part of him (welling up from a DNA source long recessive in the Lorenz genotype, but active in Zik) feels like he should decline. I don't give him a chance to act on his better instincts— I inch the car forward enough to knock him out of it, then lean over and close the door. He hops in the rain for a second, keeps his balance, then flips me off with a grin as he dashes toward the house.

All's right in the world.

I was hoping for some peace and quiet at home so that I could gather my thoughts and assemble choice phrases for my diatribe on the injustice of my latest suspension, but strangely enough Mom and Dad's cars are both in the driveway when I pull up.

Inside, I hear voices—Mom is upset, Dad is calm. Can't quite make out what they're talking about. The usual scenario.

My mother seems like those moms you see on the commercials—the ones who are cool and collected, who launch flotillas of children from battleship-size SUVs and have a ready jug of sweetened fruit punch on deck at all times. She works as a research assistant to one of the professors at Lake Eliot College. She lives for facts.

Dad, though, is one of those guys you see on the really bad sitcoms where you think, *How did he end up married to the hottie?* He works in marketing, and his slogan is "Convincing the world it's wrong, one product at a time." He deals in fantasy. And he wallows in it.

So it's not particularly out of the ordinary to hear Mom arguing and Dad grunting occasionally as the near-silent partner. What *is* weird is having them both home so early in the day.

They're in the kitchen as I come in. Mom standing by the

counter, leaning on it for support, Dad at the table, the newspaper spread out before him.

"Who are you people and what have you done with my parents?" I demand, trying to break the ice. It hits me almost as the words leave my mouth: the school called them. Good old Roland decided to bend me over and screw me in advance.

Mom gives Dad a look that says, "Well?" but Dad just shrugs. Mom sighs. "We have to talk to you."

"I'm sure." Before I can launch into my defense, though, she goes on:

"This is very serious, Josh. This is difficult for us."

This can't be about my suspension. I've been suspended before.

Letters came from the Holy Trinity? *That* could be it. I didn't check the mail, so maybe one of them did and this is it. My future's been decided.

She starts to talk, then bites her lip. She's been crying. Her arms shake, bearing her weight as she leans into the counter. Mom's slim and ageless, but she looks a hundred right now.

"I can't believe this. I can't believe it."

"What, Mom? Tell me."

She nods and stands up straight, then takes my hand the way she used to when I was a kid. "We wanted you to hear it from us. That's why we came home. They're letting her out, Joshua. They're letting that woman out of prison." Mom's voice goes from reedy to boiling over by the time she hits the word "prison."

She doesn't have to tell me who "that woman" is—

—*tongue tracing a line of cool heat up*—

and I blink, actually jerking my head at the power of it. Mom thinks I'm upset—she pulls at me, and I'm disoriented enough to let her do it. Suddenly I'm being hugged by my mom for the first time in years. It's a weird feeling; these days, I'm five inches taller than she is. I go to put my arms around her in return, but I end up crushing her to me, flattening her breasts against my chest, too aware of them, letting go—

Mom won't let go. I let her hug me, my arms lamely akimbo. She's sobbing.

"Mom, it's . . . It's OK . . ." I look to Dad for help again. He's strumming his fingers on the table.

"She's a sick woman." He says it very calmly, and at first I think he means Mom.

She breaks away from me and screams, "Then they should leave her where she is!"

"She has to see a shrink twice a week," he says, again very calmly. I think of my sessions with Dr. Kennedy. I started out at twice a week, too. I wonder who Eve will be seeing. Wouldn't it be bizarre if it ended up being Dr. Kennedy? Could that even happen? Are there laws about that?

"She didn't even serve half her sentence!" Mom rants.

"Hell, these days we're lucky she was in that long." Dad taps his pen against his upper teeth for a second, turning into the Spermling for that brief moment. "You OK with this, Josh? You want to talk about it?"

Mom fixes Dad with a glare like something from an abstract comic book: hate vision, instead of heat vision.

"I'm seeing Dr. Kennedy tomorrow."

He nods. Mom seems mollified. A bit.

I assure them I'm all right and I do my best to keep my legs from shaking as I head to my room. Eve. Eve is getting

—do you like—
out of prison. When? I forgot to ask. I should have
   —move over like that and—
asked them when, but I didn't even think to
   —guuuhhh! Ohhhhhh!—
ask and the flickers are strobing as I make it to my room and collapse on the bed, as I flip back and forth between the present and multiple pasts, and I realize I never even told them I was suspended.

Dr. Kennedy: Still worried about college?

J. Mendel: Yeah. Still haven't heard from the Holy Trinity.

Kennedy: You've already been accepted to Georgia Tech and College Park and Clemson, right?

Mendel: Yeah, but those were my safety schools. MIT, Yale, and Stanford are the ones I'm really waiting on. It's like, every day I run to the mailbox, but . . . nothing. It's tough because the money at those schools is, you know, a lot. My parents don't have a lot of money. I don't know how it's going to work out.

Kennedy: It's natural that you're going to be anxious about this. I'm not going to tell you to relax about it, but I do want you to try to remember that three good schools have already accepted you and you can afford to attend each of them. Just remember that, OK?

Mendel: Yeah.

Kennedy: Now. Why did you hit your coach?

Mendel: You ever do any sports, doc?

Kennedy: I rowed crew in college.

Mendel: Then you know—sometimes coaches just need to be hit.

Kennedy: Be that as it may—

Mendel: I love that expression.

Kennedy: Glad to brighten your day. Be that as it may, was it worth a three-day suspension? Was it worth the possible legal ramifications?

Mendel: There won't be any legal ramifications.

Kennedy: For hitting a teacher? That seems pretty serious. They usually don't let things like that slide. Not these days.

Mendel: If they make a big deal out of it, they'll have to take it to court, right? And if they take it to court, then I'll testify as to what he said. Believe me, he doesn't want that to get out.

Kennedy: See, now we're getting somewhere. You hit him because he said something to you. You didn't mention that before.

Mendel: You didn't ask.

Kennedy: We've been doing this too long for games. You know damn well I asked why you hit him. So what did he say, Josh? What ticked you off?

Mendel: We were running laps and the little prick was goading us on and when I ran past him, he dropped his voice so that I was the only one who could hear him, and he said, "Pick it up, Mendel! You never slept with me, so I ain't about to take it easy on you!"

Kennedy: He said that? He actually said that to you? Well, you were right: He needed to be hit. What a piece of shit.

Mendel: My sentiments exactly.

Kennedy: You can't let this stand. You should report what he said.

Mendel: Why bother? It'll just open up the whole thing again.

And at least now I know what everyone's thinking. I have confirmation.

Kennedy: Confirmation of what you've always expected?

Mendel: Yeah.

Kennedy: Do you think *everyone* at your school thinks like Coach Kaltenbach?

Mendel: I don't know. I see the looks I get sometimes. Especially from the female teachers. It's like they're afraid of me. Like they have to avoid touching me or they'll catch the molester virus.

Kennedy: You haven't molested anyone. You are the victim . . . the target of molestation.

Mendel: Once you've been touched—

Kennedy: You said the female teachers in particular. Why them?

Mendel: I don't know.

Kennedy: Until you punched out your coach, you've never harmed a teacher, right? So why would they be afraid of you?

Mendel: Maybe they don't want to spend five years in jail like, y'know. Like . . .

Kennedy: Like Mrs. Sherman. Hmm?

Mendel: I guess.

Kennedy: What do *you* have to do with that? She chose you, Josh. Not the other way around.

Mendel: I guess.

Kennedy: Do you think there's a teacher at the school who's interested in you? Sexually?

Mendel: No! No.

Kennedy: It's not uncommon for a sexual predator to latch on to a previous—

Mendel: No. No one. It's me. They're afraid of me.

Kennedy: That just doesn't make sense. I think you're projecting something onto them.

Mendel: Oh, God. Psychobabble bullshit. You're not supposed to—

Kennedy: I know, I broke the rule. Here's a dollar. But look, clearly there's still some residual worry about Mrs. Sherman and about what she did. It's perfectly natural for you to fear the same reaction from women in similar positions. Are any of these teachers young? Attractive?

Mendel: Every school's got at least one like that. You're not listening to me. But I appreciate the buck.

Kennedy: Josh, don't be obtuse. I know how bright you are. Think about it: What are the odds you're so concerned about this just as Mrs. Sherman is being released from prison? How do you feel about that? Scared? It's OK to be scared.

Mendel: I'm not scared.

Kennedy: There's already a protective order in place. She's not allowed within a hundred yards of you.

Mendel: Why? What's she going to do to me? I'm not twelve anymore. I'm six-one. I outweigh her by a hundred pounds. I could—

Kennedy: What? What could you do? Hurt her? Is that it? Did you want to hit her? Is that why you hit your coach? He was there and she wasn't.

Mendel: No. I don't want to hurt her. I hit Kaltenbach because he was a fucking douchebag, OK?

Kennedy: There's no doubt in my mind that Kaltenbach is a fucking douchebag. But you have every right to be angry at Evelyn Sherman. Every right to want to hurt her. I don't want you to *act* on that anger, but I want you to know that it's OK, that it's understandable.

Mendel: [unintelligible]

Kennedy: What's that?

Mendel: I said—I said, she liked to be called "Eve." Not Evelyn. Eve.

CHAPTER 3
Tell Me

AFTER MY SESSION WITH DR. KENNEDY, I head over to South Brook High and wait in the parking lot for Zik, who comes running up from behind the building—the rain ended last night, so practice was outside. He spots me, waves.

"Watch the mud," I tell him when he opens the passenger-side door. I drive a crappy little Escort from before the Precambrian era, but I like to keep it clean. Zik's cleats are caked with mud and grass. Kaltenbach's an idiot for having outdoor practice without waiting for the field to dry.

"No fear," Zik says. He leans against the car and pries off his shoes, then dumps them into a plastic bag. We've done this routine before.

"Dinner?" I ask him, once he's strapped in and ready for takeoff. It's a rhetorical question. Zik would be up for driving to the moon if I asked—it would keep him out of his house.

"Yeah, let's hit the Narc."

"I don't want to."

"Oh, come on, man! They've got the best fried chicken!"

The Narc is a big local grocery store off 54 on the north side of Brookdale. It's actually called "Nat's Market," but at some point in teen history that got shortened and corrupted to "the Narc." Har-har. Its defining characteristic is the ancient lunch counter tucked away in the back, open from noon to midnight. Throwback to a rumored time when such things were common. The only other time I've seen a lunch counter is in old footage of the civil rights movement.

But I have a rule about the Narc: I don't go there before midnight.

"You want Narc fried chicken, I'll sit in the car while you go get it."

"Man . . . Never mind. Drive-through anything's fine. Except for Taco Smell."

I drive aimlessly for a while. No rush. I like being in the car, as long as traffic isn't too bad. Cars are little privacy cocoons that we take with us. If you could refuel while driving you could, theoretically, stay moving forever.

Zik's usually a chatterbox, but he's saying nothing right now, so I figure it's on me.

"So, how was dickhead at practice today?"

Zik snorts laughter. "You gave him a black eye."

"No shit!" Score one for me!

"And he was wearing his cap different. Forward, you know? Like this?" Zik demonstrates with his own ball cap, tilting it forward at an odd angle. It's just right to avoid brushing, say, a big ol' goose egg on the back of your head. I can't help it—I giggle like a five-year-old who just heard someone say "poop."

"Then it was all worth it. My sacrifice has not been in vain."

"Yeah, speaking of . . ." Zik stops to point out the drive-through for Lake Side, a pretentious local joint with fries to die for. I agree with a shrug. "Speaking of sacrifice, man—how'd your parents take the news?"

Eve. My heart jackhammers for a second, and I think a flicker's coming on. "The news?"

"Getting suspended?"

Oh. That. "They're OK with it."

He shakes his head. "You've got the coolest parents in the world."

It's our turn at the window, so I get to avoid responding to that. The truth of the matter is that by the time I decided to go tell them last night, Mom and Dad were in the middle of a fight, and next thing I knew Mom was out the door and backing out of the driveway. That's her usual response to their fights—flight. I figured that wasn't the best time to tell Dad. In the morning, while he was eating breakfast, I told him, including what Kaltenbach had said to set me off.

"He really said that? You're sure you didn't misunderstand him?"

"Yeah, Dad."

He shook his head sadly. "You're seeing Kennedy today, right?"

"Right."

"OK. Good."

And, mission accomplished. If Mom had been home, there'd have been a scene.

The girl at the drive-through window hands me our change and two bags of food. We keep going north up 54. Route 54 is the main road through Brookdale, bisecting the town into east and west halves almost perfectly. Go north far enough and you end up in Canterstown, which is such a small hick town that even people in Brookdale make fun of it. The Canterstown

Sledgehammers, though, are a kick-ass ball team. They've beaten us ten times out of the last ten games, and four out of five before that. Kinda sucks to get your ass kicked by shit-kickers.

Zik dives into his bag, and the smell of perfectly fried fries makes my mouth water. I drive with one hand and stuff my face with the other. As we enter Canterstown, Zik rolls down the window and hurls his soda at the sign that says "Welcome to Canterstown, Home of the Mighty Sledgehammers!" He can't help it—you can never *completely* escape your DNA.

"You're pretty quiet, man." Zik rolls up the window. "Usually you've got something to say."

He's right. But entering Canterstown has sparked a memory. Not a flicker; a memory. Eve—Mrs. Sherman—whatever—brought me here to a little family restaurant once. Late in the day, right after school. The waitress thought I was Eve's little brother, and Eve didn't say anything to disabuse her of the notion.

Awesome restaurant. Best turkey pot pie I've ever had in my life, and the strawberry pie for dessert was made with fresh strawberries that they picked from a patch a half-mile away . . .

". . . the newspaper," Zik's saying.

"Huh? Sorry, man, I missed that."

He sucks in his breath. "I said I—I saw the article. The one in the newspaper. About her."

"Oh." *Former teacher released from jail.* That was the headline in this morning's edition. Simple and to the point. Buried on page seven.

"I'm just saying, that's all." He's dancing close to the edge here. We've never talked about it. Not once. Not even about what happened at Rachel's that night five years ago; he was ten feet away and he never asked me. But I bet he asked Rachel. Or Michelle told him. Flicker

—*little bastard!*—

"Shit!" Zik shouts, as I twist at the last second to avoid the kid on the bike.

My breath comes fast. "Little fucker! Shot out at me like that!"

"Dude, I saw him coming. He fucking *signaled*. It's like you wanted to plow him down."

Is that true? Is that what happened? Did I miss something while in the flicker?

"I better take you home." The dash clock says it's not even seven yet, and I hate to dump Zik at home while his parents will still be up.

He's morose, but he understands. Or at least he pretends to understand, which is good enough for me. Sometimes that's the mark of a best friend—someone who puts up with your shit and pretends it doesn't bother him.

Former teacher released from jail.

That's it. My name's nowhere in the article, of course. I'm "a local minor male." I was a minor, so my name was out of the papers, but everyone still knew. After Rachel's closet, how could everyone *not* know?

According to the article, her family was there in the court-room, but said nothing. I guess that was her brother and her mother, then. Her father's dead. I wonder if her husband was there? Are they still married?

—fucking little perv!—

—you maniac!—

I pull over to the side of the road amid honking horns. Hit the hazard lights. I just need a second to collect myself. Just a

—listen to me!—

—fucking ruined my life!—

Just a second.

CHAPTER 4
Walking Backwards

WITHOUT REALIZING WHAT I'M DOING, I drive to her apartment.

I have the address memorized: 1033 Fire Station Road, Apt. B. There's no fire station there—there used to be, back when Brookdale was founded, but now it's a collection of apartment complexes and condos. I remember the address from the subscription to *Electronic Gaming*.

I pull up at around eight. It's dark by now, dark enough to need headlights, dark enough for streetlamps to glow.

Former teacher released from jail.

Why wasn't I there? Shouldn't someone from my family have been there? Isn't that how it works with parole?

I find a parking spot and sit there for a while. So this is déjà vu, huh? Not like the flickers at all. The flickers are real, like sci-fi time travel, only for a second. This déjà vu is just . . . creepy. Creepy as hell.

It's imperfect, though, because this place isn't the same as five or six years ago. There's a little island of grass between the parking lot and Fire Station Road—six years ago, they had just planted these spindly bushes there, and now it's like a green barrier of thorns.

Other things have changed, too. The retaining wall on the

south end of the complex has been freshly painted a cheerful blue—it used to be naked gray cinderblock. The yellow stripes on the parking lot tarmac are bright and straight.

—not much, is it—

Potted plants line the walkways. They weren't there before. I'm *on* the walkway. I somehow got out of the car without realizing. God, am I losing my mind?

OK, so, potted plants. The big crack in the sidewalk, the one I used to jump over, is gone. She used to hold my hand as we walked from the car, and every time I would come to that crack, I'd jump over it as if it were an endless chasm...

She used to hold my hand...

My fingers twitch. There's a brick archway that leads into a little outdoor alcove with a row of steel mailboxes. Beyond, through another archway, are the stairs, concrete risers that go up for six steps to a landing, then a half-turn, six more steps to the first floor. Twelve steps in total. I know because I counted them and the number was the same as my age—

Don't go so fast. I'm an old lady.

You're not old, Mrs. Sherman.

That's sweet of you, Joshua.

—and when I turned thirteen, I started counting the landing, too, and then a couple of days later, in the closet with Rachel...

It's like I'm walking backwards through time, propelled by memory, receiving the occasional rocket boost from a particularly powerful flicker.

I lean against the alcove wall. There's a new security light that shines directly on the mailboxes, and a bulb of opaque glass suspended from a corner, way up high. Camera. I stand there awhile until I catch my breath, then scan the mailboxes.

Unit B.

The little black tape from a label maker spells out: Maguire, S.

I touch it, just to make sure it's real. The raised white letters bump my fingers. Fuck the camera. I prod at the label with my fingernail until I find a loose corner, then slowly peel it back, but there's nothing underneath.

I'm tempted to go upstairs. To walk up those twelve/thirteen stairs, down the corridor to Unit B. Knock on the door.

And . . . what? Ask S. Maguire if I can walk around? See if the inside of the apartment has changed as much as the outside of the building? Relive the memories of—

This is fucked. What am I *doing* here? She's not here. She hasn't been here in years.

Back in the car, the remains of my fries and burger from Lake Side have gone cold and the ice has melted in my soda. I toss it all in a trash can. I shouldn't have come here. It was stupid. What did I expect to find? I pound a fist against the steering wheel—the Escort is old, but tough enough to handle the occasional temper tantrum.

I'm in no hurry to go home. By now, Dad will have mentioned my suspension to Mom, so I'm scheduled for a severe talking-to when I walk through the door. Not my favorite way to kill time. Besides, since I had to chuck my food, I'm still hungry. Might as well have one final meal before being hassled.

The way home from the old apartment takes me past the Narc. My stomach rumbles. Fried chicken sounds really good right now. I pull in and get halfway to the lunch counter before I realize what I'm doing.

I'm in the Narc before midnight.

OK, calm down, Josh. Chill out. Maybe *she's* not working today.

I'm frozen in the canned goods aisle, unable to move. A woman with a squealing kid stares at me like I'm a sasquatch stumbling in from the wild. I have to get out of here.

But I'm too terrified to move. She could be here, around any corner. She doesn't *have* to be at the lunch counter; she could be on a checkout aisle or stocking shelves or something.

She could, in fact, be about to come around the corner into the canned goods aisle.

I bug out. I head back to the doors, forget that I can't go back out the way I came in, then dodge for an empty checkout aisle. Quick scan: she's not at any of the registers. I breeze through the empty aisle and blow through the automatic doors, back into the humid April night and straight into Rachel Madison, who's standing there in her red Nat's Market apron, nursing a Coke.

We stare at each other for a second. We're maybe two feet from each other, closer than we've been since that day five years ago. I want to run like hell—I'm not track-and-field fast, but I could get pretty far before she could say anything.

Instead, I stand rooted to the spot, wondering with sick horror what she'll say. I realize—and honest to God, this is the first time I've realized this—that I never apologized to her. I never got the chance back when it all happened, and I've tried to stay away from her since then. Too difficult to be near her. And she never works past midnight, so . . .

It's my first time really looking at her in years. She never did finish filling out. When she got too old to play baseball with the boys in Little League, she shifted over to softball, which kept strengthening her legs into a muscled dream. Her hips have rounded a bit—helps her on the pitcher's mound, and makes it fun to watch her walk away. Her breasts topped out at A cups, but she makes the most of them.

I'm staring. I have to stop that.

—*look all you want*—

Gah! She's gazing at me, worried. "Josh? Are you OK?"

Flickers! Goddamned flickers! "Yeah. Yeah, I'm all right. Sorry." There we go—an apology after five years. Think it counts? No, me neither.

"You looked a little . . . spacey for a second there." She narrows her eyes, pulling the freckles in toward the bridge of her nose. They've lightened a little bit over the years. Or maybe it's just makeup?

"Yeah, I guess . . ."

"Don't usually see you around here," she goes on. "I always thought you were the one guy in Brookdale who didn't like the Narc."

I don't know what to say.

"Or maybe you're just avoiding me? Like in school?"

Something to say pops into my head: "I saw you in the game against East Brook last week. Your fastball is unreal."

She leans against the wall and takes a sip of her Coke. "It's even better than when you couldn't hit it." She grins at me, and I want to kill myself for her kindness. How can I deserve that?

"That was overhand," I tell her, remembering her blistering fastball as a kid. "Underhand isn't the same."

She checks her watch. "I'm off break now, but I'll take you up on that." She heads for the entrance.

Take me up on that? On what? She saunters away—the hip sway that she hadn't perfected at thirteen is effortless now at eighteen. What the hell is she talking about?

"What do you mean?" I call after her. I start to follow her, then stop when I realize how bizarre it is to be chasing after the girl—the woman—I molested.

"I'll call you," she says, half turning to mime holding a phone to her ear, then slipping back through the automatic door and into the store. I stand there for a while, my hunger forgotten, my confusion overwhelming.

After a minute or two, I go back inside to buy a newspaper, then head home.

Mom and Dad (mostly Mom) used to get sketchy about me reading about the case in the newspaper. By the time I get home, Mom has already tossed out the newspaper; I read the story this morning, but she can't know that. I sneak my copy into my room and hide it for later. Mom calls out to me from the laundry room downstairs, where she proceeds to give me all kinds of holy hell about being suspended again. Where Dad was blasé, she's in a fury.

I promise to try harder and to avoid further suspensions, which should be easy considering that there's only another six weeks of school. Even *I've* never managed multiple suspensions in that period of time. Mom seems mollified and swishes off to bed, leaving me to fold the laundry. I could have lived my entire life a happy and fulfilled man without learning that my mother has a thong—

—*push it aside*—

Ah, Christ. Like Eve. I don't need this. I really don't.

In my room, I take out the newspaper and read the article:

Former Teacher Released from Jail

by Stephanie Gould, Times Staff Writer

With members of her family in attendance, Evelyn Sherman appeared before Judge Eric L. Fletch, who suspended the remaining time of her sentence and ruled that her probation would begin immediately. Sherman had served nearly five years.

Four years and ten months earlier, Fletch sentenced Sherman to serve fifteen years in the State Women's Correctional Facility. In February, Sherman's attorney, Danielle G. Cresswell, filed a motion for a reduction of her sentence. A hearing took place in March, at which time Fletch said that he would make a decision later.

Last Friday, Fletch told Sherman that, based on reports from her therapist, the prison psychologist, and guards at the prison, he felt it would be a waste of the correctional system to keep her in jail.

"This woman has made enormous strides," Fletch said in court today. "Leaving her behind bars serves no one's interest, and certainly not the interests of justice."

Sherman wept in court on Friday at the news that she would be released. She said that she is remorseful for what she has done.

"I have learned an enormous amount in the past five years," she said, "both about myself and about the situations I failed to react to successfully. I'm grateful for this opportunity to prove myself to the community and to my friends and family again."

Cresswell submitted to the court letters from Dr. Judith

Fraser, who has been Sherman's therapist since her arrest five years ago.

According to Cresswell, Fraser rated the odds of Sherman re-offending at zero. James B. Olsen, warden of the prison, also submitted an affidavit calling Sherman "a model prisoner," citing her work teaching illiterate inmates to read and write.

With her release, Sherman begins five years of supervised probation. Under the terms of her parole, she must register as a sex offender, complete a sex offender program, and have no un-supervised contact with children. She must also attend therapy sessions twice per week.

"We're very grateful for the judge's compassion and that this nightmare is over and this young woman can go on with her life," Cresswell said.

Sherman was twenty-four at the time of her arrest. She will turn thirty later this year.

Gil B. Purdy, the district attorney who prosecuted Sherman, appeared in court to protest her release.

"This woman is a sexual predator. She preys on young men. I don't see how we can let her out on the streets," Purdy told the press immediately after the hearing.

State police arrested Sherman five years ago based on allegations that she had engaged in sexual activity with a local minor male while she taught at South Brook Middle School. She was also accused of providing that same student with alcohol. Sherman initially pleaded not guilty, but later changed her plea to guilty.

Reach staff writer Stephanie Gould at stegould@lowecotimes.com.

Remorseful? Really? I have a hard time believing that. That just doesn't sound like her. I'm tempted to call the reporter and get a first-person account of what happened in the courtroom, but she probably wouldn't even talk to me.

I carefully clip the article from the paper and throw away everything else.

At the bottom of my closet is a fire safe I bought at Staples, hidden under some gym clothes and old toys. Within is a sea of tiny plastic cases—microcassettes. A copy of every tape Dr. Kennedy has made of our sessions. Five years of my life, completely documented on tape. Not many people can say they have that.

Also in the safe is a clipping of every article from the *Lowe County Times* about Eve Sherman. I look through them for the first time in years; there haven't been many articles since she went into prison. Headlines jump out at me:

Sherman to Serve Jail Time

Sex, Lies, and Videogames

Sherman Attorney: "No Insanity Plea"

Sex-scandal Teacher Changes Plea

Eve is out of prison. She's out. She's . . . somewhere. Is she staying in the state? She can't teach anymore, so what is she doing? What about her husband? The article is a piss-poor source of information.

I lock the safe again, now including the new clipping, then cover it with its camouflage, lie back, and drift off to sleep, flickers sparking and wheeling off into the dark.

Session Transcript: #1

Dr. Kennedy: My name is Dr. Kennedy. I don't know if you remember, but I saw you at the courthouse the other day. Do you remember that?

J. Mendel: Yeah. What's your name?

Kennedy: I just told you: Dr. Kennedy.

Mendel: That's not what I mean. What's your first name? You know mine.

Kennedy: My first name is Gene. Do you always want to know adults' first names?

Mendel: I don't know.

Kennedy: Can we talk a little bit about Mrs. Sherman?

Mendel: No.

Kennedy: Don't you want to know why I want to talk about her?

Mendel: It's like the police and my parents. You want to know everything.

Kennedy: Well, look. I want to know things, but only so that I can help you.

Mendel: I don't need help.

Kennedy: Do you understand what's happened to you?

Mendel: I'm not stupid.

Kennedy: I didn't say you were. Your grades are very good—

Mendel: Do you have everything about me in that file?

Kennedy: Not everything. Not the important things. I need you to tell those things to me.

Mendel: I don't want to.

Kennedy: Well, let's start slow. Why don't you just tell me how it started?

Mendel: Are you going to tell everyone else? Are you going to tell my parents?

Kennedy: Oh, is that what you're—? No. There's something called . . . Do you know what doctor-patient privilege is?

Mendel: Yeah. I saw it on TV.

Kennedy: Well, that's what we have between us. Anything you tell me, I can't tell anyone else. Not the judge. Not your parents.

Mendel: But you tape-record it.

Kennedy: What?

Mendel: You tape-record it. I saw you push the button before. Anyone can listen to what I say.

Kennedy: The tapes are just to help me remember what you say. That's all. See this door here? See the lock? I'm the only one with the key. Your tapes will be locked up at all times. No one will get to them.

Mendel: I want them.

Kennedy: Excuse me?

Mendel: I want copies. Of the tapes.

Kennedy: That's not—

Mendel: That's how I want it. I'll tell you everything, but I get copies of the tapes. This way, if you tell someone what I said someday and you lie, I'll have proof.

CHAPTER 5

Waking Games

I AWAKEN TO THE SOUNDS. I hate it when this happens.

Through the ductwork that runs along the ceiling of the house, you can hear a lot at night when it's still. And, yes, that means I can hear my parents having what they call sex.

This isn't quite as creepy as it seems; I've been hearing this every once in a while as long as I can remember, though the frequency over the past few years has been nearly nonexistent. It usually doesn't keep me up, but tonight I must be on edge, every nerve ready to fire, as if someone's stalking me.

After some rustling of bedclothes and squeaking of bedsprings, there's silence until Mom starts to complain and Dad says, "I'm sorry, honey. I'm sorry," and I turn over in bed, pull the pillow around my ears, and force myself back into sleep before I can finish the thought, before I can finish thinking, *I do it better*.

Later, bang! I'm up again, suddenly, as if an alarm's gone off in my skull. Clock says it's three a.m. My brain is fuzzing and buzzing. I don't even remember sleeping, but I guess I must have been. The house is quiet, still. It's like there's no one here at all. Or maybe like the entire world disappeared while I was asleep, leaving nothing but a silent black void outside my bedroom door.

Through the vent, Dad snorts out a sudden burst of ragged breath that ends as soon as it began. The world is still out there.

Remorseful.

What the hell does that actually *mean,* anyway? How did she say that? Did she actually say, "I'm remorseful for what I've done"? Or did she say something vague that sort of *sounded* remorseful and the reporter just paraphrased it?

And wouldn't she say "I *regret*" instead of "I'm remorseful"? They're two different things. I mean, remorse is . . . Remorse . . .

I kick off the covers and switch on my light. According to my online dictionary, remorse is about having a sense of guilt for something in the past. Regret is about being sorry. Two different things. It's subtle, but they *are* different. Which one did Eve claim? Did the reporter get it wrong?

And what's up with that prosecutor? I remember him—he interrogated me five years ago. He was a real dick; he was an assistant DA back then, but he thought he was hot shit. And let me tell you—he *loves* the word "predator." He used it so often when he was interrogating me that I started keeping count.

Here's what amuses me about the whole "predator" angle: Predation is a part of the natural world order. You don't get pissed at a lion for eating a gazelle; that's just what lions do. They prey. So by calling Eve a "sexual predator," aren't we saying that she's doing something that's part of the natural order? It isn't that we have to like it, any more than we have to like the idea of some poor eland bleeding to death on the veldt. But it's nature.

I have learned an enormous amount in the past five years.

Like what? What did she learn in the past five years, other than how to teach inmates how to read and how to avoid getting stabbed in the showers? How do the other prisoners treat a woman who did what she did? Is it like being a child molester? I read somewhere that child molesters are considered the lowest of the low in prison; even mass murderers hate them. Everyone is out to kill them.

Did someone try to kill her in jail? Did she have to fight to protect herself?

What did she learn?

And who was her teacher?

And then I'm awake again. Still feel like I haven't slept at all. I only know I did because there's a big chunk of *blank* in my memory and the clock has jumped ahead to almost six.

Rachel...

What did she mean by "I'll take you up on that"? I told her underhand wasn't the same as overhand. You don't "take someone up" on that; you either agree or disagree with them.

And underhand *isn't* the same as overhand. It just isn't. I've seen Rachel pitch a couple of times when I ended up at softball games, and the style is completely different. We first met when we were kids, playing rec center baseball and Little League together. She had a decent fastball back then, but her slider was an absolute killer. I rarely hit off her, but she had control issues—she walked me a lot. My on-base percentage was sort of ridiculous, but I was pretty small until a big growth spurt hit me in middle school; my strike zone was tough to nail, so I got walked a lot. I had to teach myself to swing at a lot of bad pitches if I ever wanted to hit the ball, and then I had to un-teach myself the same thing.

Once we got older . . . Well, we would have gone into sepa-rate sports anyway. Brookdale is just barely progressive enough to let boys and girls play baseball together through sixth grade. But after that, it's "separate but equal." Even if the nightmare at Rachel's house hadn't happened five years ago, we still would have been seeing less of each other.

By now I'm too keyed up to go back to sleep. My alarm will be going off in half an hour anyway. I do some crunches, some pushups, some curls and flies with the resistance bands I keep under the bed. Exercise is good—it's tough to think *too* much when you're exercising. You get all caught up in the repetition and the counting and focusing on your form, and there's no room for flickers or memories or recriminations.

My stomach rumbles, but I hear Mom and Dad bustling around in the kitchen, getting their lunches ready and drink-ing coffee. I feel awkward seeing them in the morning after I've heard them through the vent. As if they'll be able to tell that I could hear. Or that there will be some weird sign of failed sex on them—like the scarlet letter, almost—that I'll have to pre-tend not to see.

I wait until I can't wait any longer; I don't want to be late picking up Zik and condemn him to the indignity of taking the bus. Even though I haven't heard Dad leave yet, I head out to the kitchen.

He's sitting at the table, stirring the contents of a big metal-lic coffee mug.

"You're up early for someone who doesn't have to go to school," he says.

"I'm taking Zik to school." *Like yesterday,* I want to add, but don't. Dad's not known for the quantity of clues in his possession.

"That's nice of you." He frowns and peers into his mug. His eyes go to the creamer, and I can almost see the conflict within him.

"Look," he goes on, reaching for the creamer, "your mother is going to be out late tonight. Some baby shower or wedding shower or . . ." He regards the creamer in his hands, then tips it enough to let a few drops into his coffee. This seems to make him happy. "Some damn shower or other. Anyway, I was thinking we'd just do pizza for dinner. Does that work for you?"

"Sure, Dad. Whatever you want. Can Zik come over?"

"Sure, sure. How is Zik these days?"

I love how he says "these days," as if he hasn't seen Zik in years, as if Zik is some stranger from a remote land who shows up on the summer solstice and that's it.

"He's doing OK. Pissed at me for getting suspended. He says I'm gonna lose my swing without practice."

Dad grunts. "You won't lose your swing in three days. That's stupid."

My dad is not one for idle chitchat.

Dad leaves for work and I slug down a granola bar and milk before heading out to the car.

CHAPTER 6
I Am Iron Man

WHEN ZIK CLIMBS IN next to me a few minutes later, he has a weird look on his face. Almost as if he's trying not to smile.

"You OK?" I ask him.

"Oh, yeah. Sure." He gives me the once-over. "How about you? You OK?"

Is this about the newspaper article again? "Yeah, man, I'm fine."

Zik nods as if he doesn't believe me. There's an anticipatory silence in the car as I pull away from Zik's house, as if we're each waiting for the other to say something. After a few moments, Zik breaks the silence.

"Here, J." He pulls a spiral-bound notebook out of his backpack and holds it up to me.

"What's that?"

"Eyes on the road!"

I tap the brake and come nowhere near to rear-ending a Honda. Nowhere near. Seriously.

"Well, don't fucking wave shit in my face while I'm driving!"

He tosses the notebook into the back seat. "I copied all my notes from bio, history, and English last night. For the last two days, you know? Sorry I couldn't go to your math class for you. Or physics." He pauses. "Or Spanish."

Zik and I share most of our classes, but there are a couple of the really high-level math and science classes that I'm in alone. But in the meantime, he's saved me from having to hunt down all of this stuff from my teachers in most of my classes.

"You saved my life, man. Or my GPA, at least."

He grins. "Gotta keep the Streak alive, Iron Man."

Years ago, a ballplayer named Cal Ripken Jr. became known as the Iron Man because he had this ungodly streak of consecutive played games: 2,632 by the time he was finished. People who like baseball like to talk about home run records and hitting records and pitching records—they bring up Bonds and McGwire and Clemens and Wood; all that. But people who *love* baseball know that Ripken's record is *the* record, the record that will go unbroken as long as we live. Why? It's simple: Anyone can have a good season and hit enough homers to kick Barry Bonds out of the record books. Anyone can have a lucky game and get twenty-one strikeouts in nine innings, thereby eclipsing Clemens, Wood, and Johnson at once. But Ripken's record spans *seventeen seasons*. It's not a case where you can have a good game or a good season or juice yourself up on steroids and break a record. You can't break Ripken's record with luck or a burst of skill. You have to be dedicated. You have to have a superhuman focus that pushes you through injuries, bad days, and all the petty stupidities the world throws at you . . . all the while maintaining a level of ability that suits the major leagues.

Zik calls me Iron Man because I haven't had less than an A in any class since third grade.

It's nothing I set out to do. I wasn't trying, at least, not at first. But somewhere around sixth grade, Zik noticed; that's when he started calling me Iron Man. It was just an in-joke between friends, so it didn't mean much. And I figured that once I hit high school I would, inevitably, get a B at some point.

But it didn't happen. Or, at least, it hasn't happened yet, and given that it's April of my senior year, the odds are on my side. The longer I went on my personal streak, though, the more intense it became. For most of my life, I got straight A's as a matter of course. I never even thought about it. Schoolwork just came easily to me, and it was no problem to hit my scores. But once I became aware of my own success, it started to gnaw at me. I started to obsess over it. Every paper, every test, had to be an A. I couldn't get a B on something and then pull it up with a bunch of A's later—no, I had to get all A's, all the time, or else I'd start to panic. One slip could lead to more, after all.

I wonder if that's how it was for Ripken? At first was it just fun playing the game? And some breed of stubbornness or persistence or overblown work ethic that compelled him to play through injuries? And when did he first realize that he might be able to challenge Lou Gehrig's old record of 2,130 games? That record stood for fifty-six years before Ripken broke it—it was so inviolable that it was practically a law of physics. And then Cal Ripken, the Iron Man, did the baseball equivalent of discovering cold fusion.

So sometimes I wonder—when was that moment that it occurred to him that not only *could* he break Gehrig's record . . . but he *had* to? In press interviews, Ripken always said that the streak and the record were secondary to the game, and I've always said that the learning and the process of learning are superior to the actual grades . . .

But honestly, the one thing Cal Ripken and I have in common is this: We're both full of shit. Because streaks and records have a way of worming into your mind whether you want them there or not.

I've got six weeks left of school. I could bag my classes and end up with a B average in most of them and still go to college. And that would be a lot less pressure on myself. But I can't do that. My parents don't understand that. Hell, even some of my teachers have told me to take a break.

But Zik gets it. Zik gets it, and he sat up last night copying his notes into a second notebook. Because Zik wants to see the Streak continue.

And unlike most people, Zik knows that I earned each and every one of those grades. Even the ones in seventh grade, when Eve was my history teacher. Even those.

CHAPTER 7
OK, Baseball

HERE'S THE THING ABOUT BASEBALL—at the end of the day, it's not really a team sport.

Which is just as well, because I'm not one for teams. Teams generally are a collection of loosely aligned assholes who all think they have something in common when they really don't. Jocks are jerks, plain and simple. I've seen it my whole life. Just because I have a talent with a bat, I've been witness to some real primo acts of assholery—front-row center seat, let me tell you. Freshman year, I saw a new kid just about dunked headfirst into a flushing toilet for the ever-popular swirly.

I say "just about" because I intervened. I was only a freshman, but even then I was somewhat legendary to the upperclassmen. I was the only freshman that year to start on the varsity team, and in the early practices I had batted well against the senior pitchers, going 6 for 7 with a double and a triple for a whopping .857 batting average and an unheard of 1.286 slugging average. Now, granted, that was just in practice, but I was a freshman hitting against seniors. It got people's attention. Early on, Coach Kaltenbach set me aside for "special attention."

I took a few licks rescuing that hapless new kid, but it was worth it. Given my history and my skills on the field, I get treated with a certain deference at South Brook, a deference bordering on fear, but I'll take what I can get.

Coach's "special attention" turned out to be nothing more and nothing less than a series of concerted efforts to screw up everything I was doing right and replace it with his own half-assed ideas of how to play the game. It was *enormously* frustrating. He messed up my swing something fierce, and he couldn't understand why I suddenly started hitting only around .300 by the time the season started.

Finally I had to tell him to shove it and I went back to doing things my own way. In our first game of the season, I kicked serious ass, hitting the ball every time at bat for a perfect 1.000 batting average. I drove in two runs with a double and a triple, then hit a home run in the bottom of the seventh, racking up a godlike 3.000 slugging average, all of it by ignoring everything he'd tried to teach me. If there's a better, more effective way of telling someone to fuck off, I have yet to discover it.

It was in that first season that I also managed to get Coach to agree to make me permanent DH. I can't stand playing in the field. I'm a good defensive player, but to me it just ties you into that whole "team" thing and makes you lose focus on what's important: the hitting. Coach didn't know how to deal with me—he was used to dealing with jocks, and I'm not a jock. I guess if you wanted to call me something, you could call me a scholar-athlete, though I hate that term too. It's like a bizarre species of human that only exists, at most, for eight years—high school and college—before vanishing, collapsing like light into one or the other, particle or wave.

Other than having Coach on my ass for four years, constantly trying to get me to change something about my stance or trying to get me to play in the field for a game or two ("Just to see how you do," he says), baseball's been one of my few pleasures in high school. Because I don't let myself fall into that team trap. I don't let myself think of it as a team effort. It's not.

In football or basketball or any of those "bunch of guys try to get a widget to the other end of the field" games, you *have* to be a team. You have to think like a team and subordinate yourself to the team ethic and structure. It's the only way to accomplish anything.

But in baseball . . .

In baseball, when you get into the batter's box, that's *it*. It's just you. It's one man against the world. All that matters in that moment is your individual achievement and your individual skill. There is literally nothing that anyone else on your team can do for you. Hell, they're all sitting on the bench, waiting to see what happens, just like the fans in the crowd! It's just you and your bat.

And the ball.

It's the best, most sublime, purest and truest moment in all of sport. There is nothing in this world more impressive than a good hitter in baseball. Pitchers get all sorts of attention when they strike you out, but here's a secret: Pitching is *nothing* compared to batting. Striking someone out isn't *nearly* as impressive as getting a hit. Want proof? Tell me how many major leaguers hit the ball more often than not. Don't bother to look it up—I'll tell you. There hasn't been a .400 hitter in more than sixty years, since Ted Williams, much less someone hitting over .500. Hitting the ball is infinitely tougher than pitching it. And as far as getting on base period, Williams was the best *ever* and even he only did it 48.3 percent of the time. As a pitcher, you have the entire field backing you up, which I guess brings me right back to where I started.

At the end of the day, it's a series of individual challenges played out against a team defense. It's a personal test every time I step into the batter's box: Can I do better than the last time? And that's why I love it.

CHAPTER 8

Eve

I DRIVE BY THE NARC on my way home. It's weird to think that I can go there now, even when Rachel's working. For a long time now, it's been like the Narc's a church and I'm a vampire. But now I can go inside. Redeemed. Or something like that.

I pull in to try out my newfound freedom. I'm in the breakfast foods aisle when I see her.

She's at the far end of the aisle, but I would know her anywhere, at any distance. She's wearing a pair of jeans that are loose and baggy, along with a sleeveless blouse. Her hair is shorter and lighter than it used to be.

Eve.

And then I'm suddenly *aware* of my heart, with Eve standing ten, fifteen feet away and my heart starts to announce itself to me, to the world, pounding like

—Xbox controller vibrates in my hands—

dinosaur footsteps or

—you're good at this one, Josh—

the thunder of big cannons on a gigantic movie screen, in Dolby surround sound

—come here come here—

or . . . God! Goddamn it!

I lean against the shelf. My heart won't stop pounding. I

can't breathe. I can't focus on the world anymore. The past keeps intruding on the present.

—like this, not like . . . yes—

And I notice that she has a kid.

A kid.

A pudgy little boy, maybe three years old,

—do you have any—

—no, not yet, maybe someday—

clings to her right hand, wearing a red and white striped shirt and khaki shorts. His cheeks are shiny, his dark brown hair fastidiously combed back except for a stubborn cowlick that points starward.

Oh my God. Is that . . . ? Could that be *my*—

No. No. I swallow hard, try to force my breath back into my chest, try to force my heart to stop leaping around like a kitten trapped in a sack. It can't be my son. It can't be. That kid's too young. How the hell did she get pregnant in jail? Is she still married? I never knew. No one would tell me if her husband left her or not. Was he allowed to visit her in jail? Was she raped by a guard? God, why won't my heart stop doing that? Is this a heart attack? Is this what a heart attack feels like? Why can't I catch my breath? What's that ringing in my ears?

I want her not to turn, not to see me. Especially like this, weak. But at the same time, I need her to turn. I need to see her eyes. I need—

And then she turns.

And looks down the aisle.

And I realize, suddenly, that it's all wrong. The shape of her torso, the set of her shoulders. And her eyes—brown, not green.

Things that don't change even after five years in prison. It's not Eve. It's just some cute twenty-something mom with a brat tagging along.

My heart, my lungs, my ears, my brain—they all start to come online and cooperate again. I take a deep, shaky breath and push myself from the shelf to stand unaided again. She looks at me strangely, so I offer her what's intended to be a reassuring smile, but I think it comes out creepy instead because she suddenly hauls her kid up onto her hip like a sack of laundry and says, "Come on, sweetie," and ducks around the corner to the next aisle.

The Narc is dangerous ground, still. Rachel's forgiveness notwithstanding.

I thought it was over, but it's not. She's out now. She could be here.

And then it hits me: She could be *anywhere*.

The realization almost drives me to my knees. I feel like gagging right here in the store, right here in the breakfast food aisle, next to the Count Chocula and the Honey Grahams. She could be

—over here—

—move there—

anywhere at all. And I have no way of knowing. I don't know where she is. I don't know how to find her.

—here—

—here—

—here here here—

Damnit! Fuck! Fuck! Fuck!

Almost as soon as the flickers overwhelm me, they're gone

again, and I'm just an idiot in the cereal aisle, wiping sweat from his forehead and praying that there are no security cameras trained on me right now.

I make my way to the front of the store. The Not-Eve is nowhere in sight, having no doubt taken her child and ducked out a back door, to where it's safe from random, spastic teenagers.

Still, I find myself looking around everywhere, as I walk through the automatic doors, as I cross the parking lot to my car. She's *out*. She could be everywhere and anywhere.

I stop for gas on the way home and sit like a scared kid in my car as the pump chugs away. She could be filling up at the next tank. She could be inside the convenience store, buying orange juice, and walk through the door any minute . . .

—come here—

Any minute . . .

—I want to see you in the light—

Right now

—to the left—

or now

—over more—

or now.

The gas pump thunks to a stop, shaking the car, and I almost leap through the roof.

Everywhere I go—she could be there. At a stoplight. She has to drive places, right? Fast food joints. Stores. She could come to my baseball games, right? Or is she allowed near the school at all? Probably not. But what if it's an away game?

Like next week's game. We play a team from Finn's Crossing. They're 2–6 and their starting pitcher was busted a week ago for smoking pot at a party, so they're like a winged duck on open water. We'll mop them up no problem. But despite the court order, what's to stop Eve from sitting at the top of the bleachers, or maybe way out in left field? That would be far enough, I think. And she'd still be there, right?

My palms are slick on the steering wheel. I'm glad it's early in the day; everyone's at work, the roads are nearly empty, and there's less of a chance of me accidentally killing someone. I don't even know if she's in the state anymore, remember? She could be long gone. That's what *I* would have done—I would have left as soon as I got paroled.

Hell, that's what I *am* planning. It's just that it's taken five years because there's that whole "turning eighteen and graduating from high school" thing to deal with. I would have run like hell from this town when I was thirteen if I could have. I begged my parents to move us away. I couldn't stand walking down the street or the bus aisle or the school hallways, feeling people's eyes on me, knowing what they were thinking, knowing that they knew everything. I wanted to yell at them, to hit them, to *beat* them, to run away screaming . . .

Mom and Dad tried a bunch of things. There were the regular sessions with Dr. Kennedy, but also some New Age woman who explained to me that virginity was a state of mind and that if I didn't think of myself as "violated," then I wouldn't be. Um, OK.

In the end, it was Dr. Kennedy who helped. And even then, I couldn't tell him everything. I couldn't get him to understand all of it.

Session Transcript: #155

Dr. Kennedy: How are you doing, Josh?

J. Mendel: OK.

Kennedy: That's a nice shiner you've got there. Care to tell me how you got it?

Mendel: You already know.

Kennedy: What makes you think that?

Mendel: You get reports. You talk to people. You know everything before I even come in here.

Kennedy: That's true, in some cases. You're still getting into a lot of fights, aren't you? Why don't you tell me about it in your words.

Mendel: I don't feel like telling it in my words, OK?

Kennedy: You're translating your mischanneled erotic feelings into rage and—

Mendel: I hate that. I hate that shit.

Kennedy: What's that?

Mendel: That psychological bullshit. It's all a bunch of crap.

Kennedy: To be fair, some of it is. Tell you what—if you catch me slipping into psychobabble, I'll give you a buck. How about that?

Mendel: Seriously?

Kennedy: Seriously.

Mendel: It's your money.

Kennedy: OK. Let me try to explain this: Sometimes, when children are sexually abused, they become incapable of what's considered a "normal" sexual response. Make sense so far?

Mendel: You mean they can only have sex with the person who abused them?

Kennedy: Well, no. But close. Look, as people grow older, they come to develop responses for situations, including sex, OK? But if you're abused when you're young, sometimes those responses can be twisted or changed. It could make it difficult for you to respond sexually to someone your own age, for example.

Mendel: This is bull. I don't go crazy for every woman who's older than me.

Kennedy: Do you have a girlfriend, Josh?

Mendel: No. I don't. OK?

Kennedy: Why not?

Mendel: I was . . . I was supposed to go out on this date. A double date. With my friend Zik.

Kennedy: This is Zik who's dating . . . Melissa?

Mendel: Michelle.

Kennedy: Right. I'm sorry. And Michelle is best friends with—

Mendel: Rachel.

Kennedy: The girl you—

Mendel: Right. Anyway, we were supposed to go out. It was going to be Zik and Michelle and me and this girl, Lisa Carter.

Kennedy: Why didn't you go?

Mendel: Zik told me . . . Zik told me that he was going to sit apart from us. With Michelle, you know? So that they could be alone and, you know, kiss and stuff. So I would be with Lisa. And he told me that Lisa thought I was cute.

Kennedy: And?

Mendel: And then he . . . He didn't mean anything by it. He's my best friend. He was just trying to help. He told me that Lisa was really nervous and I should just be cool.

Kennedy: Was it her first date?

Mendel: No—don't you *get* it? It wasn't that she was nervous because it was a date! It was *me*. She knew about Rachel and the closet and E— Mrs. Sherman and *all* of it. Everyone knew. Everyone in town.

Kennedy: Your name wasn't in the paper.

Mendel: So what? Everyone knows anyway. That's what I'm trying to explain to you. Rachel's parents told people about what happened in the closet, and then the word got out *why* things happened in the closet, and then the trial and *everything*. And Lisa Carter was *afraid*.

Kennedy: You did nothing wrong. In this whole . . . this whole *thing*—you're the one person who never did anything wrong.

Mendel: No. That's not true. I shouldn't have touched Rachel like that. I shouldn't have—

Kennedy: Have you ever talked to Rachel about this? Have you ever apologized to her?

Mendel: She doesn't want an apology. She hates me. She's afraid of me.

Kennedy: And you think Lisa Carter is afraid of you, too?

Mendel: Wouldn't you be?

Kennedy: I think you're assuming that everyone knows—

Mendel: There's this website. I found it one day. It has scans of all these public documents, you know? For big cases, for anything that hits the news. It has all these scans about Mrs. Sherman and me. From her allocution. And because

I'm under eighteen, my name is blocked out, but it doesn't matter. Because everyone knows it's *me*, so it doesn't matter. And everyone knows everything. How can I kiss a girl? How can I touch a girl? What are they expecting? What do they know? How—

Kennedy: There's no question . . . Look, I need you to take a moment, OK? There's tissues in the . . . Right. Do you want some water?

Mendel: No.

Kennedy: OK, just . . . That's it. Deep breaths, like we talked about. What are you doing in your head right now?

Mendel: Figuring out Zik's IPA.

Kennedy: Which is . . . ?

Mendel: Isolated power average.

Kennedy: And that helps calm you down?

Mendel: Sometimes.

Kennedy: I'm not going to lie to you. You've got a tough road ahead of you. But you've got a tough road *behind* you, too. You've come so far in the past couple of years, Josh. The road doesn't go on forever, and you've already made a lot of headway.

Mendel: I feel like I'll never be normal.

Kennedy: It's perfectly natural for you to feel like you're always going to feel this way. That's part of being a teenager, and it's particularly strong for you, given the circumstances. But you'll date girls, Josh. Yes, some of them may react strangely. Some of them will break your heart. But not all of them. You'll go to college someday and there will be people who've never even heard of Brookdale, much less Evelyn Sherman.

Mendel: God, that sounds good.

CHAPTER 9

Michelle's Perfect World

AROUND FIVE, I go to pick up Zik from practice. He looks at me expectantly, then settles back and says nothing, alternating between looking out the window and looking over at me. So we go that way for a little bit.

"How was practice?"

He just shrugs. "You know." He looks over at me again like he's expecting some great wisdom, some epiphany or sermon. What's with him?

"Dude, you feelin' all right?"

"Yeah. How 'bout you?"

"Yeah, I'm good."

"Huh." He settles back again and looks out the window.

We're almost at my house by the time the silence drives me completely insane. "So, I, uh, saw Rachel yesterday."

Which, y'know, is the kind of thing that *should* spontaneously shoot Zik through the roof like an ejector seat. Instead, he just sits up straight and grins. "Oh, yeah? Really? How was that?"

He already knew. Of course—I'm an idiot. Michelle and Rachel are still best friends, after all. That's why I don't hang out with Zik when Michelle's around, because Rachel would usually be a step behind.

"Shit, Zik! Why didn't you say something to me?"

He looks wounded. "I was waiting for you to tell me, J. I don't push you, man. So," he goes on, grinning, "how'd it go?"

"What do you mean?"

"What did you guys talk about? How did you end up talking to her?"

"Oh, come on. Michelle must've told you—"

"No, seriously. She just said that Rachel IM'd her late last night and said that she talked to you. That's it."

I can't believe that they didn't exchange any more information during school today. Rachel and Michelle are, according to Zik, world-class experts at texting each other between classes—they can communicate entire bibles in the four-minute commute. Exactly *what* they need to say in those four minutes is beyond me, but teenage girls have always been something of a mystery to me.

"Look, it's nothing exciting," I tell him, hoping that this message will work its way back to Michelle. Michelle has always harbored a secret hope that Rachel and I will get together and be as hot and heavy a couple as she and Zik are. That way she can be with her boy toy and hang around with her best friend, too. In Michelle's perfect world, every night is a double date involving her, Zik, and Rachel. I'm the missing piece that makes the theorem come together, the sole variable that balances the equation in Michelle's social life algebra.

We head inside. "How did it happen?" he asks.

"Man, you make it sound like I cured cancer."

"J, you talked to *Rachel*. This is *huge*. You've been avoiding her for five years."

"Yeah, well . . . I went to the Narc last night."

Zik's eyes pop. *Now* he's excited. "You went to her? Why?"

"No, no. You've got it all wrong. It was an accident. I wasn't thinking."

I recount for Zik the brief, awkward conversation, and we both agree that it didn't make much sense, which is good because I thought it was just me.

"I'll call Michelle."

I grab Zik's hand before he can snatch up the telephone. "What? Are you *nuts*?"

"Dude, it's gonna clear the whole thing up in less than five minutes. You'll see. Even if Rache didn't call Michelle, Michelle'll still have a better idea of what was going on than either of us."

"Forget it." I tighten my hold on his wrist and pull it back a bit farther from the phone. "She might call Rachel."

"Yeah, I know!" Zik says cheerily, not getting it at all. "That's even better; then we'll know exactly what—Ow!" He yelps and pulls away from me. "Shit!"

"Sorry. But I don't want you to call Michelle. Not about this."

"J, I realize you're, like, a social retard and all, but trust me—this is how it works, man. A girl looks your way, you look her way, then you find out through each other's friends what it all means. You'd know this shit if you weren't practically a—" He stops, gulps, and trails off weakly. "You know . . ."

"Practically a what?"

"A virgin." To his credit, he looks me straight in the eye when he says it.

I laugh because, let's face it, I'm no virgin. Zik laughs along with me after a moment. It's the closest we've come to talking about Eve and what happened five years ago.

"Look, J, this is how it works. Seriously. You've been like a, a *monk* or a *priest* or something. I mean, there've been plenty of girls interested in you. Like Lisa Carter—"

"Yeah, and I remember how that worked out."

"That wasn't her fault."

"No, it was mine. And I get that. This isn't 'how it works,' OK? Seeing Rachel, that was a fluke. I got out with my skin and that's cool."

"But—"

"But nothing. This isn't a case of a girl being interested in me. This is *Rachel*, OK? And Michelle's little fantasy world where Rachel and I get together is really getting old, man, OK?"

He bristles, real anger gathered in his eyes and the set of his jaw. I've seen him like this before, when he talks about his father or his brother. I stepped over the line—I shouldn't have dragged Michelle into it.

"It's not . . . It's not some fantasy of Michelle's. It's not . . . You make it sound like she's—"

"I'm sorry, Zik."

"No, listen to me. There's fantasies, OK, I get that. And then there are just things that people want really bad. And this is one of those things. And Michelle's not the only one, get it?"

"What—Rachel?" I can't believe that Rachel would want to date me.

"*Me*, you asshole!" he yells, his face flushing red. "Me! Jesus Christ, why do you have to be such a dense asshole sometimes?"

My fists ball up on their own; it's just a reaction to being yelled at, to Zik's flushed face. I would never take a swing at him. I tell myself that. Never. Even though I can see the perfect opening.

So, Zik shares Michelle's fantasy. I should have realized.

"I mean . . . God!" He turns away from me, throwing his hands up in the air in frustration. "I hang out with Rachel all. The. Time. Do you even *realize* that? She's Michelle's best friend. I see her all the time!

"It's like I'm . . . It's like I'm schizophrenic or something. I mean, I can't talk about Rachel when I'm around you, and I *won't* talk about you around Rachel. And I have to think about who I'm going to see on which days and for what events and can I wave to Michelle at a game if Rachel's standing next to her . . . I mean, thank God Rachel's softball games are usually at the same time as ours so I don't have to worry about *that,* but . . ."

I had no idea. I never gave it a single thought. But for five years, Zik's been living two lives, like a kid with divorced parents. No wonder he never asked me about Eve; it would open the whole thing up—Rachel's closet and everything else that happened.

The phone rings just then. Caller ID says "Out of area," but that could be Mom or Dad's cell phone, so I answer it.

"Hi, Josh?" says the voice at the other end.

"Uh, yeah." And I realize, as I say it, that it's Rachel. I flicker back to the closet for half a second. Zik arches an eyebrow, and I wonder if I looked like I was going to pass out.

"So," she goes on, "I'm at work, but I get off at midnight. Do you have to get up in the morning, or are you ready to put your money where your mouth is?"

"What are you talking about?" I mouth "Rachel" to Zik and his eyebrows jut skyward.

"It's just a figure of speech," she says. "Look, I have to go. Meet me at SAMMPark? Like, twelve-fifteen. I'll see you. Bye."

I hang up. Zik's swaying back and forth like a potty-training toddler. I almost ask him if needs to pee-pee like a big boy.

"Well? What was *that* about?" You can tell that if he could ask the question louder or somehow bigger, he would.

I'm honest with him: "I have no clue."

Zik, of course, wants to call Michelle right away and get the 411 from the closest thing we have to the source itself. He's certain that Michelle has a series of text messages that, once decoded through the Michelle-inator, will spell out exactly what's going on.

"Nothing's going on," I tell him as Dad pulls into the driveway. "This is over, Zik. Rachel's just . . . She's just messing with me. Which is fine. She's entitled."

But over takeout pizza, while Dad and Zik chatter about the Orioles' chances this year, I sit in silence, wondering, *Why now?* Why would Rachel wait until now, until the ass-end of senior year, to start fucking with my head? I mean, yeah, she's entitled, as far as I'm concerned. But five years is a long time to wait, even if you think revenge is a dish best served cold.

Some part of me always dreaded this. Rachel never talked about that night in the closet (other than to her parents that exact night, of course, and to the police later, and, I assume, to Michelle); there's always been plenty of school gossip and the hick-town equivalent of urban legends surrounding that night and much of what happened with Eve, but as far as I can tell, none of it is close enough to the mark to have come from Rachel herself. She's been pretty circumspect about the whole thing, as is her right as the victim. But even though I've walked five years with the guilt of that night like a squat bar on my shoulders, I never really thought Rachel would retaliate.

I always figured I *deserved* some sort of retribution, but now that it's here (or at least peeking around the corner and grinning diabolically), I'm a bit peeved. Couldn't she just have left well enough alone?

Or maybe I'm just scared. Scared of what could happen now. Or maybe . . .

Maybe *this* is what guilt really feels like. Maybe the past five years have just been proto-guilt, guilt-in-training. Maybe this sense of dread is the real thing. Maybe I'm only disappointed in Rachel because I'm scared shitless and she's the only one who can decide to make it all go away.

"Dude, you want the last piece?"

Zik's pointing at the last piece of pizza. I realize, in a spasm that twists my guts, that if I even *touch* food, I'm going to vomit my intestines and my stomach right out of my body.

"Take it." I push the box to him like it's laden with anthrax.

"Your plate's clean," Dad says, suddenly noticing. "Didn't you eat anything?"

The thought of food makes my stomach lurch again. "No. No, I'm . . ."

"Are you feeling OK?" Dad's concern is mitigated by his plan to take the last piece before Zik can get to it.

"Yeah, I'm fine. I—" And the phone rings. I almost jump out

of my skin. Zik's eyes widen. Dad shovels the pizza into his mouth.

"Get that, Josh," he manages around a mouthful.

Zik follows me to the phone. "What if it's her?"

"It's not," I tell him, forcing a confidence I don't have into my voice. But Caller ID says "Out of area" again, and my stomach groans in protest and I flicker

—like this—

long enough that the phone gets to the fourth ring and the answering machine cuts in, while I'm standing there like an idiot, coming back to the present to see Zik staring at me like I just dropped my pants or something. I shake it off and grab the phone before the message gets to the second sentence.

It's not Rachel, just Mom, calling to tell me that she and a bunch of her friends have already had too much to drink so they're planning to stay at a hotel for the night.

Michelle pulls up at the house a little while later. It's Friday, so she and Zik have their standing date. Zik doesn't have much in the way of dough, but Michelle insists that they at least rent a movie and watch it at her house on Fridays. Couplehood. Togetherness. How cute.

I watch Zik scamper off to Michelle's electric blue Cobalt. I shouldn't be so mean about Zik and Michelle, about her whipping him, about the stupid movie dates. It's jealousy in part, I admit. Zik's got a regular warm body at his disposal, and what a hell of a body it is. Michelle's been blessed with the Jurgens Asset, a rack that makes grown men weep and teenagers faint dead away from the sudden rush of blood away from the brain. I'd never tell Zik that I love sneaking looks at Michelle's tits (especially in the summer, when she wears these thin little halter tops that are completely and gloriously inappropriate for someone so well endowed), because you just don't talk about a guy's girlfriend like that.

I try to imagine the conversation Zik and Michelle are having as he gets into the car. Michelle waves to me from the driver's-side window and I wave back. What's he telling her? What's *she* telling *him?* No way to know.

Meet me at SAMMPark?

Well, what else do I have to do?

CHAPTER 10
Rachel's Pitch

SAMMPARK WAS BUILT a few years back. Some old shoddy buildings were torn down and the whole area was resodded and landscaped. It all started around the same time as Eve's trial; for a while there, it was like dueling headlines in the *Times,* with one crowding out the other on occasion but nothing else interfering with the front page.

They originally would shut the whole thing down at eleven, but some local religious group wanted to hold a midnight prayer vigil there and then the ACLU got involved and eventually it was just easier to leave the park open, with a Rent-A-Cop stationed at the main gate. Hell, Zik and I had been hopping the fence on the east side of the park to play midnight baseball anyway, and judging by the scattering of Coke cans, beer bottles, used condoms, and burger wrappers, we weren't the only ones in violation.

I wait in my car by the gate. It's cool out, so I roll down the window to catch the breeze and lean out the window. I look up at the sky.

Ursa Major and Ursa Minor are both really bright tonight. I pick out Venus, twinkling away like a star ... to the uninitiated eye. Venus, 67.2 million miles away from the sun, is technically the closest planet to Earth, but it's usually on the *other side* of the sun, so for all intents and purposes it's much farther away than you'd think. You couldn't send a manned mission there—the pressure from the superhumid atmosphere would kill any astronauts, assuming that the 900-degree heat didn't do it first. Still, spacecraft have been sent there, and I like to imagine that someday we'll figure out a way to put a person there, in a protected environment. I like to think I'll help work that one out.

I love the stars. Love them for *how* they are almost as much as for *what* they are. Stars are just mathematical equations, when you get right down to it. Precise ratios of helium and hydrogen, heated and lit just the right way, all of it balanced and perfect for billions of years as they slowly churn their way toward iron, toward entropy. Space is one big mathematical construct. It's just figuring out gravity and electromagnetism and thrust and lift and BOOM you're off the earth, you're walking the moon like Neil Armstrong in those old, old videos.

Just when I figure Rachel has either stood me up, died in a car accident, or never planned to come here after all, I hear tires crunch the parking lot gravel and catch headlights in my rearview.

I get out as she pulls up next to me. She's wearing a gray South Brook Bobcats cap, a yellow shirt, and a pair of green shorts. The shirt is cut loose, the shorts tight.

"Sorry I'm late," she says, waving to me as she goes around back to her trunk. "I had to change from work."

"That's OK."

She digs into her trunk. "Get your bat."

"My *bat?*"

She slams down the trunk; she has a glove in one hand and

a softball in the other. It looks like a pumpkin compared to the balls I'm used to hitting.

"Yeah, your bat. Time to measure up, big guy."

You're kidding me. She wants to *pitch* to me?

"Rachel, I don't—"

"I know you keep a bat in your trunk. Come on." She doesn't even wait for me to finish—she just heads off toward the gate.

I pop the trunk and grab my bat and glove, then hustle to catch up to her. No need to run, though—turns out she's waiting just inside the park entrance, near the nurse statue and the big bronze plaque that reads "Susan Ann Marchetti Memorial Park." Spotlights shine up from the ground, shrouding the statue's upper half in shadows.

"Hey, Rache, can we talk?"

"You ever think about her?"

Shit. She's not even looking at me but at the statue of the nurse. On the way here, I sort of decided that I was coming for one reason and one reason only—to apologize. To look her in the eye and say, in no uncertain terms, that I'm sorry for what I did all those years ago. But now she's got me toting baseball gear and looking at statues.

But I figure it's her game and her rules. For now, at least.

"Not really, Rache." I take a good long look at the statue. It's just a chunk of stone. Marble, maybe. I don't know. I've walked past it a million times.

"You ever read the plaque?"

"Just her name."

She sighs and offers me an exasperated frown. "God, Josh.

How many times have you walked through this park or played in this park, and you never wondered about the woman they named it after?"

"I just said I read her name!"

"Read the rest of it."

So I read it: *Dedicated and built in her name by the man who gave her life and the man who gave her death.*

"Whoa!"

Rachel smiles smugly. "See?"

"What does *that* mean?"

"What do you *think* it means?"

"I don't know." I think about it for a second. "I mean, the 'man who gave her life' would have to be her father, right?"

She nods. "Yeah, that's what I always figured."

"But the 'man who gave her death' . . . Does that mean the same guy? Or is it another guy?"

Rachel shrugs. "I don't know. There was a whole big story about it when they first built it, but there was, y'know, another story that sort of overshadowed it at the time."

My face burns. It's now or never.

"Rachel, look, this isn't easy for me . . ."

She cocks her head to one side like a curious dog.

"Rachel, I'm just gonna say it." My heart, interestingly, has decided to switch into calm mode, reliably thudding along and doing little else. My pulse can't be more than seventy-five bpm. I resist the urge to check.

"I'm sorry, Rache." As soon as the words are out, my heart starts up, kicking up a storm, blasting out a panic serenade. I can barely hear myself speak for the rushing thrum of blood in my ears. "I'm so sorry. I'm just so, so sorry." I can't stop saying it, and I can't even summon up any sort of variation on the theme. I just keep blabbing "I'm sorry" over and over again, like some kind of deranged parrot.

She regards me, impassive, saying nothing, not even moving until I somehow ramble to a stop in the middle of the word "sorry," like a car drifting onto sand.

"You done?" she asks.

I'm out of breath. My heart has settled down, but my lungs are protesting. She just stares at me.

"Yeah." I gasp it, as though I'm rounding third and heading for home and the ball is sailing *right overhead* and the catcher looks *really* confident.

She slams the ball into her glove. "Good. Let's go."

The SAMMPark baseball diamond isn't lit at night unless there's an official game and someone's paying for the juice, but it's a clear night and the moon and the stars and the big billboard that faces the highway offer plenty of light.

"Let's warm up." Rachel jogs out to the mound, spins around, and tosses the ball to me at the plate, overhand. I snag it with my glove—not. What *really* happens is that I snap at it with the glove and knock it out of the air, missing my chance to catch it because I misjudged its size.

"Good catch," she calls out.

If Zik made a comment like that, I would know he was just kidding and I would probably call him a douchebag, but I don't know if she's just busting on me or being mean, so I say nothing as I retrieve the ball and toss it back to her, adding a little more heat than is strictly necessary. She catches it effortlessly, barely looking at it, her glove darting out to one side.

She fires it back, overhand again, and I don't know why I'm so surprised by that—they only *pitch* underhanded in softball. For fielding and everything else, it's just like in baseball, except the ball's the size of a goddamn grapefruit.

I get used to it quickly and manage to keep my glove open wide enough to avoid embarrassing myself further. She starts tossing some deliberately off to the left or right, making me chase them, and I return the favor, and soon we're running all over the infield, firing the ball back and forth, running it down until we're loosened up and I'm sweating a little bit.

I'm standing on second, waiting for her to throw the ball from third, when she stops.

"Here's the deal, Josh. I heard you before. OK?" She waits. "OK?"

"Yeah." This is the part where she tells me to shove my apology up my ass.

"I heard you," she says again. "But we don't talk about it until *I* say. Got it?"

I don't know about that. On the one hand, I guess it's her right. On the other hand, though, I don't want to be standing here all night with spin-the-bottle and the closet hanging between us like dense fog.

"I said, 'Got it?'" And she fires the ball at me, hard. It stings my palm when it lands in the glove.

"I got it." I throw it back. "It's just that—"

"Jesus!" She jumps a little to catch it—I threw it high. "What part of this don't you understand?"

"I understand all of it, Rache, but I can't just stand here and play catch with you when there's all of this other shit between us."

She hurls the ball again, this time so hard she goes wild and I have to run into center field for it. "God, Josh, you don't get it, do you? We were friends, remember? Good friends."

Yeah, I remember. Our mothers thought it was so cute, a boy and a girl being such good friends like that. They teased us sometimes, said we'd end up married. "I know. But then I—"

"Will you stop talking about that time in the closet? That's all you think about. What about what happened *afterward?*"

Afterward? I don't get it. "What do you mean? *Nothing* happened. Not with us, at least."

"That's my point, you jackass! You disappeared on me! You stopped talking to me, you wouldn't come around anymore—"

"Your parents wouldn't let me near you! And I don't even blame them."

"Shit, that lasted all of a year. Once the truth came out, once the trial started, they felt sorry for you. But me, I lost one of my best friends in the world. All because you were so damn worried about what you did that you never stopped for a minute to think about what I needed or wanted. Throw the goddamn ball!"

I realize I've been standing in shallow center, holding the ball, staring at her. I hop into the base path and toss it to her. She grabs it out of the air, savagely.

"You never tried to call me!" She fires the ball back. *Hard.* "You never look at me in school! You never talk to me. You won't talk to Michelle or Zik about me or go anywhere you think I'll be. God!"

I just stand there holding the ball. She starts pacing, flinging her arms out to punctuate her points. "It was like being exiled or something! And I couldn't figure out why. My parents would watch the news and see Mrs. Sherman and they'd say, 'That poor boy,' and ask if I'd talked to you, and I would always have to say no. I got so sick and tired of hearing about her, about you. It's like you died, but people wouldn't stop talking about you, wouldn't stop bringing you up, so I couldn't even . . ." She plants her feet. "Throw the goddamn ball!"

I toss it weakly. She grabs it and fires it back, almost clipping my head before I duck out of the way and knock it down with my glove.

"I couldn't even *mourn* you!" she says. "I couldn't even forget you."

I retrieve the ball. She's not even watching me now. She's wandering around home plate, facing the backstop. If this were Zik, I'd pitch it right over his shoulder and rattle the backstop to scare the shit out of him.

Instead, I tuck it into my glove and walk over to her. She turns when I'm about halfway there and I expect her to tell me to back off and keep playing extreme catch. But instead, she just slumps her shoulders and watches me.

I hand her the ball. "Are we at the part where I can apologize now?"

She shakes her head, but she's chuckling. "Sorry about all that. It's been building up for a long time. I had to get it all out."

"You don't have anything to apologize for."

"You caught me off-guard back then. I wasn't expecting you to tear my panties—"

"I said I'm sorry, Rachel. I swear to God."

"I mean, we were thirteen! And it's not like no one goes to third or hits a homer at thirteen, but it's usually not so aggressive."

"Look, it's what I was used to. It's what . . . It's what she—" God, I don't think I can talk about it. Here I have my chance, at last, to make amends, and I can't even talk about it.

"I understand. I didn't know that then, though. And I'm sorry too."

I blink. "For what?"

"For freaking out the way I did. For starting the whole thing. If I hadn't gone screaming out of the basement—"

"Rachel, it's not your—"

"If I hadn't gone screaming out of the basement like that," she insists, "no one would have known. No one would have known and Mrs. Sherman would still have her job and maybe you wouldn't hate me."

"Hate you?" It's like a line drive to the balls. "Hate you? Jesus! How could I hate you?"

"You never talked to me after that day. You avoided me everywhere. Michelle tried to get Zik to talk to you about it, but he wouldn't . . ." Good old Zik. "And you wouldn't even *look* at me. As soon as I'd see you somewhere, you'd leave or look away or find some excuse to talk to someone else."

"Rachel! God! I was—I was *embarrassed*. I practically raped you in that closet! I couldn't even *think* about looking you in the eye."

"You didn't practically rape me, you bonehead! I was coming on to you!"

"Oh, right. Like you wanted to have sex with me right there in the closet, with Zik and Michelle on the other side of the door!"

She glares at me and tugs her cap. It's somehow adorable. "I would have."

"What?" Did I just think *adorable?*

"Well . . ." She shrugs. "I might have. I don't know. You were—I was really into you, Josh. I don't know how far I would have let you go if you'd gone about it differently."

I swoon into a flicker, Rachel's lipstick smudging my cheek in the closet, all those years ago.

"Josh? Josh?"

"I'm OK."

Under the brim of the cap, her eyebrows have come together in concern. She comes closer, reaching out. "You looked like you were going to pass out. Don't blow a blood vessel over this."

Her freckles are soft in the moonlight, a faded tattoo over the bridge of her nose. Her eyes glow blue-green. No makeup or eye shadow or mascara. I think of Eve's long lashes, the smoky gray shadow that made her eyes look so deep.

"There's no reason to be afraid," Rachel says, and she's whispering, and I don't know why.

"I'm not afraid," I whisper back, and it's a lie that even I don't believe.

There's a thumping sound, a single, solid *plop.* The ball has dropped to the ground, along with Rachel's glove. She's so close to me that I can count the freckles. I can smell the sweat soaked into her cap. She leans in closer and kisses me on the lips.

It's not like last time. Her lips are dry, naked, firmer than before. I fight the warring urges in my body; I want to grab her and pull her closer, but that would scare the living shit out of her, so I also want to break away and run like hell. It's been like this with *every* girl. I flicker, seeing Eve before me, and my reflexes rear up, telling me what to do, what needs to be done, what she needs, what I need, what she *insists* be done. My hands tremble and the tremble reminds me I'm wearing a glove, and that somehow brings me back to the real world as Rachel pulls back.

"It's better if you open your mouth," she says.

"Yeah. I know."

"I know you do."

Has she read the documents online? Does she know everything I did with Eve? What does she expect from me? How do I act with her?

"I don't know what you want from me, Rache." And I don't. I get that she missed me. I get that I was a jerk for years. And it ends there.

"I want you back." She blurts it out, then turns away from me, embarrassed. "I mean . . . You were a big part of my life. And then you were gone. I always wondered . . ."

"We were too young for . . . for what I tried to do."

"Says who? You had a hell of a lot of experience by then, didn't you?"

"I don't want to talk about that. We're not going to talk about that."

"Why not, Josh? I was a part of it, wasn't I? I brought it to light."

—running from the closet—

—the hell is going on down there?—

And Rachel, at my side all of a sudden, holding my arm to steady me. "Are you OK? You look like—"

"Fine. I'm fine." But I let her help me to the backstop, where I lean against it before sliding down to sit in the dirt behind home. She stands over me.

"What was it like, Josh? With her? You owe me that much."

I shake my head. How can I sum it up? How can I describe it? I'm a completely different person now. It's a different world. Eve's thirty and free and a registered sex offender, and me? I'm just muddling through, hitting the ball, slamming straight A's, doing all the easy things in life.

"I really can't talk about it."

"Things are different now," Rachel says. "For one thing, I'm more experienced."

As experienced as I am? Who knows? How are we counting? Other than Eve, my experience amounts to a slew of aborted attempts over the years, each time arrested by my own fear or something I communicate invisibly and inaudibly that drives the girl away. Like standing perfectly still and close-mouthed while Rachel tries to kiss me.

"Well, that's good."

"We're on equal footing now. Cal Willingham took care of the whole virginity thing two years ago."

"Oh?" She seems to take a perverse pleasure in making me uncomfortable, in talking about this. My sex life is practically an open book to anyone with the time and patience to browse the Internet. Hers is a mystery. As it should be. A mystery she wants to reveal. But why? To shock me?

"Is that all you have to say? Oh?"

I cast about for something, anything. "Is it true what they say about black guys?"

She rolls her eyes in disgust. "Stop changing the subject."

"I've forgotten the subject." Which is true. At this point, my mind is cranking at a thousand rpm.

"Tell you what—I'll make you a bet."

"A bet?"

She stoops to pick up her glove and the ball, giving me a glimpse of her butt as it tenses under the tight shorts. I don't think there's an ounce of unneeded flesh on her. It's all lean muscle, perfectly toned, and I have to stop thinking like this—it's no good.

"Yeah, a bet." She smiles at me knowingly; she knew I was checking out her ass. What's more, she didn't mind. But she should. Doesn't she know I'm a sex fiend?

"Grab your bat," she goes on, and heads out to the mound. I obediently rise and switch my glove for my bat.

At the mound, she turns. "Here's the bet. Here's where you get to put your money where your mouth is. I'm going to pitch to you, underhanded. If Mr. Hotshot Batter can get a base hit off me, I'll stop bugging you. I'll leave you completely alone and never speak to you again, if that's what you want."

And that's *not* what I want, I realize with no small amount of surprise. I wasn't sure until right now what I want, but her terms have made me realize: I just want things to be OK, to be like they used to be, before I had to hide my face in shame from Rachel and from everyone else in Brookdale and all of Lowe County and half the state.

"If I strike you out, though, you have to tell me all about you and Mrs. Sherman."

For the first time since Babe Ruth League, I freeze in the batter's box. She could pitch a big, fat slow ball in my strike zone right now and I wouldn't have the presence of mind to swing at it.

"What?"

"Come on, big shot! Didn't you say underhand is different

from overhand? Are you really afraid of me and this oversize thing?" She waves the ball at me. It's as big as the moon.

She's right; this is no challenge, really. My batting average is .502, and that's against guys who pitch overhand. Even if she was throwing overhand, she'd have less than even odds on striking me out. And if I just score a hit off her—which the odds say I will—I can make her stop asking about Eve. And maybe we can move on somehow.

"What if you walk me?"

"I won't walk you," she promises. "But if I do, you win the bet."

"What if I pop up or line drive to the mound?" I have no intention of doing either one, but it can't hurt to check.

She grins. "We should count those as outs, but we'll just call them strikes, OK?"

Sounds fair. "Deal."

She takes a step back on the mound, finding the rubber. I go through my batting ritual—step out of the box, knock dirt off my left shoe with the bat, step forward, knock dirt off the other shoe, step into the box, rotate my bat a quarter-turn in my hands. I usually tug my helmet's brim once, then push it back up into position, but I'm not wearing a helmet. I'm embarrassed to find myself miming the action through sheer muscle memory. Rachel doesn't crack a grin. She's a ballplayer; she understands.

"Batter up!" I yell.

She's all legs up there; can't say I've ever been distracted by a pitcher's calves before, but I guess there's a first time for everything. I redirect my attention above the waist, which is nothing special. She goes into her wind-up—it looks weird and backwards from the plate.

I tell myself—I *command* myself—not to swing at the first pitch. I've never seen her pitch softball up close, never studied her, so I have to have at least one pitch to learn her form, puzzle out the way she tilts her shoulders for a curve or a slider.

But then the ball's right in front of me, it's right over the goddamn plate, just hanging there, fat and slow, like a fucking piñata. I can't resist. *No one* with a bat in his hands could resist this thing!

I swing with all my might, ready to drive the ball out into the home-run bushes in deep left. But the ball has other ideas— as if it has a mind of its own, as if it has *eyes* and can see my bat coming, it suddenly drops a good three inches. My bat whiffs where the ball used to be, pulling me around so hard that I think for a second I might have dislocated my shoulder.

That sound I hear? That's Rachel, laughing.

"Thanks for the breeze!" she shouts, spreading her arms out as if I've generated a gale-force wind.

I retrieve the ball from the ground near the backstop. "You're welcome." I toss it back to her, a little harder than necessary.

The ball smacks into her glove. If it hurts, she doesn't show it, which I like.

"You ready for the second pitch?" she asks.

"I'm standing in the batter's box, aren't I?" It comes out meaner than I'd intended.

"Someone's on the rag," she chides, then grabs her crotch as if adjusting a cup. "And it's not me."

"Throw the ball." I twist my palms on the bat, tightening my grip.

Her shoulder cocks back in a blur of motion. Slider? Fastball? I can't tell—the signs are all wrong. *Zing!* The ball comes sailing toward me at ten million miles an hour, setting the atmosphere on fire and burning a hole in the space-time continuum.

I resist the temptation to swing, even though every muscle in my body wants to lean in and smack the ball into orbit.

"Shit!" she says from the mound. "High."

"Ball one," I tell her.

"Yeah, yeah, you've got one ball." She sniggers as I throw the ball back to her.

"And so do you," I point out as she catches it in her glove.

"Wow, between the two of us, we're a full scrotum!"

"Pitch."

She clears her throat and cocks her shoulder. It's weird, seeing her full-on like this. Distracting. Usually, pitchers stand to the side for the wind-up, then come forward to release. But not for underhanded pitching. She's in my face the whole time. Nothing helps. I'm used to looking over the pitcher's shoulder for the ball, but Rachel's pitch comes from down near the waist. Or the hip. Depending.

The ball whips toward me. Slider. I can tell. It just floats there for a second, then spins off, cutting the outside corner of the plate. I reach for it with the bat and feel the connection, but it's not enough. I just nicked it, just got a piece of it. The ball jerks up into the air and soars off to my right.

"Foul ball!" she calls out, running for it.

Shit.

"Strike two," she tells me when she returns to the mound, as if she has to remind me.

"I know."

The next pitch is another ball—low and inside enough to make me jump back. Rachel giggles. Was that intentional? Was she trying to brush me back?

I foul off the pitch after that, this time popping it up and over the backstop. Two and two.

It's OK, though. I've got her rhythm now. I see how her shoulders work and how her delivery changes for the curve balls. Not a problem.

The next pitch makes the second one look like a slowpoke—I've never seen anything move so fast in my life. I could swear I hear an engine revving as the ball rockets toward me.

It's going to hit right over the plate. It's a perfect goddamn pitch, the kind of pitch I take to the moon on a regular basis. I dig in my right heel for balance, twist, bring the bat around, and listen for the sound of wood on horsehide.

And miss.

The ball slams against the backstop with a clatter like a dropped drawer of silverware.

"Yes!" Rachel cries from the mound, pumping her fist in the air. "*Steeeee*-rike three! You're out!" She winds up her pitching arm and spikes a finger to the ground. "Out! Outta here, Mendel! Back to the dugout!"

I toss the ball back to the mound. "You got lucky," I tell her, and I regret it as soon as it's out of my mouth. It's the one thing I've said that really gets to her.

Her eyes flare. "Fuck you, Josh!"

"Rachel, wait. I didn't mean—"

"No, *fuck* you!" She hurls the ball at me, but she's angry, so she throws overhand and has zero control. I don't even flinch, and the ball misses me by miles. "Fuck you, and fuck you again! I didn't get lucky, you asshole! I struck you *out*. And I can do it again and again and a thousand times again because I'm the best fucking pitcher in the state."

"I know. I know. I'm sorry. I shouldn't have said that."

"Fuck you!" she says again, this time over her shoulder as she stalks off the mound and heads toward the gate.

Shit. How did I get into this? *Why* did I get into this?

I chase after her, which isn't difficult since I'm running and she's walking—walking with that fast, pissed-off gait people use when they want to get the hell out of the area, but walking nonetheless.

"Wait, Rache." I grab her arm without realizing what I'm doing.

"Get the fuck off me!" she spins around, jerking out of my grasp. At least she didn't say, "You freak!" or "You pervert!"

"God, I'm sorry. I really am. I shouldn't have touched you."

She crosses her arms over her chest, her glove hanging down. "Why did you have to say that? Huh? Why did you have to be such a dick about it?"

"I don't know. Stupidity. I'm a fucking imbecile, OK?"

She glares.

"But, look, Rache . . ." God, I don't want to fuck this up. It feels like, for the first time in years, I can actually communicate with someone other than Zik. And maybe even *more* than Zik. I don't know. If you'd asked me a week ago, I would have told you the odds of me ever speaking to Rachel Madison, much less having an in-depth heart-to-heart with her, were somewhere between zero and none. Of course, I would have given the same odds that she could strike me out.

Maybe that means something.

I don't know. It's not the forgiveness. Or at least, it's not *just* the forgiveness. I'm not sure what it is.

"Rache, look. You won the bet, OK? Fair and square. You won."

She narrows her eyes, but she stays put.

I take in a deep breath, but my lungs won't let me hold it for long, and it all comes dribbling out in a series of weak sighs.

"You won. I'll tell you. I'll tell you everything."

But I'm not ready to. Not at all. I'm scared. Not the sort of "Oh, what am I going to do?" scared or the hand-wringing "How do I get out of this?" scared. This is full-on piss-your-pants, shit-your-drawers, "Who do I kill to get out of here?" terror. Sweat's running down my back and gathering under my balls, which have shriveled to tight grapes for protection.

She has to know. She has to see the fear writ large on my face, because there can't be anything else there right now—there's no room for it . . .

And

—*Whoever gets the bottle pointed at them*—

—*pouted again, but went ahead and spun the bottle once more*—
I realize that I never

—*The bottle has to spin all the way*—
stood a chance. Not with Rachel.

"Josh? You OK?"

"I'm fine."

"You look like you're"

—*I've been practicing spinning that bottle all week*—

"spacing out again."

"No." I shake my head, sending flickers off into space. "No, I'm fine."

Never stood a chance. She's always ten steps ahead of me. Always has been. On the field and off.

Flashbacks, Not Flickers (I)

1

"HE'S OLD ENOUGH NOW."

That's what I remember my mom saying at the time. She and Dad were arguing about her going back to work. She saw an ad on a bulletin board for an assistant to a professor at LEC, and she wanted to go for it.

"Damn it, Jenna," Dad said. They didn't know I could hear them through the vents. "We agreed that until he goes off to college—"

"That was a stupid agreement," Mom shot back. Mom was hard-core. Tough. I always thought it was cool, as a kid, that my mother could kick ass. "He's old enough to look after himself for two lousy hours in the afternoons. You think a twelve-year-old can't look after himself for a couple of hours?"

"What if you have to work late? What if there's an emergency?"

"Oh, for God's sake, LEC is only twenty minutes away!"

"Twenty minutes away from *here*. It's more like forty-five minutes from his school."

My dad has always been master of the nitpick.

"How do you plan on paying for college on your salary alone?" I was only twelve, but I recognized that Mom had just scored the verbal equivalent of castration.

"There are scholarships . . ." Dad said, but I could tell he was weakening. Money was always tight around the house. Not like we were poor or anything, but just enough that I knew my parents thought about it a lot. College was six years away for me, and I hadn't given it much thought at this point. My dad had always talked about me getting a baseball scholarship somewhere, which never made sense to me. If I was going to play baseball, why not go pro? But he was my dad, and I figured he knew something I didn't, so I would just nod whenever he brought it up.

"You can't expect him to go four years on scholarships. He could get injured. Or he might lose interest in baseball."

Mom was nuts. Lose interest in baseball? Impossible. That was like saying someday I would get tired of sneaking peeks at the high school girls who practiced cheerleading at our field. Give me a break!

They argued for a while longer and I got bored with it when they started tossing numbers out there, because in those days unless it was a batting average, an ERA, or algebra homework, it just didn't interest me. I drifted off to sleep, and at breakfast Mom said, "Honey, would you mind if I wasn't here when you got home from school?"

I shrugged. "Why?"

"Well, I might go back to work. So I wouldn't get home until closer to when Dad gets home."

"Who'll pick me up when baseball starts?" Practice could run until six or so.

"One of us will. Whoever gets home sooner. Does that sound OK?"

"I don't care." And I really didn't.

□ □ □ □

Zik lived too far away for us to get together back in those pre-driving days. There were a bunch of kids in the neighborhood I was friends with, but I had hoped that Mom's absence would mean something *cool*, something *new*, something *forbidden*.

Instead, it just meant that I had to fix my own snack, and then go outside and play with the usual suspects.

Rachel was one of the regulars, though we were getting to the point where a lot of the guys had decided that it wasn't cool to play with a girl anymore, especially one who could strike out just about everyone and also run a football at the speed of sound. I used to worry about hurting Rachel when we played football (we played tackle), but it was never an issue—if she had the pigskin, none of us could catch her.

That fall introduced me to the wonders of being completely alone, if I wanted.

It also introduced me to Evelyn Sherman.

MRS. SHERMAN WAS MY HISTORY TEACHER that year. It was her second year as a teacher, I learned later, and her first year at South Brook Middle. She had been at the high school the previous year and transferred when the history position opened up at South Brook Middle.

It's difficult, now, to describe her as I first saw her. How to recapture that initial blend of adolescent lust and childlike innocence, that mixture of "God, she's hot!" and "Look at the pretty lady!" and "I think I'm in love," the same combination of emotions that hit all of the boys in her history class. With the perspective of six years and a relationship that went far beyond teacher/pupil, it would be easy to give a certain picture of her. But that wouldn't explain the impact she had on me at that moment, right then.

So I'll do my best.

I guess the first thing that I noticed, really, was her hair. It was black. Jet black. So black that it shone like onyx under the fluorescent lights of the classroom. It was long, tumbling over her shoulders. I wanted to run my fingers through it. Somehow I thought it would be warm to the touch, like cookies just out of the oven.

I noticed her hair first only because she was sitting down at her desk, bent over a book, making a tick mark occasionally. As we filed into the room, she glanced up, but then went back to her book, so all I saw at first was that lustrous hair.

When we were all sitting down and the bell to start class rang, she looked up from her work and smiled. I noticed the smile third because in looking up, she straightened and her chest came into view, tight against her blouse, and that's when a sort of sigh went up from the male contingent.

It wasn't that she had enormous breasts or that they were perfectly formed or anything like that. It's that they were just a little bit *too* big for her frame, just slightly out of proportion, so that no matter how much you wanted to, you couldn't stop yourself from looking at them over and over, thinking, "I must have seen them wrong," and going back to them to make sure.

I was glad she wasn't my math teacher; in history, I wouldn't have to get up and go to the blackboard, which would have been beyond mortifying.

But, third, that smile . . .

Red lips, full and soft-looking, revealing bright white teeth. She had one dimple when she smiled, on the left cheek only, and it made her somehow imperfect and more beautiful for it. Her eyes were a bright green, smoky under the slim black arches of her eyebrows. They seemed to glow.

"Good morning," she said, and smiled even more broadly, and then took roll. When she got to me, I responded "Here" and dutifully raised my hand. She hesitated, then went on to the next person.

By the time she stood up and went to the overhead projector to start explaining what this class would be about this year, I was pretty sure I'd fallen in love. Her blouse was a creamy white and very loose, though it seemed to cling every time she moved. Her skirt was straight and black, hitting just about the knee, with no slit, but it clung to her so that you could see her legs moving beneath, see the swell of her hips, which I'd never, ever noticed in a woman before. I was a typical American adolescent male—I had zeroed in on any number of chests and rear ends in my life, but Mrs. Sherman's were the first hips to make me go, *Wow!*

3

SEVENTH GRADE WAS A GOOD YEAR for me, a year when I really came into my own on the ball field. I went 16 for 32 at the plate for a flat .500 batting average, but my on-base percentage was even higher—.754. I think I would have done even better if I'd had more playing time, but there were always more kids who wanted to play than time and positions and our league emphasized participation over victory, so I ended up playing half games most of the time.

In the field, I played shortstop, like Cal Ripken had for most of his career. I did well there, though I didn't like it. I threw ten outs at first, four at second, and assisted on two double plays. It should have been four double plays, but the first baseman dropped the ball once and got knocked over by the runner the second time.

But the big thing about Fall Ball that year was, well, big. And that was me. I had always been a small guy, but as seventh grade kicked off, I had just experienced a massive summer growth spurt. I looked more like a high school freshman than a seventh-grader, towering over most of the kids in my class, with shoulders as broad as a kindergartener was tall. My voice cracked on occasion, but since I tended to think things through before speaking, it wasn't that much of a problem; I knew where the danger syllables were, and I could compensate for them.

I'd always possessed the skills and, I suppose, a certain level of natural talent, but now I could actually get decent pitches in or near the strike zone, and I took them into the bushes a good deal of the time.

I never played baseball for ego stroking, but I have to admit that when I started knocking the horsehide all over creation, it gave me a good feeling. After all, this is what I'd been training for ever since my dad handed me a Wiffle ball bat and pitched me my first little blooper back when I was a little kid. Now I was finally using the skills I'd developed, and it felt great.

Just as great was having my best friends around me while it happened. Zik was coming along as a catcher, making some decent plays at the plate. He was sort of fearless in a way that marveled me. A kid twice his size could be barreling down the base path from third toward home, murder in his eyes, and Zik would set his feet in front of the plate, clutching the ball like it was his own child, and let the kid plow right into him and never, ever lose the ball. He got the out every time, along with a reputation for being willing to get the shit knocked out of him as long as it meant a win for the team.

Rachel was playing softball now, and for the first time the Three Musketeers were divided. (We called ourselves the Four Musketeers when Michelle was around, but by unspoken agreement between the athletes, we shifted to Three when discussing sports, which Michelle avoided.) The girls' softball field was near our practice field, though, so Zik and I would sneak over whenever we could to watch. We'd tease Rachel about her bizarre (to us) underhanded wind-up and delivery, but in private we agreed that she was the best of the players we'd seen. We missed having her play baseball—even though she'd usually ended up on an opposing team, she was fun to practice with and play against.

Now, her reassignment to the depths of girls' softball was as much evidence as my sudden growth spurt that we were, inevitably, growing up.

4

HISTORY WAS MY FAVORITE SUBJECT that year, and not just because Mrs. Sherman was so much fun to look at. We were being taught all kinds of cool stuff—the Black Plague, the Crusades, stuff like that. Disease, death, brutal warfare—throw in some sex and music and you would have hit the jackpot.

Mrs. Sherman had, two weeks into the year, suddenly dowdied herself down. Zik and I talked about it on the bus for a while, trying to figure out why she'd foregone the clingy skirts and filmy blouses for heavier dresses and slacks and sweaters. Sure, it was getting cooler out, but it wasn't *cold* yet. She was still beautiful, her eyes warm and almost too intense for her face, her single dimple showing up whenever she smiled, and those lips . . .

But her body was becoming more and more of a mystery.

"Maybe she's pregnant," Zik said one day on the bus.

I hadn't even thought of that. I didn't even realize she was married. Or, rather, it hadn't firmly locked into my brain that she was married. We called her "Mrs. Sherman," so of course we knew that she was married, but the home lives of teachers were, at our age, purely theoretical constructs. Evidence pointed to their existence, but we had no concrete proof.

"Maybe." For some reason, I didn't like the idea of her being pregnant. I couldn't explain it, so I didn't say it.

"That would be awesome," Zik said. "I remember when my aunt was pregnant." He cupped his hands in front of his chest. "Huge, man! *Huge!*"

We laughed over that until some eighth-grader behind us told us to shut up, and then we just reduced ourselves to giggles.

As Fall Ball wrapped up, parent-teacher conferences kicked in. Mom and Dad went together back then. I had to go, too, since there would be no one to watch me at home. By now Mom had been working at Lake Eliot College for two months, but they weren't about to give me free rein in the house all day, so I ended up grumbling and complaining in the back seat on the way to school on a day that was *supposed* to be a vacation for me.

I sat in the back of each classroom as Mom and Dad held hushed conversations with my teachers up at their desks. Mom did most of the talking.

They spent the most time with Mrs. Sherman, who had dressed up that day, wearing a sleek gray skirt suit. From my position in the back of the room, I had a terrific view of her legs. It was intoxicating; I thought I might pass out.

On the way home, while Dad drove, Mom turned to me. "All of your teachers say you're doing very well."

"I know." And I did. I couldn't figure out the point of these conferences; I had an A in every class. The Streak was only three years old at that point, but I was still pretty confident.

"I don't know about these things," Mom said to Dad,

echoing my thoughts. "They never have anything to say except, 'He's a great student. He's a good kid.' I'm starting to feel weird about it."

"You feel weird hearing good things about your kid?" Dad asked.

Mom sighed. "No. Don't you notice how they look at you? Like 'Are you so egotistical you have to come here to hear me gush about your son?'"

"I think you're overthinking this."

"Maybe you're underthinking it," Mom said.

Dad grunted. Mom turned back to me. "So, Josh, who's your favorite teacher?"

It was no contest; history was just too cool a class. "Mrs. Sherman."

Mom laughed. "Yeah, I bet," she said.

Dad chuckled like he knew a secret. "Well, that's one thing we don't have to worry about, I guess," and Mom snorted more laughter.

"What do you mean?" I asked.

"Nothing, honey. Don't worry about it."

Seventh grade was also the year I got *really* sick and tired of stuff like that from my parents. "No." I leaned forward, straining against the seat belt. "Come on, Mom. What did he mean?"

"Nothing."

"Dad?"

"It's an adult thing." One of Dad's favorite phrases back then.

"Come on, you guys!" My voice cracked there, which ruined what I was about to say, which was "I'm almost an adult!" So I tried a different tactic instead. "It's not nice to talk about me like that while I'm right here."

Mom and Dad shared a glance.

"We just . . ." Mom hesitated, thinking. "All we meant was that it makes sense that you like Mrs. Sherman, because she likes you."

Huh? In a kid's lexicon, *like* can mean many things and is used as a substitute for *lust after* and *love,* as in: "I like her. I mean, I *like* like her." Even suffering from a brand of puppy love, I knew that Mrs. Sherman didn't *like* like me.

"She said that you're her best student, but she was worried at first because you look so much older and more mature than most of the other kids. She thought you had been held back a year and she couldn't figure out why you were in the advanced class. So she was relieved when you turned out to be a smart kid. What did she call him, Bill?"

"'My little historian,'" Dad said, without missing a beat.

Her little historian? From their reactions, my parents clearly thought it was cute, but I was horrified. It sounded like I was a doll or an action figure.

"I like history," I told them stubbornly, because they seemed to find the idea of me being a historian funny. And even though I didn't like being a doll, I liked amusing my parents even less.

"I'm sure, honey," Mom said, but she said it in the same tone that she'd said, "Yeah, I bet."

No one expected the snow.

Flakes hit early on the Tuesday after Thanksgiving when I was on the bus. The weather report, though, said that the big stuff wouldn't come until later that night.

Instead, by ten o' clock or so, someone shouted, "Look at that!"

The soccer field was visible from Mr. Tunney's classroom. We couldn't see the turf at all. Snow had drifted up to half the height of the goals.

"Holy crap!" someone else said with all the fervor a seventh-grader can muster.

"That's enough of that!" Mr. Tunney said sharply, but by now twenty twelve-year-olds had gotten up and begun to congregate at the window.

"That's enough!" he said again, coming over to the window to shoo us back into our seats. "It's just snow; you've seen it before. Back to your seats."

Just as Mr. Tunney managed to get us back to our seats, the PA crackled and Mrs. Cameron, the principal, told us that schools were closing early. A cheer went up and Mr. Tunney threw his hands up in defeat.

I've thought about this next part a lot, and I'm still not entirely sure about it. I know that the storm ended up getting caught between two fronts and just kept spinning over our area, dumping more and more snow by the minute. I have vivid memories of watching the news that night, the weatherman gesturing clockwise over an image of the storm clouds as they spun like a pottery wheel.

I understand the storm just fine. I *don't* understand how I missed my bus.

We had to get to our lockers and pack up. The halls were a bustle of activity, kids shouting and laughing, teachers trying to ride herd on the whole thing. The PA would blare to life at random intervals, announcing this bus or that bus had arrived at this or that spot on the parking circle. I filled up my backpack and headed outside.

Snow swirled around me, thick like dust in a shaft of light. I was scared and thrilled at the same time. It was like being caught in a whirlwind. My heart pounded with excitement. I thought of snowballs, snow forts, snowmen.

Crunching the three inches of white powder under my feet, I made my way to the spot where my bus usually waited. But something was wrong—the kids getting on weren't kids who lived near me. And when I looked up into the bus, the driver was a stranger.

I backed up a step. The bus number was wrong.

I walked down the line of buses, looking for number 481. Nothing.

Well, OK, I figured. It's snowing. The roads are bad. It's just running late or backed up somewhere.

I fought against the press of kids heading for their buses until I was back in school. The PA announced that bus 10 was ready at the end of the parking circle.

I was waiting for 481, which, by some strange coincidence, was my batting average in sixth grade, the previous year. I had gone 26 for 54 with five doubles and two triples. What annoyed me, though, is that I *know* I could have broken .500 that year. Just one more hit—one more lousy hit—would have put me at .500. Two more hits would have been . . .

I did the math in my head: .519. Wow! Two more hits. Just two hits! If I'd been left in a couple more games and gotten, say, five more at bats . . . I would have easily hit two or three times, no question. That would have made me . . . Let's see . . . that would have made me 29 for 59 . . . which is only a .493 average, which is still higher than .481. Coach should have let me play those extra innings. If I'd played, say, *ten* more at bats and hit half the time, I'd be at . . . 31 for 64, which is . . . not much better. So I'd need to hit more than half the time, which I could have done, especially late in the season, when I was really into my swing. I went 4 for 4 in the last game of the season, 2 for 3 before that, 2 for 2 before *that* . . .

That was when I realized how quiet the hall had gotten. There was no one else there. I looked around. Maybe everyone was clustered around the door?

No. No one there.

What was going on? I wasn't the only kid on my bus! There had to be other kids here, even if my bus was the last one.

Maybe everyone was outside. Maybe I'd missed the announcement for my bus!

I ran outside, bursting through the doors into the swirling chaos of the storm. The snow was easily four inches deep now, and I almost lost my footing as I stepped into it.

The parking circle was empty except for slushy gray ruts carved into the snow by the tires and exhaust fumes of departed buses.

Maybe my bus was on its way? Maybe . . .

No. Even as a desperate seventh-grader, I knew that was wishful thinking. I'd missed the bus, plain and simple.

What could I do now? Could I walk home? I was pretty sure I could walk the distance—I was in good shape, after all—but I wasn't sure *how* to get home. Especially on foot. And the snow made the prospect all the more daunting. How high would it get by the time I got home?

I allowed myself a few seconds of panic, standing in the snow, alone in the whole wide world as far as I could tell. How would I get home? Would my parents be coming home early, trying to figure out where I was? What was going to happen to me?

I went back into school. It was so strange and so quiet in there, every footstep echoing off the lockers like the sounds monster feet make in movies.

A wall clock told me that it was just a little bit past twelve-thirty. There still had to be *someone* here, right?

I made my way through the corridors. It felt like being in a haunted house, only one with flickering fluorescent lights. The classrooms were all closed and dark. I tried a door—it was locked.

I walked faster. There had to be *someone*—

Just then, I turned a corner into the main lobby. Across the way, I saw the lights of the office.

In the office were the school secretary, the principal, and Mrs. Sherman, who was bundled up in a heavy coat and wool hat, tugging on a pair of very red leather gloves. "—like two years ago," she was saying. The secretary was pretty much ignoring her, typing on her keyboard.

"Um, excuse me?"

It was like I'd pulled a pistol and shouted, "No one move!" All three of them froze and turned to look at me.

Mrs. Sherman was the first to speak: "Josh, what are you *doing* here?"

"My bus isn't—"

"We called all of the buses," the secretary said with a little snappish edge to her voice. "All of them."

"Which bus are you?" the principal asked.

"Four eighty-one."

"That was one of the first ones we called," the secretary said. "Didn't you hear it?"

Now I was getting pissed. How was this my fault? "I went to the stop, but it wasn't there."

"We *announced* it," she said again, as if that would reverse time and put me on the bus. "We had different stops for them all because they were . . . Oh, who cares?" And she turned to look helplessly at the principal.

Who sighed and said, "Come into my office, Josh. I'll try to figure out what we're going to do. Don't worry—we'll get you home." She didn't seem terribly happy about it.

"Wait a minute," said Mrs. Sherman as I was following the

principal. "Look, you have to stay, right?" The principal and the secretary nodded miserably. "Then let me take care of this. I'll call the parents and get them to come pick him up."

The principal narrowed her eyes, but I could tell she wanted to jump on this opportunity to ditch me and get back to whatever it was she had to do. I guess principals don't get snow days. "You sure?" she asked Mrs. Sherman.

"Of course. I'm only five minutes from here; I can spend a few more minutes here to square things away." She held out one red hand to me. "Come on, Josh."

I knew Mrs. Sherman a hell of a lot better than I knew the principal, whom I'd only seen in the halls and heard speak at the occasional assembly. I felt a little weird holding a teacher's hand, but I took the one Mrs. Sherman offered. She smiled at me. "All right, let's take care of this."

Mrs. Sherman got my emergency procedure card from the secretary and took me out into the lobby. "Who do we want to try first?" she asked, squinting at Mom's tiny handwriting on the card. "Mom or Dad?"

Dad's job was pretty far away. I knew that because he regularly complained about his commute. But Mom was just down in Lake Eliot. "Mom."

"OK." She rummaged in her purse and pulled out a cell phone. Those were some tight-fitting gloves, because she was able to flip it open and punch out the number without taking them off.

I thought about how much Mom loved this job, how she had argued with Dad about vacation time. "She's gonna be pretty pissed," I told Mrs. Sherman, and then clapped a hand over my mouth as I realized what I'd said.

Mrs. Sherman tried to look angry, but she couldn't help herself. She giggled, rolled her eyes at me, and ruffled my hair. "Watch your mouth, goofball. And don't worry." She flashed me a reassuring smile—her dimple winked at me—and then she spoke into the phone:

"Hello, Mrs. Mendel? This is Mrs. Sherman, Josh's history teacher? Yes. No, no, there's nothing—Yeah, the snow. I know. Look, there was . . ." She looked over at me, chewed the corner of her lip for a second. "The buses got mixed up and some kids missed their buses. Is there any way you can come get—

"Oh. Oh, my God. Really?" Mrs. Sherman looked concerned. I guess something in my eyes echoed that concern, because she took my hand in hers and squeezed it tight. It didn't hurt—it felt kind of nice. "Yeah, yeah. I can see how that . . . No, there's, uh, there aren't any of Josh's friends here. And I don't think we're allowed to send him home with one of them anyway. Is there a friend or a relative who could—I see. Right, right. No, I wouldn't want that, either."

Mrs. Sherman took a deep breath. "Look, Mrs. Mendel, if it's just going to be a few hours, why don't I just take Josh home with me?" I think my eyes might have popped out of my head, but Mrs. Sherman wasn't looking at me anymore.

"No, it's no bother. Really. I'm only five minutes from here. Let me give you my address and then you can just pick him up when you're ready."

They exchanged address and phone information. I felt a little weird thinking that I was going to see a teacher's home. I was going to go *home* with her. Was she going to make me do homework?

She hung up with Mom and put her cell away. "All right, Josh. You're coming home with me. Is that cool?"

The way she cocked her head and grinned at me as she said it, I couldn't help but say, "Yeah, sure."

Together, we cleared the inches of snow off her car and she explained what Mom had told her: The roads were even worse down in Lake Eliot and many of them had been closed to anything but emergency vehicles. Mom figured it was going to be a few hours before she could get out of Lake Eliot and back home, and Dad would take even longer.

"This just makes the most sense, don't you think?" She swept a big floe of snow off the windshield onto the ground. "Better than bothering the principal again."

"Yeah."

She was a careful, slow driver, focusing on the road, which meant I could look at her. It was weird how a coat and scarf and boots can make a woman's body look totally different, all straight and bulky and uncomplicated.

She looked over to check on me. "You OK?"

"Yep. Thanks for not telling my mom that I was the only kid who missed the bus."

She laughed. "I was a kid once, too, y'know. I know how parents flip out over little things. Don't worry about it."

And, strangely enough, that's what happened—I settled back in the seat and didn't worry about it.

She may have lived five minutes from school, but between traffic, snow, and plenty of time with the brake, it took more like twenty to get to her apartment complex.

I wasn't sure what to expect inside her apartment. It was basically normal and, therefore, sort of disappointing. I guess I'd been expecting something exotic. I had to remind myself that teachers are just normal people when they're not teaching.

The door opened into a living room–type area with a sofa facing a big entertainment center and a couple of chairs. There was a little round table with chairs tucked into a corner, and a big opening in the wall that showed the kitchen. A hallway ran back into darkness.

"Not much, is it? Make yourself comfortable," she said. "Are you tired? Do you want to take a nap? The bedroom's right down the hall."

I wasn't sure what to do. I had never been to a teacher's house before. I was afraid of doing something wrong. "No, thank you."

"Well, what do you normally do when you get home? Do you want to watch TV or something?"

"I guess."

"OK, well, take off your coat and your boots and sit down. Remote's on the table."

A minute later I had MTV2 going. Mrs. Sherman struggled out of her coat and tugged at her boots. One came off suddenly, flying out of her hands and hitting the wall, where it left a black scuffmark.

"Oh, goddamn." She caught her breath and turned to me. "I'm sorry. I'm sorry. I shouldn't have said that."

Dad said it all the time, but I felt bad for her because *she* felt bad. "It's OK."

"Please don't tell your parents I said that. They'll think I'm horrible."

Nah. They'd probably welcome her into the family. "I won't."

She grinned, "Our secret, right?"

"Yep."

"Want something to drink?"

I didn't want to say yes; it seemed like imposing. But I was really thirsty. "OK."

She ruffled my hair as she walked past me on the way to the kitchen.

"I don't have much!" she called from the kitchen. "Is OJ OK?"

I giggled at "OJ OK." "Sure."

A minute later she came in with a tall glass of orange juice for me and a wineglass for herself.

"Do you mind?" she asked, sitting across from me on a chair. She gestured with the wineglass. "It's not like I'm an alcoholic or anything. It's just that I always have a glass of wine when I get home from school. It's like a tradition."

"No, I don't mind."

I watched MTV a little while longer in silence. It wasn't very good, but I didn't know if she wanted to watch it or not, so I didn't say anything about changing the channel. After a few minutes, she got up and went into the kitchen, where I heard her use the phone.

"No, the roads weren't too bad yet. One of my students is here with me. Missed his bus. Yeah. I don't know. His mother works down near you, so who knows?" She opened the refrigerator. "I think we're OK. Maybe soda or something like that. We don't have anything to drink."

It was weird seeing her putter around in the kitchen, occasionally drifting out into the hallway. She wasn't wearing any shoes and her toenails were painted a vivid pink. She had tiny toes.

"You doing OK, Josh?" she called, craning her neck to look around the corner at me.

"Yeah!" I turned back to the TV quickly. Didn't want her to know I'd been looking at her feet.

I got bored with the TV, so I just looked around the room. It was almost all in black and white, with clear glass for accents. I had never seen a room so neat and . . . *straight*. It just seemed like the whole room was set in a specific order. The artwork on the walls wasn't pictures or anything like that—it was patterns of colors. At first, they just sort of looked like someone had randomly splashed paint all over them, but the more I looked at them, the more I could detect a pattern of some sort. I wasn't sure *what* the pattern was, but I knew that it was deliberate. Cool.

I wandered to the entertainment center. On a shelf at eye-level there were a bunch of framed pictures. One of them was a little girl—kindergarten, maybe?—with pigtails, sticking her tongue out adorably at the camera. Another showed a guy around my age in a football uniform, sullen. There was a frame with two pictures in it, both of old people, but two *different* pairs of old people.

One picture, though, took my breath away. It was a photo of Mrs. Sherman in her wedding gown. I don't know enough about dresses to describe it, other than to say that it fit her down to the waist like a second skin made of shimmering, neon white, where it flared into a wide skirt that seemed to be made of overlapping clouds. It was so low-cut in front that I couldn't imagine how her breasts stayed put or how there could be any more breast to cover in the first place. She seemed almost completely exposed, yet still covered. Her skin glowed bronze against the white of the gown, except for the darker valley where her breasts came together and seemed somehow to gesture below and between them.

And her *smile*. Her smile was hypnotic. It was as if she loved the camera itself and couldn't help letting it know.

I stared at it for a long time, memorizing every detail, looking for new details. My God! Zik and I had thought she was gorgeous before, but we hadn't had any clue! She wasn't just beautiful—she was *supernatural*.

I think if I'd stared any longer, there would have been a waterfall of drool running down my chin and puddling around my feet. I forced myself to stop looking at the photo.

Under the TV, on a shelf on the entertainment center, was another kind of heaven. I couldn't believe it—I crouched down to make sure I wasn't seeing things.

"Something wrong?" I almost jumped out of my skin. Mrs. Sherman was standing right behind me! The phone was nowhere in sight.

"Yes! I mean, no!" I got up and scurried back to the sofa. "I'm sorry. I didn't mean to—"

She shook her head. "What are you *apologizing* for?"

For staring at the picture, really, I guess. But I couldn't tell *her* that. "Nothing. I don't know. I just . . ." I pointed. "I can't believe you have them! Xbox, PlayStation, *and* Nintendo!"

"Oh, I should have known!" She rolled her eyes. "Yeah, we've got them all. They're George's."

"Wow! You let your son have all of these? My parents won't let me get any video games."

"Not my *son*. I don't have any kids. George is my husband. He's a game tester. That's why we have all these things. We don't even have a DVD player—we just use the game machines."

Now something clicked: The coffee table, I realized, was covered with video-game magazines—*Official Xbox, PSM, EGM* . . .

"He's the luckiest man in the world," I said gravely, and meant every syllable of it. To play video games for a living *and* be married to Mrs. Sherman? How could one man be so fortunate?

She laughed. "If you say so. Do you want to play something? He won't mind. We've got . . . I think we've got *all* the games. Sure seems that way, at least." She pointed to a closed cabinet door. "Help yourself."

I couldn't believe it! Mom and Dad wouldn't let me have a console in the house; they didn't even like to buy me games for the computer, though they'd usually relent for my birthday or something like that. I opened the cabinet door and beheld more video-game cases than I've ever seen before in my life. I usually played Xbox at Zik's house, but only when his dad and older brother weren't hogging it. Here was an Xbox and about a million games, and they were all mine!

Pretty soon I was sprawled out on the floor, frantically blasting zombies. The game was rated T—there were a bunch of M-rated games, too, but I didn't want to push it or get Mrs. Sherman angry at me.

Mrs. Sherman came up to me and I hit Pause so that I wouldn't get killed while she told me my mom had called and she was on her way. I was so absorbed in the game that I hadn't even heard the phone ring. I looked at the clock; hours had passed while I was submerged in the digital world.

"Keep playing. I'm going to start dinner. If your mom gets here first, fine. Otherwise, you can eat with us."

Us? That's right—her husband.

As if he heard my thoughts, he opened the door just then. "Fuck! It's crazy out there!" he shouted. He was tall and stoop-shouldered, his gut a little knot that protruded out from over his belt. He shook snow out of his sandy, unruly hair as he stripped off his coat.

"George!" Mrs. Sherman ran in from the kitchen.

"What? What did I do?"

She pointed to me. "Meet Josh, my student."

George's face fell when he saw me. "Whoops! Sorry about that, kid. Pardon my *français*."

"De nada," I said. It was the only foreign language I knew at all. They both laughed.

"Josh, this is my husband, George," Mrs. Sherman said, gesturing vaguely between the two of us. "Josh is using the Xbox."

"I don't have to—" I started.

"What are you playing?" He glanced at the screen. "Ah, cool. Want some help?"

"Sure."

He looked at Mrs. Sherman. "Honey, I'm gonna . . ."

"Go ahead," she said with the tone of someone who's used to it and returned to the kitchen.

"Let's kick some zombie butt," George said, dropping to the floor next to me and grabbing another controller.

We played Xbox for another hour or so, and just as Mrs. Sherman was ready to serve dinner, the doorbell rang and it was Mom, standing in a good six inches of snow that had blown onto the entrance balcony. I gathered up my stuff and put on my coat and went to stand with Mom.

"I hope he wasn't any trouble," Mom said.

"No, God, not at all," Mrs. Sherman said.

"Hey, Josh," George said, holding out his hand to me. "You can save the world from the undead with me any time you want." He grinned and winked at me as I shook his hand.

"Boys," Mom and Mrs. Sherman said at the same time, and laughed.

THE SNOW DIDN'T LET UP all night, and school ended up canceled for the rest of the week. Mom stayed home with me for two days since classes were canceled at LEC, too. That first night, though, I lay awake and listened through the vents as Mom and Dad argued. Dad was pissed and not afraid to say so. He had *warned* her about emergencies. He had pointed out that she would be far from me if there was a problem.

Mom told him that everything was fine, that I hadn't been in any danger. She found me playing video games and ready to eat dinner, for Christ's sake! "He was having the time of his life!" she said.

"I don't know about this job of yours," Dad said. He sounded like he was talking about a pet.

Friday, schools were still closed while Lowe County cleaned up the last of the snow. The roads were OK for most vehicles, but not school buses. Mom had to go back to work, but she arranged to drop me off at Zik's since his mother would be home. I usually avoided hanging out at Zik's house (so did Zik), but his dad wouldn't be home, so that was good. We stayed away from Mike and went outside instead. We played catch with snowballs, trying to throw them hard enough to make them explode against our palms when caught, scoring points for intact catches.

"What happened the other day, J? Why weren't you on the bus when we got out early?"

I gave him an edited version of the truth, one that involved me being in the bathroom when the bus was called so that I wouldn't have to admit that I was trying to calculate a better retroactive batting average for myself. When I told him that I'd gone to Mrs. Sherman's apartment, his jaw dropped and he didn't even try to catch the snowball I'd just thrown. It exploded against his shoulder.

"Holy fucking shit!" Zik's vocabulary at an early age was heavily influenced by his father and brother. Even his mother dropped the f-bomb on occasion. My mom hated me being around the Lorenzes, so I was always careful to watch my language; the last thing I needed to do was give her one more reason to try to keep me away from Zik.

"Goddamn!" he said, scooping up some snow and mashing it into a ball. "What was it like?"

"Her apartment?" I thought about the art on the walls. The video games. That picture . . . "Just an apartment. Jeez, man."

"What did she wear?"

"What are you talking about? She wore her clothes. Just like at school." I didn't tell him about seeing her naked feet, the little pink-tipped toes. That was mine.

He threw the snowball at me. I managed to catch it without it falling apart. Another point for me.

"Did you see her bedroom?"

"No, you doofus! Why would I see that?" But in the back of

my mind, it danced there . . . *Do you want to take a nap? The bedroom's right down the hall.*

"Man," Zik went on, "if it was *me*, I woulda seen the bedroom. I woulda gone there and snooped around, you know? See if she has any porn or lingerie."

"You're a perv," I told him, hurling the snowball back. It disintegrated in midair. I deducted a point for myself.

"I met her husband."

Zik clutched his chest. "That lucky fucker!" he moaned. "I don't even know him and I hate him."

"He was nice. He let me play Xbox."

"I hate him!" Zik ranted. "Hate him hate him hate him!" And on and on until I pelted him with snowballs, rapid-fire, and we dissolved into giggling grunting snowmen, hurling snow and kicking it up as we chased each other around the yard.

School reopened on Monday, and I guess I expected Mrs. Sherman to act different somehow, but she didn't. She was just my history teacher again (my *hot* history teacher). No more little giggles and little secrets. As I left class that day, I wanted to go up to her and tell her to thank her husband for letting me play with his Xbox, but she was talking to another teacher who had come in, so I left.

But a couple of days after that, Mrs. Sherman returned papers we'd turned in earlier in the year. Mine had no grade on it, just "See me after class" written in red.

My heart went into triple time, like that burst you get when you realize the ball is going over the heads of all the outfielders.

What had I done wrong? The Streak was solid at this point—was I going to blow it here?

I flipped through the pages (there were only three of them—it was seventh grade, after all), but there was no indication as to why she wanted to see me. No grade. No notes. Nothing.

I actually started to *sweat;* it gathered at the nape of my neck and trickled down between my shoulder blades like when I stood out on the field and waited for a new pitcher to warm up. Only I didn't mind it then—I was playing baseball; I was supposed to sweat. But not here in school.

I had trouble paying attention that day; all I could think was, *I'm going to get a bad grade. I might not get straight A's this year.* Over and over. I barely heard Mrs. Sherman speaking. I robotically copied what she wrote on the board and the overhead.

At the end of class, I pretended to be having trouble getting everything into my backpack. Once most of the kids had filtered out, I heaved the pack over my shoulder and walked up to Mrs. Sherman's desk, where she was busily writing something in her gradebook.

I waited for a minute. Nothing. Then, as the last kid filed out of the classroom, she looked up and smiled at me. Smiled that broad, half-dimpling smile, smiled so close to the smile from the wedding picture that I thought I might just lean forward . . .

No. No!

"What's up, Josh?"

I gaped for a second, but recovered. Didn't she remember? "Here." I thrust the paper at her. "You said to—"

"Oh, right! *Right!*" She sounded excited as she grabbed the paper. "I *love* this paper, Josh! Your insights on medieval Europe are . . . I don't think you can understand how exceptional this is for someone your age."

What? I just kept staring while she chattered on happily.

". . . so anyway," she went on, "I'm taking this grad class on cognitive development and adolescence and I thought that your paper would be a great topic for me to write about. So I was wondering if you would mind if I used your paper for my research topic."

I guess I was supposed to say something here, but I was busy staring in shock.

"Josh?" She waved a hand at me and the smile turned into concern. The dimple smoothed away. "Josh, are you OK?"

"Yeah. Yeah, I'm fine. I just didn't know—I thought I got a bad grade. I thought that's why you wanted to see me."

She blinked in genuine surprise. "A *bad* grade? This is better than some of the papers I saw teaching high school last year!" She held it out to me. "You should be very proud of yourself."

"But—"

"But what?"

I couldn't speak. I just pointed to the paper.

Her brow furrowed as she looked at it. "What do you—Oh! Oh, my God! I'm such an idiot!" She barked out a huff of laughter, slammed the paper down on her desk, and scrawled something on it with a red pen. "Sorry about that." She slid the paper back to me, with a big, bright, red "A+" across the top.

That night, Mrs. Sherman called at home and talked to Mom to get permission to use my paper and me as the subject of her research paper. She also asked Mom if it would be OK for me to stay after school with her sometimes so that she could interview me and do questionnaires and stuff. She promised to bring me home at a reasonable time.

Mom was thrilled, I later learned through the vents. Ever since the snowstorm, Dad had been pressuring her about quitting her job—he called it "ending the experiment"—since I didn't have baseball practice to occupy me after school. But now that I would be with an adult, he didn't have a leg to stand on. Mom shut him down early in the evening; chilly silence mingled with heated air through the vent into my room.

So a couple of days later, after the last bell, I went to Mrs. Sherman's room. She gave me a test to fill out. "Remember, this isn't for a grade, Josh."

It wasn't a very difficult test; it had some vocabulary and some multiple-choice stuff. Nothing complicated. Mrs. Sherman sat at her desk and did stuff on the computer while I finished the test, but a couple of times I looked up and saw her watching me.

"Just take your time," she said. "There's no prize for finishing first." And then we laughed, since I was the only one taking the test—I would be first, last, and everything in between.

Even without trying to break any speed records, it didn't take very long to finish the test. Mrs. Sherman had me home with a good hour to spare before Mom got home from work.

The next day, she gave me another test—this one was written and might take a little longer, she said. I plunged into it. I wanted to impress her even more. I wanted to blow her mind.

By the time I was finished, it was almost time for Mom to be home from work. Mrs. Sherman drove me home and talked to Mom briefly. Mrs. Sherman was worried that the later testing and interviewing would take longer. Would it bother Mom if she brought me home a little bit later?

Mom didn't mind, as long as I wasn't bothering Mrs. Sherman. Oh, no, Mrs. Sherman assured Mom: Josh was *delightful*. She was enjoying this project.

And Mom couldn't have been happier—there had been some opportunities to work a little later at work, but she'd always declined because she already felt guilty about getting home when she did. But if I was with Mrs. Sherman a little later, then she could stay at work a little later and get home closer to the time Dad got home.

I drifted off that night, thinking how this was working out for everyone—Mom got to keep her job and do it better, Mrs. Sherman got her help, Dad didn't have to worry, and me . . . I got to spend more time with the most beautiful teacher on the planet.

That same night, I had the first dream.

I don't remember many of the details except that it started with Mom and Mrs. Sherman talking about something, talking very loudly, even though I was right there. I knew they were talking about me, but for some reason I couldn't understand them. It was like they were speaking a foreign language.

At some point, my dad called out to my mom and she left. Mrs. Sherman kept talking to thin air and then she started to get undressed, even though I was standing nearby. She kicked off her shoes first and I couldn't stop staring at her toes.

When I woke up, my pajamas were sticky and wet. At first I thought I'd wet the bed, but then I realized. I sneaked into the bathroom to clean up, then changed into fresh pajamas. I balled up the old ones and jammed them deep into the hamper, hoping that Mom wouldn't notice when she did the wash.

It was tough to focus in history that day—I felt like Mrs. Sherman could tell that I dreamed about her. I avoided eye contact with her, looking down at my desk. I did too good a job—as class ended, she asked if I was feeling OK and even put a cool palm against my forehead to see if I had a temperature. I think I blushed; at the very least my face felt so hot that I thought for sure she'd rush me to the nurse's office, but instead she just said, "You don't feel hot. Are you sure you're OK?" to which I said, "Yes," and shuffled off to science.

By the end of the school day, I'd gotten over the guilt and instead stole every glance I could, wondering how accurate my dream had been. I imagined Mrs. Sherman standing up at her desk while it was just the two of us in her classroom, unbuttoning her blouse, slowly, letting it slide down her shoulders and arms like water from a pool or a bath, then reaching around to unfasten her bra—

"Stop daydreaming, Josh," she teased from her desk. I jumped and banged my knee against the desk, but I didn't let it show. "You only have twenty minutes to finish this part of the test. You can think about your little girlfriends later."

God! If she knew *what* I was daydreaming about . . . ! I turned my attention back to the test and finished it. I hated the way she'd said "little girlfriends."

I handed the test to her. She thanked me and looked at the clock. "It's still early, Josh. Your mom won't be home yet."

"I know."

"How about this—let's go back to my apartment and I'll get the next test. You can do it right away. We'll get ahead that way."

"Sure."

On the way to her apartment, I said, "I don't have any, you know. Girlfriends."

"What do you mean?"

"Before. During the test. You said about my 'little—'"

"Oh, Josh!" She laughed. "I was just teasing you. Don't take everything so seriously."

"But—"

"And besides, I can't believe you don't have a girlfriend. What about Michelle?"

"Michelle *Jurgens*?"

"Yes. She's cute, don't you think?"

"Michelle likes Zik."

"Oh. Well, who's that other girl I always see you hanging out with? Rachel?"

"Rachel's just my friend. And a really good baseball player."

"Good for her." She looked over at me. "Don't worry, Josh—there'll be plenty of time for girls."

I wasn't worried. Not particularly.

"You're a good-looking kid. And you're very mature and respectful. Just wait until you get to high school—the girls are going to love you."

Well, that was nice to hear.

At her apartment, she rummaged through a stack of papers on the coffee table until she found the one she wanted. It was a really short, really easy questionnaire about my reading habits. I had done something like it on the first day for her, so I couldn't figure out why she wanted me to do it again. But she kicked off her shoes and went into the kitchen, returning with her glass of wine, so I didn't ask questions. She sat across from me in a chair, her legs tucked up under her, and leafed through a book while I answered the questions and sneaked the occasional glance at her exposed knees.

When I finished, she unfolded herself from the chair (giving me a quick and painful glimpse of the inside of one thigh, down low near the knee) and put the questionnaire on top of a stack of papers. It was still early.

"Do you want to play Xbox to kill time before I take you home?" she asked.

Duh! I scrambled for the controller while she went back into the kitchen.

There was already a game in the machine—I checked the empty box on top of the Xbox to see what it was. "Is it OK if I play the one that's already in here?"

She came back from the kitchen, her wineglass refreshed. "I don't see why not. Just don't save over George's game or he'll get all huffy."

Well, I could understand that! "But . . ." I showed her the box. I figured I should at least ask. The game was rated M.

She read it: "Blood and gore. Strong language. Violence." She sighed. "Probably nothing worse than you've seen on TV, right? Just don't tell your parents, OK? Our secret."

I mimed turning a key over my lips and then tossing it over my shoulder. She laughed and settled back and I switched on the Xbox.

7

THAT'S HOW IT WENT for a little while—I would stay after school and, if it was an early test day, Mrs. Sherman would drive me back to her apartment. I would switch on the Xbox and settle in to play while she sat nearby, shoeless, sometimes in a chair, sometimes on the sofa, grading papers and occasionally egging me on when I did something stupid that got my character killed on-screen. Her toenails went from pink to naked to a funky electric blue to red and then back to pink. She must have spent a ridiculous amount of time on them.

After a few days of this, we just skipped the school part altogether and went straight to her apartment. It was easier to do the tests there, she said. Quieter. No distractions. I filled out surveys, answered interview questions, told her about how I learned to read, about my school experiences. She carefully noted everything I did, took notes, filed everything.

I have to admit that I had some more wet dreams and it got pretty embarrassing. I'm pretty sure Mom had to realize, since I was putting my pajamas in the laundry a lot more often than usual. But she didn't say anything, so I didn't say anything.

I got to see more of the apartment—after all, my bladder couldn't hold out forever. I went down the hallway to the bathroom and resisted plundering the medicine cabinet. But I did get a quick peek at the bedroom on my way back—nothing to write home about. Just a bed, some furniture, and some more of that cool artwork on the walls. I liked the artwork and I told her so.

"Really?" She seemed surprised. She was in the kitchen, pouring the last of a bottle of wine into her glass. I grabbed a Coke from the fridge. By now I was pretty comfortable here. On a couple of nights when my mom and dad had to work really late, I even ate dinner with Mrs. Sherman and George. (He wouldn't let me call him "Mr. Sherman." "I'm not your teacher, Josh. And besides, you can kick my ass on half these games. I should be calling you Mr. Mendel.")

"Yeah. It's cool. I've never seen anything like it before." As if I had extensive art experience! But I was feeling quite grown up. Mrs. Sherman treated me like an adult, not like a kid, and it was just the two of us hanging out in her apartment, like friends. George wouldn't be home for a while yet.

"That's because it's original," she said. "A friend of mine from college paints them."

"Really?" I wandered into the living room and stood before one of the bigger paintings. I had never seen *real* art before, art that someone actually painted. Except for a field trip to the museum, but that didn't count.

"Yes." I almost spilled my Coke—Mrs. Sherman had come up right behind me, her bare feet silent on the carpet. "She's really talented. We roomed together junior year and stayed in touch."

And then . . .

I don't know why.

She put an arm around my shoulders. "What do you like about the art?" She sipped at her wine.

But...

Her boob...

Her *breast*...

Was just *resting* against my shoulder!

I could *feel* it, the side of it! Her breast lay there, heavy against me, yielding just slightly. My vision swam—the riot of color before me didn't help. My lungs, suddenly tight, had trouble getting air. And when I *did* breathe in, I smelled...

Strawberry.

And wine.

"It's chaotic," I said in a whisper, because a whisper was all I could manage. Her *breast*.

"Wow," she said, and pulled me tight against her for a brief, glorious moment. Her breast just *smashed* against me for that instant and my throat tightened and I was *rock hard* in no time flat, near to hyperventilating, and then she pulled away. "That's a really, really amazing viewpoint from someone your age, Josh. I mean... That's exactly the point of this series: chaos." She looked over at me shook her head. "You know, I have to keep reminding myself that you're only twelve. You look and act much older."

Right now, I was just acting like I had to turn away from her; if she looked down, she would see... *everything*.

I held my Coke can strategically to block her view and started to head back to the Xbox. "Thanks." It seemed inadequate, though. She was telling me I was a grownup. Or close. That I wasn't like the other kids in school. I knew that already, of course. My grades. Teacher comments over the years. Even my focus in baseball, which coaches had always called "beyond advanced." Mom and Dad used to worry that I wasn't having enough fun, until I convinced them that working hard in school, on the diamond, *was* fun for me.

Just wait until you get to high school—the girls are going to love you.

You're very mature.

You're a good-looking kid.

I sat in front of the TV and prayed that she wouldn't sit where she could see my lap, but she did. I held the Xbox controller there and unpaused the game just as a dinosaur came on screen and made the controller vibrate with the shaking of its footsteps.

"Does that *vibrate?*" she asked, as if discovering this for the first time. How could George play all these games and she still have no idea about it at all?

"Um, yeah." And, in fact, it was vibrating against me right now, and I wanted very much for it to stop.

"Let me see."

I handed over the controller, leaning in such a way as to conceal (I hoped) my lap. She took the controller and jumped a little at its vibration, then laughed and said, "No wonder George likes this one," before handing it back immediately.

I sat there with the controller and an erection and my eyes locked on her left foot and its pink toenails. "You can . . ." God, my mouth was dry even though I'd just drunk a Coke. "You can play if you want."

She laughed again. "God, no. That's OK, but it's sweet of you to offer." She got up (quick flash of thigh again) and ruffled my hair on her way back to the kitchen.

On the screen, my character was eaten by a dinosaur, with much gnashing of teeth and squirts of blood and dino spittle.

I reloaded the game and played until it was time to go home. That night, I lay in bed and replayed the breast, the pull closer, the toenails, the hair-ruffling over and over in my mind. To my shame, I had to change my pajamas before I even fell asleep.

At lunch and during recess, I'd let Zik in on selected details. There were some things I just couldn't tell him, even though he was my best friend. I told him I got to play M-rated video games, that I'd seen the bedroom and bathroom in the apartment, and that Mrs. Sherman thought I was very grown up and mature for my age. (This last sent him into a paroxysm of air-smooching and self-hugging, accompanied by "Oh, Josh! Oh, Josh!" until I beaned him with a dodgeball.)

In early December, we got hit with more snow. Nothing like the near-blizzard that shut schools down a few weeks earlier, but just enough to make it a pain in the ass to drive and walk. When we got to Mrs. Sherman's apartment, the sidewalk was covered. She made us hold each other for support, sliding an arm around my waist, and I decided that needing to lean on someone wasn't such a bad thing. I put my arm around her waist in turn, aware of how close to her breast and hip my hand was, midpoint between two things I wanted to touch *very* badly. On the other side, her breast and hip pressed against me, making me dizzy, the very opposite of what hanging on to each other was supposed to accomplish. I was glad for the long winter coat that hid my hard-on, and the slippery stairs that made it OK for me to walk a little funny.

At the stairs, I started counting, my usual routine, ticking off the first six steps in my mind, then a half-turn on the landing, then one (seven) two (eight) three (nine) four (ten) five (eleven) six (twelve) . . .

"Don't go so fast," Mrs. Sherman said, laughing. "I'm an old lady."

"You're not old, Mrs. Sherman."

"That's sweet of you, Joshua." For some reason, hearing her use my full name made me feel . . . adult. I don't know why. When my mom used it, I was usually in trouble.

But Mrs. Sherman didn't come down hard on the word, didn't draw out the end of it. She said it . . .

I don't know. She said it like she said "George."

Once inside the apartment, we enacted our latest ritual: I would go to the kitchen and pour her a glass of wine and get a Coke for myself. She would disappear into the bedroom while I was doing this and reappear shoeless, usually with a button or two unbuttoned on her blouse.

We sat in the living room and she quizzed me on some general knowledge–type questions: current events, terrorism, things like that. Then I was free to play Xbox. I was doing much better in the game than George was, but then again, I had more time to play it. He had to test a bunch of games at work; I could focus on this one.

Mrs. Sherman sat nearby in the living room, grading her papers or reading a book while I played. She never asked me to turn the volume down.

After one particularly loud dino-roar and explosion, I looked over at her to see if I was bothering her. What I saw made me dizzy and rock hard all over again. Mrs. Sherman was sitting on the sofa, leaning back and reading a test paper. It wasn't just that by leaning back her breasts pushed up and strained against the material of her blouse. No. It's that her legs were slightly apart, and thanks to the reflection in the glass-topped coffee table, I could see . . .

I could see.

Right up her skirt.

Right up to her *panties*.

At least, I *think* they were panties. There was almost nothing there, just a strip of shiny black material. I thought I would explode. I was like an animal trying to cross the highway, caught halfway, terrified by the loud sounds and zooming metal things but unable to move for all that fear. I couldn't make myself look away, but at the same time I knew I *had* to look away, that at any moment she could look down or look over at me and see me doing this, doing this horrible, horrible thing.

My mouth went dry and I licked my lips. I was losing my mind.

A scream from the Xbox brought me back to reality. I hadn't paused the game and my character was dead. I jerked around to the TV so fast that I thought my head would just keep spinning from sheer inertia and snap right off. It didn't.

I restarted the level, my breath coming fast now, my heart pounding. I couldn't even see the screen. All I could see was that reflection in my mind's eye, the smooth skin of her thighs, the darkening under the skirt, leading to that shiny patch of black material. God! I knew I would never be soft again.

"Josh?" she said suddenly, and my heart skipped not one, but two or maybe even three beats.

I ignored her, pretending to be engrossed in the game. So engrossed that I couldn't *possibly* have just been looking up her skirt five seconds ago.

"Josh!"

"Hmm? What?" I asked innocently, clicking away on the controller.

"Would you mind getting me another glass of wine?"

I paused the game and looked over my shoulder. She was sitting up, holding the glass out to me. Her breasts had returned to their normal positions and her legs were primly set together.

"Sure, Mrs. Sherman."

I unfolded myself from the floor and, miracle of all miracles, my erection had subsided. I took the wineglass.

"You know, Josh, when it's just the two of us and we're here, you don't have to call me Mrs. Sherman."

I had heard George call her "Evelyn" and "Evvy" in the past. I didn't think my parents would like me calling a teacher by her first name, but what they didn't know wouldn't hurt them.

"Are you sure?" I took the wineglass.

"Yes. It's just silly. You're helping me with my project. You're not just a student; you're like my research partner." She favored me with a brilliant full-wattage smile and that left dimple.

"OK . . . Evelyn." It felt weird coming out of my mouth.

She frowned, her face scrunching up like she'd bitten into something sour and bitter at the same time. "God, no. Not *that*. I *hate* my name. 'Evelyn.' Yuck." She made a gagging sound and I couldn't help laughing. "Sounds like some old lady from a million years ago."

"OK. Evvy?"

"No. No, that's no good either. How about..." She thought for just a second. "How about Eve?"

"Eve."

She smiled when I said it, her entire face coming more alive. "Yes! Perfect! I always wanted people to call me that."

"OK." I said it again. "Eve."

She clapped her hands like I'd just given her a present. Maybe I had. I don't know.

I filled her wineglass and brought it back to her. She sipped and sighed in contentment.

"What's it taste like?" I asked her.

"Do you want to try some?" She held it out to me.

"Are you serious?"

"Sure." She shrugged. "Just take a little sip. And promise me you won't tell your parents I let you try this." She looked over at the clock. "You won't still be drunk by the time I take you home."

"Ha, ha," I said. "Very funny." But I took the glass and sniffed it carefully.

"Oh, so you're a connoisseur!"

I had seen people drink wine in movies, so I went along with the joke—swirled the wine in the glass, sniffed it pretentiously. "A passable bouquet," I said in a snooty tone, causing Mrs.—Eve to throw her head back and roar with laughter. I grinned at her and waggled my eyebrows, then took a sip.

It actually tasted pretty bad, but Eve seemed to like it, so I didn't want to say so. I don't know what I expected, but from the smell, I thought it would be more like fruit juice. Instead, it tasted like fruit juice gone bad. And it burned my throat as it went down.

"Well?" she asked.

"It's OK." Ever the diplomat.

She took the glass back. "OK, so you're not a red man. I can tell. See? You've learned something. Next time you're on a hot date, don't order the red wine."

"Got it."

She looked serious all of a sudden. "But really, Josh—you can't tell your parents I let you do this, OK? I could get in a lot of trouble."

Over a little sip of wine? Puh-lease. But whatever—I wasn't going to tell my parents anyway. "Don't worry about it."

That night at dinner, my mother asked me why I had a grin plastered on my face. I didn't realize I did. "No reason," I told her.

But the truth is this: Until I ate my second helping of mashed potatoes, I could still catch a lingering taste of the wine on my lips when I licked them. And for some reason, it tasted better now.

That night, I did my best not to think of Eve as I lay in bed. It was pure torture; she had become a part of my nightly ritual, to the point that I didn't put on my pajamas until I'd already added another wad of tissues to the trash can.

I was getting home later and later each day; Mom was working late to show her professor (that's what she called him, "my professor," not "my boss") that he had made a good choice when he'd hired her. George had loads of deadlines, multiple games coming out at once ("going to golden master," they called it), so I stayed at Eve's for hours after school each day, playing Xbox, stealing looks whenever, wherever, and however I could. Dad started coming home late, too, since there was no one home anyway.

You'd think that we'd be sullen and sort of miserable, what with all of us seeing each other just for an hour or so at night before I went off to blast through my homework. But the opposite was true: Mom was ecstatic because she was doing so well at her new job; Dad was happy to have some peace and quiet. And me? I was playing video games and getting the chance to memorize a beautiful body on the sly. What's there not to be happy about? I even heard Mom through the vents one night saying, "Thank God for this. It's like free babysitting."

School was, for a little while, difficult. I had to remind myself to call her "Mrs. Sherman," for one thing. For another, it was tough to be just another student to her, to not be able to joke with her or be silly like we were in her apartment. She made it more difficult—every now and then, with no warning, she would toss me a big, secret smile, her left cheek dimpled, her eyes shining.

Zik smuggled one of his brother's *Playboys* into school one day and we sneaked off during recess to page through it, saving the centerfold for last. As we unfolded it, our eyes drinking in the seemingly impossibly smooth skin and endless acres of bared flesh, Zik whistled low and quiet. "Why isn't there a girl like that around here?" he begged. "Why?"

We checked the Playmate biography to see if, by chance, this girl *was* around here, but she was from Canada.

"What do these numbers mean?" I asked. "Thirty-four C—"

As usual, Zik had the scoop—his dad and brother were a font of this sort of information. "Those are measurements.

Here, here, and here," he said, cupping imaginary breasts, then hands to his waist, then his hips.

"I don't get it. What do the numbers *mean?*"

"Thirty-four C is, like, her bra size, J. Thirty-four C is good."

We caressed the centerfold with our eyes again. "Well, obviously. But what does it *mean?*"

"I don't know! What is it with you? Can't you just stare at the tits?"

There were other numbers on the bio sheet. I did some quick mental math. "She's twenty."

"OK. Twenty is good. That's not too old."

"Mrs. Sherman is twenty-four," I said, and maybe I shouldn't have, but Zik knew I was going there almost every day after school.

"Huh." He thought about that. "Twenty-four. That's pretty old."

"No, it isn't." A thrill of unexplainable anger riffled through me. "And anyway, just because someone is old doesn't mean they aren't hot."

"Like your mother."

"Shut up about my mother!" I punched him in the shoulder, but it was just kidding. I knew what my mom looked like, and Zik never meant anything mean by it.

That afternoon at Eve's, she retreated to the bedroom as usual while I switched on the Xbox and then went to pour her a glass of wine and get my Coke. But this time, there was a new wrinkle.

"Something wrong?" Eve asked, poking her head into the kitchen. She had worn a rather shapeless and severe dress at school, but now was changed into a pair of sweatpants and a loose T-shirt. She'd added some more lipstick—she had told me once that it wore off during the day at school and her lips felt dry without it. Her hair was tied back—it changed the whole complexity of her face, drawing back her cheekbones, making her look like an entirely different person. Still beautiful, but in a different way.

Her feet, of course, were bare. Bright red toenail polish.

"There's two kinds of wine." I pointed. Next to Eve's red wine was another bottle of white. "Which one do you want?"

"Let's try the white today." She padded into the living room. I poured the white and followed her, gave her the wine, and settled down for some serious Xbox action. She was wearing pants, so there'd be no panty shots today, and that shirt was too loose to make her chest interesting. Fortunately, I was twelve years old and easily distracted by video games.

I was ostensibly at the apartment to help Eve with her project, but in truth it was done now and we basically just hung out together. I can't remember a time when we definitively stated that I would keep coming over. Neither, now that I think about it, can I remember when she officially said that the project was over. My time there just sort of morphed over a period of a few weeks from test subject to test subject/video-game guest to video-game guest/afterschool buddy.

"Do you want to try this one?"

I looked up from the game. Eve was sitting on one of the big stuffed chairs, holding her wineglass out a little. "Me?" I asked stupidly.

"Sure. You wanted to know what the other tasted like."

True. "OK." I took the wineglass and sipped. It was *much* better than the red! It didn't taste as fruity—it was cleaner, somehow, with bubbles like club soda or ginger ale. And it didn't burn my throat as much going down.

"That's pretty good!" I took another sip, then another.

"OK, that's enough!" she said, laughing. "I don't need you getting drunk on me."

I handed the glass back to her, embarrassed. "Sorry."

"Don't be sorry. It's OK." She chewed on her bottom lip for a moment. "Josh, you really can't let your parents know that I let you—"

"I won't tell them! I haven't told anybody anything."

I noticed another taste, another feeling—something waxy and slippery. I licked my lips.

"Oh, you've got . . . Come here," said Eve. I leaned toward her and she did the same. From the greater height of the chair, it made her loose T-shirt gape open at the neck, revealing some of that cleavage that the wedding picture promised. "You've got some of my lipstick from the glass right . . . Ah." She stroked the pad of her thumb across my lips, wiping away the lipstick. It took all my willpower not open my mouth and taste her thumb.

"There," she said, showing me the thumb, imprinted with a light burgundy smear. "Now you don't look like you've been kissing someone."

Kissing . . . It felt like forever as I watched her raise the glass to those lips and drink. I *wanted* to be kissing someone, I realized.

"Why doesn't it make you drunk?" I asked, pointing to the wine. "Drunk" I knew—I'd seen Mom and Dad come home from friends' houses sometimes, Mom stumbling a little bit or giggling too much. Those were usually nights when I closed the vent to my room and tried not to listen.

"Not everybody gets drunk quickly," she said. "Your size and weight have a lot to . . ." She stopped. "Well, you're practically as big as I am, so that doesn't really apply, does it? But I've built up a tolerance because I'm older and I've been drinking for a few years. You haven't been drinking . . . have you?" This last asked like a cop, her jaw set and her lips pressed into a thin, shimmering line.

I laughed. "No. Why do you drink it if it doesn't make you drunk?"

"Getting drunk isn't the only reason to drink wine. It relaxes me."

"I guess you need to relax after being with us all day, huh?"

She laughed. "Not you, but the others, yeah. God, Josh—you're so grown up sometimes . . ." She cocked her head and gazed at me over the rim of the wineglass. Those shining green eyes held mine for what seemed forever. I stared until I no longer felt uncomfortable doing so, and then until I felt uncomfortable again.

I was the one who broke contact, clearing my throat (it seemed like a gallon of saliva had suddenly settled there) and turning back to the Xbox. I could still feel her eyes on me.

Later, when she dropped me off at home, she leaned over to the passenger seat before I got out and said, "Have a good night, Josh."

And then she kissed me goodbye.

It was just on the cheek. And I knew it was just a friendly

goodbye kiss, but I wanted it to be more. I wanted it to be more so badly.

I fumbled for the door, finally pushing it open. I didn't trust my legs to carry me out onto the driveway and into the house.

"Josh, wait a sec."

I turned back to her.

"Do this." She mimed wiping at her cheek.

I obeyed, then looked down at my fingers—her lipstick blurred the tips.

"Good night," she said.

"Good night." I realized I was whispering.

It was dark out. I stood in the cold night air and watched her pull away, watched until her car's lights disappeared over a hill. Then I went inside.

Dad wasn't home yet, but Mom was eating a TV dinner by herself in the kitchen. I washed my hands and checked my cheek in the bathroom mirror, just to be sure.

"Hungry?" she asked.

"No. Mrs. Sherman made something."

In bed a little while later, I thought about the kiss. I focused on the memory, trying to transfer the sensation of her lips from my cheek to my lips, but I couldn't do it. I couldn't stop thinking about the taste of her lipstick.

I lay awake a long time and went through many tissues before I slept.

8

DECEMBER 15 IS THE DAY everything changed for good, though I didn't realize it until much later.

As usual, I went home with Eve. In the car, she told me she had a small headache and that she was going to lie down when we got to the apartment.

"Kids acting up today?" I asked.

"More like the teachers," she said. I knew that she didn't get along well with the other teachers. She was new to the school and they didn't like her for some reason. She always ate lunch alone, in her room, not in the teachers' lounge. Sometimes the assistant principal came by to talk to her, but she always asked him to leave.

I counted six—half-turn on the landing—and six again going up the steps. She sighed with relief when the door opened.

"Do you want me to get your wine?" I asked.

"No, Josh. I'm just going to lie down. Let me sleep a little bit, OK?"

She retreated to the bedroom and I went into my usual routine—switched on the Xbox and got my Coke from the refrigerator.

Something was wrong, though. The Xbox usually announced itself with a dinosaur roar as the game loaded. I knew that sound, knew how long it took to come up. It always came up while I was in the kitchen. Was the disk broken? Had George taken the disk out last night?

I heard something else. Something unfamiliar. I went into the living room.

On the TV, there were three people. A man and two women. They were naked.

And they weren't sitting around talking about the weather.

My breath got locked up somewhere deep in my lungs and I almost dropped the Coke.

I had seen naked bodies before, thanks to Zik's filching of his Dad's and Mike's porn, but never in motion. And never with sound. I stood, paralyzed, as the three people on screen entwined themselves into something that looked almost painful. The sounds they were making didn't sound painful, though. They were quite the Happy Trio.

I grabbed the Xbox controller and turned it off. My breath, restored, was making up for lost time by coming hard and fast. What the hell—?

I remembered Eve saying that they didn't have a DVD player; they just used the Xbox.

This was hers? She watched it?

Well, of course she did. This was her apartment—who else would be watching it?

I slowly came to realize that my heart was pounding ferociously and I was fiercely erect at the same time. The images and sounds from the DVD seemed to be imprinted on my brain itself, pressed there like a fossilized footprint. What should I do? Take out the movie and play Xbox like nothing had happened?

But where would I put the DVD in the meantime? Eve would see it when she came out.

Or should I leave the movie in and just not do anything at all? Maybe that was the best thing to do.

Or maybe . . .

Maybe Eve didn't even know about it. Maybe this was *George's* DVD. Maybe he watched it alone. Zik had told me that his father hid his porn from Zik's mom. So maybe it was something like that.

Yeah, that could be it. Maybe Eve didn't even know about it. That was a lot better than the idea that she was watching it *with* George.

With George . . .

Anger suddenly burbled up from deep within me like water foaming as it boiled over on the stove. I didn't understand it or anticipate it—it was just *there*. It was there as I thought of Eve curled up on the sofa with George, watching naked people have sex, kissing him with those lips, kissing him *on* the lips, not caring if he had a smear of lipstick on his cheek or lips.

It had to be George's. I had to tell her about it.

I went down the hallway. The bedroom door was open.

Eve lay on the bed, turned on her stomach, one leg brought up, the knee bent. The room was dark, but I could make out the smooth curve of her calf, the crook of her knee before her leg disappeared up her skirt.

I trembled in the doorway. I had meant to tell her about the DVD, but she was sleeping, her back softly rising and falling with each breath. I took a step into the room; she didn't move.

What did her leg feel like?

I was possessed by a sudden urge to lay my palm flat on her calf and run it up to her knee, taking the curve into the hollow there, then running up—

I swallowed, hard. A memory slammed into me from nowhere, hitting me like a line drive: When I was little, maybe five or six, Mom used to have me rub lotion on the backs of her legs at night before I went to sleep. My dad didn't like the greasy feel of the lotion, so I did it.

That memory—along with the sense of touching the leg—came back to me. My fingers twitched. I *knew* what her leg would feel like. I knew. And looking at her while knowing . . .

My breath was so loud that I thought she had to hear me. She would wake up and turn to see me standing there, evidence of my lust tenting the front of my jeans.

But I didn't care. I *wanted* her to see. Somehow, imagining her seeing drove the image of her and George on the sofa out of my mind, and it was *very* important that I kill that image.

I took another step. My feet made no sound on the carpet. *My hand, running up her leg, up under the skirt . . . fingertips brushing against . . . against . . . shiny black—*

I stopped before I could take another step. What the *hell* was I thinking? Before I could imagine any further, I backed away slowly, making no noise as I retreated to the hallway and then the living room. I sat on the sofa, shivering as I drank my Coke.

I didn't touch the Xbox.

It was none of my business, I decided. I just watched TV for a while, surfing the sports channels mostly, until my breathing and trembling subsided and I felt like I was, if not in the strike zone of normal, at least close enough to fool an ump.

After maybe an hour, Eve came out of the bedroom. I heard

her in the kitchen, pouring herself a glass of wine. My heart kicked into high gear again.

She came into the living room. She had a sort of sleepy vibe about her. It was strange and exciting. Her hair was fuller somehow; her eyes were enormous.

"What's this?" she asked. "Did you beat the game or something?"

I shook my head. I didn't trust my voice. My heart pounded.

She sat down on the sofa, at the end opposite me. "Then what's wrong? Why aren't you playing?"

And I realized that I would have to tell her. I could stonewall for a while, but not forever. And if she didn't know about the DVD, then seeing it might make her angry at George, and that would kill the image in my mind . . . and the weird anger that went with it.

I've never been one for theatrics, but for some reason, instead of telling her, I hit a couple of buttons on the remote, and suddenly there was the Happy Trio again, bucking and moaning.

"Oh my God!" she shrieked and covered her mouth with her free hand. The wineglass shook and threatened to spill. "Oh, God! Josh, turn it off! Turn it off!"

I obeyed.

"Oh, Lord," she groaned, pulling her legs up under her on the sofa. "I'm so embarrassed."

And that was that. I knew. It *was* hers. Hers and George's. They watched it together. They *liked* it.

I was stupid.

I was an idiot.

Eve was *married*. Like my mom and dad. She loved George. They had sex.

Stupid. I was just a kid.

"I'm so sorry," she mumbled, setting down the wineglass so that she could go retrieve the DVD. My anger, which had flared bright and hot, now cooled. But it didn't go away. It didn't vanish. It just dimmed and settled and became a dull, nerveless ache in the center of my chest, throbbing there in time with my heartbeat.

As I watched her go back down the hallway with the DVD, I realized what the anger meant: I was in love with Eve.

I hated her, too, of course. Hated her for loving George, for kissing him, for having sex with him. The love and the hate got all tangled up and twisted together until they became the anger.

We sat in silence as I played the Xbox game. Eve started out on the sofa, but then moved to a chair, then back to the sofa, clearly nervous and upset. I played terribly, constantly getting killed performing routine combos, reloading over and over again. I hardly saw the game—I was seeing the Happy Trio, seeing George and Eve in my mind.

Seeing Eve and *me* in my mind.

Earlier than usual, she said it was time to go. I didn't protest. I just gathered up my things and got in the car.

About halfway to my house, she said, "Do you want to talk about it?"

"About what?" As if there was anything else to talk about!

She sighed. It was already dark out and I could barely make out her lips parting. "About the—about the movie you saw."

Talk about it? How? I didn't get it. "I don't know what you mean."

"Well, I imagine it was a shock for you. If you want to talk about it—"

"I don't have anything to say—"

"—about how it made you feel—"

And that was when I had my first flicker.

It was so weird—one second, I was in the car, fuming in the dark. The next, I was back in Eve's apartment, two steps into her bedroom, my hand twitching as I contemplated touching her calf and running my hand up her skirt . . .

I blinked and I was back in the car. I gasped at the shock. It had been so *real*. I hadn't just *remembered* the moment in her bedroom. I had *relived* it. I was *there* again, for just a second.

"Josh? Josh?" Eve's voice had jumped up into panic altitudes. She looked over at me, back to the road, over at me. "Are you OK? What's wrong? Can you breathe?"

"I'm fine." And I was. With the flicker over, everything was back to normal, except for the ball of pulsating lead where my heart used to be.

"You got so quiet. I thought—" She cut herself off. I never learned what she thought.

At my house, I waited for my usual kiss on the cheek, but nothing came. Eve watched me, worrying her bottom lip. I flickered again

—taste of her lipstick—

but it was so fast that she didn't notice and all I did was blink and lick my lips, expecting to taste the lipstick and wine. But nothing.

I went inside. No one was home yet. I went to bed without eating. It wasn't even seven o'clock yet.

I dreamed of Eve, of course. Dreamed of her sleek and free like the women in the Happy Trio.

Mom and Dad coming home woke me up. I told them the first thing I could think of—I had a headache and wanted to sleep. Mom kissed my forehead and left my room. I thought of the backs of her legs, of the scent of the lotion, the feel of it, slippery. Dozing, they became Eve's legs.

I woke up again at four in the morning, this time wide awake, reeling from a dream that I could barely remember but that still had its hooks in me. Something about George, yelling, and Eve stepping on grapes to make wine, the juice painting her toenails blood red.

I lay there, panting, until the sky outside my window began to lighten on a new day.

But in school that day, Eve called me up to her desk as history class ended. She looked tired, drawn. Her face was pale, her eyes dim.

"Josh, I think it's probably for the best if you don't come over to my apartment anymore."

"Why?"

"Keep your voice down." She got up and closed the door. I hadn't realized my voice had been loud.

"Look, Josh, after what happened yesterday . . . last night . . . Maybe it's just best if you don't come over."

"But . . . But, Eve!" Her name was out of my mouth before I could stop it.

"Josh, I could get in a lot of trouble if anyone knew that you saw that. Plus, it was very embarrassing for me."

"I didn't tell anyone. I *won't* tell anyone. I promise!" She didn't look convinced. "And you don't have to be embarrassed. It's just, you know, it's just a movie. That's all. I've seen pictures before. Of naked people. It's no big deal."

Her eyebrow lifted and I thought some light came back into her eyes. "No, Josh. It was a lot of fun, but I don't think—" Someone knocked on the door. "That's my next class. Here." She scribbled out a hall pass and handed it to me. "Don't be late."

I wanted to stay and argue, but I knew I couldn't. I raced to my next class and spent the day in a whirl of confusion. What had I done wrong? I wasn't the one who put the movie in the Xbox, so why should I be punished for it? Why should I lose out on something?

The flickers came back at the end of school; one hit me while I was getting my books from my locker. I staggered away from the locker, aware that I was being watched by the kids around me, who no doubt thought I was about to collapse. Instead, I marshaled my guts and managed to walk out the door into the cold December afternoon.

The bus driver looked at me suspiciously. It had been a while since I'd ridden the bus on the way home.

It was like being on an alien planet. No one sat with me, and why should they? I was a stranger now. It was loud and obnoxious and annoying, not like driving home with Eve, where she'd play some soft music or NPR and we'd talk about how my day was and how her day was . . . The bus was just a big, stupid chaos of noise and idiocy. God, no wonder Eve didn't want to spend more time with me—I was one of *them!* I was one of these stupid *kids.*

At home, I wanted to call her, but I couldn't. It's not that I didn't know her phone number—I did, and her cell, too. It's just that I couldn't bring myself to do it. I couldn't bring myself to hear her voice telling me, again, that I wasn't wanted.

I puttered around the house, miserable, until Dad got home many hours later.

"You not going to Mrs. Sherman's anymore?" he asked. I'd been home before him two days in a row now.

"She dropped me off early." I don't know why I lied. I didn't intend to—it just happened. And now I couldn't take it back.

"Have you eaten?"

I didn't feel like eating, but two days without dinner in a row would have really raised his suspicions, so I made myself eat when I really felt like throwing up.

When Mom came home, Dad told her how I'd been home alone "for two days now, for God knows how long" and asked "Weren't you supposed to be home earlier?" while Mom kept trying to explain, over and over, that she'd gotten caught up in things, couldn't he just understand that she'd—

I went to the family room and turned up the TV loud enough to drown them out.

I woke up the following morning with only one emotion running through me: fear. Fear that Mom would have to quit her job. That my parents would never stop arguing. Hell, fear that I'd have to give up the Xbox.

But most of all, fear of Eve.

Fear that she knew about my dreams. Fear that she'd seen me looking down her blouse or up her skirt. Fear of what happened to me when I was around her—I didn't understand the rising welter of guilt, shame, and terror that somehow, in some twisted way, made me feel *good* . . . for a little while, at least.

As soon as the bus dropped me off, I headed straight for Eve's room. All I knew was that I had to get my friend back.

Eve jerked like someone had stabbed her when she saw me come into her room that early. Maybe it was the determination in my eyes. The fear. She glanced at the kids in her homeroom, who weren't paying the least bit of attention. But they would snap to attention *real* fast if something interesting started to happen at the front of the room.

I only had a minute or two before the homeroom bell rang. I leaned over her desk. "Mrs. Sherman, I *really* need to talk to you."

I can't describe the look on her face. I think at that age I lacked the emotional vocabulary—it was an utterly *adult* expression, one I'd never seen or made before. I have no idea what she was thinking in that moment.

"Josh, I think you took a wrong turn somewhere. You need to be in homeroom." She was trying to sound lighthearted, but it wasn't working.

"*Please.*" I was all but down on my knees.

She sighed. "There's no time now. Come see me at the end of the day."

It wasn't the victory I hoped for, but it was *hope* for victory. I made it to homeroom right before the bell and somehow got through the rest of the day with a raw thrill of hope vibrating in me like an aluminum bat that's just smacked a homer.

She would talk to me. At the end of the day. But she would *talk* to me.

History was tough, of course. I had trouble paying attention because I was too distracted by Eve, wondering what she would say to me. She looked past me or through me the entire time, never calling on me to answer a question, even if I had my hand up. One time, when we were supposed to be writing something down, I looked up suddenly and caught her at her desk, staring at me. She didn't flinch or turn away—she just took a breath, nodded, and then started working on her computer.

As soon as bus dismissal was called, I raced from homeroom to Eve's room. Kids were streaming out, babbling and chattering as they headed for the buses. I fought against the tide and made my way inside; Eve was packing up a bag at her desk, loading it with the papers she usually took home for grading. She didn't see me there.

"You said—you said I should talk to you at the end—" The room was almost empty, but I wanted to be careful.

"Shh!" She massaged her temples as she looked down at the desk. Her lips moved in silence. I'd seen this before; she was talking to herself, making sure she'd packed up everything she needed. I shut up.

Soon, she muttered, "OK." I heard them call my bus number, but I didn't move.

"Come on," she said. "We can't talk here."

WE DROVE IN SILENCE back to her apartment. Six steps up. Half-turn on the landing. Six steps. Inside, she told me to sit on the sofa and wait for her. She went into the kitchen for her wine.

"Do you want a Coke?" she asked.

I fidgeted on the sofa. It felt like I was being punished. Usually *I* got the drinks. "OK." I tried not to look at the Xbox.

She came back with our drinks, gave me my Coke, and sat down next to me on the sofa. I smelled strawberries.

"OK, Josh. You said you had to talk to me. Talk."

I fumbled with the Coke can. What was I going to say? It had all flown out of my brain somehow. I couldn't even form words. Managing to get the can open without spraying Coke all over was a major achievement.

I waited for her to say something instead, but she didn't. She just sat there, sipping her wine, watching me.

"I don't want to go," I blurted out.

She raised an eyebrow.

"I like being here. I like spending time with you."

"Yes, Josh, and I . . ." She sighed. "I like spending time with you, too. We have good conversations. We've become friends."

Friends! That was it! That was how to—"Right! We're

friends. I mean, you let me play with the Xbox . . ." Mistake! I shouldn't have mentioned the Xbox! That conjured the moaning ghosts of the Happy Trio.

But instead she laughed, like she used to, before I saw the movie. "Is that what this is all about? Playing video games because your parents won't buy them for you?"

"No! I just . . ." I cast about, looking for answers in the furniture, the air, the paint on the walls and ceiling. "I just like being here. It's . . ."

What *was* it? Yes, the Xbox was part of it. And Eve's beauty. And being—

And being treated like a grownup.

Like I wasn't a little kid.

I poured the wine. I got the drinks. When Eve cooked dinner, I helped, and she didn't boss me around like Mom did, ordering me to do this or that.

I looked at the artwork and I noticed things and Eve appreciated it.

"You don't treat me like a kid," I told her. "You act like you respect me."

"It's not an act." She sat up suddenly and leaned toward me. "I think you're an amazing young man, Josh. Your mind . . . The way you think, the way you express yourself . . . You're years ahead of your classmates."

"I know."

"It's tough, isn't it?" She stared at me with those blazing green eyes, eyes like an explosion of tropical leaves. "It's tough being different."

"Yeah."

"I know. When I was a kid . . ." She stopped and took a big gulp of the wine, almost draining the glass.

"What? What happened when you were a kid?"

She smiled at me and held out her glass. "Nothing. Will you refill this?"

My cheeks hurt from the broad grin plastered across my face. Things were coming back to normal. I hustled to the kitchen and came back with her glass of wine in record time. Back on the sofa.

"We still need to talk, though."

"Can I keep coming here after school?"

"Yes, Josh. But we need to talk. Seriously."

"OK."

"You have to understand that I could get in—"

"—a lot of trouble. I know. I get it. But it was an accident. And if anyone ever found out, I would tell them that—"

"No one can ever find out!" She practically screamed it, her eyes wide, veins standing out from her neck. I jumped back.

"I'm sorry, Josh." She put down her wineglass and leaned over, very close to me. "I'm sorry. I didn't mean to scare you." She took my face in her hands and made me gaze into her eyes. "I'm sorry. I was just worried. I'm sorry."

"It's OK," I whispered, as if speaking at a normal volume would somehow break us or cause the fragile, tense quiet in the inches between us to shatter. "It's OK," I said again, hyperaware of how close we were.

"Sorry . . ." she murmured, still holding my face, then leaned forward and pressed her lips to my forehead, as if checking for a fever. She lingered there and it was like I *did* have a fever, a fever confined to the space of her lips, where my forehead burned hot.

"I don't want you to be afraid of me." She pulled away, her voice soft.

"I'm not. No one will ever know. No one will ever find out," I swore.

She said nothing. She just nodded once, slowly, and that was it.

I wondered: Would it be cool to play Xbox now? But she still looked out of sorts, so I didn't want to move.

"Josh . . ." She hesitated, and then: "Look, we still need to talk about what you saw." She held up a hand when I started to protest. "I know that you're much more mature than most people your age, but I'm still the adult and I have a responsibility to make sure that you're not . . ." She gestured like she was trying to make a rabbit appear from a hat—only there was no hat. "Scarred—"

I laughed. "Scarred? From what?"

"Don't laugh! This is serious!" She nudged me with a foot. "I'm trying to find out how it made you feel."

The truth . . . God, the truth was tough! It made me horny in the way that Zik's near-endless supply of *Playboys* did. But it was different because Zik wasn't around. Because there was motion and sound. Because it was in Eve's apartment, with Eve sleeping down the hall, on her stomach on the bed, one leg cocked—

I shook my head. I couldn't tell her *that*.

"I was just surprised," I told her, and my voice . . . my voice *fucking cracked! Very* convincing. "I was surprised." And angry, I remembered. Angry that she watched it with George.

She regarded me for so long that I got nervous and drank some Coke just as an excuse to do something. I had to pee all of a sudden.

"Anything else?" she asked.

"Like what?"

"Anything. There are a whole range of reactions that would make sense."

"Like what?" I wasn't going to answer the question until I had some idea of where this was going.

"Well . . . Did it make you think of anything? Or anyone?"

God! "No." Lying through my teeth and anything else I could lie through.

"Josh . . ." She grinned at me, her dimple forming in her left cheek. She knew I was lying. Hell, the paintings on the wall knew and they weren't even alive.

"It made me think of you." I said it quickly, hoping that it would come out so fast that she wouldn't even realize it, like a split-fingered fastball that moves so quickly that you're struck out before you knew it was pitched.

"That's perfectly natural, Josh. You saw it in my house, after all." She didn't seem upset. "What did it make you think about me?"

I swallowed. No. I would not. I wouldn't say it.

She sipped wine and her eyes flicked to the TV. "They were touching and hugging, weren't they?"

If you want to call it that, sure. But I think the Happy Trio had other words for it.

"They were kissing . . ."

Yes, they were definitely doing that.

"Do you want to kiss me, Josh? Is that it?"

"I can't—I can't—you're my *teacher*." I wanted to kill myself right then and there. After all this talk of me being so grown up and so not a kid!

"I'm your friend, too. And friends tell each other things."

I stuttered for the first time in my life. I just couldn't get the words out. But finally, eventually, tortuously, I told her about the dreams. I didn't tell her about the ones I had when I was awake, or at least, I didn't tell her that that's what they were. I told her about them and lied and said they happened when I was asleep.

"Oh, Josh . . ." she said, only it was more like a groan, like she'd been hurt somehow. I could hear her breathing, *panting*, like she was running a race or carrying some heavy, awful weight. She leaned closer to me, and I could smell strawberries and the wine on her breath. "Josh, I'm so sorry. I'm so sorry . . ."

I was trying to figure out what she was sorry about when she kissed me. Not on the cheek this time. Not for just a second. Her lips against my lips. My head exploded. My heart stopped and started again in triple time. I flickered

—hand running up—

and rallied back just as I felt something warmer and softer and stronger than her lips pressing against my lips. Her tongue *oh wow shouldn't that be gross someone's tongue but it isn't it is glorious* pressing against my lips, prying them open, and then her tongue inside my mouth like in the movies—I realized, *This is how they kiss in the movies* and sparks flew in my brain, ricocheting in my consciousness and igniting me all over.

I probed at her tongue with my own. Yow! It was like sticking a fork in a socket. My mind melted. Everything I was or would be boiled down to the tip of my tongue.

Our tongues danced around each other. I tasted the wine on hers. Could she taste the Coke on mine? She traced the edges of my teeth, slid around the confines of my mouth as if seeking out every last trace of taste from me.

I couldn't stand it. I had to—

I pushed forward the tiniest bit and forced her tongue out of my mouth . . . following it back into her mouth with my own, our lips fused as if with glue.

I followed her lead, exploring the inside of her mouth, dueling with her tongue, rooting out the flavor of the white wine and the even sweeter taste of her own saliva. It should have been gross. I always imagined it would be gross. But it wasn't.

She leaned back a little, breaking contact. We were still so close that a movement from either of us would mean touching the other, but I froze. It was like an electrical field had come up between us and to disrupt it would mean . . . I don't know. I was afraid to find out. I was dying to find out.

I was woozy. So was she. She was still panting, having trouble catching her breath.

"Was . . . was . . . was . . ." She gulped air and laughed. "Was that what you wanted?" Her voice was low, not a whisper, just *low*. "Was that what you wanted, Josh?"

I fought for breath, swaying back and forth.

"Don't pass out on me, Josh," she said, her voice still low, like it was for me and no one else in the universe. "Was that what you wanted?" There was a desperation in her tone.

"Yes," I managed to gasp.

She sighed like someone who's been given an unexpected gift.

I don't know where it came from, but it popped into my

head and I said: "Let me guess: I can't tell my parents about that, either."

She collapsed against me. We held each other and laughed.

George was coming home early that day, so there was no time for further discussion. I wanted to stay, but Eve said that I had to go. We bundled up against the cold outside and she drove me home.

"Listen to me very carefully," she said on the way. "What we did was fine. We care about each other, and when people care about each other, they kiss. You know that, right?"

I was a little annoyed. I wasn't a baby. "Yes."

"But you know I could get in trouble for it, right? I mean, I could lose my job. I could go to jail." Her fingers strummed on the steering wheel.

"I know."

"So—and I know I've said this before—you can't tell anyone what we talked about or what we did. OK?"

"Uh-huh."

"Promise me, Josh. Promise me you'll never tell anyone."

I promised. Why would I tell anyone? If I told anyone, they would know what I had thought and seen. They would know I'd lusted after Eve, know that I'd spied on her while she slept, that I'd dreamed about her even while awake. I couldn't tell anyone.

"OK." We pulled into my driveway. The house was dark, the driveway bare. I started to open the door, but Eve stopped me with a hand on my shoulder. The dome light dimmed and we were in darkness.

She looked around for a second, then leaned toward me. I

met her halfway and she kissed me again, a shorter but no less electric version of what we'd shared in the apartment.

"To keep you warm tonight." She giggled. I don't know why—I felt like I'd be warm forever.

I hugged her and said good night and went inside.

I thought for sure that something about me would scream "I kissed Eve!" to everyone in a twenty-foot radius, but Mom and Dad seemed oblivious when they got home. (I had checked myself in the bathroom mirror a hundred times, it seemed, before Mom got home, making sure that there was no lipstick on me anywhere.)

Mom made dinner, which I barely tasted. I went to my room to do my homework, and close to my bedtime, the phone rang. My door was open, so I heard Mom pick it up out in the kitchen.

"Hello? Yes, this—Oh! Mrs. Sherman! How nice to hear from you!"

What? I crept out of my bedroom like a ninja. What the hell was going on?

"Really?" Mom said.

Oh, God! She was going to tell Mom! She was going to tell Mom what I said, about the dreams . . . I was *dead. Mrs. Mendel, your little perv of a son kissed me tonight* . . .

"Well, that's so nice of you to check," Mom went on. "No, I got home just a little bit after six today, so he was only here for forty-five minutes or so."

I tried to imagine a way to get Mom off the phone. Maybe I could scream and pretend I hurt myself? But that wouldn't work unless I *really* hurt myself.

"Oh, of course you can. Just a minute." Mom put her hand over the phone and turned right to me. I stepped back into the hallway quickly so that she wouldn't see me.

"JOSH!" she yelled. "Josh! Telephone!"

My heart hammered in the darkness. How could she not hear it?

"OK!" I shouted back, forgetting that I was only standing about five feet away.

Mom poked her head around the corner. "What are you doing there?"

Busted! God, I was an idiot! My heart kept pounding. How could Mom not see the word *GUILTY!* emblazoned across my forehead?

"I was ... coming ... to get a ... *glassofwater!*" It came out of me in a rush of triumph, like a sliding stolen base. Lie completed! The runner is safe!

"Well, here." She thrust the phone at me. "Your teacher wants to talk to you."

I had the presence of mind to enhance my lie by saying, "Which teacher?" as if I couldn't possibly imagine *which* teacher would be calling me.

"Mrs. Sherman," Mom said, with a little eye roll, as if I were a bumbling idiot child, and in that moment, I was.

I took the phone. "Hi, Josh," Eve said. "Is your mom standing there?"

Mom had wandered back into the kitchen to empty the dishwasher, but she was still pretty close by. "Yes."

"OK. I just wanted to say good night to you."

"Oh." I felt warm again.

"I can't wait to see you tomorrow."

My head swam.

"Now say 'OK, Mrs. Sherman.'"

"OK, Mrs. Sherman." I was a robot, operating each line of code as it came to me.

"Say 'Thanks.'"

"Thanks."

"Are you looking forward to seeing me tomorrow?"

I flickered to her lips, her tongue, then reached out to steady myself against the wall.

"Yes," I whispered.

"Good. I'm glad." She sounded like a kid on her birthday. "If she asks, tell your mother that I called to let you know that you left a book here, but that I'll bring it in to school for you."

"OK."

"I'll see you tomorrow."

"OK."

"Good night."

"Good night."

She hung up and I went into the kitchen to put the phone in its cradle. "What did she want?" Mom asked.

"She, uh, I left a book at her apartment." Wow! Eve thought of *everything*. "She's bringing it to school for me."

Mom *tsk*ed. "Well, you're lucky she's looking out for you, Josh."

No kidding.

It took me a long time to fall asleep that night.

10

FOR THE NEXT COUPLE OF DAYS, this is how it went: I would go home with Eve after school and we would spend an hour or so on the sofa, kissing. She taught me what she liked, training my lips and tongue, an education in when to thrust and be aggressive and when to tease, passive. Her hands roamed my upper body the whole time, tracing electric charges over my chest and stomach and back and shoulders. Everywhere she touched me felt supercharged. I put my arms around her, touching only her back, exulting in the glory of her body pressed tightly to mine.

After that hour, Eve would excuse herself to the bedroom while I sprawled on the sofa and played Xbox. It took a while, but eventually my erection would subside. My Xbox play suffered; I really sucked after a make-out session with Eve. I couldn't concentrate. I flickered like the images on the screen.

If George was working late, we would cook dinner together, like we were married or something, and have another brief make-out session on the sofa while dinner cooked, stopping with the buzz of the oven timer. Sometimes she unbuttoned my shirt or (if it was a pullover) pulled it out of my waistband and skipped her nails lightly across my chest, a sensation I can only describe as ... indescribable. (I tried running my own fingernails along my chest at home, but it didn't feel remotely the same.) Then we would eat, clean up, and get into the car to take me home for the evening. We would stop up the road from my house out of range of the streetlights and nosy neighbors, for one last brief kiss. Then Eve would check me over for lipstick and general disarray and drop me off at my house.

I was getting home later now, but my parents didn't seem to mind. I lied to them and told them that I was doing my homework at Eve's, so they saw nothing amiss. Instead, I would set my alarm for early in the morning and do my homework then.

School was tough. I thought of Eve constantly, flickered regularly. It made it difficult to pay attention in class, and almost impossible in history, where Eve dressed down and acted like I was just another student. School had always been easy for me, almost intuitively so, and I was able to get by and keep the Streak going, but only barely.

Eve hated that there was no way for her to talk to me at home without raising my parents' suspicions. They had Caller ID and also monitored my e-mail.

Right before Christmas break, things changed again.

It was a Friday afternoon, and Eve seemed particularly aggressive, moaning deep in her throat as we kissed and clawing at my back through my shirt. The lights were off, the room lit by candles placed on the coffee table. As Eve pulled back from me, her face was a gorgeous painting, sections drenched in black, others lit in a flickery orange. She was gasping, and so was I. Her hand lingered on my belly, stroking gently back and forth.

I waited for her to get up and go into the bedroom, like she usually did. Instead, she leaned in and nibbled on my ear (another thing I never would have imagined could feel good . . . but did) and whispered, "You poor thing."

I liked the way her voice went husky and breathy when we were alone. "What do you mean?"

"I think I've been torturing you. I'm so sorry. I didn't mean to."

"What?" My head was spinning as her tongue found its way into the shell of my ear, flicking lightly, sending sparks down into my brain.

"It's so selfish of me," she whispered, and her hand moved farther south. When she touched my belt, I hitched up a breath and jerked involuntarily. "Shh! Shh!" she said. "It's OK."

"I'm sorr—" I started to say, but then her hand went lower, touching me through my jeans. Oh, God! She knew! She knew I had an erection! I wanted to melt away from embarrassment then and there.

"Don't be sorry. What are you sorry for?" It had to be a rhetorical question, because she shoved her tongue into my mouth just then and I was helpless as she found my zipper and pulled it down.

If I'd thought that the feel of her tongue on my ear or her nails on my naked chest were phenomenal, then I had absolutely no idea what to expect and no way to be prepared when her hand slipped into my fly. There was nothing tentative about it—her fingers didn't brush against me gently, they sought me out and *grabbed*. I groaned into Eve's mouth, was greeted with a groan in return.

It only took a few seconds for her to navigate the fly of my boxers and then her fingers were on me directly. I saw explosions of light against my eyelids as my eyes squeezed tightly shut. Before I knew it, she had me out in the open and broke our kiss.

I looked at her as she looked down into my lap. "Well," she said. "Well."

And started to do to me what I had been doing to myself two, sometimes three, times a day. Only it was so much better.

"Can you . . ." She stopped. Stopped *talking*, that is.

"What?" I was shocked I could even speak.

"Never mind," she whispered. "I want to be surprised."

I didn't understand, but seconds later I didn't even understand how to breathe as a kaleidoscope of stars exploded behind my eyes, leaving fire trails like bottle rockets.

Eve giggled a little and murmured something that sounded like, "That answers *that*." She kissed me on the cheek and went to the bathroom to wash her hands. I slumped on the sofa in something like shock until I heard her open the bathroom door and close the bedroom door. Then I went to clean myself up and straighten my clothes.

When I emerged, Eve was still in the bedroom, so I turned on the Xbox. Even though my play wasn't as good, I made up for it in sheer hours—I was kicking ass in the game because I was playing it so much, and I had promised George that I would get to the end before Christmas break and show it to him.

Eve came out of the bedroom a little while later. She looked at the TV and at me with the controller in my hand, sighed, and said, "Men," then kissed the top of my head in a way that was creepily like Mom. I pushed it out of my mind.

I heard her rummaging around in the kitchen. "Do you want me to help?" I shouted.

"No, that's OK, honey. Keep playing your game."

Usually only Mom called me "honey," and I hated it. But I liked it when Eve said it because she didn't *have* to say it.

I played Xbox until George got home. Eve came out of the kitchen to greet him with, I noticed, a dry, brief peck on the cheek. Did she ever kiss him like she kissed me? I thought about it—I had never seen my parents kiss like that, either. Maybe...

Maybe what? I couldn't wrap my brain around it. I knew married people had sex because I'd heard my parents. But they didn't seem to kiss a lot. And Eve and George weren't kissing. Maybe they didn't have sex, either?

George took off his coat and kicked off his shoes, then joined me in front of the Xbox. "How's it going, bud?"

"Fine. I got into the pyramid." I didn't let my eyes waver from the screen.

"Excellent!"

My manners kicked in. "I can stop, if you want to play."

He shook his head. "Nah. I've been playing games all day. My thumbs are killing me. I'll just watch."

The three of us ate dinner together at the little table in the corner where the kitchen met the living room. George talked about the games he'd tested, some of which sounded really cool, although I discovered that he also had to test games for little kids, which sounded boring.

On the way home, Eve drove with one hand; we held hands over the armrest.

"Did you like tonight, Josh? Please tell me." She pouted.

"Yes." Deep down, though, I felt bad. Bad that I'd made her do it. Guilty that she'd felt compelled. Guilty for making a mess, of all things.

"Good. Look, this went farther than kissing, you know. I wouldn't just lose my job if this got out. I would go to jail. You don't want me to go to jail, do you?"

"No way!" I was getting tired of her constantly reminding me not to tell anyone, though. Of course I wouldn't tell anyone. I wouldn't do that.

"I'm going to miss you this weekend, honey."

"Me, too."

She sighed heavily. "Maybe I could buy you a cell phone or something?"

"My parents would wonder about that. I'd have to hide it."

"I figured that," she said, exasperated. "You'd have to leave it off at home, but you could go outside and call me, right?"

"I don't know. During the day, maybe. But it's getting—" I didn't want to continue. As the weather got darker and colder, my parents wouldn't let me go out as much at night. But I didn't want to advertise that I was a freakin' baby. "Maybe," I said.

"I'll think about it," she said, chewing her lip.

We had our usual make-out session in our usual secluded spot and then she dropped me off.

Mom and Dad were arguing when I got home, so I just slipped into my bedroom. They were fighting about money, which bored me, so I tuned them out. It was a good hour or so until Dad poked his head into my room and asked, "How long have you been home?"

"A little while. Mrs. Sherman brought me home."

Dad frowned. "You should have told us you were home. It's late. You should eat something."

"I ate already."

"OK."

I heard the front door close. "Where's Mom going?"

Dad's eyes narrowed. He didn't answer. I thought maybe he didn't hear me. "Dad, where—"

"Shopping," he said, and left.

As always, Zik was my font of knowledge for all things sexual. He eavesdropped on his brother and father all the time, got to watch Kevin Smith movies on cable at home, and had that nigh-endless supply of fresh nudie magazines to consult. I bugged my parents until they drove me over to Zik's to spend the day. I told them we were going to play baseball with some other guys, despite the cold.

Zik and I spent the day out of the house, wandering his neighborhood. Anything to stay away from his parents. It was freezing outside, with a bitter wind, but we just jammed our hands into our pockets and roamed up and down the streets.

I didn't specifically tell him anything about Eve and me, just sort of made some calculated, seemingly random musings, and learned that I had been the recipient of my first "hand job," which sounded exactly like what it had been.

At dinner that night, Mom said, "You're awful quiet, Josh."

I shrugged. Only on the weekends did we all sit down as a family for dinner; we did it so rarely that it felt awkward and wrong somehow. I wasn't the only one being "awful quiet." Mom and Dad barely said a word through the whole meal.

"Is everything OK?" she asked. Dad was just watching the whole exchange like a prison guard or a scientist. I shrugged again. I figured that if I just gave her nothing, she'd get bored and give up.

Instead, she flicked her eyes to Dad, who nodded. Mom took a deep breath. "Josh, honey?"

"Don't call me 'honey,'" I said in the lowest growl my adolescent voice had ever mustered. I don't know where it came from, some deep, secret place low down in my heart or gut. But when I heard "honey" now, I thought of Eve and her lips and everything else, and the thought of that and my mother's voice and—

I just couldn't handle it.

Mom was taken aback. It was as if she'd gone to pet a cat and been snapped at by a wolverine. "OK," she said after a moment. "Josh, do you . . ."

And I knew, in that moment, what had happened. Someone had seen me kissing Eve in her car and told Mom. I was about to get into more trouble than any human being had ever conceived of.

"Josh," she said, starting again, "do you want me to quit my job?"

Huh?

"So that I can be here when you get home from school? So that you can come right home and not have to spend so much time with your teacher?" She was unsure, tentative, and I wasn't used to hearing my mother like that; it definitely got my attention.

But . . . give up Eve? Unlimited Xbox? Give up being treated like an adult and not a child? Was she *nuts*?

"No, Mom. Everything's fine."

"You've been quiet lately." Dad jumped in. "Spending a lot of time alone in your room. More than usual."

"Yeah, but—"

"I want you to think about what your mother said very carefully," Dad said. "Very carefully."

"I know, Dad. But I'm fine. I just . . . I just have a lot more homework this year, that's all."

I don't know where the lie came from—my homework was no more burdensome or difficult than it had been the previous year, and spending time with Eve instead of doing my homework in the afternoons hadn't made much of a difference. I was used to cramming in my homework after baseball practice two seasons a year anyway.

But the lie worked. Mom's maternal instincts came online. "Are they giving you too much work? Should you cut back on one of your academic classes?"

"He's not cutting back on a class," Dad told her. "That's stupid. He can't just change his schedule. This isn't college."

"If my son is having trouble, we'll talk to the principal and—"

"They aren't going to—"

"Guys!" I said. They stopped bickering. "It's no big deal. Really. It's just tougher, that's all. I saw my progress reports the other day and I'm still getting straight A's. I just have to work harder for them, that's all."

We finished dinner in a chilly silence, Mom and Dad barely looking at each other.

▫ ▫ ▫ ▫

It was a long weekend and, for some reason, the phone rang a lot. Caller ID said "Caller Blocked," so no one picked it up, but Mom became increasingly annoyed at the constant ringing. Finally, late on Sunday afternoon, I picked up the extension in the basement just to find out who was bothering us.

"Hi, Josh," Eve said.

I checked my surroundings; no one was around and the basement door was shut. I would hear the creak of the steps if my parents came down and have time to hang up.

"Have you been calling all weekend?" I asked.

"I blocked my cell phone number," she said, "and figured I'd just hang up if your parents answered."

"You've been driving my mom nuts." I meant it as a scolding, but halfway through I started giggling. Eve laughed, too.

"Oh, well," she said.

"Why did you call?"

"I just missed you. I wanted to hear your voice."

That didn't make any sense to me. She just wanted to hear my voice? Now what was I supposed to do? What if I didn't have anything to say? Was I supposed to just say random words so that she could hear me?

"Do you miss me?" she asked.

"Sure."

"That's nice. I like to hear that."

"I miss you," I told her.

"You can be very literal-minded, Josh."

"I was making a joke."

"Look, you have my cell number, right?"

"Yep." I had written it down for my mom, and once I write down a number, it pretty much sticks in my head forever. I used to think everyone was like that, which made things weird because I would get frustrated at people, thinking they were lying to me or being stupid by pretending they couldn't remember the number of strikes in the previous night's game or the page number of a homework assignment or the answer to the third question on last week's math test. Eventually, though, I learned that not everyone had my memory, poor suckers.

"Well, call me whenever you want, OK? Unless George is around, I'll pick up. Leave me a voicemail if I don't."

"OK."

"I'll see you tomorrow."

"OK."

She paused, like she was either waiting for me to say something or for herself to say something that she hadn't settled on yet. And then: "Sweet dreams, Josh."

I shivered.

It was the week before Christmas break. I went to Eve's every day after school, as usual, and for the first few days, we had our usual make-out session, now bolstered by the mind-blowing hand jobs that I replayed each night at home.

Over the weekend, Eve and George had decorated for Christmas, and the apartment was adorned with holly and wreaths. The living room had sprouted a Christmas tree, and Eve turned off the lamps so that only the glow of the tree's lights lit the room.

"It's going to be a whole week," Eve said Wednesday night, pouting at the calendar as I zipped up. "Actually, *more* than a week."

The next day, on her sofa, she did something different. She

fished me out of my fly and then, to my astonishment and complete disbelief, leaned down and took me into her mouth. I thought my eyes would melt out of their sockets.

When she was finished (and *I* was finished), I lay half on and half off the sofa, my body limp and weak, my ears ringing. Eve disappeared into the bedroom for a while, and when she came out, I was still lying there, my pants open, in shock, flickering in and out of the present as I relived moments that had just passed. She slipped next to me on the sofa and slid her arms around me, holding me, her lips pressed to my hair.

"I guess you liked that," she murmured.

"You could—you could say that."

"Good. I wanted to make sure you wouldn't forget about me over break."

"Not after *that!*"

She laughed and brought us drinks, letting me have some of her wine. "To relax you a bit," she said. And I *was* breathing pretty hard, both from what she'd done and from the flickers, which kept catapulting me back to those delicious moments.

I hadn't figured out the flickers and I hadn't told anyone about them, either. I thought they were temporary. Or maybe they were a part of growing up, something that happened when you became . . . active. In that case, mentioning it to my parents would be a clear sign of what I'd been up to. And mentioning it to Eve would make me look like a clueless little kid, not her mature young man.

"Do you know what we're doing, Josh?"

I wasn't sure of the name for it, exactly. I knew about making out and stuff like that, but it seemed like we weren't in that ballpark anymore. We weren't quite in the majors, but we sure weren't in Little League, either.

"Look," she said, "we're making each other feel good. Like when you play with your friends. When you play baseball, you feel good, right?"

"Yeah."

"This is like that." It wasn't *anything* like that, but I got her point. "But it's just for us, OK? This is for grownups, and you're so grown up that it's OK, but not for anyone else, do you understand?"

I understood.

At recess the next day, I once again employed some seemingly random discussion to tease out of Zik what had happened to me the previous afternoon. So now I had a name to go with the feeling and the act.

That afternoon, the last time we'd be together before Christmas break, lit by the usual candles, I received my second one, which was even better than the first because I was prepared to enjoy it. Eve once again withdrew into the bedroom while I lay about in a stupor of flickering recollection and pleasure aftershocks.

She wasn't in the bedroom as long as usual, but when she came out, she wasn't wearing her outfit from school. She was wearing a robe, but it wasn't a thick, heavy, shapeless thing like my mom wore. It was red and black, light and filmy, shiny, and it clung to her like it couldn't bear not to touch her. In that moment, I empathized.

In the soft light of the Christmas tree, she looked completely smooth and flawless, as if the robe were a part of her body and she was actually standing before me naked. My eyes couldn't decide where to look, so they tried to go everywhere at once. She struck a pose, cocking one hip, her arms out, hands palm up like a model. "You like?"

I could only nod.

"I can tell," she said, nodding toward my exposed lap. Her eyes glinted with mischief and something else.

She sat down next to me. I hadn't even had time to zip up my pants. She put her arms around me and we went hurtling into an unprecedented second make-out session. My mind spun and bounced and ricocheted against invisible walls of pleasure. The robe was slippery and smooth under my hands. Touching her back, I realized that I couldn't feel a bra strap.

She pulled back after a moment and dropped one shoulder, causing the robe to slip down. I stared at her shoulder, smooth and naked in the candlelight. I flickered

—lotion on Mom's leg—

and forced myself back to the present. On the side where she had bared her shoulder, her robe was still slipping down, until she was exposed on that side from her throat to midbelly, a perfect triangle of naked flesh that included one breast. I stared. I'd seen Zik's magazines, of course, and I'd seen the Happy Trio and I'd seen R-rated movies at Zik's house, but I'd never in my life been within arm's reach like this.

For some reason, I thought of the Playmate and the numbers that Zik told me meant so much. What was Eve's number?

"And this?" she asked in a husky voice. "Do you like this?"

There was only one answer, but I had no voice with which to give it. "Come here," she said, putting her arms around me again, her hands at my neck, pulling me toward her, pulling my head down, pulling my mouth to her.

She shuddered and caught her breath. I thought I'd done something wrong and tried to pull away, but she held me tight and I continued, going on instinct. I smelled something.

"Strawberries . . ." I mumbled.

"My body wash," she whispered, and pulled me closer, shuddering again as I worked my mouth and tongue, shuddering, gasping, groaning quietly, almost whimpering. Then one hand left my head and migrated to my lap, where I was ready.

"You'll remember me, won't you?" she whispered, her voice desperate and ragged. "You'll remember me over break, right?"

I couldn't speak. I couldn't even think. My mouth was full, my brain was full. I moaned and she moaned and that was good.

CHRISTMAS BREAK WAS TOUGHER than I thought it would be.

The first weekend was fine—it was like any other weekend. But as Monday morning crawled toward Monday afternoon, it hit me that I wouldn't be seeing Eve today or *any* day until after New Year's.

I would have called Eve, but Mom was home all day and would be home all week, LEC being closed for winter break.

I suppose I should have been happy; there were presents under the tree and I knew that cards stuffed with checks, cash, and gift certificates would be arriving from relatives all week. But instead, I felt sick to my stomach. It was as if I'd drunk something that had turned solid and expanded once it hit my stomach. Something that moved. Something that wanted out.

For Christmas Eve, my mom always makes my favorite: baked ham, green beans, corn bread, and cranberries. But I sat at the table, toyed with my food, and then begged off, claiming my stomach hurt.

And it did.

I lay awake for a long, long time. Long enough to have heard Santa Claus, if he existed. I eventually fell asleep wondering what Eve had done on Christmas Eve.

□ □ □ □

The day after Christmas, Rachel showed up at my door with Michelle in tow. She wanted to play catch. Michelle just wanted to know if Zik was visiting me. I got Mom to drive the three of us to his house.

We walked up to a construction site near Zik's house, where new houses were being built. One lot had been cleared down to the dirt, so Rachel and I set up and started hurling fastballs at each other. Zik and Michelle disappeared into the half-complete shell of a nearby house.

"What d'ya think they're doing?" Rachel asked, in a tone that told me she knew *exactly* what they were doing.

I knew, too. Zik didn't know how to keep his mouth shut around me. When he'd told me he'd gotten to first base with Michelle over the summer, I'd been sort of jealous. Now, though . . . Now I felt the way parents must feel when their kids walk for the first time. Yeah, it's an accomplishment, but, really—big deal, right?

"Playing smoochie-face," I said sarcastically.

"That's just a single," she said. "They're on second base. Didn't you know?"

"On second? Really?" I didn't know that, in fact. I hadn't been hanging out with Zik as much because I was spending so much time with Eve. But Rachel couldn't know that.

"But I guess you're not up on all the latest, are you?" she said, skewering my theory as I even formed it.

"What do you mean?" I asked cautiously. Had she seen something? Heard something?

"Zik says you've been spending all your time with Mrs. Sherman. What's up with *that*?"

"I'm just helping her with a grad school project." I tried to sound as casual as I could. We hadn't worked on that project in weeks.

Rachel laughed. "Yeah, right. Even *you're* not that smart, Josh."

"I'm like her test subject or something. She does tests and interviews me. It's boring," I threw in for good measure.

"Then why do you do it?"

The ball sailed past me. I didn't even reach for it. The time it took me to chase it down let me think of an answer that would shut her up. *What, you mean besides the sips of wine, the Xbox, and the fringe benefits?*

Which made me think: What base was I on with Eve, anyway? Was Zik *really* on second with Michelle? The base-running schematic was pretty simple:

First Base = Kissing

Second Base = Touching above the waist

Third Base = Touching below the waist

Home Run = All the way

We all knew what "all the way" meant, thanks to health class. But what base was there for Eve and me? We were past third, obviously, but hadn't hit a home run. You can't just stand there between third and the plate! You have to be stealing the base or running toward home.

Is that what we were doing? Were we headed toward home? Was Eve going to have sex with me?

No, that was impossible.

"Hey! Have you found it yet?" Rachel shouted from behind me.

I scrambled for the ball, which was lying among some scraggly weeds and broken bottles left behind by the construction crews. I hurled it back to her and changed the topic.

"What did you get for Christmas?"

"New glove. A dress. Some girly stuff. Stop avoiding the subject: What's the deal with Mrs. Sherman?"

Tough to pull the wool over Rachel's eyes! "I'm just helping her out, OK?"

Rachel held the ball, chewing over that. "Do you think she's pretty?"

I flickered. Rachel threw the ball midflicker, so when I blinked my eyes the ball was suddenly halfway to me. My heart raced as I lunged, snagging the ball.

"Good catch! Come on, Josh, answer me: Is she pretty?"

It was an impossible question. Anyone with eyes could tell that Eve was pretty, beautiful, gorgeous. If I said no, Rachel would know I was lying and be pissed at me. If I said yes, though, would she be jealous?

I threw the ball back. I settled on "She's OK."

Rachel caught the ball. "Is it because she has, you know . . . ?" And she looked down at her own chest.

There was just no comparing Eve to Rachel. Not without hurting Rachel's feelings.

"I bet she can't pitch worth a damn!" I shouted back.

Rachel studied her chest for another moment. When she looked up, her face was split with a wide grin and she went into her wind-up.

Days were OK—during the day, I was usually busy. Either Michelle and Rachel would come over (sometimes with Zik, sometimes to wheedle a ride to Zik's with Mom) or Mom would have me busy helping her with chores around the house. With Mom working, our normally neat and tidy house had become something of a wreck, cluttered with outdated mail and piles of laundry that had never been folded and put away after coming out of the dryer.

But I didn't mind. It kept me busy. But each day, around 3:45, I'd feel this ache, as if something had gone wrong or missing. It didn't matter where I was or what I was doing; I would get that feeling, look up at the clock, and there it was—3:45. Unfailingly. Every time.

I wondered if Eve missed me.

So one morning while Mom was in the shower, I grabbed the cordless phone and headed into my bedroom. I left the door open a crack and sat near it so that I could hear the shower when it stopped.

"Hello?" Eve sounded out of breath when she answered her cell phone.

"Hi . . ." I said. I realized I had nothing to say.

"Josh? Is that you, Josh?"

"Yes."

"You have to speak up, honey. I can't hear you."

The water was still going in the shower, so I raised my voice. "I wanted to say Merry Christmas."

"Merry Christmas to you, too. I miss you, Josh."

I closed my eyes and pictured the tree-lit living room in the apartment. The Xbox. A glass of half-drunk wine on the coffee table, its brim marred by a smudge of lipstick.

"Do you miss me?" she went on.

"Yes."

"I miss you a lot, Josh. I miss the fun we had together. Do you remember?"

"Yes." Water still running.

"I really want to see you. Is your mom still home from work?"

"Yeah. She doesn't go back until I go back to school."

"Damn! How are we going to get you over here, Josh?"

"I don't know."

"Can you ask your mom to take you to the mall? I could pick you up there."

I wasn't sure about that. Mom might drop me off at the mall, but . . . It seemed wrong. I didn't mind lying to Mom and Dad about what I was doing with my afternoons—at least they knew where I was and who I was with, right? But this would be a *big* lie. "I don't know," I told her. "I don't think I can lie to them about *that*."

Her voice picked up speed and urgency, sort of like a base runner pouring it on even though he sees that the baseman has the ball already. "But, Josh, you would just be with me. And you already know that they don't mind you being with me."

"I know, but—"

Just then, the water cut off in the bathroom.

"I have to go."

"Josh! Wait! Not yet! Look, let's arrange some—"

"I really have to go." I couldn't let Mom catch me on the phone and ask who I was talking to.

"Josh, promise me that you'll think about it, OK? I know you want to see me."

"I have to go!" I could hear the shower door opening. Mom would be toweling off.

"Promise me, Josh. Honey? Promise me."

"I—"

"Josh. Please. For me."

"OK. I promise." The tension started to bleed away.

Her voice went smooth. "Oh, thank you, Josh. Thank you," she said, as if I'd just saved her life. "Call me back tomorrow morning, OK?"

"I have to go. I really do!" I heard the bathroom door open. I risked peeking out my door, down the hall. Mom came out of the bathroom in her robe.

"Call me tomorrow, Josh. I'll be waiting for your call."

Mom went into her bedroom and closed the door behind her.

"OK," I whispered, panicking now that Mom would go straight for the phone in her bedroom. "I have to go."

I crept down the hall and made it past Mom's door safely, then replaced the phone on its cradle.

To my surprise, that night when I broached the topic of spending a few hours at the mall, Mom readily agreed. She thought I was going to meet Zik and Rachel and Michelle there, watch a movie, and spend the day goofing off. She thought this because it's what I told her.

I had thought she would have me slaving away in the basement, but she said she would be happy to drop me off in the morning when the mall opened, as long as I got up early enough to help her clean the downstairs bathroom.

I couldn't call Eve that night, and in the morning Mom woke me up and was with me every minute from then until we left, except for the ten minutes I took grabbing a quick shower. She dropped me off at the mall a little bit after ten and the place was already packed.

"Either your father or I will pick you up at three right here," she said.

"OK."

"Right here. Three o'clock."

"I heard you, Mom."

As soon as Mom was out of sight, I dashed for the pay phones. But as I punched Eve's cell phone number in, I realized something: The mall was right near her apartment! I never realized it before because you have to take all these windy roads and crazy turns, but the mall is only a couple of minutes from Eve's apartment if you just walk over a hill. No wonder she wanted me to come here—it was closer to her apartment than school, even.

She picked up. "Hello?"

"It's me," I said. "I'm on my way."

"What do you mean?"

"I'm at the mall, but I just realized I can walk over the hill and be there in five minutes."

"Be careful."

"I will."

I hung up and checked quickly to make sure that no one I knew was around, watching. Then I ducked out of the mall.

Up six steps. Half-turn. Six more.

I knocked at Eve's door. She opened the door in her slinky robe, her hair falling around her face and down to her shoulders.

She pulled me into the apartment and slammed the door, pressing herself against me, slippery and soft in the robe. She nibbled at my ear, breathing into it, gasping out her words: "Oh, baby, I missed you. I missed you so much. I need you so bad."

"Me, too."

She dropped to her knees and unbuckled my belt, then skinned down my pants and underpants. I was ready for her already, and she dived down, darting her head like a starving bird. I hissed out my breath and clenched my fists and leaned my head back against the door.

She stopped. "Watch me," she groaned. "Watch." And she took my hands and put them on her head. I gripped her hair and looked down. She looked up at me, our eyes locked as she descended again.

Later, we lay intertwined on the sofa while I played video games. She dozed, her robe open from throat to waist, her chest warm against my naked thigh.

LUCKY 13

CHRISTMAS BREAK WAS THE TURNING POINT for me. That was when I realized that I needed to be with Eve, as if she'd injected me with something and only she had the antidote. Away from her, I felt sick and miserable. With her, I felt pleasure; the pleasure brought its own sort of guilt, but I could live with it. It was certainly better than the illness I felt away from her, and the horrible wracking guilt of knowing that she wanted to be with me and I was preventing that. So I just gave in.

I called her every morning while Mom was in the shower and we whispered to each other the way I imagine Zik and Michelle whispered. I couldn't get Mom to take me to the mall every day, but two more times I went over to Eve's—she picked me up in her car when I told Mom I was going outside to play. It was frigid by now, even with the sun out, but Mom thought I was going over to Michelle's to see Rachel and Zik, so she said nothing. Looking back, I'm lucky that she never called Michelle's house on those two occasions.

When school started again, things became easier and more difficult at the same time. I could once again spend every afternoon with Eve, but I was having trouble focusing in school, especially in history. I told Eve at one point how much I liked her toenails and she asked which polish was my favorite. I told her about the time I'd noticed her electric blue polish and she laughed.

The next day, even though it was the end of January, she wore open-toed sandals in school, her nails a brilliant blue. I didn't hear a word she said in class—my notebook was completely blank. That afternoon, after our usual session (she called it "petting," and she was letting me touch her freely now—a stand-up triple, easy), she snuggled up to me on the sofa and let me copy her notes into my notebook so that I wouldn't fall behind.

Sometimes she would take me places. Never in Brookdale, of course. We'd make out in her apartment and then drive out to Canterstown or down to Finn's Crossing, where she'd treat me to dinner or hot chocolate or a movie. For those excursions, she would always call Mom from her cell phone and pretend that we were staying late at school to change the bulletin boards in the classroom or set up something for a lesson. "He's just a terrific little helper," she would say in complete innocence, usually while we were half-naked together on the sofa or floor.

The more time Eve and I spent together, the guiltier I started to feel, though I knew that the alternative—not seeing her at all—would be even worse. Eve was my friend. She had talked about how our "playing" together made us both feel good, but I knew that I was getting more out of this than she was. I was getting mind-shattering bliss and pleasure every time we were together, sometimes twice. She wasn't getting anything like that.

"Why don't you let me make you feel good, too?"

"Do you want to, Josh?"

"It just doesn't seem fair. You do all of these things for me and I don't—"

"But do you *want* to, Josh?"

I got frustrated. Why didn't she understand? I wasn't talking about what I wanted to do or didn't want to do. I was talking about what was *fair*. About me always getting and never giving anything back. Feeling *guilty* for that.

But sometimes she was like this—she wanted to hear what she wanted to hear and that was that.

"Yes. I want to."

That afternoon and for the rest of the week, she taught me her body. She was a very good teacher, and I suppose I was a good student.

There was only one other lesson to learn, I guess.

A week or so later, she asked me if I wanted to see the Happy Trio again. (She didn't call them the Happy Trio. That's just how I thought of them.)

I was curious, I have to admit, so I told her yes. She went into the bedroom and got the DVD. We watched it from the beginning, when it was just a Happy Duo, not a Happy Trio. It was amazing to see it with the perspective of the last few weeks. I *knew* that. And that. And that, too.

Except for when they pressed together, as close as Eve and I had pressed, but without clothing. I stared.

"Are you OK?" Eve was lying on the sofa, her head on my lap. I absently stroked her lustrous black hair while watching.

"I'm fine," I said, unable to turn away from the TV. I knew the sounds of lovemaking from listening to my parents through the vents. But I'd never had the visuals to go with it.

"I want to do that," I whispered.

Eve sat upright. "Are you sure?"

I kept staring at the screen. Eve paused the DVD and made me look at her. "Are you sure that's what you want?"

I swallowed. Was she saying that we could . . . She was *married* . . .

"Yes," I whispered. I realized I was shaking. I had something else to say, something I could barely bring myself to say. I wanted to tell her that I wanted to do it with *her,* but I knew that was too far, too much. She was *married.* Married people have sex with each other. I knew that much.

"Yes," I said again. "But I don't know how."

There were tears in her eyes. She held me tight to her and kissed me deep and long. "That's OK." Her tongue flicked at my ear. "I'll teach you."

And she did. From then on, we moved our sessions from the sofa to the bedroom. My Xbox time dropped almost to nil.

I learned every curve, nook, and niche of her body, every inch of smooth skin, every bump and turn. I learned what to touch, when to touch it, how to touch it, and for how long. I learned; I watched.

I never, ever stopped thrilling to the sight each time I saw her naked. Every time, it was new. Never boring. Never old.

She taught me how to make love and she taught me how to fuck and she taught me the difference. We ended up doing more of the latter than the former.

One time, in the panting aftermath of our afternoon session, she lay on the bed in unconscious imitation of that Playmate from Zik's *Playboy* an eternity ago.

"What are your numbers?" I asked her.

She looked at me sleepily over her shoulder. "My what?"

"Your numbers." I gestured at her chest, her waist.

"Oh." She laughed. "Why do you care all of a sudden?"

"Numbers are important."

"Come on, Josh."

"Numbers are important."

She relented at the seriousness in my expression. She took my hand and made me touch breast, waist, hip, as she recited "Thirty-four, twenty-six, thirty-five."

"Are those good numbers?"

Her eyebrows shot up. "Well, *I* like to think so! What do *you* think?" And she sprawled out on the bed, unashamed, completely open to me.

"I like them," I conceded. "But what do they mean?"

She explained the measurements to me, the way bra and cup sizes worked, the way women's clothes were measured differently then men's. Satisfied at last, I drifted off to sleep in her arms, catching an hour nap before the alarm woke us up in time to change the sheets, make the bed, and get dressed before George got home.

"Are you OK, Josh?" she asked me as we put fresh sheets on the bed. I was being quieter than usual, I guess.

"Yeah."

"Are you all right with what we're doing?" Her eyes and her voice were filled with concern.

"Yes. I'm fine with it."

"Because if you want to stop—"

"No. I don't want to stop."

I couldn't tell her the truth: that I felt terrible for what I was doing. Guilty for making her do what I wanted. Guilty for making her do it my way. Guilty for making her cheat on her husband. Every time I saw George, every time his eyes lit up at the sight of me and he slapped me on the back and said, "How's it going, champ?" I felt like a part of me had died.

I hated myself for being too weak to stop it.

"You know, Josh, what we're doing is fine when two people love each other. Do you love me, Josh?"

And of course I had no choice. Not in terms of what to say—no choice but to love her. How could I do anything but? It was impossible.

"Yes. I do."

She came to me and hugged me, our bodies still slightly sticky with sweat. She was a few inches taller than I, and my head nestled—perfectly, as if designed that way, she always said—in the hollow of her throat, just above her breasts.

She kissed the top of my head, just like Mom. "And I love you, Josh. I really do. I wish . . ." Her body hitched, and I realized she was crying. "I wish things were different. I wish people would understand . . ."

I held her tightly as she cried.

The weather warmed—a little bit—and the days lengthened by some small but noticeable amount. One day over dinner, Mom suddenly said, "Poor Mrs. Sherman."

My heart hammered like I was facing Randy Johnson on the mound. I said absolutely nothing.

"I said," Mom said when no one rose to the bait, "'Poor Mrs. Sherman.'"

"We heard you," Dad said.

"Baseball practice starts in a couple of weeks. She's going to lose her little helper."

Baseball practice! How could I have forgotten about it?

Well, that was a silly question, actually. I knew *exactly* how I could have forgotten about it. I wasn't hanging out with Zik and Rachel all the time like I used to. We would have started our spring training countdown a few days ago and begun obsessing over the new season. But time was a strange, plastic thing when I was with Eve—it went slowly when it was just the two of us together, whether in the apartment or out somewhere in another town together. Then, when I came back home, it seemed like weeks had gone by in the interim, and I was late with homework or a project or something else.

Baseball practice. Man! It wasn't every day, but it was three times a week, plus Saturdays. Eve had been talking about trying to figure out a way to steal an entire Saturday together, but she hadn't come up with anything yet. Now there would be no way for that to happen.

"This project," Dad said, bringing me back to the moment. "This project of hers is taking a hell of a long time, isn't it?"

I opened my mouth to answer, terrified that I was going to throw up instead.

Mom rescued me. "The project's been over for *weeks*, Bill."

"Then why's he over there all the time?"

She rolled her eyes. "He's helping her with school stuff. Making bulletin boards, grading papers . . ."

"Grading *papers*?" Dad didn't believe it. Neither did I. Of course, I had the added benefit of knowing that it wasn't true.

"She teaches a sixth grade history class, too. He can grade

those. They're just true-false. She gives him an answer key." She laughed lightly. "For God's sake, Bill, stop worrying. I talk to the woman every week. Everything's fine."

Mom looked over at me. "Josh? Are you OK?"

I think I'd gone pale the minute Mom said that she talked to Eve every week. My mouth didn't work; my voice wouldn't come.

"Josh?"

I said the first thing that came to mind: "I have to pee."

Dad grunted. Mom gave me her most exasperated look. "Well, for—Go to the bathroom, then! What are you waiting for, an engraved invitation?"

I scrambled up from my chair. "Honestly," I heard Mom say as I left the kitchen, "if I hadn't seen the IQ scores myself, sometimes I would wonder . . ."

"He seems distracted . . ." Dad's voice faded as I closed the bathroom door behind me.

I looked in the mirror. My face screamed, "I've been lying to you and I've been kissing Eve and I've been having sex and I've been FUCKING." I don't know how they could have missed it. They must have been complete idiots.

"Of course I've been talking to your mother," Eve said the next day on the way to the apartment. "Did you think she was just clueless and didn't notice how much time you've been spending at my apartment?"

Well, yeah, I had, to tell the truth. Still, I was mad. How could Eve let me get caught off-guard like that? What if my mom . . . What if she . . .

I don't know what, actually. But if Mom was talking to Eve, *something* could have happened.

"I'm still trying to come up with a way for us to have a whole day together, honey. I have to be friends with your mom, don't you see? So that we can keep playing together." She stole glances at me as she talked; I sat there with my arms folded over my chest and stared out the windshield.

"Oh, honey, don't be angry." She put her hand on my leg and I shook it off.

"Talking to my mother . . . It's like I'm a baby or something."

"Honey, I know you're not a baby. You *know* I know that. Don't be angry. We only have two hours today—George is coming home at his usual time."

"I don't care."

"I'm going to make this up to you," she promised. "You'll see."

At the apartment, she told me to wait while she went into the bedroom. After a few minutes, she came and strutted down the hallway toward me on heels. She was wearing a kind of bra and stockings I'd never seen before, festooned with straps and bands of color, something complicated and almost not there at all.

"Now," she said, standing before me, towering over me on her heels, "I'll make it up to you." She took my hand and led me into the bedroom.

Later, we lay together on the bed, each trying to catch our breath.

"You know what I like about us, Josh?"

"What?" I gasped.

"Our names. We both have biblical names. Did you notice that?" She turned her head to me and kissed my heaving shoulder. "You're Joshua. Strong. My king. And me . . .

"I'm Eve. The first woman." She snuggled close to me. "*Your* first woman."

I forgave her.

As baseball season started, Eve became more and more obsessed with figuring out a way for us to have an entire day—and, she said sometimes, an entire night—together. I could have told my mom I was spending the night at Zik's house, but Mom didn't really like Mr. and Mrs. Lorenz (then again, Zik and I didn't like them, either), so she would have asked a lot of questions and probably called over there once or twice just to check up on me.

The first game of the season, I went 2 for 3 and fielded three outs at shortstop. I had an RBI when I went for a double on a long drive into center left. Dad was at the game, but Mom had to work late, so she missed it.

I was surprised when I saw Eve on the third-base line, sitting in a fold-out lawn chair behind a group of parents. When I was hit to third, she winked at me, then pretended she was watching the rest of the game.

After the game, she came up to me—right in front of Dad!—hugged me, and congratulated me on such a great game.

If Dad noticed the look of terror I was sure had pounced on my face, he didn't let on. He offered her his right hand; she shook it with her free one. "Bill Mendel," Dad said.

"Evelyn Sherman. We actually met at parent-teacher conferences last year," she reminded him. "But that was a while ago, and I'm not very memorable."

Who was she kidding? She was wearing a light yellow tank top that I'd never seen before and a little pleated skirt along with sandals that showed off—yes—electric blue toenails. Her black hair was tied back in a ponytail, sunglasses pushed up on her head. She was smiling broadly, her dimple out in full force.

"Of course," Dad said. "Of course. Josh speaks highly of you."

Huh? I never talked about Eve.

"Well, he's just a delight in class," she said. "And such a great helper, too!"

"I'm glad he's making productive use of his time."

I coughed. Productive use! How could he not tell? My God! Her standing there with her arm around me . . . ! It took every ounce of willpower in my body to resist leaning into her and pressing against her like I usually did. My knees were so locked in place that I thought I might faint. I couldn't figure out how no one could tell what was going on between us. But people just milled around as if nothing had happened, nothing would happen.

"You know, my nephew's on the rec center team," Eve said, "and their schedule mirrors the school's. So if you and Jenna are ever too busy, I can always bring Josh home for you."

"That's nice of you. Thanks."

It was like Eve had multiple personalities or something. She could talk to my dad as if she were really nothing more than my teacher, all the while angling to get me back to her apartment on a regular basis. I was impressed, despite my fear that simply standing next to her would reveal the truth to the world.

I also knew that she didn't have a nephew.

"Well, I've got to get going. It was good seeing you again." She shook Dad's hand again and disengaged from me. "Bye, Josh. See you in school tomorrow."

I couldn't speak. I finally grunted, "Bye."

"Sorry," Dad said. "He's been quiet lately. Is he like that in school?"

Eve looked right at me, her green eyes seeming to take me over, commandeer my soul. "No," she said, smiling cheerfully, innocently, her voice light and airy while her eyes plumbed my skull. "He's very different around me."

My thirteenth birthday was a Friday. Mom and Dad said I was too old for a big party with lots of people, so I invited Zik to spend the night instead. Of course, I went home with Eve first, and we celebrated in our own way. She gave me a card that said "I love you," but didn't sign it. I read it as we lay in bed together.

"I can't sign it if you take it home with you," she said. "If your parents see it, tell them that you found it in your locker and it must be from a secret admirer."

Eve was happy because she'd finally figured out how to get us more time together. In two weeks, my team had an away game on a Saturday afternoon. Eve was going to come to the game and, just before we got on the bus to come back home, tell the coach that she'd gotten a call from my parents on her cell phone—there was an emergency and no one would be able to pick me up at the school when the bus dropped me off. Eve would volunteer to take me home. She knew the coach (he was our phys ed teacher), so she knew she could pull it off. Meanwhile, she had already told my parents that she was going to be working at school on that Saturday, so she would be more than happy to bring me home for them.

In reality, of course, we would be heading straight for a hotel room she'd already booked. We would get back to Brookdale late that night—she planned to call Mom and Dad and tell them that her car broke down on the way back and we were waiting for a tow truck. She was positively giddy about her plan.

So my birthday came. "Lucky thirteen," Dad said. "Oh, Bill," Mom said. That night, while my parents and Zik slept, I crept out of my room and swiped the cordless from the kitchen. I took it out on the back porch, where you could still get a signal, and I called Eve. Her voice mail picked up. I don't know what made me do it, but I said, "Hi, it's Josh. I can't wait for two Saturdays from now." I had her card in my hand, and looking at it filled me with an empty want for her. "I love you," I said, and hung up.

And four days later, I went to Rachel's birthday party.

And she spun a bottle.

And we went into the closet.

And that was the beginning and the end of it all.

Strike
Two

CHAPTER 11

Back to Life

RACHEL PEERS AT ME in the gloomy morning dark. According to my watch, it's 3:14 and SAMMPark is a mass of shadows, a thousand different shades of gray all commingling in the murk, broken up by the light of the moon.

Zik's freshman season batting average was .314. He went 33 for 105, with 10 walks and 34 strikeouts. A woman with measurements 33-105-34 would look mighty strange.

"I didn't know any of that," Rachel says softly. We've been sitting on the grass midway between the diamond and the gate for hours, and my ass is numb. Hers must be too, because she stands and stretches, her legs wide apart. Touches her toes a couple of times. "I mean, once you mentioned it, I remembered that Christmas at the construction site. But I didn't know *any* of that."

"It was in the papers."

"Not the details. Not that stuff. It just said that she abused you and then she confessed, and—"

"And within a week, her whole confession was on a website because someone in the county courthouse thought they were doing the world a favor by leaking it. Don't tell me you never read the confession."

She stops midstretch, her body contorted, her face twisted to match. "Fine, then. I won't tell you."

And then she yawns.

"Sorry to bore you." It comes out snide and mean and shitty, and I wish I could say that it's a mistake, but it's not. In that moment, I want to hurt Rachel and I don't know why. Maybe because I told her things I swore I'd never tell anyone. Maybe because, in the end, it *is* her fault that it all came out, her and that stupid party and that stupid game.

"I don't deserve that," she says quietly, folding herself up into a ball on the ground, knees drawn to her chest, chin resting on knees, watching me sadly. "I'm tired, is all. I worked all night, then I came here, and I have to be up for work again in five hours."

"I'm sorry."

"Five hours," she goes on, as if I've said nothing, "and I'm not going anywhere."

"I'm sorry." I say it again, this time louder, and more contritely. I've apologized more in the past three hours than in my whole life, it seems.

"I'll tell you my part of it," she says, now looking up at the sky. The moon's gigantic, pregnant. "It was all my mother's fault."

"What?"

"I missed you. I liked you a lot. The way kids like each other and maybe a little bit more. I don't know. I was thirteen. I wasn't experiencing what you were experiencing. All I knew was that you suddenly weren't around anymore. Zik said you were helping Mrs. Sherman with a project, and I couldn't understand how that could occupy every last minute of your time.

"Michelle was getting tired of me moping around. She was on cloud nine with Zik and I think I was bringing her down. So now I'd lost this guy I liked a lot and on top of that my best friend was acting like she had better things to do."

She shrugs. "So. Enter: my mother." She says it like the reveal of a villain in a movie, and I can't help but chuckle. Rachel shakes her head. "Yeah, yeah . . . She saw I was depressed. Like an idiot, I told her what was bothering me. God, Josh. You should have *seen* her eyes light up! I mean, it's like she suddenly saw a lever that read 'For Mother of the Year Award, pull here!' I've spent my whole life being called a tomboy and my mother always hated it. She wanted a life-size Barbie doll she could play dress-up with. She said, 'Don't worry, honey. We can fix this up, no problem.'

"It was supposed to be the last year for me to have a big birthday party with lots of friends over. Instead, Mom suggested I just have Michelle and Zik and you. It was so devious; she said that Michelle and Zik would spend all their time together, so you would *have* to talk to me."

"Your *mother* planned all that?"

"Well, she didn't tell me to play spin-the-bottle or get you into the closet. That was Michelle's idea. She came over early and we practiced it until we had it down pat."

"You manipulated me." I don't know why I'm so angry over it; it was ages ago.

"I wasn't the only one," she shoots back.

And we stare at each other over the silence for a little while.

"You want me to finish this story or not?" she asks.

"Go ahead."

"Yes. Yes, I manipulated you. Believe it or not, I wanted to just talk to you. But my mom—I think she was living out some fantasy of hers, rewriting or editing something from her own life. You know what that's like?"

She bites her lip. Her front two teeth are just slightly oversize, but it's fetching in a weird sort of way. *Yes, Rachel,* I think but don't say. *Yes, I know what it's like. More than that, I was the rewrite, the edit. I was the fantasy.*

We walk back to the cars together. By now it's half-past four—4:31, to be precise, which happens to be the record for errorless chances by a major league shortstop, set by—you got it—Cal Ripken in 1990.

"I'm really sorry," Rachel says. We're standing at our cars, keys out, unready to get in and drive off.

"For what?"

"For my mother's stupidity. If she hadn't—"

"Rache, it was probably . . . You know, it would have come out eventually anyway. I really believe that." It's true. We were pretty good at keeping our secret, but we were getting more and more indiscreet as time went on. Eventually someone would've twigged to what was going on.

"Yeah, but I think about everything you missed out on. The dates . . ."

"I wouldn't have been dating anyone anyway, not if I was still—"

"You never even went to a single *homecoming.*"

"Homecoming's stupid." And it is. Bunch of kids looking for excuses to grope each other all night.

"Or any dances or anything."

But I never cared about any of that stuff, and I tell her so. I understand that some people see school as a social outlet, but I've never been that way, even before I met Eve. It's what made me stand out, I guess. Even what made me stand out to Eve, for all I know.

To me, school is a means to an end: You get the work done (and truthfully, the work isn't hard) so that you can get through and move on to more important things. Anything else is a waste of time.

"What about prom?" Rachel asks.

"What about it?"

"Who are you going with?"

"No one."

"You're going alone?" It's like I've announced my intention to open a crystal meth stand in the cafeteria.

"No, I'm not going at all."

She walks over to me, takes my hands in hers, and looks up into my eyes. She's only a couple of inches shorter than me, but it might as well be a mile. So strange to look down into her eyes; for years, we were nearly the same height.

"Go with *me*."

It takes a second for me to realize what she's saying. She's asking me to *prom*. Insane.

"Rachel, you don't have to—"

"Remember how I kissed you before?" she asks.

"Yeah. What does that have to do with—"

"I'm going to do it again. I wanted to warn you this time."

Part of me figures I should fight her off, but that seems ridiculous. She's smaller than I am. She can't *hurt* me. But she leans up and in, and then she's doing it. And I want to struggle against it like before, but she somehow teases my mouth open, and then I'm kissing her back.

Kissing Rachel is different from kissing Eve. Eve kissed like her life depended on it, as if kissing me were the only way to sate some urgent hunger, with moans and sudden breaks for gulps of air before attacking me again. Rachel kisses like she's looking for something. It's the difference between swinging for the fences and going for a guaranteed base hit.

I flicker. I'm in the closet, in Eve's bed, on the sofa.

I'm standing outside SAMMPark, fighting against the sick urge inside me, the urge that says to let go of her hands, enfold her in my arms, explore every part of her with my hands, devour her with my tongue—

She pulls back. "So tense. Lighten up, Josh. How are you going to dance with me at prom if you tense up so close to me?"

"What? No way. Look, find someone else. I'm not going."

She drops my hands and takes a couple of steps back, her lips wet, shining, her eyes dancing. "I could always strike you out again."

"I don't know about that."

"Try me?"

"It's late."

"You don't get what's going on, do you?" She asks it with genuine concern in her voice, and I feel like I'm a three-year-old having a Band-Aid put on a boo-boo.

"What do you mean?"

She boosts herself onto the hood of her car, crossing those strong, magnificent legs. "This isn't about you and me hanging out and throwing the ball around. This is about missing five years. About Zik and Michelle."

"What do *they* have to do with it?"

"They're our best friends, you moron. They've been waiting five years for us to talk to each other. You think they're gonna keep going the way they've been going for five years now that we've talked? You think they're going to let you avoid me? Not gonna happen."

I think of all the times I couldn't hang out with Zik because he was with Michelle and Rachel. There must have been just as many times that Rachel couldn't see *her* best friend because Michelle was with Zik and me.

"You're part of the group now. There *is* a group now. Like when we were kids. The Four Musketeers ride again." She slides off the car and opens the door. "Get used to it. You might as well agree to go to the prom with me—Zik won't have it any other way."

She blows me a kiss and leaves me standing there, stunned and confused and wondering what the hell I've gotten into.

CHAPTER 12
Cincinnati Joe

I'M HOME BY 5:22, which is the same number of shortstops used by the rest of the major leagues during Ripken's streak. Can you imagine that? He's on the job twenty-four/seven for the Orioles and the other twenty-seven teams in the league each needed nineteen or twenty players to do that same job.

I sit on my bed for a minute, still feeling Rachel's kiss on my lips, my teeth, my tongue. I'm hard. I want to beat off, but I'm dead tired, exhausted mentally and physically. All those years of dreading this conversation with Rachel and it ended up not being as bad as it could have been. I don't know what I expected. I guess I was thinking there'd be tears and screaming and a couple of fists thrown.

I guess I didn't give her enough credit.

Forgiveness is a funny thing. Dr. Kennedy wants to know if I've forgiven Eve. I've never answered that question directly. I always hem and haw and poke around it like it's a snake trapped in a bag and I'm not sure if it's dead yet. Because I figure there's a lot more to the question, to that topic, and I don't want to get into it. There are other people in need of forgiveness, after all.

See, forgiveness doesn't happen all at once. It's not an event—it's a process. Forgiveness happens while you're asleep, while you're dreaming, while you're in line at the coffee shop, while you're showering, eating, farting, jerking off. It happens in the back of your mind, and then one day you realize that you don't hate the person anymore, that your anger has gone away somewhere. And you understand. You've forgiven them. You don't know how or why. It sneaked up on you. It happened in the small spaces between thoughts and in the seconds between ideas and blinks. That's where forgiveness happens. Because anger and hatred, when left unfed, bleed away like air from a punctured tire, over time and days and years.

Forgiveness is stealth.

At least, that's what I hope.

Surprise, surprise, the phone rings at nine a.m. sharp. Of course it's Zik. I'm a bit surprised that he and Michelle weren't camped out on my front porch all night and all morning, waiting for me to come home. Then again, maybe they were camped out at Rachel's.

I can still taste Rachel's spit in my mouth, but I think I dreamed of Eve. I feel like my brain has vacated and all that's left is bleary vision, a head stuffed with wet cotton, and truly cruel morning wood.

"How'd it go?" Zik demands.

"Didn't Michelle fill you in?"

"Dude, she was texting Rachel *all night*." I hear something in the background—a rambling, urgent sort of growl. I check Caller ID—he's calling from home, which means that the growl is Zik's dad. "All night and Rachel's offline, you know? And she's working this morning, so 'chelle won't be able to talk to her until this afternoon, so *tell me*—Ow! Fuck! All right, Dad. Give me a minute."

Anger blossoms in the wet cotton packed in my skull and cuts through the fatigue and residual horniness. "Tell your dad I'm coming over to drop-kick his ass through a window."

"I have to help him clear some shit out of the basement," Zik says. "Fuck, I can't wait to get out of this place."

Zik and I share the desire to get the fuck out of Brookdale. Different reasons, same passion.

"He smacking you around again? Because I'll beat the shit out of him." Zik can take care of himself, but I'm two inches taller and twenty pounds heavier. Plus, it's not *my* father.

"Nah, he's just flicking my earlobe. Fucking around. Look, what happened, J? I gotta go soon."

I give him a quick version—I apologized, she accepted. I don't get into the kissy-face shit because I don't even know how I feel about it yet. I don't want to think about Rachel *that way*, but a couple of kisses have a way of cementing a girl in your glands as a sexual possibility.

"Oh, man, this is awesome," Zik says, and there's such a joy in his voice, such a light, that I just know it's got to be bad news for me.

Witness my power of foresight: The first double date takes place that very night at Cincinnati Joe's. It's my first date in three years.

Cincinnati Joe's is this dive-y sort of wings-and-beer joint in an old shack on Route 27, which is off Route 54. Every time I think about it, I'm struck, for some reason, by the fact that 27 is half of 54, and I can't help thinking that Route 27 is somehow half the road Route 54 is. What can I say—I'm weird.

High-schoolers hang out at Cincinnati Joe's in terrifying

droves. I hate the place, but I love the wings. Still, I don't like crowds, especially crowds of people my age. I can't help wondering which ones are thinking about what they know about Eve and me.

The place smells like hot sauce and stale beer and stale cigarettes. Fortunately, the minute you get a wing within proximity of your mouth and nose, the heat of the peppers instantly destroys your ability to smell anything else for a week and a half, and you're spared the beer-and-cigs.

Zik and Michelle sit on one side of the table, and on the other side of the scarred, pitted, wooden surface there's Rache and there's me, sitting ramrod stiff and trying not to brush against her accidentally. Rachel knows I'm uncomfortable. *Zik* knows I'm uncomfortable.

The only person who doesn't know is Michelle, but that's because Michelle has the ability to *edit reality*. When she wants them to be, left is right and black is white in Michelle's world, and that's because Michelle is *beautiful*.

Let me back up for a second. Michelle is not beautiful. Michelle is *fucking hot*. It runs in the family. As *hot* as Michelle is, her older sister Dina was *supernaturally hot*. And the oldest in the family, Stacia, went off to college years ago, but some still whisper legends. Mama Jurgens ain't too bad herself, but that could just be me—I may have a thing for older women.

All this genetic largesse means that the world revolves around Michelle and reconfigures itself at her will. She gets extra wings at Joe's without asking for them. She gets super-sized at fast food joints. She gets the sale price at stores even if the sale ended yesterday.

So while Zik eats wings and Rachel eats wings and I sit like

I'm a condemned man offered a last meal of liver and onions, Michelle burbles on about prom.

"... think we should all go to *Paradis*," she says, "and have a long, romantic dinner there. Doesn't that sound great, honey?" She grabs Zik's free hand—the one not smeared with wing sauce—and squeezes.

"Yeah, I guess so." Zik is, of course, helpless to do anything but agree. And I'm still not sure how everyone decided that I was definitely going to prom. Because I'm not.

"You'll never get reservations," Rachel says. "Prom's in three weeks. They're booked up."

Paradis is a new French restaurant in Finn's Crossing. There isn't room for anything quite that fancy or interesting here in Brookdale—we have to emigrate for anything remotely cultural. (Unless you consider wings hot enough to burn your tongue to ash haute cuisine.) And Rachel is right, except ...

"I'll take care of it," Michelle says nonchalantly, as if describing a hangnail and not an impossible reservation on prom night. She grins and daintily plucks a wing from the plate, managing to eat it without smearing sauce on her cheeks, chin, or fingers.

"Well, have fun," I say, my first contribution of the evening, chased with a wing (eaten sloppily—I'm a guy).

Michelle glares at me, then at Rachel. "I thought you said—"

"Josh thinks he's not going to prom," Rachel says.

"I'm right here!"

"I know." She pats my leg and I

—*hand on my*—

almost drop my wing into my lap.

Michelle's never seen a flicker. She's looking at me, bug-eyed, from across the table. "Are you OK, Josh? Josh? Do you need help? Josh?"

Zik calms her down and explains that I space out sometimes, which really is the easiest explanation and the one I tend to stick with.

"*Are* you all right?" Rachel asks in a low voice, leaning in close.

"Yeah. It happens."

"It better not happen when we're dancing at prom." Her voice has a lilt to it. Her fingers are slightly orange from wing sauce, and so are mine. How nice it would be to hold hands with her. Just hold hands.

But it can never be just that anymore, can it?

"I don't want to go to prom."

"I know. Give up now."

I look over at Zik, who's worshipfully tangling his fingers with Michelle's. "I know I'm not as hot as Michelle," Rachel says, her voice still low, "but I like to think I make up for it with other attributes."

"Yeah, like a fastball hotter than these wings."

She laughs loud and raucous. I wish I had the guts to laugh like that, to not care if everyone heard me and turned.

"Yeah," she says. "Yeah, that's one of 'em."

Zik drives us all in Michelle's car, which is marginally roomier than mine or Rachel's. I end up in the back seat with Rachel, of course.

"Who do you guys play on Tuesday?" Rachel asks.

"East Brook."

"No challenge there."

She's right. East Brook is strictly Z-league.

"We've got Canterstown," she goes on.

I wince. Even the Canterstown softball team is hard-core. They do something in Canterstown, I think, where they genetically engineer the kids to have superior ball-playing skills. The Sledgehammers and the ironically named Lady Sledgehammers are brutal.

"Good luck," I tell her, and I mean it.

"Wish I could see you play."

I grunt something noncommittal. I've seen Rachel play, and I know she's been in the stands when I've played over the years. It *is* terrific to watch her, strictly from a logical and platonic point of view, of course. She's a phenomenal player, and my appreciation for her talents has only gone up in the wake of her striking me out. I wouldn't mind seeing her pitch, but I don't want to have her think there's something more to it.

She leans over toward me. "I don't bite, Josh. You can talk to me. You can even sit a little closer so it's easier to hear."

I turn to answer and realize that she's practically on top of me, her face close to mine. "Jeez, Rache."

From the front seat, Zik sees us in the rearview and kills the moment, unintentionally, I'm sure: "Hey, you two! Get a room!"

Michelle giggles. I sit up straight. Rachel sighs and leans back in her original position.

"Canterstown," I say.

"Lady Sledgehammers," she confirms.

"Good luck," I tell her again.

CHAPTER 13

Back to School

MONDAY MORNING, Roland the Spermling demands an audience. I'm not even in the building five minutes when he spots me in the hallway and calls out, "Joshua! Joshua Mendel!"

In the chaos and tug-of-war that is a high school corridor, everyone manages to find time to turn and look at me. By now, the South Brook verbal Internet will have propagated the story like a virus: Josh Mendel beat up Coach Kaltenbach. No one will have been surprised by it, given that my history of beating the crap out of people, my excellent grades, and my admittedly standoffish behavior have combined to make me an almost-pariah. *Almost.* The fact that I'm magic with a good piece of lathed ash in my hands makes me tolerable.

That's not ego speaking; it's raw numbers. My batting average this year alone is .526 and over my high school career it's .494. I've got a .600 on-base percentage, a 1.070 slugging average. In the majors, I'd be walking on water. In high school, it just means I'm damn good. School pride—that invisible, amorphous, ultimately useless glue that holds South Brook together—prevents me from being a complete and total reject. I'm seen as contributing something to the school, and for that reason alone, I'm tolerated.

"Roland!" I shout back to him. "Roland Sperling!"

He flushes redder than usual and gestures impatiently for me to come with him. "I gotta go," I tell a random student nearby. "Roland needs help tying his shoes again."

I push through the crowd, but Roland is already playing his pathetic bullshit passive-aggressive game by walking away before I've caught up to him. Fat-ass *needs* a hundred students to block for him if he's going to try to move faster than me.

It's no mystery where he's going anyway—his office. I blend in as best I can, slipping by and moving ahead, then run like hell down the hall that passes the cafeteria, turn right, and haul ass up toward the music room. The hallway here is nearly empty, and it's a straight shot to the office. It's a longer route, but I can run, unlike the Spermling. I weave my way into the office and wave to Miss Channing, the school secretary.

"I'm here to see Roland," I tell her, and then duck into Roland's office and sit down behind his desk. I've got ten seconds before he's here, easy.

A few seconds later, I hear Roland bitching and complaining out in the outer office. ". . . want her here ASAP, OK, Miss Channing?" And she says, "Yes," and he says, "And page Josh Mendel for me. He was supposed to be right behind me."

I miss the next part, but I hear Roland loud and clear—"What?"—and then the heave and huff of his breath as he tromps down the short hall. His bulk fills the doorway to the office.

"Roland!" I exclaim. "I'm so glad you could make it. Have a seat." I gesture generously to one of the two guest chairs.

His nostrils flare and his face is so red that it's damn near purple, but he's not about to let me get to him. "Good to see you, too, Josh. Take your appropriate seat, please."

"This one's comfortable." I bounce up and down a little bit on the chair that is no doubt reinforced to hold a man of Roland's considerable bulk. "I can see why you like it."

"We've spoken about respect before, Josh."

"Yeah, we have. Like not screaming my name out in a crowd of students. That the sort of thing you mean?"

He bristles at the comment because it's true and I'm right and if there's one thing authority figures can't stand, it's being called on their own bullshit.

"Out of the chair. Now."

I relinquish the seat and sit in one of the guest chairs. Roland closes the door and squeezes around me to take up position on the Throne of Power. He takes a moment to check everything, making sure I haven't messed with his stuff.

"Did you enjoy your time off?"

"Oh, yeah, it was a blast."

"As promised, I've had your teachers hold your work for you. You shouldn't have any problems making up the work. If anyone gives you trouble, just let me know."

I'm dying to say, *Why bother suspending me if you're going to make it so easy for me to get caught up again?* But I already know the answer—it's all about appearances. About taking a stand and saying that a student can't hit a teacher, but without really hurting me. Stupid.

"I hope you took your time off to think about what you did," he goes on.

I didn't really think about it much at all, and when I did, I thought about how good it felt. But I don't tell Roland that. "I did spend some time wondering why a jerk-off like Coach Kaltenbach is allowed to teach at all, but I guess it has to do with tenure, huh?"

Roland starts drumming his fingers on his desk. "Joshua, I have cut you more slack in your four years here than I've ever cut for anyone in the ten years prior. I wish you would appreciate what I'm trying to do for you."

"What exactly *are* you trying to do for me, Roland? I haven't figured out what I've done to deserve any favors from you." I drop my voice low and give him a coy look. "Unless you're sweet on me . . ."

He harrumphs and knocks a pen off his desk. "I know you enjoy getting my goat, Joshua, but the truth is that I simply believe that a young man with your potential should not be held back due to . . . issues that may arise from certain . . . incidents in your past." He laces his fingers over his considerable gut and leans back in his chair, satisfied.

I force a smile to my face, but what I really want to do is lunge over the desk and force-feed his hands to him. It's such a palpable urge that I can almost feel my body launched over the desk, scattering papers and pens and knickknacks as Roland's face turns into a round badge of terror and then I'm on him, pounding—

Sigh. Not a chance.

I want to say, *So, getting fucked on a regular basis when I was twelve buys me a free pass from you? Is that it? Do you get some kind of Good Samaritan award for helping the poor abused child, Roland? Do you feel like your life amounts to something? Like you're somehow better than you are?*

"I just want you to think about your future," the Wise One goes on, smiling like a fatter version of Buddha. "You've got a few more weeks of school to go. Don't do anything to screw up at this point. You still haven't heard from all of the colleges you applied to, have you?"

I shake my head. Stanford, Yale, and MIT—the Holy Trinity —still haven't gotten back to me. And those are *the* schools.

"And be nice to Coach Kaltenbach today," he says. "He has a surprise for you."

Well, that's unexpected news. I want to ask what the surprise is, but I know Roland won't tell me; he'll just get off on having a secret from me. So I shrug like I don't care and tell him I'll be on my best behavior.

"Good," he says, and then heaves a gigantic student file onto his desk. It's the one I saw last week, the one that's bigger than mine. "You should move along to class. First period starts soon and you have to catch up. Please let Ms. Sellers know she can come in."

I leave Roland's office. In the outer office, sitting on a chair as far away from Miss Channing as possible, is a girl dressed in all black, her face as pale as a virgin Rawlings. She's wearing a necklace with a reverse smiley face on it—yellow on black.

"You Sellers?"

She glares up at me. I take it for a yes.

"He's ready for you." I jerk a thumb back toward Roland's office.

"What do I care?"

"Beats me."

"You seem happy coming out of there. Did he blow you, or was it the other way around?"

Which is what I should expect, I guess, but most people don't say it out loud. I just shrug and point to Roland's office again as I leave.

Coach kicks my ass later that day in practice.

Not literally, of course. Even he's smart enough to know better than to lay a hand on me. But he sticks me in the damn outfield and has me catching fly balls and running down line drives all day. By the end of practice, I'm exhausted and my eyes feel sunburnt from staring at the sky.

There are some perfunctory "welcome backs" from the guys when we hit the showers after practice, but nothing too emotional. Except for Zik, I don't have many friends on the team, which is fine by me. I don't like people my own age. Never have. Even before what happened with Eve. Mom used to say I was nine going on ninety. She used to joke that I was older than she was.

I spend some extra time in the shower, washing off the tired and the ache along with the dirt. I hear a sound and turn around to see Coach standing just on the other side of the tile threshold into the showers. His ball cap is jammed on his head just fine, so I guess the goose egg swelling has stopped. But there's still a massive ring of purple and black around the eye I popped.

"You gonna watch yourself from now on, Mendel?"

I grab my dick and point it at him. "Speak into the microphone, please."

"Stop fucking around, Mendel. You better watch yourself."

"You seem to be watching me just fine, Coach. How long have you liked watching boys in the shower?"

He gets flustered and makes a point of looking at something on the ceiling. "You little piece of shit. I should kick you off the team."

For a moment, there's just the sound of the shower and the water running off my body. We both know he won't kick me off the team. He needs me too badly. But it's the only threat that can make me sit up and take notice.

"Got your attention? Good. Because I got a question for you: You know the name Bill Graves?"

Bill Graves. The varsity baseball coach at Stanford. I talked to him during my recruiting trip. He was a little less psyched about me than I would have hoped.

"He's the guy at Stanford who holds your balls and your future in the palm of his hand. And guess what, Mendel? Over the weekend, he handed them over to me."

Coach grins an evil grin. "Graves is on the fence about you. Called me to ask some questions."

Oh, shit. There goes Stanford.

"They're impressed with you, Mendel. But they haven't made up their minds about an athletic scholarship. Because they've heard stories. Now . . ." He stretches and yawns as if bored with the whole thing. "Now I'm supposed to get back to him. Tell him what I think of you as a player. I can tell him a bunch of things, Mendel. I could tell him you're the best natural hitter I've ever seen. Or I can tell him that you like using your coaches like speed bags."

The water pelting me is hot, but my whole body's gone cold. "What do you want, Coach?"

He pretends to think about it for a second, but the bastard has known all along, of course. "You're playing shortstop again. Starting this week."

"What?" I would rather he pound the shit out of me! "We had a deal! I don't play in the field! I'm the DH!"

"Not for the rest of the season, Mendel. You're my bitch and I want you in the field. I need you in the field. You're a goddamn good fielder."

"So? There's ten other guys who can—"

"I need you in the field. But I'll leave it up to you—you can play in the field or not. But if you don't, then not only will I give a crappy report back to Graves, but I'll also make damn sure you don't play in the last game of the season. Against the Sledgehammers. And Fieser."

Reggie Fieser. "The Heat," as he's known throughout Lowe County. He transferred in from some school in Texas right after Christmas break and promptly started breaking school, then county, then state records left and right.

Oh, and he's a *sophomore*. He's the most feared arm in the state.

"Got your attention now, don't I?" Coach laughs. "You want a crack at him, don't you?"

"Maybe." But I have to admit my hands are trembling a little bit. Would he really bench me for that last game, the traditional "rivalry" game against the Sledgehammers? Would he do it out of nothing more than pure spite? Maybe. The real question is, am I willing to give up my only chance to go up against the Heat?

"Here's the surprise part, Mendel. Are you ready for it?"

There's more?

"There's gonna be a scout in the crowd that day."

Holy shit! I try to keep the surprise off my face, but I fail dramatically and Coach laughs. A scout? In fucking *Brookdale*?

"For Canterstown, yeah, there'll be a scout," he says in answer to my unasked question. "He's here to see Fieser, but if you want a chance to show a scout what you've got, this is it."

There are *never* scouts in Brookdale.

"You could put Brookdale on the map," Coach goes on. "I get something and *you* get something. Like an athletic scholarship. How about it, Mendel? We got a deal?"

I offer him a slick, soapy hand. "Deal."

CHAPTER 14

Girlfriend

BY THE TIME I GET HOME from practice, Dad is home from work, so we have one of our deep bonding conversations.

"Where's Mom?"

"She said she had to go to the mall after work. Probably still there. How was practice?"

"Not bad. I went five for five at the plate with two doubles."

"Who was pitching?"

"Grady."

"Oh." And he shrugs as if to say, *Big deal. Your grandmother could go five for five against Grady.* Which, you know, she probably could.

I check the pile of mail before going to my room. Nothing from the Holy Trinity. I'm getting antsy, I admit. Stanford won't base their admission decision on Coach's report to Coach Graves, but the all-important athletic scholarship hinges on that weaselly bastard.

Then again, maybe I won't get into one of the top schools. Maybe I won't get the scholarship or the financial aid. Just because I've got straight A's at South Brook High doesn't mean the world's going to drop to its knees in front of me.

I take my mind off it with my homework and catch-up work until my parents go to bed. As I'm noodling around on the Internet, the phone rings. Caller ID isn't helpful; I pounce on the phone before it can ring a second time.

"So are you planning on coming by or what?" Rachel asks.

"Rache, God! You can't call this late. My parents are in bed."

"You need to get a cell."

"Yeah, well . . ." There's no money for that, I know.

"You should come over to the Narc. I'm closing in a little while."

"I have a game tomorrow. I have to get some sleep."

"I have a game, too. I just miss you."

I don't know what to say to that. I lay back on my bed, staring at the ceiling.

"Do you miss me, Josh?"

The ceiling. Staring. Patterns in the stucco. Chaos theory in action.

"Josh? Are you there? I have to go soon. My manager is—"

"OK," I tell her.

"OK, what?"

"I'll come over."

I get to the Narc with fifteen minutes to go before closing. I scout from the parking lot quickly. There are only a couple of cars in the lot and neither of them is Eve's.

Of course, she could have gotten a new car, right? It's been five years. Would she have kept the old car all that time? Where would it be while she was in prison?

I give myself five minutes in the car, then get out and head inside.

Rachel's packing away deli meats and breads at the lunch

counter. She smiles when she sees me and gives me a little wave—the tips of her fingers jiggling in the air. I don't know how she manages all this; work, school, softball. I do some Web programming over the summer and that keeps my car insurance paid up, but that's about it.

I look around the store, just in case Eve's here. It occurs to me that if I were a famous registered sex offender, I'd probably do my shopping late at night when no one else was around.

But she's not here. Rachel finishes up and emerges from the swinging double doors behind the lunch counter, untying her stubby ponytail to let her hair down over her ears. She flashes another smile at me and holds up a paper bag. "I made us some sandwiches."

Soon we're sitting out on the hood of her car in the parking lot, eating corned beef on rye with hot mustard.

"I can never sleep after work," she tells me, then lays back and gazes up at the stars. "I always have too much energy. Takes me an hour or more to get rested enough to sleep."

"How do you go on so little sleep? I was like a zombie the other day." It's true—I'm a total sleep wuss. I need my pathetic eight hours or I feel like a slug. I already know I will pay for this little encounter tomorrow at school.

She shrugs. "I don't know. I just do. I need to work. I need to go to school. We can't all be super-geniuses with full rides to College Park."

I don't say anything. She sits up. "Oh, come on, Josh. It was a joke. I didn't mean anything by it."

"OK."

She grabs my shoulders and starts massaging them. It feels

good. "You're so serious. It's like you're a thousand years old. And Jesus! Your shoulders feel like stone! Relax."

"It's tough for me, Rache."

"I thought we went over this. There was forgiveness and apologies and—"

"I don't mean that. I mean . . . this." I gesture to the sky, the surrounding parking lot, the car. "All of this. Being out like this . . . I usually stay in when I can. I don't like being out in public."

"Shy?"

"No. It's just . . . everyone *knows*, Rachel. My name wasn't in the papers, but that didn't matter. Everyone knows. And they watch me. And *she's* out there now. She could be anywhere." Her fingers dig deeper into my shoulders, or maybe my shoulders are just bunching up more or maybe it's both. "She could be anywhere I turn."

Rachel stops kneading my shoulders and leans in against me. She drapes an arm around my chest from behind and rests her chin on my shoulder. I find myself holding her other hand.

"Are you afraid of her?" she whispers.

I can't answer. I can barely breathe. I'm fighting against a flicker, struggling to stay in the present. There should be something sexual about this, about Rachel draping herself over me like this, but there isn't, somehow. It's just warm and cozy and *safe*. Maybe it's because my back's turned. Or maybe it's that she doesn't have these gigantic breasts to push against me. Whatever it is, I feel myself relax against her and then it's just amazing because we're leaning on each other, holding each other up, like cards tilted against each other on a table.

"Are you afraid of her?" she whispers again. "You can tell me."

And I can. I realize in that moment that I *can* tell Rachel, that I can tell her anything.

"I'm not afraid of her," I say, and it's true. "I'm afraid of me. I'm afraid of what I'll do if I see her."

I spend an hour like that with Rachel, just entwined with her on the hood of her car, lit by the stars and the lampposts of the Narc's parking lot.

We talk. Nothing important. Just meaningless little things. Teachers we like or don't like. Crazy tests. Whether Zik and Michelle are having sex *right now*.

I ask her why she gave up baseball for softball in seventh grade. There's a girls' Little League and ladies' baseball teams at South Brook Middle and South Brook High.

"Because there's no career path in it." She's snuggled up tight to me from behind, lightly stroking my arm. It feels good; there's a little chill in the air. "No matter how well I played, I'd never get to play professionally in the majors. In softball, at least I can play at the top of the game."

I think about that. I think about how shitty the world is to her. She's one of the best pitchers I ever faced, and there's no room for her in a major league dugout.

But mostly I think about how good I feel right now, how for the first time in five years I'm touching and being touched by a woman and not wondering what she's going to do next.

Or what I'm going to do.

CHAPTER 15

Wrapped Up in Rachel

IN THE GAME AGAINST EAST BROOK, I go 3 for 3 with a double, a walk, and two RBIs. I'd say I'm on fire, but the fact is that East Brook's pathetic. They're 2 and 10 before we play, 2 and 11 by the time they limp off the field. We take them for 15 embarrassing runs and even Grady, our worst pitcher, almost shuts them out. He pitches six innings, walks five, but strikes out ten. It's the best game of his life.

My average is now an unreal .550, and my on base percentage is up to .620. In the field for the first time in a long time, I don't see much action given the quality of East Brook's hitting, so it's not too bad.

Zik kicks all sorts of ass. He hits two homers, one of which drives me in and one of which brings in two more runs. His isolated power average is .667, making him Zeus, Lord of Thunder and Lightning. He goes 2 for 4, which is the best he's done all season—he usually goes 1 for 3, something like that. He's a power hitter—if he can manage to get a piece of the ball, you'll never see it again, but he has trouble getting that piece sometimes. If he could settle down in the batter's box, he'd be a better overall player than I am.

Behind the plate, he catches well, calls good pitches that are executed with borderline competence by Grady. He gets a moment of rare attention when a pop fly is lost in the sun—no one in the infield can see it, but Zik somehow finds it and runs halfway to the mound, throwing his mask in the air and making the catch. In a tight or challenging game, it would be heroic. Instead, it's just . . . fun to watch.

I race through my shower and throw on my clothes as fast as I can, my shirt clinging to my still-wet torso. Rachel's softball game started thirty minutes after our game, up in Canterstown. If I hurry, I might make the last inning.

I break the speed limit on Route 54 on the way to Canterstown, but by the time I get there, I know I'm too late. The field is emptying out and there's a snarl of cars honking and inching around, trying to get onto the road. I park in a now-abandoned spot and make my way to the field, where some obnoxious Sledgehammers are chanting:

There ain't no brook!
There ain't no dale!
There's just fucking Brookdale!

The worst part of the chant is that you really can't argue with it. There *is* no brook or dale in Brookdale. I don't know where the name came from.

I wait outside the visitor's locker room for a while, watching South Brook girls come out in little clusters and pairs. The scoreboard tells the tale: Visitors 2, Lady Sledgehammers 3.

Rachel drags her duffel bag out. I've never seen her so dejected and hurt. She doesn't realize I'm there as she trudges up the path toward the bus.

"Hey!" I shout. "Hey, wet-head!"

Her face lights up when she sees me, and I feel like a superhero.

"Josh!" She comes running back down the path, but I'm already headed up the path and it's like something from a cheesy movie as we meet in the middle. Her hair is sopping wet, too. "Look at us!" She musses my hair, scattering water droplets over us. "How much of the game did you see?"

"I just got here. I'm sorry."

"Don't be sorry." She throws her arms around me and hugs me. "I can't believe you came. That's so sweet."

I can't bring myself to move my arms in turn. She doesn't say anything, just hugs the totem pole standing there in front of her, then takes a step back.

"How did you guys do?"

"Against East Brook? Heh."

"Say no more."

I point to the scoreboard. "You kept them to three runs. That's amazing. Were they earned?"

"Decent defense today, but yeah." She links her arm with mine like she's been doing it her whole life and marches me toward the bus. School policy dictates that she has to travel to and from away games on a bus, so she can't join me in the car. "I thought we had them for a little while. Struck out four in the first two innings, but then they found me and started chipping away."

"Three runs," I tell her again. "That's amazing. They haven't scored less than five in a game all season."

She stops near the bus. I'm suddenly, keenly aware of the entire South Brook varsity softball team watching through the bus windows as their star pitcher holds hands with the school pariah. "Follow the bus back to school?"

I glance at the windows.

"Don't look at them," she scolds. "Look at *me*."

And I do. Hair dripping. Spray of freckles like a constellation over the bridge of her nose. Absolutely no makeup. Just fresh-faced girl.

Woman. Not girl.

"OK."

And she leans in and kisses me, quickly, just a peck, but it's smack-dab on the lips, and I think I hear a massive, coordinated intake of breath from the bus as it happens.

"Rache . . ." I could just combust and die right here, watched by fifty eyes that know what I did with Eve.

"Shh . . ." She strokes my cheek with a palm, and then a shout from the bus:

"Madison! Get on the damn bus!"

Rachel rolls her eyes and squeezes my hand, then dashes to the door and brushes by her coach, who glares at me from the bus steps as Rachel flops into a seat near a window. I ignore Coach Kimball and find myself waving to Rachel as the bus pulls away.

I follow the bus back to South Brook, exposed, naked, and aware that at least two softball players keep looking back at me through the bus's rear windows as if I'm a stalker.

And why not? Any one of them could log on to the Web and see what I've done, see my history. Dr. Kennedy has told me for years that I shouldn't always assume that everyone I see has read the files on the Web, but I think that's naïve. Kids in particular are curious—they want to *know* things. And when knowledge—prurient, forbidden knowledge—is just a click away, how can you *not* check it out?

At school, Rachel flies off the bus and hops into my car. "Let's go!"

"Um, where?"

"Dinner, Math Boy! I'm dying. I'm starving. I'm *wasting away as we speak.*"

Dinner is suspiciously like another date, a territory I've been avoiding as much as possible. Going out with Zik and Michelle is one thing—they take some of the attention away from me. But just the two of us?

I reach for a secure rung on this weird ladder I've found myself on. "OK. We'll go to Cincinnati Joe's."

Her nose wrinkles. "C'mon, Josh. I just held Canterstown to three runs on their home field *and* hit a home run, to boot. You want me to celebrate at Joe's?"

"You hit a home run? You're hitting .367 this season, now. With a .500 slugging average and an IPA . . ." I hesitate, because her IPA is low. She hits mostly singles. But for a pitcher, she's killer at the plate.

"You're the only person on the planet who even bothers to figure out his IPA, Josh. I bet you could talk to twenty major-leaguers and most of *them* wouldn't be able to tell you their IPAs at any given moment in time."

I move on. "Your ERA is 2.20. Jesus, Rache! That's Cy Young territory!" I hate myself for saying it. Rachel could have an ERA in the negative numbers and she'd still never get a Cy Young Award.

We're at a light. I look over; she's staring at me. "Did you just do that in your *head*? Right now?"

I shrug. "Well, yeah." I still get caught off-guard by that—how can other people *not* make those calculations right away?

How can they stop themselves from doing it? I don't understand.

"Not Joe's," she says, leaning back. "You hate it there anyway."

True. But I have two reasons for wanting to go there. One is that Zik will be there and Michelle will have joined him by now, turning this into another safe double date. I can't tell her that, though, so I tell her the second reason.

"There's no chance Eve will show up at Joe's."

The light changes. I hit the gas. Rachel sighs.

"Swing by the Narc," she tells me.

At the Narc, Rachel tells me to keep the engine running. She disappears inside and comes back out with two plastic shopping bags and a big bottle of sports drink.

"SAMMPark, Math Boy!" she orders. "Quickly!"

So as the sun sets over SAMMPark, we find a quiet, secluded place near the baseball diamond and break out the impromptu picnic Rachel scored from the Narc: potato salad, apples, baked chips, fried chicken (we peel off the skin—we're in training), and carrot sticks.

We pass the big bottle back and forth, sipping from it. "Don't leave me any floaties," she warns me.

For a little while, there's nothing but the sounds of two hungry teenagers devouring food as if someone had threatened to take it away from us. We're both jocks, so it's cool to forgo manners and go totally into demolition mode while we eat and replenish our bodies after the games.

I feel a belch welling up from the depths of my gut and turn my head aside to let it go as discreetly as I can. Rachel giggles and taps her belly, then lets loose with a burp-roar that sounds like a wounded lion.

"Holy shit!"

"Not bad, huh?"

She sidles up to me. We both smell like fried chicken and mayonnaise, and since we both do, it doesn't matter. A part of me wants to snuggle up to her, to entwine with her like the other night on the hood of the car. But I just hold myself still.

"Loosen up. You got screwed, Josh. No question about it. Literally and figuratively. So what? It was five years ago."

"I guess I should just move on, huh?" I ask sarcastically.

"I'm not saying that what happened wasn't a big deal. Just that it's not *the* deal. It's not the only thing in your life. You've got college to think about. Prom."

I groan. "Please, Rachel, please stop talking about prom. I don't want to go."

She gnaws at a carrot. "You don't have a choice. I bought my dress already. It's gorgeous. Green. I'll bring you a swatch so you can match your tie and cummerbund."

Match my tie and cummerbund? Match my *tie* and *cummerbund?* Is she insane?

I think I've let this go on long enough. I have to let her down easy, but I absolutely have to let her down.

"We're going away to college, soon, Rache. We're gonna be apart. Does it really make sense to start something now?"

She toys with her carrot, not looking up at me. "We're not starting something," she says quietly. "We're *continuing* something. Something that was interrupted. The question really is: Do you want to? Or not?"

"Rache . . ."

"No, let me finish. You're avoiding it. You're avoiding all of it. Why? Is it her? Is it because she's out of jail? Do you think she's going to show up and pick up where you left off? Why can't you pick up where you left off with me?"

"Because it doesn't make any *sense*—"

"Damn, Josh, why do you have to be so *logical* all the time?" Her eyes flash as she finally looks up at me. "Why can't you just enjoy the moment? We missed out on five years, on what could have been. Why can't you let us at least experience what *is*? Why do you always have to worry about what could be or what might be?"

She leans in and kisses me on the lips again; she wants more. She wants me to open my mouth and let her in, but I can't, I won't, but then I do because as much as I try not to be, I'm still me. I'm a horny guy. I try not to act on it because that way lies disaster, but I'm still just a guy at the end of the day. A guy wrapped up in Rachel as SAMMPark goes dark around us.

CHAPTER 16
MIT, Stanford, Yale

I STAY WITH RACHEL longer than I should. We don't go any further than kissing and a little tongue-action on necks and ears, but it makes me dizzy and almost sick. Rachel doesn't groan like Eve did—she makes little sounds that are almost like whimpers, but somehow sexy.

I'm hard as a rock the whole time and I don't want her to know, but I think that's probably impossible.

It's past midnight when I get home. My brain is sloshing around in my head like a cork on the ocean. I don't know how Rachel manages on so little sleep. She's like a robot or something.

I creep into the kitchen for a quick snack—it's always time to feed the machine, even late at night. If I'm up, I need fuel. But in the light from the refrigerator, I notice a collection of shadows on the living room sofa. Now that I've seen it, I hear it, too—softly breathing.

I sneak over. It's Mom, wrapped up in an old afghan, fast asleep. The afghan's too short and her feet and calves poke out from the bottom.

Well, *this* can't be good.

In my bedroom, I figure I'm good for passing out as soon

as my head hits the pillow, but instead I just lie there on top of the covers, my mind spinning, my chest too tight for my heart.

I'm a dickhead.

I call Rachel on her cell phone. I have an inkling she'll be up. Probably texting Michelle about me.

"Hey, Rache. It's me."

"I know."

"Did I wake you up?"

"Are you kidding?"

Deep breath. And: "I'm sorry I'm such a dick."

"You're not a dick. What are you talking about?"

"Everything. I'm distracted these days. College stuff." I'm beating around the bush. I'm not talking about what I *really* need to talk about. Why? Why can't I just open up and tell her?

It's like dead air on her end, and for a second I think she's lost the connection. Then she says, "Hang on a sec, OK? I want to tell Michelle I'm on with you and I'll get back to her later."

I hear a click. I lay in the dark. What the hell am I doing? How did I get to this point? Seeking forgiveness from Rachel was one thing. Telling her about Eve was too far. And then the double dates. And now . . . Am I really considering going to the prom with her?

"I'm back," she says.

"Maybe I should just go. Let you sleep."

"*You're* the weakling who needs sleep," she reminds me. "C'mon, why did you call me all apologetic?"

I tell her about Coach confronting me in the shower, about the deal we made. "Zik thinks I should just try to impress the scout, see if I can go out for the minors or maybe even straight to the majors. My parents want me to play ball in college."

"What do *you* want?"

Well, that's the problem, isn't it? "I want to play baseball. I want to go to a good school. Somewhere where I can really use math, you know? Change the world a little bit. Send someone to Mars."

"So, college, then. Zik can't control your life, Josh. He'll get over it."

But it's not as simple as that. "It's not just a choice between the league and college, though. You know how it is. Most of the really good math schools, the ones that would change my life— they're not exactly renowned for baseball."

"What about Georgia Tech?"

I considered Georgia Tech. Good school, ranked consistently in the Top 15 nationally for college ball.

"Clemson?" she goes on. "USC?"

Decent schools. Good for baseball.

"Stanford," I tell her.

She doesn't say anything for a second. "Not exactly *renowned* for baseball," she says. "Might as well go to USC if you're looking that far away."

Does she realize what she just said? "Where are *you* going, Rache?"

I can almost hear her shrugging. "Probably Maryland. They've offered me a great scholarship as long as I pitch. Still a chance that financial aid might come in from Michigan or Iowa. I don't have the options you have."

I laugh at that. "God, Rache, it's all speculation right now. I haven't even heard from Stanford or MIT or Yale."

"All known mostly for their baseball teams," she jokes.

"Seriously, Rache. I might end up at Maryland with you.

Especially if I don't get the baseball scholarship for Stanford. If I don't get it . . . Really, it's like 'College Park, here I come.'"

"That's not going to happen."

"Why not?"

"Because you've got skills, Josh. Beyond me or Zik. I'm not talking about baseball. I mean the way your head's like a computer. It's unreal."

"But if I want to play baseball—"

"Josh, if you want to play baseball, no one can stop you. But you'd be wasting your brain if you went to college based on who has the best ball team."

She's not telling me anything I haven't told myself over the past couple of years, but I guess it helps to hear it in another voice. And to hear the other side. Zik thinks he and I are headed to the Show. He thinks we're going to get drafted right out of school. And he's spent a good percentage of his time convincing me that this is a good thing. "You can always go back to college," he tells me. "You can do online classes and stuff like that. Your brain isn't going anywhere, but in ten years, your swing will be slower, your eyes will be weaker, and your shoulders won't be as strong. Play now. Think later."

"Rache . . . All those schools you mentioned, the ones I mentioned . . ."

"What about them?"

"They're all pretty far away. From here. From each other." There. It's out.

"Yeah," she says after a bit. "Yeah, I know."

"So, not to be a dickhead again, but what I said tonight about how it doesn't make sense—"

"You were doing really well, Josh. Just shut up now."

"But—"

"Look, my dad has a saying—we'll burn that bridge when we get to it. OK? You get it? Worry about tomorrow, tomorrow."

"But—"

"No. No buts." She's serious. "We'll only talk about *now*. Right now. This moment. Prom. The summer. Everything after that is *after that*. We'll burn that bridge when we get to it."

I'm silent long enough that she checks in: "Josh? You still there?"

"Yeah."

"Then say something. Something *here and now*."

I don't know what to say. I'm thinking of Georgia Tech and Stanford and MIT and hitting the ball and quantum theory and the Mandelbrot Set and NASA and modeling simulations and why is it that the world gives you so many options, so many choices, and then forces you to cut them all away?

"Did you fall asleep? Talk to me, Josh."

I say the first thing that pops into my head about *right now*. "My mom's asleep on the sofa."

Silence for a moment. "It doesn't . . . It doesn't necessarily . . . My parents went through something like that a few years ago," she says. "But they're still together."

It shouldn't make me feel any better, but it does. "They've been through a lot. They used to fight all the time, even before the stuff with Eve. It's just gotten worse. My mom's out of the house a lot."

"It'll get better," she promises me. And for some reason, I believe her, and it lets me sleep at last.

Session Transcript #215

Dr. Kennedy: I didn't think we were originally scheduled until next week.

J. Mendel: I asked your secretary if she could fit me in earlier. Is that all right?

Kennedy: It's fine. What's on your mind, Josh? Last time we talked, Evelyn Sherman was being released from jail. How are you handling that? Are you thinking about her? Worrying about her?

Mendel: Not really.

Kennedy: Thinking about revenge?

Mendel: No. No. Look, I guess I *am* thinking about her a lot.

Kennedy: I thought you might be. What are you thinking?

Mendel: But that's not why I came in today.

Kennedy: All right. I think it's bothering you more than you think, but we can move on.

Mendel: It's about Rachel.

Kennedy: Ah.

Mendel: This is weird, but . . . Well, I've been sort of . . . *dating* her, I guess.

Kennedy: Really? Well, that's . . . For how long?

Mendel: About three weeks. Pretty much since the last time I saw you.

Kennedy: And how did this come about?

Mendel: I'm not even sure. She pretty much tricked me into it, I think. But that's OK. I'm . . . It's OK.

Kennedy: But something's bothering you.

Mendel: She . . . She sees us picking up where we left off, OK? Five years ago, when everyone thought we'd—I don't know— be boyfriend and girlfriend someday.

Kennedy: Do you enjoy spending time with her?

Mendel: Yeah. I mean, it's tough. She, uh, she kisses me and sometimes I freeze up. You know.

Kennedy: You're having trouble trusting your instincts.

Mendel: Yeah. I mean, a part of me wants to . . . I can't . . .

Kennedy: Take your time. I get paid by the hour.

Mendel: Heh. I can't . . . I want to throw her down and . . . That's what Eve—Eve wanted things a certain . . .

Kennedy: So you fight against yourself. You're afraid to do anything at all because it might be the *wrong* thing.

Mendel: Yeah. It's like the one time Zik set me up on that double date. And I couldn't even hold the girl's hand—

Kennedy: That was, what, three years ago?

Mendel: About, yeah.

Kennedy: Don't you think you've changed since then?

Mendel: I'm still afraid.

Kennedy: Have you tried talking to Rachel about this?

Mendel: How? "Hey, Rachel, remember how I almost raped you a while back? Would it freak you out if that happened again?"

Kennedy: Just by talking about it, you're going to demystify it and take away a lot of its power. If she's able to approach you at all, then she's able to talk about this.

Mendel: I don't know.

Kennedy: You're eighteen. How old is Rachel?

Mendel: The same.

Kennedy: You say she pursued you for this relationship. Don't you think she might at least be interested in the possibility of some sort of physical intimacy?

Mendel: We kiss . . .

Kennedy: I mean beyond that.

Mendel: I know.

Kennedy: What Evelyn Sherman did to you wasn't about intimacy. There may have been times that she made you feel like it was, but it was all about satisfying her needs. You were a means to that end. You've had a lot of experience in the physical actions that comprise sex and sexuality, but you have next to no experience in the emotional component. Evelyn Sherman was an authority figure. She was able to manipulate you into doing things that you wouldn't have done under normal circumstances. It's like . . . Look, how do you hit a baseball?

Mendel: What?

Kennedy: Humor me. How do you hit a baseball?

Mendel: It's complicated.

Kennedy: Start with the easy stuff. How did you learn how to do it?

Mendel: God, you—you square your shoulders, OK? And you watch the pitcher's movements. They telegraph what kind of pitch—

Kennedy: No.

Mendel: I think I know how to—

Kennedy: What's the *most important* thing you learned about hitting a ball? Weren't you told to keep your eye on the ball?

Mendel: OK.

Kennedy: Everything else follows from that, right?

Mendel: Yeah.

Kennedy: Think of keeping your eye on the ball as the most basic precept you have to understand before you can succeed. Everything else—squaring your shoulders, watching the pitcher, whatever—comes later. You can learn it all, but if you can't keep your eye on the ball, you'll never be a hitter. Right now, when it comes to issues of intimacy, you're like a player who's learned everything there is to know about hitting ... except to keep your eye on the ball.

Mendel: Sounds like you're trying to help me score.

Kennedy: You can make jokes all you want, but this is serious, Josh. I've been wondering when we would get to this point. You're in a relationship now, only you don't know *how* to be in a relationship. You don't trust yourself. You know too much. But you need to get back to basics. Keep your eye on the ball. Don't worry about everything else.

Mendel: But I can't help myself. It's like I want to swing even though I'm blindfolded. Or something. I don't know. That didn't make any sense.

Kennedy: It made perfect sense. When you get a bad pitch, you don't swing, do you?

Mendel: No.

Kennedy: Then think of this as the same situation. You want to swing. You know how to swing. But you're going about it all wrong. You're locking up when Rachel needs you to be receptive. Don't swing at the bad pitches, but that doesn't mean you shouldn't swing at *any* pitch.

Mendel: So you're saying I should wait for my pitch.

Kennedy: Exactly.

Mendel: It's just that . . . Prom is on Saturday. And I'm nervous.

Kennedy: Why? It should be a great time. What are you doing?

Mendel: We're going with Zik and Michelle to this restaurant first . . . And, see, here's the problem. Michelle booked a hotel room for the night, so that we could all go there after the prom. Stay off the roads, you know?

Kennedy: That sounds responsible.

Mendel: I—It's a suite, OK? And Zik and Michelle are getting the bedroom. And the sofa folds out and I guess that's where Rachel and I are supposed to sleep, but . . . I don't know if I'm ready for that.

Kennedy: Have you talked to Rachel about this?

Mendel: No.

Kennedy: You need to.

Mendel: It just—It all seems so *pointless!* I tried telling Rachel, but she got upset and I don't blame her, but . . . We're graduating in a couple of weeks. And then we're all going off to college—

Kennedy: Have you heard from all your schools?

Mendel: No. Not yet. Still waiting for the Holy Trinity.

Kennedy: Where is Rachel going to school? Does she know?

Mendel: Probably College Park.

Kennedy: So she'll be near home and you'll be . . . in Massachusetts. Or California.

Mendel: Maybe. I haven't gotten in yet. And the money—

Kennedy: You'll get in. You're a smart, talented guy.

Mendel: Well, I hope so, because I want to get the hell out of this town. This *state*. But if I'm going to be so far away, then how can Rachel and I keep seeing each other? What's the point of getting all involved now, when we're going to have to split up anyway?

Kennedy: Do you have to split up?

Mendel: Come on. Three thousand miles apart, if I'm at Stanford? Eight hundred at MIT?

Kennedy: Maybe the better question is: Do you *want* to split up?

Mendel: I don't see what the choice is.

Kennedy: Keep your eye on the ball, Josh.

Mendel: Yeah, right.

Kennedy: And have fun at prom.

CHAPTER 17

Prom

AS MUCH AS I TRY TO MAKE IT NOT HAPPEN, despite my best efforts to bend the space-time continuum with the force of my brain alone, it happens: prom arrives.

It's the last thing in the world I'm ready for right now. I still haven't heard from the Holy Trinity of colleges, and Mom and Dad are getting antsy. Antsier than usual, at least. Dad has dropped several broad hints that maybe I should just take the College Park offer for the first year or so, see how baseball treats me there, and then transfer after that. Or go to Lake Eliot, where I've got a full ride since Mom works there. All of which just sounds like a nightmare to me, besides the fact that I want to get as far from here as humanly possible. Half of Lowe County's graduating seniors will be at College Park next year—what's the point of just putting myself right into a situation where everyone knows me again, where everyone knows about Eve?

And they don't know about my deal with Kaltenbach. Unless he's totally messing with me, I have to figure that Graves's interest means I'm in at Stanford. It's just a question of the money now.

Rachel drives to my house on prom night, where Michelle and Zik are going to pick us up in Michelle's dad's big Mercedes SUV. For a little while, things are cool at my house again—Mom's actually home on a Saturday, and she runs around like I'm two years old and just figured out the whole talking thing. Dad acts like I just hit my first single. They both scramble for cameras—Mom the still, Dad the video.

"So adorable together," Mom gushes, snapping away. "For God's sake, Josh, put your arm around her!"

I edge closer to Rachel and put my arm around her waist. Rachel sighs and leans into me.

"Turn this way," Dad coaches, filming away like a pudgy Spielberg. "Say something for posterity."

"My tux itches," I announce.

"Do the corsage," Mom urges.

I didn't know what Rachel's dress would be like, so I played it safe and went with a wrist corsage. It doesn't make for terribly dramatic footage when I slip it onto her wrist, but Mom and Dad are there to record the event for future Mendel generations anyway. Rachel pins on my boutonnière without jabbing me, even though Mom and Dad's constant exhortations to "be careful, careful, don't stick him!" make her hands tremble. We somehow come through without bloodshed or the need for an EMT unit.

Just when I've hit my boiling point for pictures being taken, at the exact moment that I'm about to scream bloody murder, a horn beeps. Zik and Michelle, waiting in the driveway. Thank God.

Once in the car, things go from annoying to bad. Because now we have to go to Rachel's house.

I haven't been to Rachel's house in five years. I haven't seen her parents since that day in the closet. The last time I saw them, Mr. Madison was pulling me out of the closet by my arm, bellowing, *What the hell is going on?* I saw Mrs. Madison for the last time as I was dragged out of the house; she stood in a corner, crying, holding Rachel.

Rachel wasn't crying. I remember that very well. Rachel's eyes were wide and confused, but she wasn't crying. Weeping, Mrs. Madison clung to her like I was a wild wolf ready to lunge.

I'm not looking forward to seeing them again, even though Rachel's told me all's forgiven.

Rachel sidles up to me in the back seat and squeezes my hand. "It's fine," she whispers, leaning in close. "Everything's fine."

Rachel's parents are standing out on the front porch when we pull up, waving. Michelle and Rachel are the first to get out. "Oh my God!" Mrs. Madison exclaims. "Michelle, you're a *vision!* We just *have* to get pictures of you and Isaac."

I figure this is my last chance to break free and run for the hills. But instead I sigh, square my shoulders, and come around the side of the SUV with Zik.

"Isaac, stand over here with Michelle!" Mrs. Madison says. Zik obediently lopes over to Michelle and throws his arms around her for a picture.

Mr. Madison meets me halfway to the porch. I experience a watery moment of unreality—five years ago, he seemed gigantic and powerful as he grabbed my arm and yanked me around the house. Now he's an inch shorter than I am. What seemed to be gigantic is now merely blubbery. I know I've changed. I know *he's* changed. The question is who's changed more, I guess.

"Joshua," he says, sizing me up. I feel guilty—he's the father.

He should have some sort of position of superiority here, but I'm pretty confident I could beat the crap out of him if I had to.

So I settle on giving him a little authority. "Sir," I say, as respectfully as I can muster, and extend my hand.

He shakes it. Good, firm grip. There's muscle under all that fat. Maybe I *can't* beat the crap out of him.

"It's been a while, hasn't it?"

"Yes, sir."

—the hell is going on—

His eyes narrow. "Are you OK?"

Goddamn it! "Yes, sir. I'm fine."

"You haven't been drinking, have you?"

"God, no! Sir. We're still in season."

He nods cautiously, as if he wants to believe me, but can't quite bring himself to. "Nice corsage. You have good taste."

"Thank you, sir."

He sighs. I'm pretty sure it's the sigh of a man who is painfully aware that his daughter is eighteen years old.

"Well, let's get some pictures and get you on your way."

I hop the steps up to the front porch, where Mrs. Madison already has Rachel posed against one of the oak columns. The lighting is perfect. I bet Mrs. Madison spent the past three weeks scouting locations in the house and all over the property. That's just her.

"Hello, Mrs. Madison."

She leans toward me and instigates an instant heart attack by pecking me on the cheek. "Josh. It's so good to see you. Stand there."

Rachel's beaming as the guy who almost raped her five

years ago stands next to her and—at the direction of her smiling mother—puts his arms around her. It's surreal.

"Smile, Josh," Mrs. Madison scolds. "Aren't you happy?"

Believe me when I say that no one is more surprised than I am to realize that the answer is yes. I smile for the picture.

Michelle's as good as her word and has not just gotten reservations at *Paradis,* but has managed a table on the exclusive veranda that overlooks an artificial lake and a golf course.

Michelle, of course, is breathtaking. She's wearing some sort of blue and cream gown that has straps going around her neck from the waist, the net effect being that her breasts are covered only minimally, with acres of cleavage as far as the eye can see. Her back is completely uncovered—she's been doing pilates for months, Rachel told me, and the result is an expanse of nothing but toned and sculpted back along with an exposed belly that is just the slightest bit rounded. I honestly don't know how Zik manages to keep from tackling her and dragging her under the table. The man's willpower is a marvel to behold.

Zik, meanwhile, looks like a refugee from a science fiction movie. He's wearing a metallic blue tuxedo to complement Michelle's gown, along with shirt, tie, and cummerbund in cream. I feel like I need sunglasses just to look at him, but somehow, when he stands next to Michelle, it works. Michelle had to have figured this all out; Zik's idea of high fashion is clean socks.

Me? I'm in the most boring standard black tuxedo you can imagine. The guy at the tux shop seemed a little disappointed when I rented it, as if he'd missed some opportunity to show the world something with some style. My tie and cummerbund match Rachel's dress.

Speaking of Rachel . . .

Well, she's just beautiful.

Honestly, as boner-inducing as Michelle is, it's still Rachel I can't stop looking at. I've secretly lusted after Michelle almost as long as I've understood what a penis is for, so her appearance tonight is nothing new. But *Rachel* . . . Rachel is a tomboy. Rachel is a buddy. Rachel is one of the guys.

Tonight, Rachel is a vision. Who knew?

She had her hair cut earlier today—it's too short for a pony-tail now, even the stubby one she usually has. Now it's swept up in back, short there, longer on top and in front, so that it hangs over her forehead and drapes casually to one side. Her dress is green—that much I knew before from the swatch she gave me. But it's got a subtle gold trim to it that almost makes it seem like the dress—and the body inside—are framed like a work of art. It's sleeveless and strapless, so her shoulders—strong, powerful, sprayed with a smattering of freckles—are bare, and some miracle of underwiring or internal scaffolding has actually blessed her with just the tiniest amount of cleavage. With Michelle across the table, it's sort of like a gully and the Grand Canyon, but to have the guts to wear that dress at all makes Rachel all the sexier in my eyes. It's form-fitting down to the waist, where it flares into a long tract of clingy green down the length of her legs. Complete opposite of her usual attire—focusing above the waist, hiding what's below. It's stunning, it's radical, it's beyond words.

It's fearless.

It's Rachel.

For the first time, I find myself thinking, *This is my girlfriend.* And the thought doesn't fill me with worry or with dread.

"... right, J?" Zik asks.

"Sorry, man. What did you say?" I snap out of it.

"I said, you're gonna put the Heat on ice, right?" Zik's leaning forward, eager.

"You've got as good a chance as I do of doing that."

"C'mon, J. It's gonna be you. Everyone's talking about it."

"They are?"

Michelle rolls her eyes and sighs, making every portion of her anatomy dance and jiggle. "God, Josh, even *I* know that! It's all anyone's talking about—Josh Mendel versus the Heat. You'd think it was something *important.*"

Rachel and Zik light into her good-naturedly. Somehow, Michelle has managed to stick with us (and Zik, in particular) over the years, even though she's the farthest thing from a jock you could ever imagine.

"When Iron Man takes down the Heat, that's gonna put South Brook on the map," Zik says.

"I surrender!" Michelle waves her napkin delicately like it's a white flag. "Can we move on to another subject?"

"Are people really talking about it?" I ask Rachel.

She's confused, looking at me as though I just asked if she could dip her chicken cordon bleu into my iced tea for me. "Yeah, Josh. The whole school's buzzing about it. Don't you pay attention?"

Well, I always *thought* people were talking about me. Now I know. It's not the subject I thought it was, but it's something. Take *that*, Dr. Kennedy.

Despite the sudden ball of worry that's sitting in my gut, I actually enjoy dinner. It's fun being with Michelle and Zik and Rachel, cutting up, remembering the old days, the times before "Lucky thirteen"/"Oh, Bill." I barely taste the food, though, barely even *see* it, because I keep looking to my right. I just can't keep my eyes off Rachel.

"Do I have something stuck in my teeth?" She bares her teeth at me and *grrs* like a puppy for added effect.

"No."

"You just keep looking at me, that's all."

"I can't help myself. It's like there's nothing else in the room."

"Sweet talker."

"It's not . . . I don't mean it as sweet talk. I literally can't help myself, Rache."

She strokes my jaw. "Well, I guess the dress is a hit, then, huh?"

"Grand slam."

"Nice to hear."

As dinner ends, Michelle and Rachel perform that time-honored ritual of scurrying off to the bathroom together. Zik offers me a breath mint from across the table.

"You're gonna smoke him, though, right?" he asks.

"What? Who?" I'm thinking of the way Rachel looked when she walked away, how the dress only *seemed* loose-fitting below the waist but when she moved it clung to every curve and line of her body.

"The Heat." Zik leans over the table. "The *Heat*, man! What's *with* you?"

"Sorry, Zik. Just thinking."

"C'mon. It's just us now. You feeling confident?"

"Yeah." And I am. Maybe that's just ego, or maybe it's earned. I don't know. But I feel pretty good about my chances against the Heat. "But, Zik, dude . . . What's the big deal?"

"The big deal?" It's like I've announced I'm going to throw my cherished bat into the wood chipper. "Dude, were you *listening* before? This puts South Brook on the map!"

"So? We're graduating in a couple of weeks. What do you care?"

Zik pulls back like I slapped him. "J! J, man! It's our school. And it would get us attention in the second round. Don't you care about that? Don't you want to get drafted?"

"We're going to *college*, Zik. We're gonna play college ball. See what happens from there."

He stares at me and for a second, I think I see a flash of anger. "Well, yeah," he says, calming. "I just thought . . . you know, it would be cool. To make that, like, a legacy, you know? Like our class's gift to the school—shut down Canterstown once and for all, make South Brook a stop on the scout's agenda . . ." He trails off. "Never mind, J. Just kick his ass when the time comes."

Michelle and Rachel come back to the table, not looking substantially different from when they left. Rachel leans in to kiss me and slips her tongue past my lips. We both taste minty fresh. Thanks, Zik.

"You boys ready to go?" Michelle unselfconsciously adjusts the front of her dress, causing her unencumbered breasts to bobble and collide. I tell myself that Rachel didn't see me look, but let's face it, I'm living in a dream world.

Fortunately, my girlfriend is forgiving. She hauls me out of the chair and kisses me again. "Let's go."

Prom is held at the Cantata Lounge, which is a big room at the local Hilton. The theme this year is "Over the Moon," so there are plenty of cut-out moons and stars all over the place, as well as a bunch of special decals of glowing stars pressed to the ceiling that light up when hit by the random sweep of a black light. I resist the urge to correct the positions of the constellations relative to the big papier-mâché moon.

Teachers are spread out like cops at a riot, smiling and nodding to us, but you know they're just waiting for—*anticipating*—disaster. Coach is, thankfully, absent.

Roland is in charge for the evening. He's in his glory, shuttling his bulk from one end of the lounge to the other, ordering teachers around, grinning like a fake uncle to students, pretending he's everyone's buddy, everyone's pal.

"Good to see you, Joshua," he booms to me, and claps a meaty hand on my shoulder.

"Sure, Roland."

He doesn't even bat an eye at the first name. "And you look lovely, Ms. Madison." He spasms in Rachel's direction and it takes me a second to realize that this was his version of a bow. His tie is patterned with moons and stars. Oh, so clever, Roland.

I'm not sure what I expected from prom. I guess I expected people to act slightly different from usual, but instead, it's like everyone's playing dress-up. The girls in particular seem like they're just pretending, preening and primped in their gowns. How often will they ever dress like this again? How many of them think this is what adulthood is like, despite the evidence they've seen over and over again throughout their lives? And the guys, in their tuxes, acting even less mature than usual, as if formalwear is a license for assholishness.

Rachel drags me out onto the dance floor as the DJ kicks off the first song of the evening.

I'm a terrible dancer. I'm coordinated enough to hit a baseball and run like hell on the base paths, but play some music and tell me to move and you get a statue. A statue that lurches from side to side. Fortunately, Rachel's not that much better with the fast songs (maybe it's a ballplayer thing?), and she guides me pretty well through the slow songs.

I like the slow songs better anyway. I don't feel quite as conspicuous because I have someone to hold on to (although there's a part of me that wonders if everyone is watching me, wondering when I'm going to drag Rachel into a closet or something). The slow songs are relaxing, and Rachel keeps me calm and distracted with a steady stream of meaningless, warm whispers in my ear.

As we sway against each other on the dance floor, I whisper into her ear: "You look amazing tonight, Rachel."

"Aw. That's sweet."

"I'm serious. Michelle's showing off and that gets lots of attention, but you're the most beautiful person in this room tonight. I mean it. I've never seen a more beautiful—"

"Shh." She kisses me, quickly, before a teacher can object.

"That's very sweet, Josh. Now try to relax a little bit. Enjoy yourself."

I try to loosen up, but I can't help it. Looking around, I see the usual idiots and offenders. The geeks are off in a corner by themselves, the stoners keep slipping out and then slipping back in. The jocks—the ones who are supposed to be, on some level, *my people*—are huddled in groups, busting on everyone else.

The song ends and the DJ launches right into another fast one. Rachel and I pretend we can dance for a few minutes, but we both get tired of being bumped and jostled by assholes who can't even be bothered to pretend. We step outside for a breath of fresh air.

"Are you having a *little* bit of fun?" she asks.

I shrug. Her eyes cloud over.

"It's not you," I tell her in a hurry. "Trust me, it's *not* the company! It's just . . ." I shrug again. "It's just the usual. Them." I hook a thumb toward the door.

"What do you mean?"

"I mean, we're supposed to be old enough to be on our own now," I tell her. "Look at how we celebrate. By dressing up like grownups and spinning out the fantasy that we're ready."

"It's just supposed to be fun," Rachel says.

"I don't know," I tell her. "Maybe I just don't know how to have fun anymore."

"Did you ever?"

—*Xbox controller*—

—*so good at this one*—

—*hit the ball! Hit*—

"Yeah. Yeah, once."

"What happened, gloomy guy?"

"I guess I grew up."

"The two don't have to cancel each other out."

—*there, yes, THERE*—

—*God oh God oh God*—

—stop teasing me, you naughty . . . oh God yes—

"When you grow up, I guess different things are fun."

She narrows her eyes at me. "You can stop anytime now."

"Stop what?"

"Stop acting like you're wise beyond your years. Like you know something the rest of us don't. Maybe a few years ago you did. But not anymore. You're not . . . You're not a freak, Josh. You're like one of those child prodigies, you know, the kids who are brilliant at computers or science or something?" She cocks her head at me and I nod, so she goes on, confident that she has my attention. "They skip grades or they go to college when they're fourteen, but you know what happens to them eventually? You know what happens to every single one of them?"

I shake my head. What is she getting at?

"They grow up, Josh." She squeezes my arm and leans in close. "They grow up and then they're just like everyone else."

I digest what she's said, working it over in my mind. I get it—I really, truly do—it's just that I can't *believe* it. I can't believe that I'll ever be like everyone else, that I'll ever walk down the street and not flicker or anticipate the eyes boring into my skull from behind, or wait for *her* to come around a corner.

"I'm going inside," Rachel says. "I'm giving you five minutes to collect yourself and relax. And then I'm going to dance with someone else if you're not back in there. Got it?"

Jealousy stabs at me, but it's a dull knife. I *need* some time alone right now. Just to tamp down the sudden anger that's welled up inside, if nothing else. Rachel kisses me on the cheek and goes inside. I stand out there for maybe a minute and a half before I realize I'm being a complete fucking idiot. Just chill out, Josh! God! Not everything is the end of the world!

I wheel about and head back inside. Rachel is on the dance floor, fast-dancing with Michelle. Zik's gulping down sodas at the table, rehydrating. I sit down next to him.

"We've been replaced," I tell him.

"Yeah, well, I've known for years I'm pretty unnecessary," he jokes. And it's so untrue; Michelle worships the ground Zik walks on. The feeling's mutual, of course. Those two have been inseparable since grade school. I've never seen anything like it. Then again, why would I have?

I check my watch. "Only another hour or so to go."

He looks at me, surprised. "You sad to see it end?"

"It" means one thing to him and another to me. He just means the prom. But I can't help thinking about . . . all of *it*. High school. Brookdale. It all ends for me soon, and Rachel . . . Does Rachel go with it? I don't see how she can't. Unless I stay in state. Go to College Park or Lake Eliot College, neither of which is the best choice for math *or* baseball . . .

The girls—the *ladies*—join us at the table, Rachel hugging me and saying, "Glad you came back, big guy."

"Yeah, me, too. Next dance?"

She clutches her chest as if having a heart attack. "Oh, my God! Are you *offering* to dance?"

"I guess so."

We wait for the current song to end and then get up to take the dance floor. But the DJ just riffs some chords and then leans into the microphone.

"Hey, there, Bobcats! It's *that time!* Lemme introduce Assistant Principal Sperling!"

Roland blinks into the bright light and accepts a microphone from the DJ. "Good evening!" he booms, trying to sound cheerful, but instead causing an obscene whine of feed-back that makes everyone yell out. "Good evening!" he says again, this time with the mike farther from his mouth, which is good because for a second there it looked like a turkey drum-stick he was about to eat.

"Is everyone having a great time?" he asks with the sort of enthusiasm adults think is infectious.

I can't bring myself to applaud the Spermling. My peers have no such reservations, and the Cantata Lounge reverber-ates with the stomping, clapping, and whistling of three hun-dred seniors. Michelle and Rachel clap politely—Zik gets obnoxious and bangs the table with his palms, but I forgive him. Again, you can't ever *really* escape your DNA.

"Thank you," says Roland, holding up a hand for quiet, as if the applause is somehow *for* him and not just coincidental to him. "Thank you. Quiet down, please. Settle down, seniors."

When he's got the quiet he asked for, he goes on: "Now the moment you've all been waiting for: the announcement of our prom king and queen!"

There's some more applause, even though it's a foregone conclusion.

Roland drags it out, pretending we can't possibly know: "The prom king and queen . . . for the senior class . . . as voted on by the *entire* senior class . . .

"Are . . .

"Isaac Lorenz and Michelle Jurgens!"

No kidding.

Holding hands, Zik and Michelle thread through the tables to the dance floor, where Roland and Maggie Sanchez (the senior prom committee chairperson) drape sashes over them and put cheesy crowns festooned with bulbous moon ornaments on their heads. I notice that Roland moves to put the sash over Michelle but Maggie blocks him and gets there first. Good thing for Roland—he just avoided a hell of a lawsuit.

I hold hands with Rachel at the table and watch as Zik and Michelle glide onto the dance floor together. The DJ starts up a slow number and they move sweetly and softly together. Michelle actually looks a little surprised, though I don't see how that's possible. No one could have voted for anyone *but* these two for king and queen . . . even if Maggie wasn't a good friend of Michelle's.

After a minute or so, Roland's tired of staring at Michelle and wants to be the center of attention again. Back at the mike, he announces, "Now it's time for the unveiling of our runner-up prom king and queen!"

"What," I mutter to Rachel, "in case the king and queen can't meet their obligations for the next forty-five minutes?" She giggles.

"Our runner-up king and queen are . . .

"Joshua Mendel and Rachel Madison!"

The applause for us isn't nearly as thunderous as that for Zik and Michelle. And no wonder—we're not the South Brook dream couple. If anything, we're the South Brook nightmare couple, the star softball pitcher and her freak boyfriend, the kid who fucked a teacher in seventh grade and has kept his head down ever since, the kid who beats the shit out of anyone who looks at him cross-eyed. Beauty and the Bestial.

Someone's pulling me up from my seat, and I realize with a

shock that it's Rachel. Up by the DJ, Roland is ho-ho-ho-ing like an evil Santa Claus, waving us on. "Come on, Josh! Dance with the young lady!"

I know that, technically, eyesight is weightless. But right now there are more than three hundred pairs of eyes on me, and I can feel the pressure of every single one, adding to the pull of gravity on me, combining masses to become a crushing weight. I lurch along behind Rachel, even more feral than usual, crippled by the gaze of the entire senior class and the certain knowledge of what they're thinking, that they can't believe it, that the applause is just polite and perfunctory, what the hell is he doing with *her*, how can she be with him—

Roland slips a sash that says "Prom Prince" over my shoulders. He's grinning and huffing and puffing with exertion and I figure a good, sudden shout would send him right into cardiac arrest at this point.

And then I've got a cheesy crown on my head, like Zik's only not quite as ornamented. Rachel's beaming as she comes to me, arms wide, and I make myself smile for her sake, even though the eyes have become hot now, igniting the air around me. I can barely breathe.

I take her in my arms and the world goes away. It's just her and me. I lean into her, needing her strength and her solidness to hold me up under the force of a million gravities. She whispers, "Hey, surprise, Prom Prince," and kisses the shell of my ear lightly as we start to sway. The lights leave nowhere to hide, and I shuffle my feet clumsily, managing to avoid stepping on hers.

After a minute or two that last eternities, Roland opens up the dance floor to everyone else, and a throng of bodies joins Zik, Michelle, Rachel, and me.

We dance our way close to Zik and Michelle, who are off in a world of their own, Zik's hands plastered to Michelle's naked back, Michelle pressed against him, her body conforming to his like Africa and South America before the world's plate tectonics did the geologic shuffle.

Just then the DJ segues into a new, faster song, loud with lots of percussion and a backbeat that threatens to pound my brain out my ears.

"I stuffed the ballot box!" Zik shouts over the music, but even with the shouting, only I can hear him.

"You *what?*"

"For you!" he yells. "Not me!"

And then he dances away with Michelle.

The music's changed; couples around us are breaking apart, spinning off into whirls of color and clothes. Rachel isn't changing her pace, though, still clinging to me, her head on my shoulder.

I feel a surge of anger at Zik for doing this to me, for putting me in the spotlight like this when he knows that all I've ever wanted is to be invisible.

But then Rachel adjusts herself slightly against me. She's smiling. We're slow-dancing to some hip-hop song, a bubble of quiet in a sea of thrashing bodies. I look down at my prom princess and let the anger melt away.

CHAPTER 18
Before the Past Returns

THE SUITE MICHELLE RESERVED is smaller than I thought it would be, but pleasant enough. Michelle and Rachel go into the bedroom and change into sweats. Zik and I just strip off our tux jackets and ties.

We order junk from room service before they shut down for the night: hot wings, potato skins with artery-clogging cheese and bacon, fried mozzarella sticks with marinara, and thick slices of cheesecake with fruit sauces drizzled on top.

We stuff ourselves with the lights out, the TV playing a goofy romantic comedy on pay-per-view, and as we all get more and more tired and giggly, the room devolves into stupid jokes, laughter, endless snickering at half-remembered silliness from our shared childhood. I feel like my gut's going to explode from the laughing and the enormous quantity of calories I'm inhaling, but I don't care. I'm with my friends and it feels good.

". . . the Spermling looked like he was gonna tackle you," Rachel says to Michelle.

"Oh! My! God!" Michelle squeals. "I *know!* It was *so. Creepy.* I think he *sweated* on me before Maggie got in the way."

"If he'll change my grade in sociology," Zik says, "I'd *let* him sweat on you."

"Oh, thanks for standing up for me, *sweetheart.*"

"Let him sweat on *you*," I tell Zik.

"The Spermling's not *gay*," Rache says. "He's *married*."

"The Spermling goes both ways, all ways . . ." I crack up before I can finish.

"He was like . . ." Zik starts, "'Let me help you with that sash . . .'" and mimes pawing between Michelle's breasts. Michelle squeals and bats his hands away.

"Yeah, he didn't come after *me*, you'll notice," Rachel says. "How could he resist *these?*" And she looks down her sweatshirt. "They're here *somewhere . . .*"

By four in the morning, I'm so tired that I'm laughing at things even when no one's saying anything. I'm such a sleep pussy. Rachel and Michelle are still going strong, and Zik's antsy but awake. The TV is still going, playing some HBO special on sex, so there's a constant parade of naked fat people on the screen.

Finally, Rachel and Michelle traipse off to the bedroom to change. Zik and I strip down. I sleep in boxer shorts, but I throw on a T-shirt since I'll be with Rachel. We shove the detritus of our party into the trash can, filling it to overflowing, then stack what remains next to the can. It's a precarious tower of plates, cups, bottles, and food carnage.

By the light of the TV, we unfold the couch and I put sheets on it as Zik moves some more trash around.

"Hope you didn't mind being prom prince," Zik says after a little bit. "I thought you deserved it, though. It was a nice little fuck-you to the people who've been assholes to you, you know?"

"Yeah. It's cool, Zik."

"I know you hate being the center of attention," he goes on. "But it's not like she was at the prom."

"What do you mean?" But I know what he means.

Zik punches my shoulder. "Dude, don't play games with me. I hang with you, remember? You're always looking around. I figure you're looking for, y'know, Mrs. Sherman."

"I didn't—"

"She wasn't at prom, though, OK? So you can chill."

"I'm not—"

"Dude. J. She's been out of jail for a month. If she was gonna come after you, she would have by now."

Zik has a way of cutting straight to the core of something. I don't know if Rachel told Michelle any of the stuff I told her that night at SAMMPark. If she did, then Michelle *definitely* told Zik, because Michelle tells Zik *everything*. But I don't think Rachel talked. I just think Zik's figured that it's time to tell me what he figured out a thousand years ago and has been sitting on since then.

"Maybe she would," I allow. "Maybe not."

He considers this for a moment, glancing toward the bedroom door like he's about to reveal a state secret and wants to make sure we won't be interrupted.

"If you're really worried about it," he says slowly, "you should, y'know, go all football on her."

"Huh?"

"You know—best defense is a good offense. Take the fight to her. Find her before she finds you."

"I don't get it. What do you mean?" Find Eve? Go *find* her?

"Dude, she's a registered sex offender. All you have to do is go online. You can find out where she lives and everything."

I feel like a complete moron. Of course. He's right. Eve isn't in a shadow somewhere or a hiding behind a tree. She's right where I can find her—at home. And if I go online and nothing comes up, well ... That tells me that she's not in the state anymore, right?

God! All along! All along, the answer was *literally* at my fingertips.

I can't help it—I hug Zik. "Thanks, man."

"Dude! Homo alert! Homo alert!"

I skeeve him out a bit more by planting a big wet kiss on his cheek.

"You're so gay!" he complains.

"I'm comfortable with my masculinity."

"That's fine—just don't be so comfortable with *my* masculinity, y'know?"

Just then, the bedroom door opens. I don't know what I expected, but it's just Rachel standing there in what look like pretty boring pajamas—buttoned-down top, long sleeves, long pants with frills at the cuffs, all in a soft blue. Standard girl-issue.

"She's ready for you," Rachel says, and Zik hops up, darts into the bedroom, and slams the door.

"Man, he never moves *that* fast!" I'm joking with Rachel because now this is *it*. We're getting into this bed—sofa—together. We're getting under the covers. We're turning out the light. Unless I decide to try sleeping in the car or the bathtub, this is it.

And no way in hell am I ready for it.

"If you saw how she was dressed, you would have moved that fast, too."

"Oh? Why's she all dolled up?"

She leans against the archway that leads into the bathroom. She doesn't seem to be in a hurry to come over here. "She's going to rock his world. Sorry that I'm just wearing this." She indicates her boring PJs.

"That's OK."

"It's just that, well, they're spicing up their sex life. And we don't *have* a sex life."

That does it—I freeze up. I stare at the floor.

She sits next to me on the bed and takes my hand in both of hers. "It's all right. We're gonna take this slow, OK?"

Kennedy was right; I should have talked to her. I should have been talking to her all along. But I didn't know how to bring it up without making Rachel feel like it's her fault. It's not that I don't want to be with her. It's that I'm not sure how to be with anyone other than . . .

"Turn off the TV, Josh."

I hit the remote and the room goes dark, except for an after-image of the TV screen that floats, ghostly, in naked space before fading behind my eyes.

"Rache . . ."

"Shh . . ." Leaning against me, her breath warm against my cheek. "It'll be OK."

But my heart's jackhammering and I close my eyes because it's too dark. She moves in the darkness next to me and then we're lying down next to each other, her fingers skipping over my chest, lightly. My entire body's on fire, with cool traces where she touches me.

And then her lips on mine. Her body so close, one knee coming up, sliding against my leg, God, the rustle of fabric, the weight of her leg thrown across my thighs.

Her breath quickens as we kiss, her hands touching my

chest, stomach, shoulders. She's everywhere at once. It's too familiar for me, in some ways. It's like being back in the closet with Rachel, with Zik and Michelle just a few yards away, through a door. Only now I'm not thirteen. And neither is Rachel. Now I know more. And, somehow, less.

Her hand slips under my T-shirt and I hear myself groan deep in my chest. She licks my ear and says, "Josh. Josh, unbutton my top."

I can't.

"Josh, please. Please."

I'm flickering. I'm back in the closet and in the *closet* I'm flickering, a flicker within a flicker, an infinite loop, I'm in the closet and I'm back with Eve. I'm twelve years old and I don't understand but I don't care if I understand because Eve's touching me, she's telling me what to do, how to do it, how to make it better and best.

My body jerks back into the present. Rachel's lying on top of me. Her top is unbuttoned somehow. Did I do that? In the darkness, she's an outline over me, thinly seen in the murk. My hands move of their own accord, exploring, peeling the opened top down her shoulders; her breath hisses and I flicker to Eve's bedroom, her leg cocked as she sleeps, back to the present, my hands tensed and tightened, ready to grab Eve—no—Rachel, grab and—

Stop it!

"Josh, please. God, Josh, don't you know I want you? Please?"

I push Rachel off me, my hands burning where I touch her skin. I'm cheating. I'm not supposed to do this. I don't know what I'm doing. I'm flickering in and out, of the closet, of Eve's apartment. I'm being unfaithful, cheating on Eve with Rachel, cheating on Rachel with Eve. I roll over onto my side and clench my teeth. My gut is on fire. Tears flare at the corners of my eyes.

Oh, God, I've ruined it. I've ruined it, like I always do.

Rachel lies behind me, not moving. Her weight's a tug on the sheets, on the mattress, like gravity, pulling me. I resist, curled up on my side like a baby.

"I'm sorry," I tell her. I say it so quietly that I'm not even sure she can hear me.

And it's not enough. It can never be enough. I've apologized too many times; it starts to lose its meaning after a while.

I should tell her that it's not her. That it's not her fault, that she's beautiful and warm and sexy and that any man with a brain and a working cock would be an idiot not to yearn for her, not to worship every last inch of her. That I'm damaged, broken, a bizarre temporal conjoined twin—half of me stuck here, the other half still living five years ago, connected by flickers like electric sparks in old horror movie laboratories.

"I swear to God, Rachel. I swear it has nothing to do with you."

"It's *her*, isn't it?" Her voice low and sad in the dark.

"No. Not her." My voice catches. "Me. It's just what I am."

"That's bullshit, Josh. You don't have to be anything you don't want to be. You can't keep acting like five years haven't gone by. *Something* has to have changed in five years."

I don't know what to say to that. I owe her something. I owe her an explanation. A boyfriend who's not a time-traveler. More than I am, no more than she deserves.

"Rachel, you can't unswing at a pitch. Once your wrist breaks, that's it—it's a strike. You can't take it back."

"Will you at least *look* at me?"

I roll over onto my back. My eyes have adjusted enough to the dark that I can just barely make her out, faintly luminous next to me. As I watch, she shrugs her top back on, leaving it unbuttoned, completely unselfconscious. "I think I'm in love with you, Josh. No, don't say anything. Just let me talk.

"I'm not going to pretend that I know everything or even that I know exactly how I feel. Everything in my mind tells me to run like hell away from you. But everything in my body can't stay away from you. And I've learned to trust that. You can't think through every pitch, every at bat, every line drive. You go on instinct. You go by feel and taste and smell and sound. Sometimes those things just bypass your brain and go deeper. That's how it is with you, Josh. I can't stay away from you, even though that would probably be the best for me. And I don't know if that's love or not, but it seems like it to me."

"Rache . . ."

"Shh." She covers my mouth with her hand. "Don't. If you say it back to me, it means nothing right now. And if you say you don't—I don't know. I don't know what that will do. So just don't say anything, OK?"

I nod. She releases my mouth.

She curls up next to me. "Can you put your arms around me? Is that OK? Or is that too much?"

I fold my arms around her, her body a long, firm warmth. "Yeah. This is OK." I kiss the top of her head and even as I do it, I realize that Mom and Eve both used to do that to me all the time.

We lie like that for a while. I think I drift in and out of sleep, or it might be flickers. I don't know. Pressed against me, Rachel becomes almost a part of me, our body temperatures matching, mingling, fusing as we breathe in syncopation. And then she says: "Josh?" her voice rising up from a welter of half memories and half dreams, so soft and quiet that at first I think it *is* a dream.

"Josh?"

"Yeah?"

"Tell me the rest. Tell me the stuff you didn't tell me before."

"It's not going to change anything."

"I know."

Flashbacks,
Not Flickers
(II)

14

"WHAT THE HELL IS GOING ON down there?"

That's what I remember in the eye-blinking moments of light after the closet door flung open and Rachel ran screaming up the stairs: Rachel's dad yelling from upstairs, asking pretty much the same thing I was wondering as I sat on the closet floor. *What the hell is going on down here?*

In here?

In me?

Zik and Michelle were on the sofa across the room, clutching each other tightly, caught midclinch when Rachel burst from the closet. Zik's hand was up Michelle's shirt and they were both just *frozen,* looking over at the closet.

Then they broke apart and Michelle jumped up, pulled down her shirt, and ran to the stairs. Zik scrambled over to the closet as Michelle's footsteps followed Rachel's up the stairs.

"Dude." Zik's face lurked in the rectangle of light that was the closet door. "Dude, what happened?"

I hardly knew. I stared at him.

"Hey, J? What's that?" He pointed to my right hand, which was clenched in a fist. I looked down at it as if I'd never had a right hand before in my life, as if it had just grown there as part of some puberty ritual.

I was clutching Rachel's panties, the edges torn and shredded.

"Oh, shit," Zik said, just as the boom of footsteps sounded overhead. Mrs. Madison shrieked.

"Oh, shit," he said again, and I dropped the panties and spastically lashed out with my foot, kicking them as far back into the darkness of the closet as they would go.

Zik looked over his shoulder and moved out of the way just as an enormous shadow filled the closet door. Rachel's dad snarled and reached into the closet, grabbing my wrist and yanking me to my feet with such savage strength that I thought he had pulled my arm out of the socket.

My legs, nerveless, wouldn't support me—they dangled from my hips like pants on the clothesline. He dragged me across the carpet and up the stairs. I tried to keep up with him, tried to make my feet and legs work, but I couldn't find my footing on the stairs and he just kept pulling up and on, up and on.

Upstairs, Rachel and her mom were in the corner of the living room. Michelle was near them, stroking Rachel's hair. Rachel wouldn't look up. Her mom glared at me, weeping. Rachel's brother, Bobby, came out of nowhere and grabbed my other wrist.

"You piece of shit," he said. "I should kick your fucking ass."

Together, they dragged me to the front door, which Mr. Madison opened. "Hold him," he said, and let me go.

Bobby pulled me out onto the front porch. "Don't even think about running," he hissed. He tightened his grip and I finally made my first sound—I cried out.

"Shut up! Shut the fuck up!"

I shut the fuck up.

□ □ □ □

Mom was there in minutes. She raced up the driveway and onto the front porch, where Bobby had not let go of me with his hand or his eyes. "Into the car," she said. She was trembling, her eyes red from tears. "Into the car *now!*"

While Mom watched, I went to the car and got inside. Mom went into the house. Bobby sat on the porch and glowered at me. I felt his eyes through the car window, burning me like sunlight focused through a magnifying glass.

I tried to remember exactly what had happened. But I couldn't. I'd flickered. One minute I was kissing Rachel, the next I was with Eve and she was egging me on like she liked to do, urging me to wildness—

Rachel's panties in my hand. God. Oh, God. I felt sick. My stomach tightened and I hung my head out the door. I stared at the asphalt, which swam and churned in front of me. Yeah, I was gonna puke, all right.

But even though my stomach lurched and my throat constricted, nothing happened. It was like being on the precipice of vomiting but never actually plunging over the cliff.

I don't know how long I hung suspended like that, watching the blacktop do its best merry-go-round impression. But I suddenly heard Mom's shoes on the driveway and then she slammed the driver's-side door, almost catapulting me out of the car. "Close the door," she said, her voice vibrating like kite string in a high wind. "Buckle your belt."

The car roared to life and she pulled out into the street. "They're calling the police. The *police*. And I can't even *blame* them."

"Mom—"

"Jesus, Josh!" She was weeping now. She slammed her palm against the steering wheel. "What on *earth* possessed you to do that? What is *wrong* with you, Joshua?"

I didn't say anything. I couldn't. How could I tell her that I didn't know? That I was just reacting the way *Eve* wanted me to react?

"It was that Lorenz kid. I knew it. I knew he would be a bad influence on you. That family . . . You won't be spending any more time with him, that's for sure."

Now, *that* got my attention. Zik was my best friend. And even as a child, I recognized that he didn't fit in with his family, that our friendship was a lifeline for him. I couldn't let my mother take that away.

"Mom, it wasn't Zik's fault. Me and Rachel were just playing."

"Playing? *Playing?* You ripped her underwear off. You grabbed—I don't even want to *say* what you did, and you call it *playing?* Who taught you that? Where did you learn that? I know it was from Zik. His parents are letting you watch adult cable, aren't they?"

"No, Mom! It wasn't Zik! I didn't know it was wrong. I was just playing like with E—" I stopped myself midsyllable, but it was too late.

Mom turned to me, her eyes red and puffy, her cheeks streaked with tears. "With *who?* With *who?*"

"Mom!" I screamed. A car had pulled out into traffic ahead of us. Mom stomped on the gas, jerked the steering wheel to one side, and swerved around the car.

"Who, Josh?" she screamed at the top of her lungs. We sped

down the street, whipping past slower cars. I don't think she knew what she was doing. I think, in that small moment in the car, my mother went briefly, completely insane.

"Who? Tell me! Tell me! Tell me!" Over and over again, screaming it at me, and a new scream, *my* scream joining in, a wordless scream as we weaved in and out of traffic, darting here and there, my mother a madwoman and me . . . Oh, yes, I was a madman, no doubt. A raping lunatic.

In the end, I didn't tell her. I never told her. But it didn't matter, because I had already said enough. I was so desperate to save Zik that I exposed the truth. How many people are there that I know who start with "Eee," after all?

Mom suddenly pulled over onto the shoulder and slammed on the brakes. She looked over at me with those red, red eyes, her mouth pulled down, her chin quivering. She was terrible and beautiful all at once. There was nothing maternal about her, nothing recognizable as my mother.

She flipped open her cell phone and the next thing I knew, she was talking into it: "Don't say hello to me." Her voice had gone dry and brittle. "Don't *act* with me." She stared at me the whole time and I stared back, terrified to look away. "I know what you did to my son. I know."

She snapped the phone shut.

"OK, Josh." Her voice had cleared. "OK, now we can go home."

15

HOME WAS A SWIRL OF PHONE CALLS and screaming.

There were phone calls to the Madisons and phone calls *from* the Madisons.

Mom's cell phone rang constantly. She would flip it open, look at the Caller ID, then snap it shut. It was Eve, I'm sure.

In between the cell rings and the calls to and from Rachel's house came the calls to and from the police. Mom talked herself hoarse: *My son is the victim. My son has been abused. My son doesn't know what happened. This woman has destroyed my child.*

I sat on the stairs while Mom and Dad yelled at each other and yelled into the phone. I heard all of it.

This woman has destroyed my child, her voice cracking high and strained at the end.

Yes. I felt destroyed.

Dad came to me while Mom was on the phone with the Madisons. "Josh, you have to tell us what happened."

"I don't remember," I told him.

"That's bull. You remember. You've been with Mrs. Sherman almost every day for the last four months. You need to tell us what happened or else the police are going to think you're a criminal."

"I don't remember." All I could think of was Eve telling me

how much trouble she would get in if I told anyone. How I watched her in secret, lusted after her. Watched her in her bed as she slept so innocently, slept without knowing that I was standing five feet away. It was all my fault; I'd ruined Rachel and Eve, the two people I was supposed to care for most.

"Tell me!" Dad shouted and hoisted me to my feet. "This is not a game, Josh! You could throw away your whole life! Talk to me!"

"Nothing happened!" I screamed. "Nothing happened nothing happened nothing happened!" I kicked at him and thrashed until he let me go. I ran to my room and slammed the door behind me. I threw myself onto the bed. My mind flew in a hundred directions at once: Did Rachel hate me? Was Zik angry? I had to call Eve. Was Michelle angry? Were the police going to arrest me? How could I contact Eve? Would I be sent away? Where would I go? Would I ever see Eve again? Or Rachel? Or Zik? Or my parents?

I couldn't stay on one thought—they zipped by like engines on an infinite array of parallel train tracks, catching my attention in the breeze of their wake just long enough to distract me until the next one came along.

My parents came into my room without even knocking, something they hadn't done since I was in grade school.

Mom said, "We have a meeting first thing in the morning with the police and the district attorney. You're going to tell them everything about you and Mrs. Sherman, do you hear me?"

"But you're telling *us* now," Dad said.

I shook my head.

"Goddamn it!" Dad lunged at the bed.

Mom grabbed his arm. "Bill!" For the first time in my life, I was more afraid of my father than my mother. Dad's face flushed red. He shook Mom off and stomped out of the room.

"Sleep," Mom commanded, pointing at me. It wasn't even six o'clock yet. "Do not even *think* about leaving this room. Tomorrow you're telling it all."

She slammed the door behind her as she left, leaving me there, lost on the train tracks.

That night, through the vents:

"If you'd let him get that fucking Xbox, none of this would have happened."

"What? If you hadn't gotten your damn job—"

"How else were we going to send him to college?"

"Now it'll pay for his therapy."

"Jesus, Bill! You're such a fucking asshole!"

I listened to them argue until they finally both stopped talking. It's not that they came to any sort of accord or anything like that—they just drifted into back-and-forths where neither one was responding to the other, and finally trailed off, each of them with a triumphant pronouncement that had nothing to do with what the other had said.

I slept. And then I didn't. And then I did. And then I didn't.

I crept out of bed, inching open my door as if I were one of the bomb guys on TV. It felt like it took hours to open my door enough for me to slip out.

I made my way down the hall on the tips of my toes. At my parents' bedroom door, I paused just long enough to listen at the door. There, barely audible under Dad's snores, was Mom's soft, rhythmic breathing.

I sneaked to the stairs, avoiding the third one from the top because it creaked no matter where you stepped on it.

In the basement, I picked up the extension and dialed Eve's cell. It rang and rang and rang. Voice mail. I hung up. I was afraid to leave a message.

And then I was afraid to go back upstairs. What if she saw the call on her Caller ID and tried to call back? That would wake up my parents!

I stared at the phone. I had to pee. I crossed my legs. I was terrified of leaving the phone. Maybe, if it rang, I could grab it before it woke up my parents.

I had to pee *so bad.*

I hovered my hand over the phone, willing it to ring, then willing it not to. I didn't know which was worse—having it ring and possibly waking up my parents, or standing here all night, waiting for it to ring, certainly wetting myself.

I decided: I would call Eve and leave a message telling her *not* to call.

She picked up on the first ring.

"Josh?"

"Eve," I whispered.

"Josh, I can barely hear you."

"I'm down in the basement. I have to be quiet. My parents are asleep."

"Josh, what happened? You said you would never tell—"

"I didn't!" It was a lie, but a lie of fact, not of intention. I'd never meant to tell Mom about Eve. It slipped out. It was a mistake. I didn't want her angry at me for something I couldn't control.

"I didn't tell," I told her. "My mom figured it out."

"God, Josh." I thought she might be crying. She didn't seem interested in *how* Mom figured it out. "I'm going to lose my job. I'm going to go to jail . . ."

"Where are you?" I asked. She wasn't keeping her voice down.

"I'm in the car. I haven't been able to sleep. I didn't get to the phone fast enough before and I've been sitting here staring at the phone, waiting for you to call back. Josh, this is *terrible*."

"My parents are taking me to the police tomorrow."

"Oh, shit," she said, and in that moment, something inside me broke. Eve was no longer my teacher, my confidante, my lover. She was now a scared, desperate . . . child.

"Please, Josh. Please, don't tell them anything."

My bladder felt like it would burst. It was cold in the basement and I was shaking, which didn't help the situation at all. Plus, I was absolutely terrified of getting caught at any moment.

"Please!" she begged.

"I have to go," I told her. I meant it in more ways than one. I became convinced that I'd just heard a footstep on the third stair from the top.

"I love you, Josh," she said, crying. "I love you."

"I love you, too," I told her. "I won't say anything. I have to go." And I hung up on her as quickly and as quietly as I could.

I stood there in the darkness, trembling, both hands ground into my crotch to keep myself from peeing. I *had* heard a step. I *knew* it. I waited and worried, worried and waited, the sound of my own breathing suddenly too loud and raucous. I held my breath; my heartbeat pounded my ears.

I had to breathe again. I let out my breath and stood stock-still, listening again for the footsteps.

Nothing.

My imagination.

I sneaked into the laundry room and peed into the utility sink, aiming for the drain so that it would make as little noise as possible. Then I sneaked back up the stairs, pausing again for a moment at my parents' door before returning to my room and climbing into bed, gulping and heaving air as if vomiting.

MOM POUNDED MY DOOR and shouted, "Josh! Up! Now!" I jerked awake as if electrocuted.

The first session with the police didn't go well. There was a man and a woman—both dressed in suits, both detectives. They told me their names, but I couldn't process them. I was in the *police station.*

"Tell them what you told me, Josh," Mom said. "In the car yesterday."

I said nothing.

"Josh, do you understand that we need to know what happened to you?" the woman asked.

I couldn't think straight. I thought of my promise to Eve. I thought of the horrified look on Rachel's face, of the anger on her father's, of the absolute disgust on her mother's.

And I continued to say absolutely nothing.

That was the day, pretty much. They tried a variety of tactics to get me to talk, but I wouldn't. I said nothing. Mom tried the guilt trip in various forms—"Mr. and Mrs. Madison are going to file charges against you if you don't . . ." and "How can you put your father and me through this?"—but I wouldn't say anything. I *couldn't.* I had promised.

That night, I listened through the vents again. Dad said, "Maybe this is too much for him, Jenna."

"What do you mean?" Mom's voice was cold, as if she were asking the question just to be polite.

"Look, he wasn't hurt or anything. Maybe we just keep him away from the Sherman woman, get him transferred to another class—"

"Are you *insane?*" If I closed my eyes, I could see Mom's expression, just based on her voice. It was the way she had looked in the car. "That woman *molested our son* and you think we should just drop it?"

"Jenna—"

"The Madisons are only holding off on their charges and their lawsuit because they believe Josh was molested. If we just drop it, they could still sue or have him prosecuted."

"No one's going to prosecute him for what happened."

"You don't know that. And what about a lawsuit? That would ruin us."

"I'll call a lawyer in the morning."

I drifted off to sleep on that. Dad sounded pretty confident, and talking to a lawyer sounded pretty safe.

They kept me out of school for the rest of the week. Then we all went back to the police station on Saturday. Mom took me into a room with the male detective while Dad filled out paperwork with the woman.

The room was painted a pale blue. It was pretty bare, except for a big mirror like on the cop shows and a card table with some folding chairs. Mom dragged a folding chair a few feet away and sat down, while I sat across the table from the detective.

"Josh, I know you don't want to talk to me. Maybe you're afraid. Maybe you're angry. I understand that. So I want to tell you something. I want to explain to you that we've already taken that first step, and you didn't have to say a word. We already know that something's going on between you and Mrs. Sherman. Would you like to know how?"

I was still in silent mode. Even though Mom and Dad had harangued me and yelled at me most of the previous night, I was still determined to say nothing at all to the cops. If I said nothing, then Eve wouldn't get in trouble. That's what she promised me.

"Well, I'll tell you. See, your parents gave us permission to search your house. And we also did something we call a phone dump. You know what that is, Josh?"

I said nothing. I didn't shake my head. I just stared at the table directly in front of me and clenched my hands together in my lap.

"That's where we go to the phone company and ask them for your records. The phone company keeps a record of every phone call into and out of your house. Did you know that?"

I didn't. But I wasn't about to let him know that.

"So we did a phone dump on your house, and do you know what we found?" He unfolded a piece of paper and held it up for my benefit. I refused to look at it. "Two phone calls from your house to Evelyn Sherman's cell phone on the day you attacked Rachel Madison in her closet. Well, the next morning, actually. Two-eleven in the morning and then two-sixteen. The first call lasted less than ten seconds. Did you hang up on her? Was it a prearranged signal?"

I kept my lips pressed together. My heart was hammering. I wouldn't let on.

"The second call lasted forty-seven seconds. I'm guessing you got through. What did the two of you talk about? Or did you just leave her a voice mail? Tell me, Josh—when I go to a judge and get a subpoena to have the cell phone company turn over her voice mails to me, am I going to hear a voice mail from you on that night? Hmm?"

And that's when I knew I was safe. He almost had me for a second there, but then he made the crucial mistake of giving me too much information. If he was fishing for voice mails, then he had nothing else. And I hadn't left Eve a voice mail, so I was safe. Eve was safe. He couldn't even prove that I was the one who made the phone call, just that it came from my house. Eve had been calling Mom's cell phone all day long, after all. Anyone in the house might have called her back.

"I wonder what I'll hear, Josh," he went on, but by now I knew I was safe.

"We also did a phone dump of *her* records, Josh. Don't need a search warrant for that. Not bad, huh? Did you know that?"

Again, I didn't. Something like a ball of ice settled in the pit of my stomach.

"We found repeated calls to your house right here." He pointed to a calendar. "This Saturday and Sunday, just a couple of weeks before Christmas. You remember the phone ringing a lot then, Josh? I bet you do. I bet you were waiting for a call from her, but your parents were around, so you couldn't answer."

Behind me, Mom gave a little hiccup-gasp.

"But then there's this last call, one of the ones on Sunday, that goes about . . . oh, say a minute and a half. So she finally got through to you, huh? And then, in the following week, there are calls early in the morning to *her* number from your house. Were you sneaking in little calls while Mom was getting dressed or making breakfast or in the shower or something, Josh?"

He sighed. "Josh, you can give me the silent treatment all you want. It's not going to matter. We have evidence already and we haven't even searched her house or dumped her e-mails or voice mails. It's only a matter of time. You have to believe me, Josh. And it's going to go a lot easier on your mom and your dad and on you if you just cooperate. You didn't do anything wrong, but you're doing something wrong right now. You're defending her."

He strummed his fingers on the table for a little while, waiting to see if I would look up or talk. And then:

"Want to talk to me about this?" he asked.

I looked up. He was holding a clear plastic baggie. Inside it was the birthday card Eve had given me not a week ago.

"Where did you get that?" I whispered.

"Your parents gave us permission to search your house." He looked at the card through the plastic. "You remember what it says inside, Josh?"

I can't sign it if you take it home with you, Eve whispered in my memory.

"Says, 'I love you,'" he commented, as if noticing that the sky was clouding over a bit. "Who's it from, Josh? Hmm? Not from your parents. Not from any relatives we could identify—you have cards from all of them and they're signed. So where did this one come from?"

I flickered

—If your parents see it—

and came out of it. "I found it in my locker," I heard myself say.

"Oh? Found it in your locker?"

"It must be from a secret admirer."

He dropped the card on the table in front of me and drummed his fingers. "You know what I think, Josh?" He didn't wait for me to answer, not that I would have. "I think that yesterday I went to your school and your principal gave me a piece of paper with some of Mrs. Sherman's writing on it." He opened a folder and took out another plastic bag, this one with a slip of paper inside. He held it and the card up to the light next to each other and squinted at them. "Now, I'm not a handwriting expert, but they look pretty similar to me. What do you think, Josh?" He slid them both across the table to me. "Hmm? What do you think?" He shrugged. "I'll tell you again what I think: It'll take a couple of months to come back from the handwriting lab, but when it does, that note will match that card and then we've got her."

I thought back to how Eve had wanted to give me things: Little notes. A lipstick-pressed card. Her panties. But she'd always take them back before we even left the apartment. *I don't know where you could keep it,* she would say. *I don't know how you could keep it hidden.*

My throat tightened. I closed my eyes. I was doing everything wrong. I didn't know what to do next.

The detective decided to get some coffee. He left me alone with Mom for a little while and she berated me for not cooperating. I bore it in silence. I would just have to bear *everything* in silence from now on.

When the door opened again, it was the female detective. She gave me a nice smile and asked if I wanted something to drink, which I did, but I wasn't going to tell her that. She ruffled my hair before she sat down, just like Eve used to, and I reminded myself not to say anything at all.

"Josh, I feel terrible about this. I know you care about your teacher, about Evelyn, a lot. Is that what she told you to call her? Evelyn?"

I said nothing. *Eve*, I told myself. *Eve. Eve. Eve.*

"I know that the two of you have a very special relationship. She treated you like an adult, didn't she?"

That was the closest I came to breaking then. I almost opened my mouth. I don't know what I would have said, but I came damn close to opening my mouth. Instead, I just pressed my lips together more firmly.

She noticed, though. "I know, Josh," she said, her voice low and soft. "I know. She told you you were like a grownup, didn't she? She told you that you were special, that what you and she had was special, that she could get in trouble if you told anyone. I know. I know how much that meant to you, Josh.

"And that's why I hate to do this. I really, really do. But, see . . .

"Do you think you're the first kid she's done this to, Josh?"

She pushed a closed manila folder to me across the table and tapped it with two fingers. "Why do you think she transferred out of South Brook High and into your middle school, Josh? There are two sophomores on record stating that she made advances toward them. Sexual advances, Josh."

She leaned over the table. "Josh, did she tell you she loved you? Because it's not true. She doesn't. She never did."

I couldn't let this go by without comment. Without lifting my eyes from the table, I said, "I don't believe you."

She tapped the folder again. "I know you don't. And I don't blame you. This is so hard for you. But it's not me you need to believe, Josh. It's these two guys from South Brook. Go on. Open the folder. Read it. You'll see."

"They're lying." I was whispering at this point.

She flipped open the folder. "Read it, Josh." Her voice had gone hard. Cold. "Read the file."

"No."

She pushed it closer to me, sliding it into my field of vision. I closed my eyes.

"Read the damn file." Murmuring, almost. Quiet. But like steel. Quiet steel.

A chair squeaked and Mom grabbed my wrist. "Mrs. Mendel—"

"I won't have you forcing him to read that—trash." Her voice. Just as quiet. Just as strong.

She dragged me out of there and that was it for a little while.

MOM AND DAD TOOK TURNS bringing me to the police for the next few days, though Mom ended up doing it far more often.

One day we pulled into our driveway but didn't get out of the car. Mom turned off the engine and just sat there. It was raining, and at first I thought that she was going to see if it would taper off before running through the rain to the front door.

Instead, she turned to me. "Why are you making this so difficult?"

It caught me off-guard. I wasn't the one making things difficult! The *police* were making things difficult. The *DA* was making things difficult. They were hammering away at me, trying to chip away at my resistance, but I wouldn't give them an inch, no matter how hard they made it.

"Why, Josh?"

"I'm not making it more difficult," I told her.

I expected her to be angry, but she just sighed a sad little sigh as the rain drummed around us. She rested her forehead on the steering wheel.

A swell of pity burgeoned inside me and
—*lotion on her legs*—
in that moment she was so weak and so distraught that I had

to give her *something*. Disoriented by the flicker, I reached out and tapped her shoulder. She looked over at me.

"I love her, Mom." I said it quietly, with all the seriousness I could muster. It was the biggest, most important thing I'd ever said in my life.

And Mom *laughed*.

It wasn't an amused laugh. It wasn't the sort of laugh you hear at the movies or in front of TV or during a family reunion. It was harsh, hard-edged, more a snort than actual laughter.

"Mom?"

"Don't be stupid," she said with contempt. That contempt shocked me—my mom had been angry at me in the past, but never *hateful*. "You're a *child*. You don't know what it means to be in love." And she flung open the car door as if she wished she had the strength to rip it from the hinges, and stalked off to the house through the rain.

That night, I lay in bed, troubled by what she'd said, blocking out the sounds of argument from my parents' room. Was love what my parents had? Yelling at each other, worrying about money? Never smiling? Never happy? If that was love, then I didn't want it.

I went back to school a week after Rachel's birthday party. I hadn't spoken to anyone from school the whole time. Not even Zik. He had called the house a few times, but someone was always on the other line or he called when we were out. I wasn't allowed to call back.

Mom drove me that first day so that I wouldn't have to put up with the bus. "Don't talk to anyone about this," she told me. "I've already talked to the principal. She's going to talk to you this morning, but other than that, you don't talk to anyone, do you understand?"

I understood.

The principal, clearly uncomfortable and ill at ease in my presence, told me that she'd spoken to my mother about "the recent issues" and that if anyone bothered me or approached me, I was to let her know immediately. Then, since homeroom had let out by then, she released me to first period.

And that was the first day of the rest of my life.

First period was science. The first thing I noticed was that Rachel wasn't there. The second thing I noticed was that everyone's eyes followed me everywhere I went.

And I wondered: *What do they know? How did they find out? What are they thinking?*

But I wasn't supposed to talk to anyone. I wasn't supposed to tell. So I sat in a bubble of invisible silence all day. No one tried to approach me. No teachers called on me. No students came up to me. I was like a bad smell—you know it exists, but you can't look for it or at it. You know it's there, though.

History was a shock—Eve wasn't there. I guess it clicked for me then; she had said that she could lose her job if the truth about us came out. And here the truth had begun to trickle out and she was gone. We had a substitute, the kind that stays a long time.

I sat in my seat, not hearing this new teacher as she droned on and on. I stared at my notebook.

Zik sat behind me. History was one of three classes we shared in seventh grade. I hadn't looked around to see him. I hadn't seen him or spoken to him since Mr. Madison dragged me from the closet and up the stairs.

About halfway through history class, I felt something brush against my shoulder. I jerked up just in time to see a crumpled ball of paper drop over me and into my lap. My heartbeat raced; the sub hadn't seen anything.

I uncrumpled the paper. It was small and had four words written on it:

Welcome back, Iron Man.

Lunch had the potential to be hell, but Zik saved me. I couldn't bring myself to stand in the lunch line, shoulder to shoulder with people who clearly couldn't stand to be around me but also couldn't stop staring at me. I considered going to the principal's office, pretending I was upset so that I could avoid the cafeteria.

Then Zik came up behind me and whispered in my ear, "Meet me outside."

I made for the exit door. The lunchroom monitor just glanced at me. She was one of the eighth grade teachers, but she knew. Everyone knew.

She stepped aside and let me outside without a word.

I sat on a bench near the basketball net, waiting. A few minutes later, Zik came out, walking in a funny hunched-over way, his arms crossed over his chest.

He sat down next to me and reached up his shirt and started pulling out juice boxes, ice cream sandwiches, fruit bars in wax paper.

"Bone appetite," he said.

"It's *bon apetit*," I said.

"Yeah, I know." He unwrapped a fruit bar and started to eat. We ate in silence for a few seconds, and then he said, "You think there's gonna be a players' strike this season?"

"I don't know."

"I hope not. That would suck."

"Yeah."

"Opening day is only a week away. You think your dad can get us tickets again?"

The year before, my dad had somehow managed tickets to the first game of the season. "I don't know. My dad's not doing a lot of favors for me right now."

Zik grunted, taking it in stride. He punched my shoulder. "Well, we'll watch it on TV. This is why God invented ESPN."

I guess Zik kept me sane. He didn't talk about the birthday party or the closet or anything else. It was as if we'd never gone to Rachel's that day, as if I hadn't missed a week of school, as if there were no whispered conversations held in my wake as I walked through the halls. With Zik, it was just baseball and how much of a dick his dad was and how he couldn't wait, couldn't wait, couldn't wait to get out of that place.

And me? I had never really cared one way or the other. But now *I* couldn't wait to get out either.

THE DAYS TURNED INTO WEEKS turned into months. Unlike on TV, trials in real life take a *long* time to get started, I learned.

School never felt normal—not with Eve missing—but it settled into a new rhythm at least, similar to the old one in the same way that a new tooth is similar to the old. There's that period of time where it's missing, where there's a hole, and then slowly, over time, something else fills in. And it might be just as good a tooth, but it's not the same as the one before, and you always know that.

And there's always a part of you that wonders if you'll lose *this* one, too.

I kept my head down in the halls and in classes. I hung out with Zik. I shied away from Michelle. I ran like hell from Rachel.

I thought it was all over. Except for my own guilt and shame. Other than that, I thought it was done with. There were no more trips to the police station, no more calls . . .

And then one day the handwriting analysis came back from the lab. The police called Mom and Dad to tell them that between the handwriting match and the phone records, they had gotten a search warrant. They had also questioned Eve on multiple occasions, but she wasn't saying anything. Good. We were both keeping our mouths shut.

The very next day, I was back in the police station. This time, though, it was Gil Purdy, the prosecutor, who spoke to me, while the two detectives stood off to one side, looking satisfied with themselves.

Purdy didn't mince words. As soon as I sat down, he started in on me.

"Did you ever go outside the state, Josh? Maybe to Pennsylvania or West Virginia? Hmm? Did she ever take you for a little getaway? Because if you went over state lines, then this is a *federal* case, Josh. This is a whole new ball game."

I didn't feel like playing a whole new ball game. The old one was just fine. I kept my mouth shut. But Purdy had scared the hell out of me because Eve *had* mentioned going out of state once, something about going to Delaware. I hadn't been paying attention, but he was so *close* . . .

They hammered away at me, taking turns. It was five of them—my parents included, because they sure as hell didn't seem to be on my side—against me. And they had phone call records and handwriting samples and they had testimony from some other teachers who had seen me getting into Eve's car with her and a bunch of other stuff that they hurled at me so fast that I couldn't see any of it whiz past the plate.

And they broke me.

Here's how:

Purdy kept firing questions at me, looking for details, when suddenly, out of the blue, he said, "What kind of birth control did you two use, Josh? Was she on the pill? Did she make you wear a condom? Do you know what a condom is?"

And I knew, but I wasn't going to say because suddenly it

wasn't that I didn't *want* to speak, it's that I *couldn't* speak. My stomach and my heart had twisted up and risen to my throat and I thought I was about to puke them both up.

And Purdy could tell. A crazy light went on in his eyes and he kept asking about birth control, but I didn't even hear him, not really, because all I could think was, *Is Eve pregnant? Did I make her pregnant?* Because I'd never even *thought* about birth control and Eve had never brought it up and I was just twelve when it all happened so how was I supposed to think of these things and oh my God what if I was going to be a *father—*

And Purdy just wouldn't give up and he wouldn't *shut* up, going on and on, asking about birth control, while I could only think of Zik telling me how his aunt's boobs had gotten so huge when she was pregnant, picturing Eve's belly round and tight and full, oh God.

They brought in boxes of condoms and pill packs and tubes of spermicidal jelly and stuff like that. "Just point to anything you saw in her apartment, Josh. Maybe you looked in her medicine cabinet?"

But I hadn't. I'd never looked. I'd never wondered. *I didn't know.* And Eve could be pregnant with *my baby . . .*

"What did she use, Josh?" Purdy asked for the millionth time, and that's what did it—that's what *did it.*

"I don't know!" I screamed.

Because I didn't.

And the rest followed.

I told them everything. As much as I could remember, at least. Sobbing and near incoherent, I told them all of it, just to shut them up, just to make them go away.

They gave me a yellow notepad and a pencil and made me

write down everything. I mean *everything*. Every date I could remember. Every thing she said and I said. Every . . . *thing* we did together.

I hated them. I hated all of them, my parents included, my parents *especially*. All of them, standing around me, so smug and so pleased with themselves for making me cry, for making me admit . . .

I finished the pad and they had to bring me another one. Because I remembered *everything*.

It took a few months, but when the trial started in the winter, I missed more school. I sat outside the courtroom on a bench with Mom while Dad testified, then waited with Dad while Mom testified. I had to stay outside because I was going to be a witness, so I couldn't hear any other witnesses.

And then a bailiff opened the court door and looked out into the hallway and said, "Joshua Mendel."

My legs shook like string in a breeze. I made myself walk into the courtroom.

Purdy looked at me expectantly. He had prepped me mercilessly over the past week, forcing me to recount everything in excruciating detail, making me say it all out loud again. I hated the sight of him and I think he knew it.

I walked to the witness box. The bailiff told me to raise my right hand. "Do you solemnly swear or affirm under the penalties of perjury that the testimony you are about to offer is the truth, the whole truth, and nothing but the truth, so help you God?"

I had trouble swallowing. "Yes."

"Be seated."

I sat down in the chair. Now, for the first time, I could see everyone in the courtroom—the jury off to my left, the prosecution and defense tables ahead of me, the entirety of the gallery, filled only with family and media, at the judge's orders.

My parents had moved into the front row of the gallery, right behind the prosecutor.

Eve sat at the defense table with her lawyer. George was nowhere to be seen.

Eve wasn't looking at me. She was looking down at her hands, folded over each other on the table in front of her.

Purdy came around in front of his table and leaned against it. "Good morning, Josh," he said, smiling. It was one of those smiles adults put on at parties when they're bored stiff with the person they're talking to.

"Morning," I mumbled.

"I'm going to ask you some questions today. Is that OK?"

I shrugged. I couldn't really stop him, could I?

"You need to answer out loud," he said with the air of someone who's talking to a complete moron.

"Yes," I said, leaning forward into the microphone.

"We're going to take this slow, Josh. I want to start with a simple question." He walked over to me, holding something familiar in his hand. He held it up so that the jury could see it, then held it out at arm's length in front of me.

"Do you recognize this, Josh?"

It was the birthday card Eve had given me. It was still in the plastic bag, only now there was a tag with a *C* on it. "Yes."

"What is it?"

That was a stupid question! Anyone with *eyes* could tell it was a birthday card. "It's a birthday card," I said with as much annoyance in my voice as possible. *You doofus,* I left off.

He smiled tightly. "Thank you. And who gave you this birthday card, Josh?"

I opened my mouth. But not to speak. I thought I was going to throw up right there in court, maybe hit the bailiff with some of the puke, splash the jury, I don't know. My whole body was ready to collapse into my gut like a black hole and then spew out again.

"Are you OK, Josh?" Purdy asked, a fake look of concern on his face.

I didn't trust my voice; I shook my head.

"Can we get some water for this young man?"

The bailiff brought me a glass of water. I looked at it like it was poison.

I didn't want to drink the water. I thought I would puke if I had anything at all in my stomach.

But then, the more I thought about it, the better that sounded. If I threw up, they wouldn't make me testify, right? I sipped the water. It did nothing but cool my throat on the way down and sit like a ball of ice in my gut.

"I'm going to ask the question again," Purdy said as if reading a picture book to an imbecile. "From whom did you receive the card inscribed 'I love you' that the police found in your bedroom, the card labeled 'People's Exhibit C?'"

I shook my head and looked down at my own hands.

"Your Honor . . ."

The judge sighed and said, "Mr. Mendel." Then: "Mr. Mendel, please look at me."

I looked up at Dad, who was dutifully looking at the judge.

"Mr. Mendel!" the judge snapped. "Look at me, please."

That was when I realized: "Mr. Mendel" was *me*.

I looked at the judge, who glowered at me from his bench. "Mr. Mendel, you have to answer Mr. Purdy's questions. Otherwise, I'll hold you in contempt of court. Do you know what that means?"

I shook my head.

"It means you can be fined. Or put in jail. Now, since you're so young, I would have to fine your parents, do you understand?"

Yeah, I understood.

"Now answer Mr. Purdy's questions."

I gritted my teeth together and put my palms on either side of my body on the chair, pressing down as if I could launch myself up through the ceiling.

"Answer the question, young man."

I closed my eyes. I flickered. I didn't care. I wouldn't tell them. I wouldn't tell them anything.

"Young man . . ."

"Judge, permission to treat this witness as hostile?"

A sigh. "Granted."

"Josh," Purdy said, "didn't Evelyn Sherman give you this card on the occasion of your thirteenth birthday?"

I said nothing.

"Answer the question, Josh."

It hit me then. With a sudden and painful clarity. I knew what I had to do. I've always been a lousy liar, so I only had one choice.

"Did Evelyn Sherman—" he repeated.

I opened my eyes. I cleared my throat and looked Purdy dead in the eye. "I plead the Fifth," I said.

Dead silence in the courtroom.

I looked over at Eve's table. Her lawyer was staring at me as if I'd grown a third eye in the center of my forehead. Eve looked confused. I flickered: her eyes, her bedroom.

"... can't plead the Fifth," Purdy was saying.

"Judge!" This from Eve's attorney, suddenly on her feet.

The judge waved for her to settle down and sit down. "Mr. Mendel, you're not on trial. You can't plead the Fifth. That's only for people who are on trial."

He sounded awfully convincing, but I wasn't about to cave. I had seen people do this on TV and it *always* worked. It was my only way out.

"I plead the Fifth," I said again. For good measure, I crossed my arms over my chest defiantly.

The judge sighed. "I'll see the witness, his parents, and counsel in chambers. Bailiff, please take the jury out."

"Why is *she* here?" Mom's voice had sharp edges to it. She was pointing to Eve, who was sitting next to her lawyer in the judge's chambers. I was in the chair right across from the judge's desk, and Purdy and my parents were standing behind me.

"Mrs. Mendel, we're only going to be here a few minutes, OK?" The judge gestured to a sofa against a wall. "Why don't you sit down and relax for a minute?"

Mom and Dad sat on the sofa, watching Eve. She looked down at the tips of her shoes the whole time.

"Josh, we need to talk," said the judge. "I know you're a bright young man, so you'll understand this when I explain it to you. You just can't take the Fifth in this situation. It doesn't work that way."

I shrugged. "I don't want to testify."

"It doesn't work that way, Josh," the judge said. "When you're on the witness stand, you have to testify. The Fifth Amendment is there to protect people who are accused of crimes so that they don't have to testify against themselves. It's not so that witnesses can just suddenly decide not to testify."

"Your Honor . . ." Eve's lawyer, tiptoeing into the conversation like a kid who knows she's not supposed to be up this late at night but wants a snack anyway. "Your Honor, we could be overlooking something here."

Purdy snorted. The judge shot him a look. "Go ahead, Ms. Cresswell."

"Judge, the witness has been accused of sexual assault on a minor female—"

"Those charges were dropped!" Purdy exploded. "The ink wasn't even dry before the family called the police and—"

"Counselor!" the judge barked, and I remember being impressed at how suddenly, how immediately, Purdy shut up and shut down. "In my courtroom *and* in my chambers, both sides get a chance to talk. Now shut up and let Ms. Cresswell finish."

"Thank you, Your Honor," Ms. Cresswell said. "As I was saying: The charges were dropped, but could certainly be reinstated on the basis of something in the witness's testimony. Or, should the charges be refiled at a future date, the witness's testimony could be used against him."

"Oh, for—!" Purdy couldn't help himself, but he stopped as the judge shot him another look.

"Well, Ms. Cresswell, that's an interesting approach. But my understanding is that the parents of the girl in question have no interest in pursuing the case. Isn't that true, Mr. Purdy?"

"In fact," Purdy said triumphantly, "they're on the witness list for the prosecution." He paused long enough to look down at Ms. Cresswell. "A fact the defense is *well* aware of."

This didn't faze Ms. Cresswell in the least. "Your Honor, the parents' current wishes are immaterial. The fact remains that charges could be refiled at any time within the statute of limitations. The parents could change their minds down the road. In that case, the witness has the right to protect himself."

"The only thing he needs protection from is your client!" Mom yelled all of a sudden.

"Mrs. Mendel, please!" The judge looked pained. "Please, we need to remain civil. I know this is stressful for everyone." He sighed and massaged his temples with the tips of his fingers. "The only way out that I see is if the People are willing to grant immunity to Mr. Mendel on the assault charge. Are you willing to do that, Mr. Purdy?"

Purdy hesitated. "I'd have to talk to the girl's parents."

"Do so. We're adjourned until tomorrow morning."

I had no idea what had happened. I just knew that I was— for the rest of the day, at least—off the hook.

As we all got up to go, in that momentary confusion of chairs and throat-clearing, I looked over at Eve. She was, for the first time, looking at me, her eyes moist and wide. She smiled sadly and pursed her lips for just a moment, blowing me a kiss.

And then it was over, back to reality, out the door, back to the world.

THE NEXT DAY, before the judge called the jury in, he asked, "Mr. Purdy, has there been any movement on the issue discussed in chambers yesterday?"

Purdy stood up. "Yes, Your Honor. The People have extended immunity to Josh Mendel with regards to the events of March eighteen of this year."

That was Rachel's birthday. It took me a second to realize what had just happened, but then Mom put her arm around my shoulder and squeezed me tight and whispered "Thank God," and I knew that I was in trouble. They would never prosecute me for attacking Rachel. Which meant that I had to testify.

I returned to the witness stand. Purdy once again held the card up before me. "Let's pick up where we left off yesterday, Josh: Who gave you this card for your birthday?"

I looked over at the defense table. For the first time, Eve wasn't looking down at her hands—she was looking straight at me and there was fear in her eyes. No, more than fear—terror, dread. The kinds of fear that make you bite through your own lip.

"Do you need me to repeat the question, Josh?" Purdy noticed that I was looking at Eve, who was looking at me. He stepped to one side so that the jury could see it, too. "I'm sorry, Josh—are you being distracted by something?"

I wrenched my gaze from Eve and settled on Purdy. Bastard! I knew what he was doing. Trying to make it look like . . . I knew what he was doing.

"The card, Josh." He slapped it down in front of me. "Who gave it to you?"

I gritted my teeth. "I plead the Fifth," I said, loud and clear.

"Your Honor!" Purdy exploded, spinning toward the judge.

"Young man!" The judge twisted in his chair to face me. "We discussed this yesterday. You are *not* permitted to plead the Fifth in this case! If you do so again, I will hold you in contempt of court. I will fine your parents one thousand dollars. Now answer the question."

I wanted to spit in Purdy's eye. I wanted to kick the judge in the balls. It was no one's business! It was *my* card. They were *my* secrets. And no one had a right to them.

Purdy held up a pad of yellow paper. "Josh, do you recognize this?" He slapped it down in front of me, along with another one just like it. Both were covered in my own handwriting. My gut tightened. "Isn't this your handwriting, describing events of a sexual nature that took place between you and the defendant?"

"I plead the Fifth," I said again, louder this time. I avoided looking at Mom and Dad.

The judge banged his gavel. "The contempt order is issued, one thousand dollars to Mr. and Mrs. Mendel, payable by check to the clerk's office by the close of business." I stared straight ahead. The judge told me to look at him. "That's one strike, young man. You only get two in my courtroom. If you do not answer Mr. Purdy's question, I will have you remanded to a juvenile detention facility until you *do* answer the question, do you understand?"

Sweat—cold sweat—began to collect on my scalp and run down my neck. My palms were clammy and I closed my hands until my fingertips bit into them.

"Didn't you write on these legal pads in my presence and sign and date them?" Purdy asked, this time leaning in toward me, as if daring me to plead the Fifth.

Before I could answer, I heard something from behind Purdy. Everyone else heard it, too—they all turned to look at the defense table, where Eve and her attorney whispered ferociously at each other.

"Ms. Cresswell?" *Bang!* went the gavel. "Ms. Cresswell! Keep your client quiet or—"

Cresswell shot Eve a deadly look, but Eve shot back one just as deadly. Cresswell stood up. "Your Honor, I apologize. My client has just informed me that she wishes to change her plea."

Whispers of shock filled the courtroom. The judge slammed his gavel down three times before everyone quieted down. My heart jumped with each crack of the gavel. I stared at Eve. She smiled at me, a sad smile.

The judge had the jury taken out and called the lawyers and Eve to the bench. Everyone forgot about me—I could hear everything from the witness stand.

"I won't tolerate grandstanding, Ms. Cresswell."

"This isn't grandstanding, Your Honor. Against my advice, my client wishes to change her plea."

"Your Honor," Purdy complained, "to switch to an insanity plea at this stage is an obvious and blatant abuse of—"

"She's not switching to an insanity defense," Cresswell said quietly. And then the words that changed my life forever:

"She's pleading guilty."

MY COURTROOM EXPERIENCE ENDED almost as soon as it began. They no longer needed me to testify, because only one person would be testifying: Eve.

In exchange for some sentencing considerations, Eve agreed to "allocute," which I was told meant that she would stand up in open court and describe everything she'd done wrong. Which is how my entire life's sexual experience ended up on the Internet, couched in clipped, formal, sanitized language that made it seem as dirty and as evil as bleach water.

My parents wouldn't let me into court that day. Dad went because Mom said she didn't think she could handle hearing Eve talk about how she had molested me. When Dad came home, all he would tell Mom was "It's over. It's over, Jenna."

Mom cried in relief.

He was wrong, though. It wasn't over. It couldn't be over.

The therapy started almost immediately.

Other than sending me to Dr. Kennedy and taking a stab at some other forms of therapy, my parents didn't know how to deal with me in the first few months after the trial ended so suddenly. On the one hand, I was the victim. That's what everyone kept saying. They wanted, on some level, to coddle and protect me.

But on another level . . .

On another level, it enraged them that all of this had happened, that Eve had collided with our lives and that I hadn't done anything at all to help out with damage control.

I wasn't allowed to make or receive phone calls. I wasn't allowed out of the house unless it was with Mom or Dad or to go to school. And I had to come home right away. I couldn't tell if this was for my punishment, my protection, or for both.

My prospects of playing baseball were looking grim as the new season approached in eighth grade. I'd missed the entire seventh grade spring season and eighth grade Fall Ball. My fear of my parents' anger went to war with my panic at missing *another* season, and the panic won out, just barely.

I asked them if I would ever be allowed to stay after school for baseball practice, ever be allowed to play ball again at all. They looked at each other and Mom said, "We'll see," and that was that.

A few days later, they allowed me to go to baseball practice. The coaches and teachers watched me every minute I was on the field or on the bench. Mom told me that I was going to be watched, that I wasn't even to *think* about slipping away for even a single second. I was to tell my coach if I had to use the bathroom, and Coach would send someone to go with me, as mortifying as that was.

I was under surveillance constantly. But at least I got to play baseball.

When I returned to school, I was still the Ignored Kid. Everyone walked around me, looked through me, pretended I wasn't there. Which was fine—I didn't want to talk to anyone anyway.

Things changed when a kid bumped into me in the hall one day.

I can't explain what happened. I had always been . . . quiet. Always mature and calm. But when that kid bumped into me, something broke deep inside. It was like I had a gyroscope inside my body that kept my balance, kept me on an even keel. And when he bumped into me, that gyroscope spun and tilted, trying to find the center of gravity between anger and acceptance . . . and failed. And broke forever.

I screamed and shoved him into a locker and punched him twice. Just twice. I remember that distinctly—once in the gut and once in the mouth. I didn't break anything, though I did bust his lip and cut my knuckles on his teeth.

He stood there, half ready to collapse, held up by the lockers, a look of fear and bewilderment in his eyes, his bloody mouth twisted into a shocked gape. And I felt a sense of relief and calm wash over me for just a second, a relief and a calm I hadn't felt in *months*, a tensionless bliss that hadn't existed since before I went to Eve's apartment. I wanted to hit him again and again and again, to keep that feeling alive, to pound the bliss in with my fists.

Some kids pulled me away from him. I earned my very first suspension and thereafter heard mutters that I was crazy, that Eve had made me nuts. Not just from students, either. Teachers, too. Some were sympathetic, murmuring that the "poor kid" was "dealing with what she did to him."

Others just looked at me, ever after, with worry. And angst. And fear.

◻ ◻ ◻ ◻

That year, I got into a lot of fights and beat the crap out of a lot of people. I probably should have been suspended much more than I actually was, but I did my best to fight outside of school and to tease events so that the other person ended up being the aggressor and provoker, letting me claim self-defense.

The truth is, I never particularly cared who I was fighting or even why.

I also took out my aggressions on the baseball. My batting average plummeted to .286 that year, with twenty-one at bats and a measly six hits; not bad for the majors, but pathetic against Little League pitching. My slugging average was an unbelievable .762. I wasn't hitting everything, but what I *did* hit never came back down to earth.

Other kids, older kids, baseballs—I was beating the hell out of them all.

One day, the world turned them all around and sent them back to me.

21

I WAS IN THE BACKYARD, practicing my swing. A big cherry tree grew right on the edge of our property in back, and I had climbed up to the low branches and tied a cord there, at the end of which dangled a ball. I had drilled through the ball and sunk an anchor in there to tie the cord to. It dangled just low enough to be in my strike zone.

The point wasn't to hit the ball *hard*, but just to get used to watching the ball and practice the form of my swing. I would push it out and it would come flying back more or less randomly and I would keep my stance, watch the ball, and swing away.

Zik's parents still wouldn't bring him over and my parents wouldn't let me go over there. And none of the kids in the neighborhood would even look at me (and I couldn't look at them), so this was the best way for me to practice. The only way, really.

It was getting dark and the world was getting quiet in that way that the world does when the sun starts to go down. The back porch lights were on, though, so I had plenty of light to see by, and I just kept whacking away at the ball, completely absorbed in it. I didn't want to go back into the house, where I would either listen to silence or to my parents arguing.

I didn't hear footfalls. I didn't hear anything until he said, "Hey."

I stopped swinging at the ball. I turned around.

"Hey," George Sherman said again.

I remembered the night before I'd gone to the police the first time, standing in the basement, needing to pee so badly as I waited for the phone to ring. I flickered and when I came out of it, George was saying, ". . . listen to me!" in a voice like a stone that's been heated until it hisses and sizzles.

"I'm listening." My voice cracked. It hadn't done that in months.

George's hands were clenching and unclenching in time with each other. His eyes were narrow and red. "I can't believe what you did to me. You ruined my life. Do you even know that?"

I flickered again. Eve's leg, cocked—

"Answer me!" George took a step closer to me, and even though I had a baseball bat, I was suddenly terrified. He seemed like a giant, so much taller than me. All I could think of was the Xbox games we'd played together. I was seized by a vast, almost uncontrollable urge to ask him whether he'd ever beaten the game with the dinosaurs.

"*Say* something! You fucking ruined my life! Why did you do that? Why did you have to do that?" A tear slipped down his cheek.

"I'm sorry," I said. My voice shook and cracked again.

"Sorry?" he exploded. "Sorry?"

I flickered. I was in Eve's bed for a single, glorious instant. And then the baseball bat was in the air, jerked from my grasp, spinning as it tumbled, then dropped to the ground ten feet away. I watched it land.

And George started hitting me.

He was taller than I was. Stronger. He wasn't in good shape—all those days and nights of video games and nothing else—but he was a man and I was a boy. I tried to protect myself, throwing my hands up between us, trying to block his blows. He backed me up against the tree—my head smacked into it, hard, and the next thing I knew I was down on the ground and George was crouched over me, his face a twisted mask of rage, pounding me again and again and again.

I imagine that he could have beat me to death right there under the cherry tree in my own backyard if only he could have managed to keep his mouth shut.

But instead, he couldn't seem to stop screaming, bawling at the top of his lungs, as if it wasn't enough to hurt me with his fists—he had to batter my mind with words, too. "You little fucking perv! This is your fault! You ruined my marriage! You fucking piece of shit!"

I heard something above his cries. One of my eyes was already swelling shut, but through the other I could see Dad only a few yards away, the back door standing open. He must have heard the commotion from inside.

I wanted to yell out, *Dad! Help!*, but I couldn't catch my breath. Dad stood there for a second, frozen, as George kept hitting me, popping my nose. Blood ran down my face.

And then Dad finally moved, tackling George off me. They struggled together as I lay no more than a foot away, dazed, battered, staring up at the darkening sky through the branches of the cherry tree. George's words rang in my ears, echoing over and over. *Your fault. Fucking perv. Piece of shit.*

Mom was there suddenly. "I called the police!" she yelled. "I already called 911!"

George and Dad stopped wrestling. Dad got up first, watching George carefully as he used the tree to support his way to his feet. Mom came over to me, cradling my head in her lap. "Oh, God. Oh, Josh, don't worry. They're sending an ambulance, too. Don't worry. They're coming."

My nose was bleeding. My mouth was bleeding. Both eyes felt puffy and swollen. My stomach and chest ached.

George heaved his breath, glaring at me from under the tree. Dad stepped closer to me.

"You maniac!" Mom yelled, holding me tighter. "You're an adult! He's just a child!"

George's fists tightened again. Dad took a step closer. I thought it was all going to kick off one more time.

"He fucked my wife!" George wailed. "He ruined my life!"

"Your wife was a goddamn whore!" Mom screamed, and to this day, the most shocking thing about that evening to me was hearing my mother say such a thing in my presence. "You should be beating up your wife, not my son! He's a *child!* She abused him! He's *innocent!*"

George stared at her like she'd just told him the earth is flat and she had proof. "Oh, really?" he said. "Is that what you think? Really?" He reached into his pocket. Mom shrieked and Dad jerked forward.

But he wasn't pulling a gun out of his pocket. It was a cell phone.

I recognized it. My parents couldn't, but I did. It was Eve's.

George flipped it open and dialed a number, then pressed another key to turn on the speakerphone. We all heard a voice start to ask for a password. George interrupted it by punching in the number.

A second later, my voice came out of the cell phone, loud and clear:

"Hi, it's Josh." Mom looked down at me in shock. "I can't wait for two Saturdays from now," I went on from the past.

After a brief pause, my voice continued: "I love you."

Those words. The words on Eve's card. The words I spoke to her on the phone. The words my mother said I couldn't understand.

"Innocent, huh?" George said, and cried like a baby.

A second later, sirens sounded in the air.

I made my third return to school a couple of days later, owner of a puffy lip, a swollen jaw, and a black eye. Two fingers on my left hand were broken—I wouldn't be playing baseball for a while.

No one knew what to make of me, and I didn't blame anybody. *I* didn't know what to make of me.

Dr. Kennedy told me over and over that the fight was George's fault.

I knew that.

He told me George was angry at Eve and taking it out on me.

I knew that, too.

Mom and Dad told me the same things. So did the school guidance counselor and the school district psychologist they sent to talk to me.

I knew all of it. I was tired of hearing it.

One thing they never told me, though . . .

No one ever said, *He was wrong, Josh. You're not a little fucking perv.*

Other than Zik, no one talked to me. If someone brushed up against me or bumped into me, I would just glare murder until I got an apology.

And that was it. Because I didn't want to be fucked with anymore. From then on, everyone was just better off pretending I didn't exist.

Fielder's Choice

CHAPTER 19
Distance

I WAKE UP TO CONFUSION—the bed's strange and thin, and there's someone next to me.

It takes a second for it all to click: the hotel. Rachel.

Rachel sits up next to me, pulling the open ends of her top together with one hand, whether from sudden modesty or simple reflex I can't say.

In fact, I can't say much of anything. I don't know what to say to her. I can barely look at her. I'm a eunuch in bed with a woman.

No, I'm worse than a eunuch. Eunuchs have an excuse for not performing. I don't.

"Morning," she says, using her free hand to pat down her hair, which is sticking up in every direction.

"I guess I'll, uh, get a shower . . ."

She's just about off the bed when Zik bursts through the door from the bedroom in his boxer shorts, shouting, "Firsties!" as he dashes into the bathroom.

Michelle sweeps into the room in satin pajamas and a matching robe, elegant and sexy, her makeup perfect, as if she didn't just spend the night as a willing victim of the Zik-love.

She flounces down on the bed next to Rachel, noting the

unbuttoned top. "So, how'd it go last night?" It's like I'm not even here.

How did it go last night? I can think of plenty of ways to describe it: *Pathetic. Embarrassing. Mortifying. Uneventful.* Or: *I don't know, Michelle, what's the word for holding your boyfriend on prom night while he practically cries over his last fling?*

"It was great," Rachel says, saving my sanity and the remaining tatters of my reputation in one fell swoop. I'm sure she'll give Michelle the real scoop once I'm not around.

Rachel and I get dropped off at my house, where her car awaits. She hugs me, but it's strained. I want so badly to kiss her, but I don't think I'm allowed. I don't know. I settle for the hug and then, unable to resist, I kiss her on the cheek.

"Thanks for listening," I tell her, because there's nothing else to say, at least not while Zik and Michelle are still around.

"We have a lot to talk about," she says, and then has to leave for an afternoon shift at the Narc.

Yeah. Yeah, we do.

Mom's car is missing. It's too early for her to be out shopping, and even my mom doesn't work on Sundays. She must have stayed out all night with her girlfriends.

The digital camera is sitting on the kitchen table. I flick it on and scroll through the pictures of Rachel and me. Smiling. God, I'm actually *smiling,* and it doesn't seem forced or fake! How could I have felt so good? Didn't I know what was coming?

Unreal. I'm feeling nostalgic for something that happened less than twenty-four hours ago. This has got to be a record.

Rachel's season is over, so she comes to practice Monday to watch Zik and me get ready for the Heat. She sits in the stands with Michelle and the two of them shout out obscene versions of our cheerleaders' usual chants, much to the amusement of the team. Coach, who probably lusts after Michelle as much as any other red-blooded American male, pretends he can't understand what they're saying.

Rachel and I still haven't talked since yesterday. I don't know what I would say.

"You gonna be ready, Mendel?" Coach asks me every three point two seconds.

"Yeah, Coach. I'm gonna be ready."

"I don't care about going to State," he reminds me. "I don't care about winning the championship. All I care about is that scout in the crowd on Wednesday, you got it?"

"Can you go over it one more time, Coach? I think somewhere between the fifth and sixth hundredth time you mentioned it, I got confused."

Coach turns purple. "Get your ass out there and do ten laps on the field, Mendel. You need it."

I shrug and do the laps. Michelle and Rachel cheer my laps as if I were a long-distance Olympic runner.

My laps keep me on the field longer than everyone else, so by the time I hit the locker room, everyone else is already out of the showers. Zik sees me and hoots and claps his hands until everyone's quiet.

"Ladies and gentlemen!" he shouts. "May I introduce to you the *savior* of the South Brook High Bobcats, the man who will put the Heat on ice, the man who will put Brookdale on the map . . ."

"Christ, Zik." Everyone's looking at me.

"Joshua 'Iron Man' Mendel!" He whistles through his teeth

in that loud, piercing redneck way he has and claps his hands. After a second everyone else joins in, hooting and hollering and applauding something I haven't even done yet.

"Speech! Speech!" Zik cries.

"You're an asshole."

"The man has a way with words!" Zik yells. "Two days from now," Zik goes on, even though no one's really listening anymore, "Josh 'I'm only half Jewish' Mendel will stand in the batter's box and wield a mighty Hebrew National against the *goy* Heat. We'll see who's stronger—Jesus or Moses. And let me tell you, it took some *mad skillz* to part the Red Sea, folks!"

I pummel Zik's shoulders and chest when I'm done in the shower. "You're a total dickhead. A total dickhead."

"I know! I know!" he says gleefully.

Outside, Michelle's waiting alone. "Rachel had to go to work," she says with the air of an appointment secretary, "but she says for you to call her when she's on her break, which will be around eleven." Then, with a disapproving glare: "You need to get a cell phone."

I'm exhausted by the time I get home. No one else is home, so I check the mail. In among the bills and junk mail and catalogs for Mom are three envelopes:

Stanford.

Yale.

MIT.

My heart *should* skip around, but it doesn't. It just keeps beating along reliably, as if my whole life hasn't just changed. Maybe it's because I'm too tired even to get stressed/excited/freaked out.

Dad gets home a little while later and finds me sitting at the kitchen table with the three envelopes spread out in front of me.

"Where's Mom?" I ask as he slides his briefcase onto the table.

"Had to work late. She'll be home later." He pauses. "What have you got there?"

"Stanford, MIT, Yale."

"Oh. You haven't opened them."

"Dad . . ." I point. "I don't *need* to open them."

He nods slowly. There's pain in his eyes. "Josh, look, your mother and I may not have explained this as well as we could, but money—"

"I know, Dad. Lawyers. My therapy. I know. Money's tight."

Dad sighs. "We'll try to do what we can. We—"

"I know." I gather up the envelopes and go to my bedroom, where I lay them out on my desk in alphabetical order.

I'm in at College Park. Full scholarship. Same thing at Lake Eliot. I was accepted to two other schools, both safety schools. Both affordable with decent math and decent baseball.

But don't I want more than just "decent"?

I sit at my desk, staring at the envelopes. Hours go by and Mom comes home. She comes into my room and stands behind me to hug me, her chin resting on the top of my head. It's like her boobs have become a neck brace for me. How the hell can she not be aware of it? How the hell can she *do* this? "We'll figure out something for college. Whatever we can."

I struggle a little bit, wriggling until she pulls away from me. "OK, Mom." But I don't know. I just don't know.

□ □ □ □

So at eleven, after my parents have gone to bed, I call Rachel on her cell. The three envelopes are still unopened on my desk, though now I've rearranged them: Stanford, Yale, MIT.

"You really have to get a cell," Rachel says. "This nonsense about your parents going to bed—"

"I got the envelopes today, Rache."

She doesn't say anything.

"From the Holy Trinity."

"Yeah, I figured that's what you meant. And?"

I take a deep breath.

"Don't drag it out, Josh. Tell me."

"I got into Stanford."

I can almost hear the calculations in her mind through the phone connection. Distance in miles. Distance in time. Distance in days and semesters.

"What about the others?" MIT and Yale are both a lot closer than Stanford.

"No."

"What does the letter say?"

"The letter?"

"The acceptance letter from Stanford. Read it to me."

"I haven't opened it yet."

"What? Josh! How the hell do you know that—"

"Rache, I got three envelopes today, OK? The ones from MIT and Yale are just regular business-size envelopes. The one from Stanford is a big eight by ten and heavy. Jeez! It's obvious!"

"Bring them here," she says quietly after a moment. "We'll open them together."

CHAPTER 20

3,000

AT THE FIELD at SAMMPark, we sit on a blanket from Rachel's trunk and open the two rejection letters first. They're amazingly similar. They're the only rejection letters I've gotten from colleges. MIT and Yale have decided that there's no space in their upcoming freshman classes for me.

I let Rachel open the letter from Stanford.

Dear Mr. Mendel:

I am pleased to extend to you . . .

She does well. She reads the whole letter loud and clear. Along with the letter is a bunch of brochures and a booklet on student life at Stanford. There's also a letter saying that my financial aid information has been received and is being evaluated. I should hear from the financial aid office within a week. And, of course, "the athletic department will contact you under separate cover as regards the status . . ." blah blah blah. As regards the status of Coach Kaltenbach's recommendation, that is.

"So, that's it," Rachel says, forcing a smile. "California bound." She hugs herself, even though it's not cold out.

"Not for sure. I mean, I might not get the scholarship. I might not be able to afford—"

"You'll be able to."

"Maybe. It all depends on fucking Kaltenbach."

"There's student loans."

"Yeah, I know. But they scare the hell out of me. I mean, to graduate from college and owe all that money right from the get-go?" And I don't know who I'm trying to convince, her or me. I don't know who I'm trying to reassure or what would *be* reassuring. Stanford has been, in so many respects, my dream school. An unbelievable math department and a baseball team that's good enough that I might not cut it. And let's not forget the reason I looked there in the first place: three thousand miles away from Brookdale.

Three thousand miles away from Rachel.

Three thousand is a funny number. You get three thousand hits in baseball and you're instantly a member of an elite club. Only twenty-six ballplayers have done it in history. Cal Ripken hit 3,184 in his career. Roberto Clemente hit *exactly* 3,000 in 9,454 at bats. Wade Boggs was the only 3,000 hitter to hit a home run for his three-thousandth.

I think of these things because I can't help it, because I *always* think of these things, because it's infinitely easier than thinking of the other things that are crowding my brain and clamoring for attention right now. Money problems and Rachel and Zik and being here . . .

Pete Rose has the best hit total in all of baseball: 4,256. That's superhuman, godlike, and he'll never get into the Hall of Fame because he was a dumb jackass and he gambled on baseball.

Is that how it works, in the end? You make one mistake early on and it haunts you for the rest of your life?

Rachel comes closer to me. "Josh, talk to me. Come on. Say something."

And I say the thing I've been thinking deep down, somewhere in the lizard part of the brain, the thing I've been thinking and dreading for weeks now, ever since Rachel first called me her boyfriend, really.

"Maybe I could . . ." I swallow. "Maybe I could go to College Park instead. I'd definitely get to play ball there, and their math program is decent. Maybe I don't have to decide between baseball and math. Stanford's not gonna give me the money. Coach is gonna screw me over. I know it."

"You *don't* know that. You shouldn't give up on that yet."

"Well, it's just that . . . you know, that way I'd be near Zik. And you." I look at her with all the earnestness I can muster. It's the closest I can come right now to answering her "I love you" from prom night. Staying here, so close to Brookdale, where everyone will still know me. But for her. I could do it. I *would* do it.

It's a tender moment. Rachel grimaces and stands up, throwing the Stanford papers at me. "You piece of shit."

Huh?

She looms over me. "Don't put this on me, Josh! Don't throw away your dreams and your future just to stick around here with me! God!"

"But . . . but, Rache, I thought that—"

"You didn't think at all. You idiot. If you miss out on the chance to go to Stanford just for me, I'll kick your ass. I'll never speak to you again. Worse than that, I'll tell everyone I struck you out."

As usual, I don't know what to say.

"Look." She sits next to me again and gathers up the papers that she scattered. "Here's my proposal: If your parents really can't afford it, if the money doesn't come through, then fine. You go to College Park and I go to College Park and we're right next to each other. But don't make plans until you know everything. Stanford's your dream, right? Don't give it up. Not for me. I don't deserve to carry all that guilt around."

I nod and let her kiss me. We suck face for a little while until we hit the edge of my comfort level and she backs off as though she's getting used to it.

CHAPTER 21

Even Cal Ripken Sat Down

IN THE MORNING, I haul myself out of bed, groggy and stupefied and bleary-eyed. These late nights are going to kill me, bit by bit, minute by minute.

Classes are a formality at this point—I know which colleges I'm in and which ones I'm not in, and the odds of my grades deteriorating to the point that anyone would change their minds at this point are precisely zero. But I can't help myself. I can't just slack off and get B's. I've been Iron Man too long—I kill myself for these last A's like I killed myself for the hundred or so that came before.

At home, Dad goes over the financial aid papers with me one more time.

"Stanford is doable," he says. "An athletic scholarship will make it work. Otherwise, you'd have to take out loans. Get a job, probably, at least a few hours a week."

"And what if I go to Stanford and break my leg in the first week and lose my scholarship?"

Dad sighs as if he was hoping I wouldn't think of that. "Everything's a risk, Josh. There are no guarantees. It's your decision. Your mother and I will help as much as we can, but that scholarship means no loans. You walk out at the end free and clear. I don't even see why it's a decision, honestly. You love baseball. This is a no-brainer."

I think about that all night. I lie on my bed and turn the options over and over in my mind. Every single one is like a floor laid with trapdoors that open into deadly pits. There's no clear-cut option. It's *not* a no-brainer, no matter how bad Dad wants it to be.

Because, yeah, I love baseball. But is it something I want to *have* to do? All my life, baseball has been something I did on *my* terms. And that's how I like it. Going to Stanford only seems like a no-brainer because it assumes I'm not using my brain at all. It assumes that I can play ball someone else's way, and keep at it for four years no matter what.

Or College Park, a free ride, where I'd be a big fish in a small baseball pond. But I'd be compromising baseball *and* math.

I guess that's what it comes down to: Which one am I willing to compromise? Which one means more to me?

Rachel calls just before Mom and Dad go to bed.

"I want to see you, but I know you're weak and pathetic and need your beauty sleep," she says. "So get some rest so that you can kill the Sledgehammers tomorrow, OK?"

But I lie awake, tossing and turning most of the night. Thinking of Zik. Thinking of Rachel. Thinking of college.

Thinking of Eve. Eve, who used to come to my Little League practices and games.

Eve, who's haunting me still.

And the day arrives: Last game of the season. South Brook Bobcats vs. the Canterstown Sledgehammers. Unreal.

"Where do you think you're going, Mendel?"

I'm halfway out to the field when Coach Kaltenbach stops me. I turn back to him in time to see Jerry Springfield trotting out to my "usual" position at shortstop.

"What the hell, Coach?"

"I don't want you out there yet. You could get hurt playing defense—you're back as DH."

Well, *that's* good news.

"But I'm not playing you for a couple of innings."

Which *isn't* good news.

"I want you to get a feel for this kid. Watch him from the sidelines for a little bit. Then we'll put you in and let you kick his ass all over town." Coach slaps a hand to my back and pulls me toward him like I'm a favorite nephew or something. "You're gonna make that scout shit in his pants, Mendel."

A plan that, I hate to admit, actually makes some sort of sense.

I get my first glimpse of the Heat soon enough, at the bottom of the first. The kid's a shrimp. If you saw him standing by the side of the road or huddled over a book in the library, you'd never in a million years think that this is the kid with the golden arm, the kid who makes hitters across the state weep with anxiety.

I watch him, checking his poise, his pose, his movements. It seems almost impossible that a frame so small could generate such powerful pitches, but the evidence is right in front of me.

At ninety miles an hour, it takes less than half a second for a ball to get from the mound to the plate. Your reaction time has to be shaved down to less than three-tenths of a second to have even the slightest chance of hitting the ball. That three-tenths has to comprise acquisition, assignment, adjustment, and action—the "quad-A cocktail" as my Little League coach used to put it.

Restraint is the name of the game. Ted Williams was probably the best batter in the history of the game, when you break batting down into all of its component parts. No one understood the mechanics of a bat and a ball like Williams. But he also knew when *not* to swing. The result? Twofold: Decades after he stopped playing the game and years after his death, Williams still holds the record for bases on balls, with a .208 walk average. And his career on-base percentage is a brain-numbing .483 in the majors. No one else is even close; the next closest guys are Babe Ruth at .474 and John McGraw at .466. That's not even in the same neighborhood as Williams.

Our first two guys strike out. Then Zik steps up to the plate, 29 for 75 on the season, with a .420 slugging average.

Zik spits into the dirt in front of home plate, his own little ritual. He digs in and grits his teeth, snarling at the Heat. Psychology. Baseball's all about psychology.

Zik swings at the first pitch. In retrospect (retrospect for a batter happens in the second after contact), he probably wishes he hadn't. He gets a piece of the ball, but that's all. It would have been a strike, but right now it's an out—the ball pops up and the first baseman jogs onto the grass to make an easy play.

Three up, three down. Seven pitches. I hate to admit it, but Coach was right to keep me out for now. I need to watch this kid.

I watch the first two innings go by. Canterstown scores four runs. In the bottom of the second, the Heat once again shuts us down 1-2-3, though our guys do manage to eke out a couple of foul tips and pop-ups. At least they're getting the bat on the ball.

I talk to the guys who come back from the plate and get their read on him. The kid's not human, and none of us has experience hitting against aliens or robots.

Here's the thing that gets me, too—he shows absolutely no emotion. No sneer when he fans you. No raised eyebrow when you let a good pitch go by. No concern if you pop up. He *isn't* human. It's like he's just a pitching machine. A flawless one.

Two innings is enough time for me to watch; our games are only seven innings, not nine. I usually bat as one of the first three in the rotation, but Coach has had to rejigger the lineup to accommodate Jerry Springfield at shortstop.

Pat Franklin strikes out, and then it's my turn.

No reaction from the Heat as I step into the batter's box in the third inning. He's just an impassive, immovable object. He doesn't care that the lineup's been shaken up a little bit. Doesn't care that there's an unknown factor standing in front of him. I'm just another target to him.

I go through my usual batting ritual—step out of the box, knock dirt off my left shoe with the bat, step forward, knock dirt off the other shoe, step into the box, turn my bat a quarter-turn in my hands. I tug my helmet's brim once, then push it back up into position.

I can hit the first pitch. I realize this in less time than it takes to think it, which is the only way *to* realize it. It's a fastball, emphasis on the *fast*, giving me less than a fifth of a second to

Acquire: recognize that the thing hurtling toward me
    at close to a hundred miles an hour is, in fact, a base-
    ball and not a trick of the light.

> Assign: determine the path the ball is taking and is most likely to continue taking.
>
> Adjust: determine when, how, and whether to swing.
>
> Act: I swing.

The bat vibrates in my hands and shakes my entire torso, shock waves radiating up my arms to my shoulders and across my back. The sound of the ball contacting the bat is deafening, a solid, whining *THWACK!* that rings and stings my ears. The ball spins like mad and drills over the Heat's left shoulder, sending him dodging to the right and throwing up his glove in a belated attempt to shield himself. I don't think anyone's ever taken one of his pitches right back to the mound before—that icy exterior cracks in an instant and for a split second there's just a terrified kid there.

I run like hell for first base, kicking up dust. No time to watch the ball; that's the mistake rookies make. You don't watch the ball. Not when you're heading to first. There's no point. You either make it or you don't.

And then I'm on the bag and then I'm off the bag, tearing out into right from sheer momentum, waiting to hear the ump cry, "Out!" but the cry doesn't come.

I made it.

I turn around, breathing hard, and jog back to the bag. The Brookdale crowd is going insanely wild, as if I've just hit a grand slam in the World Series or something. It's just a base hit, people. It means nothing unless we put a string of them together.

The Heat gives me a dirty look over his shoulder as Chris

Weintraub steps into the batter's box. Just a dart of *You prick*, but it's there and I love it. I rattled him. Psychology.

With one hit, my season average goes from .550 to .557! My on-base percentage goes to .625, my slugging average to 1.082.

Chris takes two strikes and a ball before swinging at an absolutely beautiful slider. It should be strike three, but someone is looking out for him and he catches a piece of the ball with the top of the bat and pops it up to deep left. No one's there because we haven't hit deep all day. I'm a couple of steps toward second, but I tag up to be safe. The left fielder is running backwards, doing a damn good job keeping his balance. At the last possible second, he jumps sideways, his arm extended. The ball drops into his glove and he crashes to the ground . . .

And the ball pops out.

I run. I'm already on second by the time the fielder has found the ball and grabbed it. Chris is racing past first and headed to second right behind me, so the fielder has to waste another tenth of a second on an important decision—throw for second and the easier out, or get the man who's headed to third?

Ahead of me, the third baseman has stepped right into the base path, waving his glove, shouting for the ball. I shoulder-check him out of the way and throw myself down on the ground, my hand slapping the bag.

At almost the same moment, I hear the slap of the ball in the third baseman's glove. He tags me, but I've got my hand on the bag.

Chris is safe back on second and I'm trying to figure out the odds of someone actually sending me home with the Heat on the mound.

Now it's Ash Heggelman in the batter's box. He takes a strike, gets a piece of a breaking ball for strike two, then exercises rare good judgment and lets the next ball go by high and outside.

Ash manages to get a chunk of the next pitch and knock it down onto the ground, which looks like the absolute weakest bunt I've ever seen in my life.

And then Ash does something sort of amazing in its stupidity and even *more* amazing in the fact that it seems to work: He takes two steps toward first and *stops*.

He just stops right there and looks at the ball, which has rolled close to the foul line on the third base side.

I doubt it's intentional, but it's a great little piece of psychological trickery. The catcher, who had been headed for the ball, pauses for just a second. After all, Ash isn't moving, right? Maybe there was a call from the ump. Maybe the ball's still moving and could roll foul. Maybe—

Maybe a lot of things, but it doesn't matter, because I'm running pell-mell from third and I need that extra second. While the catcher's distracted looking over at Ash (who now is taking an additional, doubtful step toward first), I'm halfway home.

The catcher looks up just in time to see me coming. He dives for the ball and I deliberately run right into him, knocking him down. I keep going and I cross the plate and that's it. That's it. I'm home.

A second later, the catcher spins up on one knee and rifles the ball to first, where Ash has no chance and is called out five feet from the bag. The next guy pops up to center. Inning's over, but we scored.

□ □ □ □

Somehow, our defense keeps the Sledgehammers from scoring in the top of the fourth. It's not easy, though—they rock our pitcher from start to finish, taking him deep every time. They get three men on and strand them all.

Zik's up first in the bottom of the fourth. He does something amazing. He takes the Heat's first pitch of the inning and he hits a home run.

I can't believe what I've just seen. I keep blinking, as if there's something wrong with my eyesight and the ball will reappear if I just keep blinking.

The bench goes absolutely insane, hooting, hollering, stomping, shouting. The Brookdale crowd's berserk. And Zik takes a leisurely jog around the bases, blowing kisses to the fans as he goes.

I don't move from my seat. I watch the Heat. He doesn't seem too upset. Maybe it's because he's never lost. Maybe he can't even imagine such a possibility. I used to be like that, a long time ago, when I first started to get my batting chops and I was playing against pitchers who just weren't ready for a hitter of my caliber. Every time I stepped up to the plate, I hit the damn ball. Every freakin' time. It was *easy*. And when one day I *didn't* hit the ball, I figured it was a fluke, an accident, a goof. It never occurred to me that the pitchers were catching up, getting better. Not until I started getting struck out. *Then* it hit home.

Zik pauses in front of home plate, turning to observe his worshipful public. The crowd obliges his showmanship by going even wilder, a thunderous, endless stomp of feet on the bleachers that rattles my bones. Just step on the goddamn base, Zik. Stop showing off.

Batting average: .390. Slugging average shoots up to 1.078. And the Zik Lorenz IPA towers over the world at .688, higher than when he started the game. All on one pitch.

With a flourish and a bow, Zik finally goes home—he jumps up in the air and lands on the plate with both feet, as if crushing a huge rat.

The Heat stretches a little bit, then proceeds to strike out the next three batters with pitches that get progressively faster as he delivers them. The crowd shuts the hell up and you could hear a mouse fart in the sudden silence.

Top of the fifth goes pretty well for us, all things considered. We keep them to two men on base and while the last out is a tough one, we eventually get it. In the bottom of the fifth, as if in revenge for Zik's homer, the Heat shuts us out. I manage to get on base, but no one else can find the ball and I'm stranded there.

In the top of the sixth, the Sledghammers load the bases with their best batter coming up. I figure this is all she wrote, but we get lucky and he drills a line drive to Jerry at short, who plucks it out of the air lightning fast.

The Heat retakes the mound for the bottom of the sixth. Is he going to pitch the whole damn game? No relief?

He doesn't *need* relief, it turns out. His defense lets him down and allows Jerry Springfield to take first on an error before Zik pops up to center. In a moment of comedy we desperately need at this point, the catcher drops the ball on a third strike to let a second man on, but it doesn't matter. The Heat still manages to retire us in short order.

Our bench has gone as quiet as a funeral home. We're two runs down, but it might as well be a million against the Heat.

Entering the final inning, we kill ourselves to keep them scoreless again. Coming back from a two-run deficit against this kid is bad enough; we can't let Canterstown pull any further away.

Pat Franklin leads off for Brookdale in the bottom of the seventh. Unbelievably, he gets *walked*. The Heat's first and only walk of the game. Even machinery breaks down every now and then, I guess. The Heat looks at his pitching hand like it's broken or something. I could swear I see his lips move, as if he's scolding it.

So now it's my turn at the plate.

Coach grabs me and now our faces are inches apart. His eyes are wide with anger, desperation, fear. I can smell his sweat—stale, anxious. "This is *it*, you understand? You're a guaranteed hit. You're the tying run." He licks his lips and looks over his shoulder into the stands. That must be where the scout is sitting. I look, too, though I wouldn't recognize the scout if he bit me.

I shake Coach off me. The ump's going to call us for delay of game any second now. "I know how to fucking play baseball, Coach. OK?"

He snarls. "Pick it up, Mendel," he says, his voice low. *Pick it up.* It's his favorite phrase. The one he uses when he's serious, when he wants you to pay attention, when he figures you're not bothering to listen.

Pick it up, Mendel. You never slept with me, so I ain't about to take it easy on you!

I hustle to the batter's box. The ump gives me a look that says, *About time.*

"Batter up!" he cries.

Out of the box. Knock dirt off my left shoe with the bat. Forward. Knock my right shoe. Back into the box. Turn my bat a quarter-turn. Tug helmet brim down. Push it back up.

Ready.

The Heat shoots me a nasty grin. It says, *I've got a little something I've been saving for you, asshat.*

And he does. The first pitch isn't just fast—it's *invisible.* Even my eyes, trained to watch for the fastball, can't track it. There's just a white blur, a blink, and then the horrible sound of the ball slapping the catcher's glove leather. The catcher mutters, "Ow! Damn!" under his breath. I don't think anyone here has a radar gun, but I know that ball *had* to be traveling over a hundred miles an hour. It's not impossible—a bunch of guys have thrown heat over a hundred miles an hour: Ryan, Wohlers, Benitez, Jenks, Johnson . . .

The Heat goes into his wind-up. Breaking ball this time, I'm sure.

I'm right. He cuts the corner of the plate. I resist the urge to swing, reminding myself that Ted Williams was a great hitter *and* a great not-hitter.

The ump calls it a ball. I'm one and one.

The Heat brings his fastball again. Not sure what fraction of the speed of light this one is, but it's definitely slower than the first—not that that's saying much. But I think he did his shoulder in with that first one. That's why he went to the breaking ball for the second pitch.

I let this one go by. It looks a little outside to me, and I'm right—the ump calls it ball two.

The Heat winds up and hurls a burner at me. This time I *know* he's slowing down. I can *see* this one. I swing at it and foul it off for strike two. On the mound, the Heat looks a little worried for the first time.

Yeah, that's right. You better panic, you little piss-ant. Thought you could psych me out with that first pitch, huh? Get me freaked out and scared? Doesn't work, pal. I've been threatened by cops and judges. I've had an insane husband hold me down and beat the shit out of me. I'm not scared of some skinny kid from Texas, even if his arm does come straight from God himself.

I foul off the next pitch, too. Staying alive. I've got his range now. It's only a matter of time. And he knows it. He shakes off the first two pitches his catcher suggests before nodding to the third one.

Curve ball. A beautiful thing, snapping left at the last possible instant. I should let it go. I should let it be ball three, but I can't resist. I poke it over the third baseman's head and into foul territory. The count's still two and two.

On first base, Pat's dancing about six or seven feet away from the bag, ready to dart either way depending on what I do. How long can I string along the Heat until he delivers the pitch I want, the pitch I need? The pitch I can take over the fences, like Zik did, the pitch that ties the game.

Another pitch. This makes seven, the most pitches he's

thrown to any single hitter today. There's anger and frustration in it, and his shoulder's gonna regret it later, but it's a hot, fast one. I have no choice—I swing and get a piece of it, sending the ball spinning down the first base line on the foul side.

The Heat stomps his foot like a little kid who's been told to go to bed.

Pat cups his hands over his mouth: "That's it, Josh, baby! You got him! You got him! Send me home!"

Josh, baby? Pat barely even talks to me. Who the hell is he to call me "Josh, baby"?

Another pitch, and this one's almost too easy. It's a strike, but nothing I can take to the cleaners. Still, I have to swing at it, so I manage to foul it off behind the plate. Still alive.

"Bring me home, Josh!"

The crowd starts chanting "Bring him home! Bring him home!" Over on the Brookdale bench, the team's stomping in rhythm on the ground. Zik's on his feet, his eyes alight with joy. He's clapping his hands in time to everyone else, chanting along with them.

Everyone's
Looking
At
Me

New pitch. I foul it into the stands near third base, where a mad scramble ensues to grab it as it rolls around on the bleachers. He's slowing down, but he's not throwing anything I can shoot into a hole or over the wall. I have to be patient. Have to remember Ted Williams. You don't swing at *any* pitch. You swing at the ones you can hit.

Coach is practically peeing in his pants. He's hopping up

and down, ecstatic. Anyone who knows anything about base-ball knows at this point that I've got the Heat's number. That it's just a matter of time. Now it's me and the Heat. One of us will blink. One of us will screw up, because we're both human (yes, even the Heat), and when that happens, the other one will be forgotten. It's just a matter of odds as to which one of us breaks first. It's a matter of math.

I take a quick time-out to step out of the batter's box and catch my breath. Coach gestures frantically for me to stop stalling and get back in the box.

Pick it up, Mendel.

And I realize: it wasn't just desperation and anxiety in Coach's eyes and sweat—it was greed and lust, too. His whole life changes when I hit this ball, when we tie it up. The scout came to see the Heat blow us away and instead—even if we lose in extra innings—he sees a team that made the Heat work harder than he should have. A team run by Coach Kaltenbach. A team he'll watch from now on, including visits and dinners for Coach and press attention and—

I foul away another pitch.

—and I'm starting to wonder why the hell am I going to give him everything he wants? This guy has tormented me for my entire high school ball career. Why am I going to make his life easy? Do I really think he's gonna say anything good about me to Graves? There's nothing I can do about it, after all. Like Kaltenbach's really going to forget that I punched him, that I *humiliated* him in front of the entire team. Yeah, right.

Another pitch. Another foul ball. Coach is going insane. The entire bench is up and cheering for me, something they've never done at any other moment in my life. Zik is screaming himself hoarse, veins standing out in his neck. The whole field is alive, a single living, sonic *thing* that wraps around me.

At first base, Pat dances back and forth, ready to dash for second.

The Heat shakes off the catcher, then nods. I dig in. Turn my bat a quarter-turn in my grip.

The wind-up. Watching that left leg. It's straight as a base line. No breaking ball this time.

It's a perfect strike, or it *will* be, when it reaches the plate. A *laser* doesn't move in a line this straight.

It's going to cross right over the center of plate and right at my letters. Irresistible. Impossible not to swing at it.

And it's slow. Relatively speaking, of course. Slower than his other fastballs.

You have two-tenths of a second to react. Two-tenths of a second for the quad-A cocktail.

I do what I've trained my whole life to do. I watch the ball. I keep my eye on the ball. I never stop watching.

I watch it as it sails past me and lands in the catcher's mitt, a perfect and glorious strike three.

CHAPTER 22

Aftermath (The Worst Day)

WELL.

OK.

It didn't feel as good or as liberating as I thought it would.

For the first time in my life, I *let the ball go by.*

Wow. So *this* is what that feels like.

It's weird. I let down the team, but you know what? There are a million other times when I *didn't* let down the team, when I was right there for the team, when I saved the team's ass. We let each other down every day of our lives—all of us. Whether it's Dad freezing for those crucial seconds before jumping in to stop George Sherman from kicking the shit out of me, or whether it's me ignoring Rachel for five years because I let my own guilt overwhelm my common sense and judgment.

At least, that's what I tell myself in the moment it takes for the ump to call strike three. I don't feel much better about it, though.

The crowd, both benches, the players on the field—everyone catches their breath at the same moment. Then the Heat pumps his fist in the air as if he's just won the World Series, never mind that he's got two more outs to score before he can go home a winner.

The Brookdale crowd groans as one. On the Canterstown side, a cheer goes up.

I shrug and sling my bat over my shoulder as I amble back to the bench. Chris Weintraub walks past me, glaring at me as if I just goosed him.

"What was that, Mendel? What the fuck was *that*?" Coach hisses. He grabs me and pulls me to him as I near the bench. He doesn't care who can hear him—he just starts bawling me out in front of the team. And most of 'em look like they'd like to join him. "What the fuck were you thinking?"

I grab Kaltenbach by his shirt and pull him toward me.

"Fuck you, Coach," I whisper, just loud enough for him to hear. "You don't own me. You don't *control* me. *I'm* in charge, got it? *Got it?*"

I push him away from me and, trembling, make my way to the Gatorade. At the plate, Chris pops up to the second baseman. Two outs.

No one speaks. No one looks at me as I pour some Gatorade and chug it down. My heart's pounding and my stomach's a wreck.

Zik pushes past a couple of guys to catch up to me. "What the hell did you *do*, J? You could have hit that one!"

I can't look at him. I just can't.

"Tell me you couldn't." He's pleading. He grabs my sleeve and tugs. "Come on, man. Tell me you couldn't have hit it. Tell me you didn't just—"

A cry goes up from the crowd at the same time as a cheer: Ash Heggelman just line-drived to first. The game's over.

"Oh, Christ," Zik says, looking over at the field as the

Sledgehammers jump all over each other in celebration. "Christ, man! This was *it!*"

I can't bear to tell Zik that I could have hit the ball. I drink my Gatorade.

"You ruined it!" He's near tears. I can't believe he cares *this* much about the stupid game. He hit a home run, for Christ's sake! He ought to be happy about that.

"You ruined it all!" And he shoves me once, then spins and runs away from me, from everyone.

The rest of the team files past me without looking, heading for the locker room. I realize that this is the end of my high school career. My final career numbers are a .502 batting average, an on-base percentage of .575, a slugging average of .876, and a .373 IPA. Can't be too upset with those numbers. And if Stanford's Graves is too afraid of me because of what Coach tells him or doesn't want me because I don't play defense . . . Well, fine.

But I'll always keep a mental asterisk next to those numbers because I know that, yeah, I could have hit that ball. I could have knocked it out of the park.

The locker room is . . . uncomfortable, to say the least. The place falls silent as I walk in, the last player to do so. Guys in towels, guys in the shower, guys getting dressed—they all stop whatever they're doing, whatever they're saying, and stare at me.

They don't know for sure. They *can't* know for sure. But they're pretty damn sure that I could have hit that pitch.

I don't say anything. I don't change or shower. I just grab

my stuff from my locker and head back outside, all of those eyes pushing and pressing at my back as I go.

Rachel's waiting outside. She knows, better than anyone, maybe even better than Zik, that I could have hit that ball. And she can't understand why I didn't.

The hell of it is, I'm not sure I can explain it to her.

She hugs herself as if cold. "Josh."

"Yeah?"

She exhales, blowing her bangs around. "Nothing."

"Go ahead, Rache. Ask. Ask me." And I want her to. I'm angry. Not at her, but she's the only one around, the only one who'll talk to me, so there you go—she gets to be the recipient.

But she shakes her head. "Michelle's going to drive Zik to school for the next week or so."

A "week or so" takes us right up to graduation. "So that's it, then. End of the Four Musketeers? Again. I'm sure you'll be very happy with Zik and Michelle." I push past her and head for my car.

"Hey! Hey, asshole!" she yells, chasing after me. She's fast and unencumbered—it's no great feat for her to catch me. I don't stop walking.

She falls in beside me. "Stop being a dick, Josh. This isn't Michelle and Zik and me against you."

"Oh?"

"Zik's not going to Stanford," Rachel says. She takes my hands and gently turns me from the car, forcing me to look into her eyes. "No matter what school he goes to, it's going to be half an hour from here. He won't even live on campus—he'll have to commute. But if he could get into the league . . ."

I pull my hands back. "It's not my fault, Rache. I can't be responsible for everyone."

"No one's asking you to be."

"But everyone wants to know why I didn't hit that ball, don't they?"

She says nothing.

"Everyone wants to know. Everyone wants to know why Josh didn't take the South Brook Bobcats up on his shoulders one more time and run past the finish line, don't they? Well, tough shit. I'm through explaining myself."

She says something so quietly that I don't quite catch it. "What?" She shakes her head. "Come on, Rache. Tell me. What did you say?"

She shakes her hair out of her face and looks me dead in the eye. "I said that you're through explaining yourself because you've never been *able* to explain yourself in the first place."

Now I'm the one who says nothing. Because I'm afraid of what I might say.

"You'd rather wallow in your own guilt than figure out *why* you feel guilty, Josh. You'd rather assume everyone hates you or fears you than come right out and ask them and find out for sure. You can't handle confrontation. At *all*. You can't even—" She breaks off and chokes, looks away. She hugs herself and can't look up at me. "You can't even . . ." she whispers, ". . . can't even touch me without hating yourself. And me."

A flicker hits me, strong and powerful: I'm in Eve's apartment, staring at her wedding photo.

And then I'm back. I don't know which is worse—Rachel being wrong or Rachel being right.

I've found my keys. "Goodbye, Rachel."

I leave her there in the parking lot, her arms wrapped around herself, staring down at the pavement.

I park in the driveway and sit in the car for a minute or so, taking deep breaths and telling myself that I wasn't out of line with Rachel, that I didn't do anything wrong. I'm not sure I believe it, but I say it to myself enough that it starts to sound OK.

The house is quiet. I close the door slowly and silently, looking forward to . . . I don't know. Lying in a dark, quiet room. By myself.

Mom and Dad don't even ask how the game went. Maybe they've forgotten about it. I don't know. Just to make the day absolutely perfect, they sit me down and—

We wanted to wait until you went off to college, but we felt that we had to . . .

—tell me that they're getting divorced.

I sort of sit there in shock. I don't know why—the writing's been on the wall for a million years. It shouldn't be that big a—

—and you should know that I've been—

And it gets better.

Mom's moving out next week.

Because.

Jesus.

Because she's been . . . "seeing someone."

"Seeing someone." That is, having an affair.

I should have guessed. I should have *known*. All those "trips to the mall." With "the girls." God, lies like Eve and I used to tell. I should have *known*.

"I can't believe you two."

"Josh," Mom says, "I know you're upset, but—"

"Shut your fucking mouth," I say to my mother, calmly, like I say it all the time, and I can't believe I've said it, but I have, and I can't believe that she actually *does*, but she does, and she and Dad just sit there, shocked and silent and watching me like I could explode like a suicide bomber, and you know what? I probably could. I probably could.

"I thought you . . ." I stop. The calm has all run out of me—it's all gone now, and all that's left is a cold flame of rage. "I thought you two loved each other! What the hell are you doing?"

"Sometimes—"

"Shut up, Dad! And you!" I turn to Mom, who's gone pale and frozen. "I told you I loved her!" I scream it and lean in and Mom jumps back, terrified, and I don't blame her. "I told you I loved her and you said that I didn't know what love was!" I'm crying now, but I don't care. "You guys made me tell the police everything. You ruined everything and what the hell do *you* know about love?"

Mom finds her voice. "Josh, please, honey—"

"Don't call me 'honey'! *She* called *me* 'honey'!"

And my vocabulary, my tongue, they just get overwhelmed and they can't keep up with my heart and my thoughts and my rage and I'm just blubbering, collapsing to the floor.

CHAPTER 23

The Abyss

I'M RUINED. It's in my blood—I'm broken. I'm fragmented. The flickers are proof of it. Who else goes through that? Zik can't escape his DNA . . . and neither can I. I'm the child of a cheater and a loser. What am I supposed to expect from myself?

It's late. I'm lying in bed, the phone unplugged, the door shut. I don't want to talk to anyone. I don't want to hear from anyone. What I really want, deep down, is to open my door and see nothing but a black void there, a deathless, endless abyss. And I'll know then that the world has gone away and that I'll never have to worry about it or puzzle over it or deal with it again.

Lying here, I've figured out what the flickers are. They're my punishment. It's no coincidence that they started that day that I stood in Eve's bedroom, taking my first steps toward her, toward my sin, my downfall. The flickers are my past, constantly reignited, hammering at me from below and beneath and behind.

I went to Eve. After the Happy Trio incident, she wanted to end it, but I begged her to take me back; I allowed it all to happen. I encouraged it all to happen. And I am damned for that. Eternally shattered, trapped in a world that is neither earth nor afterlife. I'm surrounded and penetrated by the ghosts of my own culpability.

I've kept a few secrets from Dr. Kennedy. Just a few. I've never told him about the flickers, for example. I've never told *anyone* about the flickers. I don't want to be hooked up to machines and pumped full of drugs while a million doctors try to figure out what the hell is wrong with me. I've just learned how to live with them.

It's late—almost ten o'clock. I sit up in bed, restless. The house is silent. I flirt with the fantasy that the abyss *is* right outside my door, but I know that it's not true. I'm not that lucky.

The combination of hours and my parents' revelation make the ballgame seem a million years away. I feel like a dick for the way I talked to Rachel. I want to plug the phone back in and call her, but she probably wouldn't answer if she saw my number on Caller ID.

Rachel's not the only one I need to talk to. There's Zik. It doesn't matter how much of a bonehead he is. Zik has been my truest, most steadfast friend, and has never, *ever* questioned me about Eve. He deserves everything I can give him and more. And I disappointed him without explaining why. Not that I really understand it myself.

I close my eyes. I see the ball sail by again. It's not a flicker—it's worse because I can control it.

I am not only broken; I am also a piece of shit.

I drive over to Zik's house. Lights are still on inside. I ring the doorbell and brace myself.

Mr. Lorenz opens the door. He sneers when he sees me, which means absolutely nothing. He sneers *every* time he sees me; it's possible Zik hasn't said anything to him about the game.

"Whattaya want?" Mr. Lorenz asks, as if I'm a Jehovah's Witness or a kid selling magazine subscriptions and not the guy who's been his son's best friend for a million years.

"Is Zik home?" Duh. Asswipe.

He shouts "IKE!" over his shoulder and then walks away, leaving the front door open. This is the Lorenz family version of an invitation to enter.

I carefully make my way down the hallway toward Zik's room. I say "carefully" because I once accidentally turned a corner in Zik's house and saw his mom in just her skirt and bra, a sight I'm not at all eager to revisit.

Zik's door is closed and loud music pumps from within. He once told me that he blares his music so that he has an excuse not to listen to the rest of his family.

I knock, but nothing happens.

I knock again.

"Go away!" Zik shouts from within. Maybe he knows it's me. Maybe he's in there with Michelle?

Nah. Not a chance. Zik never brings Michelle to his house. He's too embarrassed by his parents, and who can blame him?

I pound on the door. Zik shouts again for me to go away.

"Zik! It's me! Come on, man! Open up!"

I knock again and decide to hell with it. I open the door, praying that Zik isn't naked or jerking off or something.

He throws something at me as soon as I open the door. I duck and a copy of *The House of the Seven Gables* smacks into the door frame. Good thing it's a small book.

Zik stares at me from his bed, where he's sitting. "Thought you were my dad," he mumbles.

Zik's room is a testament to the Lorenz DNA and Zik's own strange mutation thereof: WWE posters, a naked pinup from *Playboy,* a Barry Bonds poster, and—weirdly—a giant chart of the periodic table of elements. I can barely hear myself think over the relentless thud of hip-hop bass.

"So."

"So," Zik says back to me.

"Can you turn down the music?"

He stares at me for long seconds, then, with an aggravated shrug, grabs the remote and mutes the stereo.

We watch each other for a while.

"My parents are getting divorced." I don't know why I say it. I guess it's safe. But it's strange to hear it in my voice, coming out of my mouth.

He sighs. He doesn't want to feel sympathy for me, but he can't help it. "That sucks."

"It gets worse. My mom was fucking around on my dad."

That gets his attention. His eyebrows shoot up and, in spite of himself, he leans forward a little bit. "No shit?"

I shake my head.

"How long?"

"Since around . . . since around the time I went to court."

Zik whistles. My head swims a little bit. There. Now it's real. I've told someone else. It's real.

"What are you gonna do?"

I shrug. "I don't know. Go to college. Get away."

"Must be nice," Zik says, his voice clogged with anger, pain.

"You'll get out of Brookdale, too . . ."

"I never *wanted* to get out of this town! I *like* it here." He's up in my face now and I take a step back in shock. He *what*?

"Zik. Dude." I lick my lips. The pain on his face is almost too much to take. I don't get it. "You always talked about getting *out* of this place."

He laughs, a single, short bark. "Yeah—*this place*." He gestures to encompass the entire house.

We stare at each other. I always thought . . . I always thought he hated Brookdale as much as I did. I always thought he wanted to run away like I did. I never knew . . .

"You never told me!" I complain.

"Well, there's plenty of shit you never told me, either!"

And it's true. It's *so* true. All those years of loving Zik because he never asked about Eve . . . I never realized, I never understood. It was his job as my best friend not to ask.

But it was *my* job as *his* best friend to tell him without being asked.

"God." I rub my eyes. I can't believe this.

"*You're* the one who's wanted to run away ever since the trial and the case and the newspaper stories started," he says. "That's all I've heard you talk about, is running away from here. But that's not gonna do it, J. Because you can run away from a place and from people, but you can't run away from what happened."

"I know." My voice a hush.

"Do you? Are you sure? Because you still look like you're running *away* from something, not *toward* something. Because you're afraid."

"*I'm* afraid? What about you? You've been with Michelle so long that you can't even—"

He comes right up to me, close enough to kiss, leaning in, his breath hissing. "I *love* Michelle. Don't forget that, asshole."

And here's the thing: I know that's true. I know Zik loves Michelle and Michelle loves Zik. Hell, I've seen it. But it's *high school.* It's not real love, or at least you can't be sure it's real love. Real love is messy and complicated and brutal. It's been *tested.* Zik and Michelle have never been tested by anything more than being separated by a couple of classes.

"You don't know—" I stop myself. *You don't know what it means to be in love,* I was going to say. But there was more. God, that wasn't from me. It was

—I told you I loved her—

It was Mom

—told you I loved her and you said that—

—You're a child—

I start shaking. I almost said it to Zik. Almost repeated what my mother said to me all those years ago, when she was telling me I couldn't love Eve. When she was getting ready to start cheating on her husband.

"Oh, Christ, Zik. I'm sorry. I'm sorry." It spills out of me and once it starts, I can't stop it, like with Rachel. I can't stand up; I use the wall for support, but it's no good. I start slipping, sliding down the wall, my hands scrabbling for purchase like a hamster digging in its cage, my vision fading. "I'm so sorry. I'm sorry . . ."

Zik grabs me under the arms and keeps me from collapsing. "Come on, J. You OK? You need me to call 911?"

He gets me over to the bed and helps me sit down. His lips are moving, but I'm not hearing him. I'm just hearing him say, "I *love* Michelle," and he does. He does; I know that's true. I know it like I know Rachel loves me. I know it's true. It's all true. Everything my mother told me was a lie. Everything. Everything I told *myself* was a lie. All my life, I've been waiting to be old enough, waiting to grow up and get away, imagining that it's only when you're *old enough* that you know what to do or how to do it or what's right and what's wrong.

But I *have* known something else all along. Something critical. My mother, the prosecutor, the reporters, Coach, Roland . . . All of them adults and all of them full of shit.

We *can* know what love is. It's adults who have forgotten, so they cling to their poor substitute and yell at kids who dare to live with real love. Pure love. Love without compromise or distraction. Hell, when you're a kid you've got all the energy and all the free time in the world. You'll never have the chance to devote more to love ever again in your life.

"I'm sorry I let that pitch go by." Tears stream down my face. If I could take it back, I would. If I could face the Heat again, I'd swallow my hatred for "the team" and for Kaltenbach. I'd smash that ball right down the Heat's throat for Zik.

And Zik is my best friend. He sits next to me on the bed and punches my shoulder hard, not cutting me any slack just because I'm crying. "We would have lost in extra innings," he says. Neither of us can know that, but it's a comforting fantasy.

"Zik, man, I'm sorry. I really am. I will *never* let you down again. You're my best friend in the world—"

"No, I'm not. Not any more."

It takes me a minute to realize what he's talking about. And when I do, it makes my heart feel like it's made out of pure sunlight.

CHAPTER 24

My Graduation Day, My Commencement

I DRIVE HOME, wishing I had a cell phone. Wishing, wishing, wishing.

The house is dark and it's past midnight. Rachel's off work by now and on her way home. I call her cell and get voice mail.

"Hey, Rache. Hey. It's, uh, it's Josh." That was stupid. Of course it's Josh. She knows my voice. She sees my number on her cell. "I wanted to apologize. Again. I'm, uh, I'm getting a little better at it, I think.

"Look, Rache, I have some stuff to work out. I hope you're still willing to talk to me when I'm done. If I can still talk, that is. I guess *that* didn't make much sense. Sorry—it's late, and you know how I'm such a baby about sleep.

"It's just that . . . There's some old business. I talked to Zik and there's shit going on with my parents and it made me realize some things. Some things that I never took care of, that I never finished. So I'm going to do it. I'll talk to you later."

After that masterpiece of description and explanation, I sit and stare at the phone and wonder if I should call her again. But I think I've reached my idiocy quotient for the rest of the year in a single day, so I decide to hold off.

Then I throw myself onto my bed and sleep.

For a few hours.

My dreams are many and horrifying and forgotten when I awake, which would normally be a good thing with such dreams, but not today. Today, their horror leaves me with a sense of pervasive dread, a terror that lingers just beyond conscious thought and recollection.

I think it's the fear that comes with having made a decision.

Mom has gone to work. In the kitchen, Dad's finishing up his breakfast. He looks at the clock. "You're going to be late to school."

"Not going in," I tell him. "I'm taking a mental health day."

He doesn't find it funny. He just nods gravely.

I can't just stand here and watch him finish his breakfast. Not now that I know. "Hey, Dad?"

He puts his dishes in the sink. "I really have to get going to work. We'll talk about it later, OK?"

"OK . . ." I watch him leave and I can't help wondering if what I'm seeing on the outside is what's on the inside, too. He can't possibly be so placid and accepting, can he?

But you know what? It's not for me to tell him how to deal with this, any more than it's for him to tell me how to deal with my own problems. I'm an adult now. It's time to stop running.

In my bedroom, I fire up the computer and use a search engine to find the state sex offenders database, which takes all of ten seconds. It's a simple, bland page with a state seal and some legal blurbage and a link to the database. It can't *possibly* be this easy.

I click through and get a page that lets me search by first

and last name or zip code or position in the education system. I know that Eve can't be a teacher anymore—she's forbidden. I type "Evelyn Sherman." There's a drop-down menu for the type of offense, but I'm not sure of the difference between "Child Sexual Offenders," "Sexually Violent Offenders," "Sexually Violent Predators," and plain old "Offenders."

And there it is. An address in Finn's Crossing, not forty-five minutes from here. She was never in Brookdale at all. God, all these weeks of freaking out every time I looked around . . .

There's a fuzzy, grainy picture of her, unsmiling, clearly taken in prison. It's a jolt to see her after all this time. I'm surprised that I feel nothing *but* the jolt. I expected more. But then again, the picture is so bad and so out of focus and so poorly lit that it's tough to tell that it's even her.

I print out the address and directions from Google, then go to the car.

It's a short drive. I think about Dr. Kennedy.

He always wants to know about my anger. Which is funny, because I rarely get angry around him. I rarely get upset at all. Days and weeks go by during which I get pissed off by things, and things bother me, but then when I go to see him, it doesn't seem like any of that stuff matters. I just relax in the comfortable chair and talk to him and I can't get worked up about most things. It's like I've spent all this time preparing a speech and when the time comes to deliver it . . . I realize I have nothing to say.

I think that drives him a little bit nuts. He must be able to sense the anger or something because he always asks about it. And I can never explain it to him.

One time he said, "Look, this is going to upset you, but I'm going to ask it anyway: Who are you angry at? Are you angry at Evelyn Sherman for abusing you or at yourself for letting it happen?"

The question didn't upset me. I hemmed and hawed and managed not to answer it. But he had hit the target. Actually, he'd hit the *back* of the target. Dead center, but wrong side, if that makes any sense.

I don't know if it *does* make any sense. I also don't particularly care anymore. I'm ending this. Today. Now.

The address from the website is for a rundown apartment complex in Finn's Crossing. It's on the opposite side of the town from where the Four Musketeers had dinner before prom, a billion years ago.

The parking lot's nearly empty. What if she's not home? It's early in the day. Wouldn't she be at work? *Does* she work? I don't know. I guess I'll find out.

Before I leave the car, I get my bat from the trunk. It feels heavy and lethal in my hands. I can do some serious damage with this, and not just to a baseball or a pitcher's ego.

Her apartment is on the third floor. I tell myself *not* to count the steps as I trot up them, but I can't help it: fifteen total. Meaningless number. It's not my age. It's no one's age I know. Fifteen . . .

I find the door: 3D. I stand in front of it, calm and at peace. I feel fine. I'm not flickering. I'm not shaking or nervous. I'm just . . . here. Just standing here with the weight of the bat and the bud of the doorbell in front of me.

I ring the bell.

Wait.

From within: "Hold on!"

My throat catches at the sound of her voice.

The door opens and . . .

And . . .

Ah. Ah, Jesus.

"Josh?"

I start shaking. I can't help it. She's still gorgeous and I realize how lucky I am—it's like I get to see her for the first time . . . a *second* time. Only this time I'm old enough and wise enough to appreciate it, unlike when I was a kid. She looks no older, no more worn, no worse for the wear of prison. Her hair is shorter, but those eyes are still eternal and luminous and endless.

She takes a step back. "Josh please no Josh don't please—"

The bat, I realize. I step into the apartment with her and she takes another tentative step backwards, fear radiating from every pore. I'm tight and hyperalert, my nostrils flared, my eyes darting everywhere. "Is George here?" I ask.

She stares at me.

"Is George here?" I'm close to shouting now. Not quite there, but knocking on its door and stomping on its welcome mat.

She's unable to stop staring at the bat. She shakes her head in tiny jerky motions.

It's like I've been wearing one of those heavy lead aprons you wear at the dentist's office when you get x-rays . . . and suddenly someone comes in and whisks it off. My breathing returns to normal—and I hadn't even realized how erratic it was until just now.

I lean the bat against the wall. Eve gulps loudly.

"Is it OK if I come in?" I ask.

"It's been a long time," she says, sitting down on the sofa across from me.

I recognize most of the furniture. The room, though, is smaller and dingier than in the old apartment. There are video-game machines hooked up to the TV, so I guess they're still married. I sit in the easy chair and have a brief, potent flicker of Eve and me in this chair together, the chair rocking back and forth, back and forth . . . Did she ever tell George? Does he sit in this chair, unknowing, unaware that he's sharing it with the ghost of his wife and her lover's lust? Does he know that I've made lo—*fucked* his wife on almost every piece of furniture I can see?

"Yes, it has," I say after too long a pause. She's gazing at me expectantly. He who brings the bat to the party gets to dictate the discussion, I guess.

But it's like going to Dr. Kennedy's. I suddenly have nothing to say.

We sit in silence for a few moments. She's wearing jeans and a lemon-colored tank top. I can see the outline of her bra. She looks hurried and distracted. She looks beautiful. The pull—the *lust*—that I feel at this moment is *destroying* me. It's more powerful and more potent and more *real* than anything I've ever felt around Rachel. And I know now, in this moment, that Eve has ruined me for any other woman. I'll never be able to be with anyone else.

"Josh, I don't want to upset you . . ."

Exactly like being with Dr. Kennedy.

". . . but there's a restraining order in place." She speaks slowly, choosing her words carefully. "I'm not supposed to be this close to you."

"You were *never* supposed to be this close to me," I say, and I have no idea why.

But it's like I've hit her with a Taser; she jerks and sits up straight, a wounded look on her face, in her eyes.

And then she bites her lip and looks up at the ceiling, and I realize what she's doing. She's counting to ten. Or reciting a poem in her head. Or doing calculus. Dr. Kennedy prescribed the same "medicine" for me: some sort of mental distraction that's supposed to calm me down when I get angry or hurt or upset. Looks like therapists all use the same bag of tricks.

She looks over at me. "I've had five years to think about what happened. About what I did. Five long—"

"What was it like? Prison."

She sighs and drags her palms along the tops of her thighs. I don't want her to sigh anymore. I can't stop staring at her and when her body heaves like that . . .

"It was prison, Josh. I don't know what you want to know. I worked. I taught women who never learned how to read or write. I get thank-you cards from them sometimes, now that they're on the outside. That's very . . . It's very rewarding for me." Her bottom lip quivers and she looks at me like I just called her a liar, even though I haven't said a word. "I like that, OK? I loved being a teacher. I really did. I love to teach people, to help people, and now . . ." Her breath hitches and she looks up at the ceiling again and she's got tears glimmering in the corners of her eyes.

I give her her moment to go through her mantra, whatever it is. I force myself to stare at her face, not at the hint of cleavage revealed by the tank top. I force myself to be good.

She wipes at the tears when she looks at me again. "What do you want to hear, Josh? I had to fight sometimes, OK? Is that what you want to hear?"

"Did anyone hurt you?" I mean to ask it like I care, with compassion, but it comes out flat and disinterested.

"Someone tried to stab me once. She was insane. They ended up putting her in a mental hospital. A fight broke out in the laundry room my second year there. I wasn't involved, but I got caught up in it and when the guards broke it up, they broke my left arm. I spent two days in the infirmary. I was—I was terrified until it healed. I was weak, see? I was defenseless without both arms. I thought someone..." She leans forward: more distracting cleavage, more distracting words. "I went to therapy every day for the first two years. Then three times a week, then twice a week... I still go every week." She gestures at the door. "I have to go today. That's why I'm not at work."

"Where do you work?"

"I do some proofreading for a law firm here. They have an arrangement with my parole officer. And I'm trying to get a position at the community college, teaching adult education courses." She waits, as if expecting me to say something. "Do you have any other questions, Josh?"

"You're still married." Not a question. But maybe just the hint of one.

"He was humiliated. He was—"

"He beat the hell out of me in my own backyard," I tell her, my voice tight.

She lowers her eyes. "I know. I'm so sorry. And he was, too. He really was. He told me . . . If it weren't for the restraining order, he would have . . . He wanted to tell you himself."

She shivers suddenly and I think it's an act, but I see goose bumps on her bare arms, as if the temperature has dropped twenty degrees. "Josh, I've had five years to think about this. I've waited all that time. And I thought I'd have to wait forever. I didn't think I'd ever be able to talk to you, not with your parents—"

"I'm eighteen now."

"I know. Please, let me tell you—"

"Why did you do it, Eve?"

She shivers some more and hugs herself, looking like Rachel for just the slightest moment. She rubs her arms, warming herself.

"Josh . . ." She can't look at me.

"Why, Eve?" My voice trembles. I try to force it steady, but I can't. My cheeks are wet and I wonder where the hell those tears came from. "Why, Eve? Why did you do it? Why?"

She's crying, too, great wracking sobs that shake her entire body and send streams down her face.

"Why, Eve? Goddamn it, I've been waiting forever to know. Why did you do it? *Why did you let me seduce you?*"

And time goes still.

For a little while.

My question hangs in the air between us, floats like some gossamer, luminescent cloud, drifting over the coffee table, obscuring and illuminating all at once.

I sniff and wipe my cheeks with the palm of my hand. Eve's

choking sobs stop with a single snuffle as she jerks upright and stares at me. "What?"

And now I can't stop the waterworks no matter how hard I try. The tears just explode out of me. "Why?" I practically scream it. "I ruined your marriage. I ruined your *life!*"

"I don't—I don't understand, Josh. That's not—"

And I tell her. About watching her as she slept, about those first steps taken toward her. About the wedding photo. About staring at her toes, her cleavage, her legs, her hips. About devouring her with my eyes a thousand times and a thousand ways. Everything I never told her before. Everything that was so critical, so important.

"You used to drink," I tell her. "Every day, we'd come to the apartment and you would drink and I took advantage of you . . ."

She stands up from her chair and comes halfway around the coffee table and I'm crying and willing her to come closer, yes, come closer even though it's all my fault, even though it shouldn't happen. She stops and just stands there, watching me with something like horror as I try to stop myself from crying, but I can't; it's hopeless. And here's your answer, Dr. Kennedy—here it is: me. I'm angry at *me.* But you had the *question* wrong—it's not what Eve did to me, it's what *I* did to *her.*

"Is that what you thought?" she whispers, still a few paces away. "Is that what you've been . . . Have you been carrying that around all these years? Oh, God, Josh, I'm so sorry . . ."

Hug me! I want to scream to her. *Come hold me, goddamn it! It's the only time I ever felt safe. The only time I ever felt loved, and even though it destroyed you, I want it again—I need it again now more than I need anything else in the world.*

"Josh, how could you think . . . You were a child! You were twelve years old! How can you possibly . . . Oh. Oh, my God." And she stumbles to her knees in front of me, and I burn with pain and lust at the familiar position juxtaposed to the unfamiliar emotions. "All these years you thought . . . you thought that it was *your* . . . your idea. Your fault . . . Oh, God."

I fumble in my pocket for the newspaper clipping. It's one I've read over and over. I have it memorized. "Then what about this?" I hold it out to her. She takes it. The headline reads:

Defense: Sherman Molestation "Sin of Opportunity"

The defense attorney for teacher Evelyn Sherman today told reporters in a press conference that her client acted on impulse when presented with an opportunity to act in a "sexually charged atmosphere."

"You see?" I tell her. "See what it says? The opportunity presented itself and you couldn't resist. That's what it—"

"No, Josh. No, no, no." As if she can change the world—can change *history*, can change *fact*—just by denying it. "This was . . . this was early in the trial. You hadn't testified yet. My lawyer did this. She was trying . . . I didn't want her to, but she was trying to lay the groundwork for a plea. This isn't real."

She looks up at me. I swoon, remembering her doing this years ago, looking up at me from her

—*Watch me*—

knees.

—*my hands and put them on her head*—

". . . was all *my* fault," she's saying as I blink back into the present. "I'm so sorry. It was wrong. I abused you. I'm so sorry. It wasn't your fault at all. It was all mine."

And I can only manage to say, "It was?"

"Didn't anyone ever tell you?" she yells, her frustration exploding from her. "Didn't anyone ever tell you that it *wasn't your fault?*"

I'm almost afraid to answer. But I have to. In a voice small and weak. "I didn't believe them."

"Oh, God," she moans, and puts her forehead on my knee and bawls like a newborn baby.

I want to touch her. Her forehead is like coals on my knee, burning me, like she's always burned me. Fire. She's a flame and she's always been a flame.

I hold out my hand over her hair and stop, pause an inch or so away and watch in fascination as my hand quakes in the air. I can't make it move down any farther. It won't obey me. It won't let me touch her.

"Then . . . then when?" I whisper.

She doesn't hear me. She keeps crying, shaking.

"Eve." Louder. "Eve, when?"

She lifts her head up and sits back on her heels. Her face is red, her eyes puffy and distorted and bloodshot. "When?" she asks.

"When did you *decide*? How far along did things get before you decided you were going to have sex with me, Eve?"

There's a thousand years before her answer:

"The day we met, Josh. The first time I laid eyes on you."

The first time . . . ? In class? In *history* class?

"There was no grad school project," she says. She won't look me in the eyes now—she looks down at her lap, where her hands are entwined. "I made it up—I made the whole thing up so I would have an excuse to bring you to my apartment and keep you there."

Oh, my God. What? She . . . Oh, God.

"I gave you wine. I treated you like an adult so that . . ." She sobs. "So that you would like me and want to stay . . ."

No. It's impossible. She didn't . . . She couldn't have . . .

She nods, as if she's heard something I can't hear. Meets my eyes again. "I think . . . I think you should go now. I don't think it's good for us to be together. I think it's bad for us to be together like this."

She's right. She's a thousand times right. I make my way up onto wobbly feet, swaying for a moment before I gain my balance. Without saying a word, I go to the door and pick up the bat propped against the wall.

I look back at her. Kneeling on the floor in front of the chair, her back to me. Shaking. She doesn't look over at me. I look at her and I feel . . .

I don't know.

I go outside. I force myself to close the door behind me.

Oh my God. Oh. My. God.

I was molested. When I was twelve. And everyone in the world knew it except for me.

CHAPTER 25

Joshua Makes a Decision

I SIT IN THE CAR for a while. I don't know how long. Seconds, years, centuries—they all whirl by and spin off like new galaxies uncoiling in the sudden heat/cool of the big bang.

I drive home.

It's not even noon, but I'm exhausted. I feel like I've been running laps all day, and all last night and all last week, for that matter. My brain won't work right.

I sleep.

I dream that I'm in a movie: Mom and Eve turn out to be twin sisters, the revelation made to a devastating drum sting and a blitzkrieg of strings and brass.

I wake up in a panic, wanting to scream, wanting to cry out for my mommy, aware as I think it that it's a grotesque sort of irony, but wanting to do it nonetheless.

I keep my mouth shut instead. I lie on my bed like a corpse in a casket.

Five years. Five years. What *were* these past five years? Who was I? *What* was I? Nothing as I thought it was. Nothing as it seemed.

Maybe Rachel was right all along. Maybe the past is past, history is history, and you just push it aside and look to the future...

Is that even possible? Do people really do that?

The acceptance letters and packets are on my desk. I look through them. A multitude of options. I used to think it was a curse, having so many options, so many possible end-games for each decision. But the truth is, it's a *blessing*. I *have* these options.

It's not an easy choice, but that's OK. Easy doesn't equal good. Difficult doesn't equal bad.

It's just life, is all.

So Dad's in his study and Mom's eating by herself in the kitchen and I'm in my bedroom, and in a house of three people no one's talking, no one's saying anything, because no one has decided anything.

Except for me. I've decided.

I call Rachel on her cell phone and get her voice mail. I leave her a message and then I ask my parents to join me in the family room. They sit on opposite ends of the couch, as far from each other as possible.

"I've been thinking about college," I tell them.

Midnight comes and I'm wide awake, sitting on the hood of my car and looking up at the stars from the parking lot at SAMMPark when Rachel pulls up and parks beside me. I watch her get out of the car, dressed in just a plain green T-shirt and gray shorts. Her hair's a mess and she doesn't have any makeup on at all.

God, she's beautiful.

"Got your message," she says, walking over to me. "Tried to call you a couple of times when I was on break, but your parents said you were out, and then it got too late to call."

"Sorry."

"You've *got* to get a cell phone."

That's not going to happen anytime soon, but I nod to her anyway. "Look, I'm sorry. About yesterday."

The ever-popular "pregnant pause" rears its ugly head between us.

"I'm *really* sorry," I tell her. "I said some shit that was uncalled for. I shouldn't have. You've been nothing but cool with me and I don't even deserve it. So I'm sorry. And if you want to walk away, that's fine, but I wanted to bring you here because I have a surprise for you."

She arches her eyebrow. "How can I turn that down?"

I bow and gesture into SAMMPark. "After you, madam."

She fakes a curtsy and we're off. "This isn't the part where you kill me with a hatchet, is it?"

"No."

She stops near the statue. "Hey, Josh, I'm enjoying breaking your balls, but about what *I* said yesterday—"

I hold up a hand to stop her. "You don't need to apologize, Rache. Everything you said was dead on."

"I'm not so sure about that."

"I am." I look over at the statue. "I never even looked at it twice until you pointed it out to me. Did you ever notice the dates?"

She squints at them. "Yeah. She was young."

"She was only nineteen."

"Not much older than us."

"'Gather ye rosebuds while ye may . . .'"

"Keats? Yeats?" Rachel frowns. She doesn't have my weirdly eidetic memory.

"Herrick."

"Oh."

We walk to the baseball diamond. Halfway there, she takes my hand.

Once there, I make her stand on the mound with her back to the plate. "This is when the hatchet comes out, right?"

"Stop it!" I yell back to her as I race over to the bushes behind the backstop. It's only been half an hour—at this time of night, the odds of anyone being here, much less stumbling upon my hidden stash, are pretty remote.

I drag the big cooler and the bundle of blankets and pillows stuffed into a trash bag from out of the bushes. I position everything in front of home plate and go to get Rachel. "Keep your eyes closed."

I hold one of her hands and use my other around her waist to guide her. She keeps her free hand over her eyes and giggles.

I stop near the plate and tell her to open her eyes.

"Welcome to a picnic lunch at . . ." I check my watch. "Half past midnight."

She claps her hands. "Oh, how sweet, you cooked."

I laugh a bit self-consciously. "Well, I spread hot mustard and put meat on bread, at least. Sorry—I had to buy this stuff at Sup-r-Shop because I didn't want you to see."

"That's OK. I won't dock you *too* many boyfriend points for that."

"Boyfriend, huh? Still?"

"You don't break up with someone just because of an argument, Josh. At least, *I* don't."

I spread out one of the blankets and we sit and eat. "My parents are getting divorced."

She puts down her bottle of soda. "I'm sorry."

"Well, you know. I don't know what to say. My mom was screwing around on my dad. It all started a while back."

She leans toward me and kisses me on the cheek.

"You're having a bad few days, aren't you?"

I chuckle at that because it's an understatement and an overstatement all at once. "I thought so. But, you know, I've made some decisions and that's made all of this other stuff a lot easier to deal with."

"What kind of decisions?" And I can tell from the expression on her face that she's wondering. Wondering what I've decided about *us*.

"I saw her today."

Her face goes blank. "Who? Your mother?"

I have to laugh again; *her* only means one thing in my mind, or at least it has for so many years. I just assumed . . . "No. Eve."

"Oh." She brushes some crumbs off her shirt. "I see." She starts to get up. She's upset, moving with those jerky, staccato motions that tell me she's too distracted to think straight. "Thanks for the picnic."

"Rache." I reach up and grab her hand, pulling her down to sit beside me. "Stay. Please. Listen to me."

She looks into my eyes with an anxiety I've never seen in her before. Not even when I was at my worst, refusing to look at her or speak to her. "You're old enough now. She's what you've wanted, Josh. She's what you've always wanted. It's so fucking *obvious*—"

"Look, Rache. You said yesterday that I couldn't touch you without hating you or hating myself. I'm touching you. I'm holding your hand."

"That's not what I meant."

"I know. Let me start slow, OK?"

And I tell her. About visiting Eve. About what I learned about myself that everyone else already knew.

She takes my face in her hands and kisses me hard on the lips.

"You've been telling me to get over the past five years, Rache. And it turns out that the past five years weren't even what I thought they were.

"So I'm throwing them out. That's what I've decided. To hell with it. Who needs it? I'm looking forward now, not back."

She kisses me again and something happens. Something I never expected to happen. I close my eyes and lean into the kiss and I slide my hands up her arms until I'm surrounding her, holding her, hugging her to me. Her arms slip around me and we're clenched tightly together, kissing. My hand goes up and skips past her bra strap, then runs through her hair. She digs into my back with her nails, worn short for softball. I hear myself moan into her.

And I think of nothing.

I think of nothing but Rachel.

What happens next is pure magic, and is for us and us alone.

Huddled together in the blankets, we look up at the stars together. I want to point out Mars, which you can see with the naked eye tonight if you look *just right,* but Rachel shifts against me, leans out of the blanket for a second, just long enough to tap home plate.

"Look at that. We hit a home run." She laughs, and I can't help it; I join in.

I didn't flicker once. I haven't flickered in hours. Maybe I'm done with them now. I used to think that the flickers were a consequence of losing my virginity. And maybe they were. Maybe they've gone away because this time I did it right.

"Hey, Rache?"

"Hmm?" She snuggles close to me. I'm a little worried about someone stumbling upon us here, but it's almost two in the morning now. No one's going to come out here to the ball field. And if they do . . . well, we'll worry about it then.

"Rache, I have more stuff to tell you."

"Of course you do." She kisses her way up my chest to my throat, then my lips. "You *always* have stuff."

"I'm serious."

"You're also always serious." She's giddy.

"Do you think I was wrong to let that pitch go by?"

She sighs away her giddiness.

"Tell me, Rache."

"Yes. Absolutely."

"You're right."

She tilts her head at me, confused. "Then why did you—"

"Because I didn't know it was wrong until I did it. I had to *learn*, don't you see? I had to see what would happen when I let my hatred for Coach go like that. I had to take control completely, just for once in my life, and see where it led me. And most important of all, I had to . . ." I'm getting lost in her eyes, the way I used to get lost in Eve's, but better.

"Rache, on prom night, you—"

"Don't." She puts a finger over my lips. "Don't ruin this. You don't have to. Can't you see how *happy* I am?"

I kiss her finger. "Let me talk.

"On prom night, you said you loved me. And before you stopped me, I was going to tell you that I didn't love you." Her eyes cloud over and she leans back, moving away from me. "Let me finish, Rache. Please, just let me finish."

She nods wordlessly and stares up at the sky.

"But something happened, Rache. See, I thought my mom loved my dad. I thought Eve and I loved each other. I was wrong.

"This feeling I have for you . . . I've never had it before. And I've never had a name for it. Because the name was being used—*mis*used, misappropriated—by something else."

I grab her by the shoulders and turn her to face me. "I love you, Rachel. I really do. I have for a long time. I just didn't know it."

I've dreaded this moment all day, what comes next. But I have to do it. Because it's honest and true and real.

"Rache, I love you, but—"

"You're going to Stanford," she says very calmly, as if it's the most obvious thing in the world.

And I guess it is. "Yeah. No matter what Coach does or doesn't do. Because . . . I'm going on my terms. Even if by some miracle he recommends me for the scholarship, I'm not taking it."

That surprises her. "I don't get it."

"*That's* why I had no choice but to let that pitch go by. I had to prove to myself that I could live without baseball. I can't go to college on *their* terms. I can't be the ballplayer first and the student second, and if they're giving me an athletic scholarship, believe me—that's what it would be. Athlete-scholar, not the other way around. No one can convince me otherwise.

"So, yeah. I'll have to take out student loans. I'll have to work my ass off. But that's OK. I've wanted to go to Stanford as long as I can remember. It's my dream and I want it to come true."

She shakes her head and looks up at the stars, a weird little smile on her face. "Wow. You. Not playing baseball anymore. I can't imagine it. It's strange."

"There's always intramurals. But I really want to . . . I really *need* to focus on one thing. I can't do both and be my best. For me, baseball was always a means to an end. I'm not like Zik. The game itself was always enough for him. For me, it was about the statistics, the improvement. It was a way of seeing if I measured up. But I'm tired of measuring myself that way. No matter how well I play, I'll never have a thousand average. I'll never hit a home run every time. You can't be a perfect baseball player."

"You can't be a perfect *anything*, Josh."

"I know that. But you can get a little closer than a five hundred batting average. You can fire a rocket into space and have it land on Mars and that's closer to perfect than anything else I'll ever know."

She hugs me. "I'm glad for you, then. I'm glad you decided."

I squeeze her tight. "I'm sorry. I should have told you before we . . . before we made love. I'll be far away. It'll be tough. I won't be able to call a lot or visit a lot because of the money. And I understand if you don't want to see me anymore because of it. I really do. I totally under—"

"God, Josh!" She smacks me on the arm. "Cut it out! I'm *not* giving up on you! Not after all this. In fact . . ." A devious look crosses her face and she rummages around for her purse. "This is perfect . . ."

"What's perfect?"

She hauls her purse into her lap and looks inside. "This is just perfect. I was going to give it to you soon anyway. Now it's absolutely perfect."

"*What's* perfect, Rache?"

She whips something out of her purse and presents it to me with a "Ta-da!" and a flourish. It's a cell phone.

"I don't get it."

"It's a prepaid cell phone, dummy." She pushes it into my hands, her eyes sparkling, her smile radiant and perfect. "It's got my phone number programmed into it and a hundred hours of call time."

I don't know what to say, so I just let her kiss me gently, softly.

"After that," she says, "it's up to you ..."

EPILOGUE
OK, Baseball (Reprise)

HERE'S THE THING ABOUT BASEBALL—it's not the individual sport I thought it was. Turns out I was wrong about that.

Yeah, the batter is a lone man against the world. He stands in the batter's box like a soldier and it's up to him—and him alone—what happens next.

But here's the thing I didn't understand until I was forced to, until recently: In order to hit a home run . . .

Someone else has to pitch the ball.

Acknowledgments

Thanks to Kathy and Liz at Anderson Literary; Margaret ("I've never had to tell an author this before") and the Usual Suspects at Houghton Mifflin; and the Betas: Eric, Ally, and Robin.

Extra-special thanks go out to David P. Dagget and Amy Blank Ocampo, deputy and assistant state's attorneys for Carroll County, Maryland, for their advice and counsel on legal matters pertaining to the story. Any and all errors, goof-ups, or just plain screwy legal goings-on are entirely *my* fault, not theirs.

Further thanks to Larry Meekins (head baseball coach at Franklin High School) and Randy Pentz (athletic director at Owings Mills High School) for providing high school baseball insights. Again, errors are my fault.

Last but not least, thanks to my father, Geoff Lyga, for providing baseball info, verifying facts, triple-checking my math, and raising me a Red Sox fan.